Guilty Secrets

ZOË MILLER

Guilty Secrets

HACHETTE
BOOKS
IRELAND

First published in Ireland in 2009 by Hachette Books Ireland

An Hachette UK company

2

Copyright © Zoë Miller 2009

A CIP catalogue record for this title is available
from the British Library

ISBN 978 0 340 92021 3

Typeset in Plantin Light by Ellipsis Books Limited, Glasgow

Printed and bound in the UK by CPI Mackays, Chatham, ME5 8TD

Hachette Books Ireland policy is to use papers that are natural, renewable
and recyclable products and made from wood grown in sustainable forests.
The logging and manufacturing processes are expected to conform to
the environmental regulations of the country of origin.

Hachette Books Ireland
8 Castlecourt Centre
Castleknock
Dublin 15

A division of
Hachette UK Ltd
338 Euston Road
London NW1 3BH

www.hbgi.ie

To the memory of my beloved Mum and dear friend,
Olive Morris.

ACKNOWLEDGEMENTS

A big thank you to Sheila Crowley, my agent, for her great support, commitment and friendship.

Sincere gratitude to my editor, Ciara Doorley, for her warm enthusiasm and insightful feedback. Thanks also to Breda Purdue and all the hard-working team at Hachette Books Ireland.

Much appreciation goes to my wide circle of fantastic family and friends. Your love and support, fun and kindness mean everything to me.

This book is dedicated to my Mum, who recently passed away. Mum introduced me to the wonderful world of books and encouraged my writing career with lively enthusiasm. I would like to pay tribute to the wholehearted way she always believed in me and empowered me to go confidently in the direction of my dreams.

Twenty years from now you will be more disappointed by the things that you didn't do than by the ones you did do. So throw off the bowlines. Sail away from the safe harbor. Catch the trade winds in your sails. Explore. Dream. Discover. (Mark Twain)

Guilty Secrets

PROLOGUE

She wants barefoot on the beach and sand between her toes.

He kisses her toes one by one and brushes off imaginary sand. He prefers a mountain summit, fathomless blue skies within touching distance and the feeling of being on top of the world. And flowers in her hair. Afterwards he'll pick out the petals one by one and cup them in the palm of his hand and sprinkle her body with them.

She smiles and says that it sounds lovely, but she already feels on top of the world. She could put flowers in her hair, but she couldn't very well climb a mountain in yards of white satin.

'I'll carry you,' he offers.

She shakes her head in amusement. Is this their very first argument?

Then he tells her of the perfect spot, a place they both would love.

'Small and intimate?'

'Of course. Not big or brash or noisy.'

'Silver rings?'

'Yes, if you like.'

'And music?'

'What music would you prefer?'

'Soulful songs dripping melodies into the evening air.'

He kisses her face. 'You should be a poet.'

'And dancing under the glitter of stars in the velvety night.'

'And when the last note falls away, I'll steal you off and wrap you in my love,' he says, pulling her into his arms.

'Why don't we climb a mountain anyway?' she says. 'I know a special place where we can touch the sky and taste the breeze and make our promises, just the two of us.'

And so they do. They take a winding track through scented heathers and bright yellow gorse until they reach the summit. The world is spread at their feet. They sip champagne and kiss. He picks her up and whirls her around and her laughter echoes across the green valleys that embrace the folds of the mountains. Together they reach up and touch the sky. Then he spreads out a rug and takes her into his arms.

The mist drops suddenly. It falls like a blanket of cotton wool, tender and soft, tenacious and thick, wrapping around them like a shroud. Even though they pick their way very slowly and creep along footfall by careful footfall, she senses the instant of danger before it happens, feels the moment forever frozen in her bones, hears his cry scorching across her mind before his fingers, along with hazy images of the rest of their future, slip forever from her grasp.

Afterwards, they bring his body back up a hillside and put him resting in a niche between the deep blue water and the fathomless sky. She carries white roses and plucks the petals one by one and sees them dance in the mischievous breeze.

ABBY

I

Abby Lacey stepped out of the shower, grabbed a towel with one hand and her shrieking mobile with the other and tried to predict what calamity had befallen her bride.

Maybe the flower girl's ribbon was the wrong shade of ivory, the bridesmaid couldn't find her must-have, colour-coordinated lip gloss or, horror of horrors, the mother-in-law's hat had been damaged on the flight from Dublin.

'Calm down, Megan,' she said, failing to make sense of the melodramatic outburst.

'Calm *down*?' The voice at the other end of her mobile rose to a crescendo. 'This is my *wedding* day. The wedding of my dreams! And it's going to be a *disaster*.'

'What exactly is the problem?'

Abby patted the towel around her slender body and spiky hair, which were already drying thanks to the rising heat in the apartment. No doubt she'd have Megan's little trifle sorted in a jiffy. If a tiny voice mocked that dealing meekly with such petty incidentals was a total denial of the real, authentic Abby Lacey, she desperately ignored it. Right now, she needed to be absorbed in the frothy and frivolous, for throwing her energy into the trivia of it all helped her to feel as though everything was normal, even though it wasn't.

'My musicians are missing! You *must* do something about it. I might have known there'd be a disaster.'

Missing musicians? Trust Megan to come up with

something bizarre. Still holding her mobile to her ear, Abby stepped into black lace panties, slid them up to her hips and pictured a group of musicians, complete with bulky instruments, barrelling their way confusedly through the busy, narrow streets of Sorrento. Far from constituting a disaster, she privately thought it resembled a scene from a soap opera.

Sometimes it was fun. Sometimes she was amazed at the way she still had the ability to joke and laugh. Only last week she'd said to Rosita, her colleague, 'My major learning curve over the last few months has been the revelation that brides usually fall into two categories.'

'*Ci sono?*'

'Yeah,' Abby had joked, surprising herself with her light-hearted observation. 'Those who fret over every tiny detail for months in advance and are transformed into radiant creatures on their wedding day, and those who are perfectly composed all along, only to become convulsed with last-minute hysteria as the great day finally dawns. I'm still waiting for the day when a bride changes her mind about her wonderful wedding and decides to flee to a nunnery.'

'*Grazie mille*, I'm glad you came to us,' Rosita had said. 'You have deep calm that softens the angry bride, although you are working here only three or four months.'

'Five months,' Abby had corrected. 'And if you'd known me in another life,' she'd continued, her heart skipping a beat, 'you'd have described me rather differently.' Deep calm was a new concept for her, a cloak that wrapped itself around her, numbed the overwhelming hurt and helped her to put on a smiley face.

Now there was a frenzied squeal in her ear as Megan succumbed to full-blown panic and Abby promptly decided that she fell into both categories of bride.

'I didn't come all the way to the Amalfi coast to have a

disaster like this on my wedding day,' Megan was sobbing down the phone.

'Of course you didn't,' Abby soothed. 'Just tell me what's happened and I'll see what I can do to sort it out.' She opened her wardrobe door, pulled out a pair of black cotton trousers and wriggled into them, pulling up the zip and nimbly fastening the button with one hand.

'With all due respect to your talents, even the best wedding planner in the world can't make an airplane fly any faster.'

'So it's a problem with the flight?' Abby picked out a black top, slipped it over her head and transferred her mobile from one ear to the other as she manoeuvred her arms and pulled the fabric down over her pert breasts.

'What have I been trying to tell you? It's a *major catastrophe*. There was fog at Dublin airport this morning – fog, I ask you, in the month of May? It would have to happen to me, of course. I thought the group was here. Now I've just heard that the flight was delayed by two hours. *Two hours!*'

Abby was tempted to point out that if she'd chosen the local harpist or Italian tenor, she wouldn't be having this so-called catastrophe. But Megan, a tall, spoiled brunette and a big noise in advertising, according to herself, had shown withering contempt for all the choices available on the regular wedding packages. Every last detail had to be special, unrivalled and unique. Including the musicians.

She was flying a band over from Ireland. Megan had deliberately kept all the details under the same cloak and dagger secrecy that she'd diligently applied to the design of her wedding dress. Maybe she was afraid Abby would leak the earth-shattering information to rival brides. Or the media. Maybe the band was pretentious enough to anticipate being mobbed at the airport, although why some wannabe U2s had left it until the morning of the wedding to fly from Dublin was a mystery to Abby, considering the entire bridal party had arrived en critical masse four days ago. Critical being the operative word.

Abby slid her feet into her sandals. In her living area she pressed a switch on the wall and the ceiling fan whirred into life. She reached for a pad and pencil. 'If you give me the flight details, I'll contact Naples airport to check the arrival time,' she told Megan. 'I can arrange for the transport to rush them directly to the wedding venue.'

'Do you by any chance have a helicopter waiting?' Megan snorted. 'Look, I don't care how much it costs.'

'I doubt if I can get my hands on a private helicopter at this short notice,' Abby said evenly, standing under the ripple of cooling air, 'but if I think the group might not make it on time, I'll arrange to have alternative music on stand-by. There is some local—'

'The last thing I want is a hackneyed rendition of "*O Sole Mio*",' Megan fumed.

Abby's pencil slipped from her grasp and skittered across the floor as Andrea Bocelli's version of the Italian classic drifted on the edge of her consciousness. A sliver of deeply buried memory caught her off guard and bloomed for a bittersweet instant. She felt the warmth of his arms curved around her and heard the murmur of a voice hoarse with desire . . .

Ti amo, bella Abby . . .

Abby firmly suppressed it and focused on rescuing her pencil, then forcibly injected her finest wedding planner calm into her voice. 'I can have a harpist ready and waiting,' she said. 'She plays traditional wedding music, and it can sound quite lovely rippling around the Cloisters.'

'Hmm – do you think so?'

'It lends an authenticity to the overall ambience,' Abby fished around for suitable words. 'The charming harp music is extremely romantic.'

'I suppose it'll have to do,' Megan relented. 'It's just – God, I can't believe this has happened after *all* my careful planning.'

'It'll be fine,' Abby automatically soothed. 'Your wedding day will be wonderful.'

'You're so calm. You must have been *born* for this job. You've no idea how relieved I was when I heard there was an Irish wedding planner attached to the agency. *And* multi-lingual. I knew you'd understand my needs far better than any *foreigner*.'

'Megan,' Abby immediately cut her short, 'I've important calls to make, so I'll catch you later.' She put down her mobile, crossed her living area and pushed back the wooden shutters, releasing a flood of light into the room, then stepped out onto her balcony.

Early May, and the morning temperature in the Italian resort of Sorrento was hitting the twenties. It was the kind of day that was made for living and loving, with incandescent sunshine in a pearly blue sky and everything about the world sparkling with hope. A perfect day for a wedding. She leaned back against the shutter, enjoying the sensation of the sun on her face, and closed her eyes for a moment. In her mind's eye she saw the flutter of a gauzy veil, heard the whisper of silky satin, caught the scent of a posy of roses, fresh and dewy . . . Then Abby swiftly snapped out of her reverie and blanked it.

She walked back inside and pressed the speed dial for Naples airport. She'd be glad when this particular wedding was consigned to the back of the filing cabinet. She was used to dealing with demanding brides, not to mention their equally demanding mothers, but Megan had been quite a challenge.

The Cloisters of San Francesco, a popular wedding venue, was attached to an old Franciscan monastery in Sorrento that dated back centuries. Abby stood in the office, signing off her worksheet. Registrar ready. Paperwork treble checked. Flowers and transport sorted. The bilingual hairdresser, make-up artist and photographer were long since finished in the bride's hotel.

The restaurant was obeying Megan's meticulous instructions to the letter for a canapés and Veuve Clicquot reception, six-course traditional Italian meal and colour-coordinated napery, candles and table decorations. Even the weather, mindful of Megan's wrath, was behaving itself impeccably. The groom was ready and waiting, having joked with Abby that he might be a little hungover after the previous night's celebrations, between the lure of champagne and the warm, balmy evening so different to the chilly Dublin nights, but he was all set to marry his lovely bride.

Even the obstreperous musicians had landed safely and were on their way. With a welcome relief, Abby heard the flurry of activity as they arrived, unpacked their instruments and began to tune up at the side of the open air courtyard of the Cloisters, minutes before the bride was due to arrive.

She folded her worksheet and thrust it into her pocket and remembered to put her mobile on silent mode as she slipped out of the office. She stepped briskly around the passageway surrounding the courtyard, barely glancing at the trio setting up their instruments in the corner. Wedding guests air-kissed each other, mindful of hats and expensive hair creations, radiating expectancy as they took their seats. Baskets and cornets of rose petals were aromatic inside the porch, ready for showering the newly married couple. She heard an outburst of clapping outside and hurried out to greet the bride.

Naturally, now that the crucial moment had arrived, Megan was a beatific vision in ivory silk.

'Megan, you look just fabulous.'

'Thanks, Abby.'

Megan posed regally while the photographer fired off a volley of shots, then she stepped through the entrance and glided down the passageway. Abby followed at a distance and prepared to wait in the wings until the ceremony was over.

Abby knew that she sometimes let her brides away with murder. She couldn't help it, for beyond all the trivialities and last-minute so-called disasters, there was nothing frivolous about two people putting their trust in each other. There was something very vulnerable and brave, she thought, about two people promising to love each other for the rest of their lives. Then there was the allure of it all – the rustle of the bride's beautiful dress, the scented blooming flowers, the Italian music wafting around the Cloisters . . . It held Abby captive because she found that taking care of the details and making sure everyone was happy was one way of seeking redemption in dealing with her guilt.

Then she heard the music.

It was the sheer surprise of it that was like a punch to her stomach. The resonating throb of plucked guitar notes cascaded about the Italian courtyard. A warm, mellow flute picked up the melody and then the guitar broke into a flurry of chords. For Megan's musicians were playing traditional Irish music, something she hadn't heard in eight years, and something so unexpected and yet so warmly familiar that it jolted her numbed senses, sending shockwaves around her body.

The bride reached the groom. Guests jostled in their seats to get the best view and there was the snap of camera shutters, murmurs of admiration and sighs of appreciation. Sunlight slanted across the courtyard, blazing whitely along the colonnade of pillars, throwing the series of arches into relief, filtering iridescently though the branches of the olive trees and pooling against the banks of shrubs and flower arrangements.

The music started again, the flute leading with the opening sequence, followed by the guitar and the violin. With a sense of shock, Abby recognised the haunting, beautiful melody of 'She Moved Through the Fair' all too well. She shivered in spite of the warm afternoon, moved behind the shelter of a pillar and briefly closed her eyes as the plaintive Irish love song lapped at the edges of her frozen heart. Then curiosity got the better of her, so she silently edged along the passageway to have a look at the musicians.

Her breath snagged as her past and present collided and the Cloisters dissolved around her. She didn't hear Megan and her groom exchange vows. She didn't register the round of applause or the laughter of the flower girl. Even the music slid by her raw senses as though it was coming from a distant planet.

For she only had eyes for the man strumming the guitar.

He had matured. His body had filled out and the expression on his face was more self-possessed. The memory of the carefree lad she'd hung around with for years was but a pale reflection of the handsome guy now sitting in the Italian courtyard, strumming his guitar with casual assurance.

Sam Ryan had grown up.

By some twist of destiny, he was here, now, back in her life again, bringing reminders of a time when life had been carefree and full of golden promise, and playing a love song that filtered through every layer of chilled calm in which she'd sought oblivion.

2

'Abby, I can't thank you enough! So far it's brilliant!'

Abby jumped. The ceremony was over. In a daze, she had watched the elegant wedding party as photographs, videos and lifelong memories were captured against the evocative backdrop of the Cloisters. Now the guests had drifted outside while the photographer took additional shots of the bride and groom. Abby hadn't even noticed herself handing out the paper cornets engraved with the initials of the bride and groom and full of scented petals, but obviously she had, for as she threw a startled glance at the basket she saw that it was empty.

'I'm glad you're happy.' The smile was so forced that it hurt Abby's cheekbones.

'Happy?' Megan's beaming face swam in front of her eyes. 'I'm ecstatic! It's beyond my dreams. Everything is perfect, even the group.'

The group. A sharp jolt seared her senses once more. They were still playing, sending the bride and groom on their way with another lilting Irish melody. So far, Sam hadn't noticed her, although that wasn't surprising. The Abby Lacey of today bore no resemblance to the girl he'd said goodbye to eight years ago.

'Just one thing.' Abby tried to focus on the details of her job even though her tongue felt heavy and her slender limbs stiff. She took Megan's arm. 'In true Italian tradition, the bride walks to the right of the groom as you exit. So if you'd like . . .'

Megan changed places with her new husband. Arm in arm, they sallied forth through the passageway and out to the waiting guests and the dappled shower of rose petals. Abby slipped out after them. Some instinct for survival urged her to run as far away as possible. What twist of fate had brought Sam to this place? What the hell was he doing here anyway, playing his guitar and upsetting her careful composure?

Outside, the blazing sunshine was a warm surprise on her face after the relative shelter of the Cloisters. In a swell of sumptuous style, laughter and chatter, the wedding party strolled across to the public gardens adjoining the monastery. Here, breathtaking views of the Bay of Naples were a panoramic backdrop for yet more photographs and videos. Abby stood in the shimmering heat, stuck her hand into her pocket and forced her trembling fingers to take her mobile off silent mode. She struggled to recall various arrangements, feeling that she was drifting around on some kind of shaky autopilot. The horse-drawn carriage would be there shortly to bring Megan and her husband to the restaurant hosting the reception, with the wedding party to follow in a fleet of limousines. Once she was satisfied that everything was in order at the reception, Abby's work was over.

Sam need never know that she had passed so close to him. Right now, the musicians were surely packing their equipment and preparing to move on to the champagne reception.

'Abby! Thank you so much!'

Once again, Abby's hand was grasped, this time by Maureen O'Reilly, Megan's mother, who swooped on her in acres of swirling lilac and gave her a hug. 'I know my daughter can be a bit of a handful, but you arranged everything to perfection and it's been so special,' Maureen continued. She mopped a discreet tear from her excessively mascaraed eyes before it managed to inflict any damage. 'You'll join us this evening. After the meal, that is,' she hastily clarified. 'It must be lonely for you out here, completely surrounded by foreigners.'

'I couldn't possibly—'

'Of course you can! It would do you good to have some Irish company. The music will be flying tonight as well as the champagne. Celtic Shade are terrific, aren't they? It was wonderful that they arrived just in time. Did I tell you that we heard them play at the society wedding of the year in Dublin and Megan knew she simply had to have them?'

Celtic Shade? What the hell was Sam up to? Not that it was any of her business. Abby had long ago relinquished any claims on him. Yet now she had the overwhelming urge to run back into the Cloisters and let him lift her into the shelter of his arms. She remembered exactly how they'd feel around her. Warm. Secure. Safe. She hesitated, crippled with a mixture of memories and indecision.

Then the decision was taken right out of her hands.

'Oh, here they come! Over here, Sam! I'm trying to persuade Abby to join us this evening, but maybe you'd have better luck than me, a sexy Irish man like yourself!'

Oh, God. Far from packing away his guitar and moving on to the reception, Sam Ryan, in a beautifully-cut suit, was marching through the dazzling gardens, directly towards her. Six feet tall, in his youth he had been the popular captain of the school basketball team. Now his height and athletic stride were infused with the confidence that Abby had noticed in the church. The unruly mop of blond hair was fashionably cropped. The two other musicians, whom she didn't recognise, strolled in his wake, their eyes automatically drawn to the spectacular view beyond the railings.

Sam wasn't looking at the view. The sun was in his eyes,

so she was standing in silhouette, but even so, he was staring at Abby as though he was seeing a ghost. She felt light-headed and giddy. Any minute now she would surely melt into the ground or vaporise into the warm, thick air.

'Abby?' The hazel eyes she knew so well were staring at her in amazement.

There were no words in the English language fit to describe her feelings or the look on his face. This couldn't be happening. Yet it was, right there and now, and eight years whirled like a wraith between them before fading away as they stared at each other.

'Hi, Sam,' she said, arranging her mouth into a nervous smile and forcing the greeting out though her paralysed throat.

'Do you two know each other?' Maureen clasped her hands in delight.

'No.'

'Yes.'

After his outright denial, Sam spoke first. He shoved a hand through his hair in a gesture she was all too familiar with. 'Well, sort of. We . . .' he hesitated.

'We're old friends,' Abby said, slightly shocked that she was managing to be articulate. 'We haven't seen each other in years. I'm not surprised Sam didn't recognise me at first.'

'How wonderful! Ireland truly is a village, isn't it? One big happy family. Now you simply have to join us tonight, Abby, and catch up with Sam. You'll be able to persuade her, Sam, won't you?'

Sam smiled a polite smile that didn't reach his eyes. He was clearly as thunderstruck as Abby, but not too taken by surprise to reply, 'If I know the Abby of old, Maureen, there's no way I can persuade her to do anything at all.'

Maureen batted her eyelashes at Sam. 'Oh, come on, use

your sexy charm. See you tonight, Abby. No excuses.' With a flash of her glittering fingernails, Maureen was gone in her swirl of lilac taffeta, and despite the gaiety of the wedding party flowing all around them, they were alone.

'Abby?'

'Yes?'

'Sorry, I – I just don't get this.'

She forced herself to stay still.

His eyes raked her up and down. 'You look . . . different.'

'Do I?' Trite, meaningless replies were all she could manage as a thousand unspoken questions surged between them.

'What did you do to your hair?'

Abby's slim fingers combed the spiky dark hair that framed her elfin face. The last time Sam had seen her, and indeed for most of her life, her hair had tumbled in a dark silken sheet past her shoulders.

'I had this styled, oh, a while ago.'

'Styled?'

'Yep. Change of image.' It was one way of explaining a self-inflicted penance for her guilty sins, she silently mocked herself.

'I see.' It was clear he didn't see at all. 'What are you doing here? Do you know the O'Reillys? Are you . . .' he hesitated and once more scanned all five feet two of her, looking a little uneasy. 'Are you one of the wedding guests?'

She wasn't surprised at the tone of his question. She didn't look like one of the wedding guests, not when she was wearing black cotton trousers and a matching top, her usual wedding attire. There was no point in explaining that in keeping with Italian tradition, she was wearing black to act as a perfect foil for the bride.

'Why, do I look like a wedding guest?' she asked, shocked at the impish tone in her voice and the way she slipped back into her old bantering mode with Sam.

He stared at her doubtfully.

'No, Sam, I'm not one of the guests,' she said flatly, anticipating his next question and dreading it, for she knew full well what his reaction would be.

'Then what on earth are you doing here?'

Knowing what his reaction was bound to be, and knowing he would find out sooner or later, she tilted her chin a fraction, lifted a smooth, defiant shoulder and said, 'I'm the wedding planner.'

He frowned and looked away, staring intently out across the glittering bay, and she thought the words hadn't registered, or maybe he didn't understand the concept of a wedding planner. But he'd heard all right, for he looked back, gave her a mocking glance and said, 'Yeah, sure.'

'Okay, so don't believe me, but that's what I'm doing here.'

'The *wedding planner*? Is this some kind of a wind-up?'

Although she'd expected it, his incredulity was painful in her raw state. 'No, Sam.' She dug her clenched fists into the pockets of her trousers and shifted from one foot to the other, but held his gaze. 'I help to plan and organise weddings.'

'You plan weddings,' he said flatly.

'Yes, mostly for Irish and English girls who come over here to get married,' she gabbled, anxious to get her explanation over with. 'I'm attached to Halcyon Weddings and a Sorrento travel agency, and we arrange the whole package – venue, paperwork, hotel, flowers, photographer—'

He shook his head and interrupted, 'Halcyon Weddings? Now you are taking the piss.'

She stood her ground. She'd forgotten how tall he was, how easily she'd snuggled into his chest and slotted her face into the curve under his neck all those years ago. But she'd never forgotten how secure he'd made her feel.

She gulped. 'I'm not taking the piss. That's my job, honestly.'

'And just how long have you been doing this, er, *job*?'

'Just over five months.'

His glinty expression was nothing less than she'd expected from the moment he'd stood in front of her. 'Do you seriously expect me to believe that the girl who left me to explore the world and see the seven wonders, and who laughed and told me that marriage was some kind of terminal illness, is now throwing her talents into planning halcyon *weddings*?'

She flinched at the note of derision in his voice. 'Yes.'

'Sorry, but I just don't buy this.'

'No, I don't expect you do. But what about you?' she countered, needing to hug herself with her arms to stop herself from shaking. 'I thought you were all set for the scintillating thrills of the law courts. You were mapping out a brilliant future for yourself. You certainly studied hard enough. What happened to all of that?'

Sam was silent for a moment. She watched his angry gaze flickering around the sunlit gardens, across to the glittering Bay of Naples where the backdrop of a hazy Mount Vesuvius shimmered in the afternoon and over to the wedding gathering where the photographer was trying to arrange yet another group shot. Laughter and repartee and squeals of excitement echoed in the warm air as guests positioned themselves and someone picked up the adorable little flower girl. When he looked at her, his eyes were steely flints. 'At least I'm following my dream, Abby. I haven't gone and sold my soul down the river.'

Then Sam turned on his heel and strode away.

3

Abby slipped off her sandals, feeling the cool of the marble tiles on her bare feet as she crossed the floor of her studio apartment. She stepped out onto the small balcony overlooking a side street off Corso Italia, Sorrento's main shopping thoroughfare.

She sat quite still and let the warm evening air and familiar rhythm of the neighbourhood wash over her. The sun had slid westward and the curving hills behind Sorrento were smoky shadows rimming the skyline. Rush-hour traffic hooted and snarled, and in the near distance she could hear the shouts of children playing football. Scents of olive oil, garlic and basil wafted on the air from a nearby restaurant. If you leaned out over the balcony and craned your neck to the right, you could see the silvery gleam of the Bay of Naples.

Sold your soul down the river.

Sometimes she let contrary brides away with all sorts of hissy fits, but she shouldn't have let Sam get away with that remark. She'd been stuck to the spot, though, and there had been no way she could explain. For how could she when she couldn't bear to even think about, let alone give voice to, the way her life had crumbled around her?

She couldn't begin to explain her seemingly frivolous Italian existence to Sam, how the busyness of it all kept her absorbed by day, and how the demands of her job helped her to make some kind of atonement.

But the nights were different.

In the dark hours before dawn, she lay sleepless in an empty bed, her aching limbs finding nothing but smooth, blank sheets instead of the warmth of his body, listening to the breeze that stirred through the nearby lemon grove, slipped through the gaps in her shutters and carried censuring murmurs that stole quietly around her along with the evocative scent of lemons and the sound of his name.

Raffaele . . . Raffaele . . .

Abby abruptly stood up and leaned on her wrought iron balcony. Any kind of explanation would surely begin to strip away the layers of her calm, leaving her raw and vulnerable. Today, anyway, there had been no time to answer Sam, for just as he'd stalked off in the warm afternoon, the transport arrived to bring the guests to the reception. Abby was busy rounding up everyone and at last the bride and groom trotted off in their horse-drawn carriage through the narrow Sorrento streets, followed by the tooting of car horns from the snaking line of glinting limousines. Once she'd checked that everything was in order at the restaurant, Abby had escaped to the sanctuary of her apartment.

Now she saw that the shadows had lengthened and had a sense of nervous expectation as the evening gathered in. Up at the hillside restaurant in Sorrento, with the rooftop terrace and views of the Bay of Naples, Megan's superlative six-course wedding meal would be over, speeches made and tables cleared, and everyone ready for music and dancing.

Sam's music.

Somewhere along the line he'd obviously decided to take his guitar-playing seriously. He'd sounded great. He'd looked fantastic. She couldn't believe he was really here, that they had talked, that she had stood close to him and could have reached out and touched him.

Then her mobile rang.

'Abby?'

'How did you get this number?'

'Does it matter?' Sam said. 'Why aren't you here? The party's just warming up. I thought wedding planners had to stay 'til the bitter end, making sure everyone was happy.'

'I thought you were supposed to be helping the party along with your music.'

'We do get a break, you know,' he said, then in softer tones, began, 'Abby . . .'

'Yes?'

'I'm flying back to Ireland tomorrow afternoon, but I have to see you. I'm sorry for walking away from you this afternoon. I got such a shock that I was totally dumbfounded.'

'Same here,' she admitted.

'Will I see you later? We can't leave it like this.'

He'd said more or less the same thing to her when she'd walked away from him eight years ago, Abby recalled.

She'd grown up with Sam Ryan and Elaine Stevens on Mayberry Lane, a cul de sac on the edge of a village in County Dublin. Sam was a couple of years older than she and Elaine, and they were like the sister and brother she never had. Together the three of them had shared the melee of the schoolyard, the early rumblings of teenage angst and those first exciting forays into the world of discos, music and independence. As Abby had wilfully tested the boundaries with her long-suffering mother and indulgent grandmother and got up to all sorts of waywardness with Elaine, Sam had always been there for her.

And then she'd broken his heart.

'Abby, just come.' His voice thrummed in her ear, more self-assured, yet still the familiar, comforting voice she'd listened to down through the years.

It was the comforting familiarity that beckoned her. She finished the call and had a shower. She smoothed aloe vera into her tanned, slender limbs and slid on her laciest underwear. She stepped into her long cotton skirt decorated with sequins and a matching sleeveless top. The skirt moulded her slim hips and flared at the calves. The top fitted her to perfection, showing just a small amount of cleavage. Turquoise, her favourite colour. He'd told her years ago that it matched the colour of her huge, luminous eyes. She pulled on silvery sandals and ran lightly gelled fingers through her short dark hair, teasing tendrils around her oval face, softening the effect. Pale mauve eye shadow and mascara, lips outlined in shimmering plum, a spray of perfume. Her eyes looked even bigger than normal and softly apprehensive, her whole reflection ethereal.

And lastly, she fastened a delicate turquoise bracelet around her slender wrist.

She grabbed a silver purse and hurried through warm, cobble-locked streets bustling with tourists and scooters, tiny candlelit restaurants and souvenir shops. It seemed the most natural thing in the world to be going to Sam.

Maureen O'Reilly spotted her hesitating on the threshold of the terrace and invited her in, ordering a passing waiter to bring champagne for Abby. The sunny afternoon had given way to a warm evening and the Bay of Naples was a rippling, silvery sea. Some of the wedding guests were sitting around relaxing, while others were dancing on the terrace. Celtic Shade were playing an Irish waltz, the violin and flute now replaced with a guitar and keyboard. Sam was playing the mandolin and the mellow notes throbbed across the evening air. Sometime earlier in the evening he had changed into khaki trousers and a white short-sleeved shirt and he looked relaxed and at home.

As the music paused for a moment, his eyes scanned the terrace as though he sensed her watching him. She could hardly bring herself to look at him and waves of panic rose in her throat, mixed with some kind of ridiculous delight.

The music changed. One of the groomsmen joined Celtic Shade and began to play the bodhrán and they launched into a fast rendition of 'The Irish Rover'. Abby was dragged to her feet and was soon part of a large whirling circle that quickly formed on the terrace, the lively music thrumming out across the warm Italian evening. The circle of guests stamped their feet, whooped and clapped, and the groom fastened a possessive arm around his bride's waist and tugged her into the middle of the circle. The powerful rhythm of it all, the flash of energy and charge of excitement caught Abby by surprise and sparked something inside of her. Her eyes sought out Sam's and he smiled across at her.

By the time the music came to an end, she was breathless with exertion and edgy anticipation. Through some kind of misty anxiety, she watched Sam hand his mandolin over to the groomsman and stroll across to her.

'I'm glad you came,' he said. 'Sorry for walking off on you earlier, it was just—'

'Forget it.'

It was the least she could say. Sam had never held a grudge. He'd always forgiven and forgotten, easily and big-heartedly. He'd obviously forgiven her for walking away from him eight years ago. Now she felt his touch on her arm and his eyes flicked from the top of her head to her toes. 'You look lovely.'

'Thank you.' She was pleasantly surprised as something warm reached out and touched her chilled heart.

'I just have to get used to the punky image,' he smiled as he fluffed her hair up with his hand.

'You're still a divil, Sam,' she said. It was difficult to say anything else, as her breathing was erratic. The music started up again, another waltz, and Sam held out his arms.

'Aren't you needed on stage?' she asked, torn between panic and delight.

'I think they'll manage without me for a few minutes.'

Then his arms closed around her.

'So did you climb Machu Picchu?'

'I did. It was incredible,' Abby smiled in reflection. 'I took the Inca Trail on foot and started early in the morning as the sun was rising. I went with a guided tour, of course. *Everything* was wonderful, Sam. I was three years in Australia and New Zealand, then a couple of years in America. Then it was Thailand and the Far East, and hiking through Peru, and a month on the island of Taquile on Lake Titicaca—'

'Lake what?'

'You heard,' Abby grinned. She was more relaxed with him now and had the sense of letting her guard down a little. 'I worked in restaurants, offices, hospitals. I got to swim in the Dead Sea.'

'And Africa?'

The word jolted, like someone crashing a dissonant piano chord, and she froze. Images flashed: heat and dust under a blood-red sun; her smiling reflection in his aviator shades, his hand on her hips; skin sliding against hot skin, his mouth on her breast, her indrawn breath catching in her throat . . .

'Hey, Abby?'

She struggled to be drawn back into the moment and it took a huge effort to drag all her attention to Sam's affectionate eyes. 'Africa?'

'Yeah, you wanted to set foot on all the continents. You've left Africa out.'

'I didn't leave it out,' she said, picking the words carefully. 'I spent a few weeks in South Africa before I came here, to Sorrento.' It wasn't the exact truth, but the words were spoken so assuredly that she could almost believe it herself.

By now, the wedding reception was over and they were sitting outside a small restaurant near Abby's apartment, catching up on their lives, eight years condensed into a few short sentences. Light small talk, all the time skirting around the main issues, like why legal eagle Sam was busy playing guitar and travel-the-world Abby was sorting out wish lists for truculent brides.

The owner of the restaurant knew Abby well and had put up his hands in mock surrender when she arrived at half past two in the morning with Sam in tow and persuaded him to open a bottle of wine. Gracious in defeat, Mario had produced his best Chianti and two goblets. Sensing romance for the single Irish girl, he'd changed the tablecloth and triumphantly produced a tiny vase of bud flowers and a fresh candle, which he'd lit with exaggerated flourish, then left them in peace. The streets and alleyways were quiet now, the shops long since closed and most of the tourists returned to their hotels. Only a few stragglers remained, sitting on into the scented night where the light breeze was warm and aromatic.

'You certainly got around,' Sam said. 'You always said you wanted to explore the world and see the seven wonders and do thirty things before you hit that great age.'

'I did lots of stuff, except I didn't get to Antarctica,' she said, wondering what else he remembered about the last time they'd talked all those years ago. His broken heart, for example. His plea that she was the only one for him.

'Hey, look at your mum!' Sam said. 'She's making quite a name for herself. Lia Lacey, famous crime novelist. Fair dues to her. I've seen her on TV a few times, and in the newspapers.'

Abby took a slow breath, putting to one side the blazing row she'd had with her mother the previous Christmas. 'Yeah, it's been amazing,' she said. 'Things have turned out great and I'm really glad for her. Her first novel flew off the shelves and skyrocketed into the bestseller lists and then there was no stopping her. She was hailed as an overnight success. But of course, you and I know differently.'

She paused, acutely aware of a warm sense of shared history and togetherness. A sudden longing for the past assailed her, when life was happy and uncomplicated and the future stretched ahead like a wonderful promise. She spiralled back in time and heard the rhythmic thud of Sam's basketball out on Mayberry Lane on a warm summer's evening and the click of Lia tapping away at her typewriter from a bedroom upstairs while her grandmother sat in the sunny front room and dozed over her crochet, while Alejandro, her father, was out exploring in some remote, exotic corner of the world.

Sam said, 'I'm glad it's worked out so well for your mum. Does she like living in London?'

'It suits her. She loves the whole cosmopolitan feel and it's the background for most of her novels. She leads a hectic life, always gadding to launches, charity bashes and celebrity events. And she travels abroad on book tours. It's hard to believe she'll be fifty next year.'

'Fifty?'

'Sometimes when I visit, people think we're sisters. Although she was so young when she had me, barely seventeen, that we could have been sisters. Just as well I don't take it personally.'

'No worries, I'd never make that mistake,' Sam said, warming her again with his glance. 'Have you been back to Ireland at all?' he asked.

'No, not since I left,' Abby confessed. 'I go to London every so often to see Mum. She spoils me to bits with her newfound wealth. But our family home in Mayberry Lane is still leased out.'

'We sold ours when my mother passed on,' Sam said.

It was funny to put her hand on the hard strength of his arm, the way she used to all those years ago. 'I was sorry to hear about your mum. Elaine emailed me.'

'Yeah, well, it's five years ago now. She had a lot of heart trouble and in the end it just gave up.' He stared into his glass for a few moments and Abby stayed silent beside him. 'Anyway, you have to move on with life. I'm living in Malahide now.'

'Ooh, very nice!'

'Whatever happened to the bold Elaine?' he asked, changing the subject. 'The two of you together were holy terrors. No one was safe from your escapades.'

'God, we were a riot! Elaine managed to visit me on her holidays most years until she met Colin. Now she's married and living in domestic bliss.'

'Domestic bliss? Elaine? I didn't think anyone would tame her.'

'She was married in Paris two years ago in a quiet family ceremony. I was at the wedding. Her husband is an accountant who worships the ground she walks on. She had a baby girl, Ruth, last November.'

'Jeez, that's a turn-up. And whereabouts is she living?'

'Wicklow. But I've kind of lost touch with her,' Abby reluctantly admitted.

'How could you lose touch with her in these days of instant communication?'

'We had a – I guess you could call it a bit of a falling out after Christmas.'

'You and Elaine?'

'Yeah, 'fraid so.'

Nothing like the furious row she'd had with her mother, more a chilliness that had caused a rift between them.

'And forgive my big size tens, but what could you pair have fallen out about? I would have chalked you up as bosom lifelong pals.'

'She was annoyed when I didn't go home for Ruth's christening,' Abby admitted.

'And why didn't you?'

'I was too busy.'

'Too busy planning weddings?' Sam looked at her curiously.

'Yeah, we had a lot of bookings for January and February.'

She held his gaze with all the stubbornness of the teenage Abby Lacey. For it was another glib lie, of course, but far more comfortable than trying to explain. Christmas in London had been such a disaster that she'd known it was too soon to face her friend, never mind the millions of questions that Elaine was bound to have about her life and her travels. For that would have meant thinking about the way her life had fallen apart and trying to grasp the way Raffaele had left her, as well as facing up to the stupid way she'd behaved.

She hadn't been ready then, she still wasn't prepared to go there now, and the glib lie tripped off her tongue so easily that she believed it herself, burying her secrets even deeper than before.

4

'So come on, what happened? How come you've decided to settle in Sorrento?' Sam eventually got around to asking. 'You must have celebrated the big three-oh a couple of years ago. Did that put a stop to your gallop around the world?'

'No, of course not.' Abby was deliberately casual. She twirled the tiny vase of flowers on the table, giving it her full attention in order to keep her shadows at bay. 'This is only temporary. There are still plenty of things I want to do.'

'I never saw you as a wedding planner, not in my wildest dreams. Obviously seeing other people get hitched holds an attraction for you? Or in your own inimitable words,' now his tone was teasing, '"contracting a terminal illness"?'

He hadn't forgotten anything, she realised a little uncomfortably. Not a single word. She ignored his questions, fidgeted with the turquoise bracelet on her left arm and finally said, 'I don't intend to stay here forever. I'll move on when the mood takes me.'

His eyes watched her restless fingers and he lifted her hand, the touch of his hand warm and tingly on the tender inside of her wrist. He turned her hand around and examined her ringless fingers. 'And you never felt the urge to get married yourself?'

Abby stayed silent as the sound of an Italian song drifted from an open window. She watched from somewhere deep inside herself as the couple at the next table rose to their feet and strolled down the narrow street, arm in arm. Then she said, 'Well, Sam, what do you think?' She forced herself to meet his eyes unflinchingly and held his gaze until he dropped her hand.

'I think I've said the wrong thing,' he stated calmly as he sat back and smiled at her. 'I recognise that look on your face. Maybe your hair is different, and maybe you've travelled the globe, but you're still the girl I grew up with on Mayberry Lane. And hey,' he said gently, 'I know when I've goofed.'

'You haven't goofed.' She squashed the sudden urge to cry and wondered how her calm had momentarily deserted her. It was three in the morning and she was tired, that's all, she told herself. And she was talking to Sam, her best mate who had known her since childhood and who recognised the signals in her face that she managed to hide from everyone else.

Sam reached out and his fingers brushed her face. 'If you don't want to talk about it, that's fine.'

'There's nothing to talk about,' she insisted with a shaky laugh.

'If you say so.' His eyes were kind.

'And what about you?'

'Oh, loads of women, Abby, but nothing serious. I guess no one would have me,' he lightly quipped. 'Hey, I'm still finding it hard to believe that we're even sitting here like this. It's mad, but it's bloody great to see you again. Here, let's have your glass.'

She watched him sloshing more wine into her glass, thankful that he'd changed the subject and that he'd sensed he was heading into forbidden territory. Sam had always been kind and considerate, ready to pick up her cue and follow where she led.

'I'll have to tell Mark that I met up with you, in Sorrento of all places,' he said, referring to his older brother.

'Where is he nowadays?'

'He's still over in the States. Except for Mum's funeral, he never came home.'

'I suppose he's well married by now with a few kids.'

'He's not, actually. It must be a Ryan trait,' Sam said. He stretched out his long legs scraping back a nearby chair in the process. 'Mark's had plenty of women all right from the sounds of it, but he never made it to the altar rails. He's doing extremely well for himself in the music industry – film scores, television, advertising, the works. Best of all, he received a BAFTA award earlier this year for his latest film score. It was a great recognition and he thoroughly deserved it.'

'Wow! I *am* impressed. Is that how you got involved in music? You could have knocked me for six when I spotted you in the Cloisters. Talk about a change of direction!'

'Hey, don't be under any illusions.' Sam lifted his glass of wine and slowly swirled the liquid around, then put it down again without tasting it and looked at Abby. 'Apart from seeing Mark heading up the red carpet, my life hasn't been half as exciting as yours. I went over to visit him in the States a few times, and I suppose he encouraged me.'

'So you decided to turn your back on the law courts?'

'No way. It pays the bills, but it's not the sum total of my life. I was always fooling around with a guitar but I began to take it more seriously when . . . well, I felt I needed a change. And I suppose Mark pushed me in the right direction.'

She knew by the tone of his voice that there was something he wasn't telling her. She deliberately sounded light as she said, 'Well, whatever, you're really great, you played that guitar like it was made for you. You'd give Eric Clapton a run for his money!'

'Not sure about that,' he grinned. 'Hey,' he waggled the empty bottle of wine, 'do you think Mario would have a seizure if we asked for another bottle?'

★   ★   ★

It was a quarter to four in the morning when Abby unlocked the wrought iron gate that led to the ground floor of her apartment block and turned to face him in the shadowy darkness. It was the most natural thing in the world to fall into his arms and lift her face for his goodnight kiss, much in the way she used to all those years ago. He smoothed down her hair, his fingers lingering on the curve of her neck.

'I have some free time in the morning if you'd like to meet up,' he suggested. 'I don't have to leave for the airport until two o'clock. Although perhaps you'll be busy with another wedding.'

'No, I've nothing on until the day after tomorrow. I'd love to see you, even for a couple of hours. Why don't I collect you at your hotel? Say, eleven o'clock? I could bring you around the Amalfi coast for a bit.' The invitation slipped out before she had time to think, but retracting it would only serve to give it more attention, so she stayed silent.

'I'd love that,' Sam said. He kissed her again and patted her head and she felt warmed with the familiar gestures. 'See you then. Sleep tight.'

Sleep tight? She scarcely slept a wink. The dark press of the night had long fled and the sun was already high in the sky and squinting through her shutters by the time she rose just after nine o'clock. She was waiting for Sam when he emerged from his hotel into the sunlit morning.

'What the hell is this?' he asked, halting on the sidewalk.

She took off her Gucci sunglasses – a present from her mother – and once again, her eyes absorbed him, noticing his air of sexy maturity, his solid confidence and behind that, the gentleness and good humour she'd so often taken for granted. She sat astride her scooter and watched the bemused expression on his face.

'What does it look like?' she asked.

'Some kind of motorbike. Don't tell me we're going on that.'

'Why not? It's the best way to get around,' she smiled.

'Tell me about it. I've never seen as many of them in my life as I have in the last twenty-four hours.' His lopsided grin made her feel light-hearted all of a sudden.

'This is my pride and joy,' Abby said, revving the engine. Her pride and joy was silver and dotted with colourful dragonfly appliqués, with a helmet to match. She jumped nimbly off the saddle, opened the storage box on the back and lifted out a spare helmet. 'Put that on and hold tight,' she ordered, his bemusement giving her a victorious thrill.

'Are you serious?'

Silently, she handed him the helmet.

'I suppose. At least it's plain white and not covered in some girly design,' he relented.

Abby swung back into the saddle and felt the weight of Sam settle behind her and the warmth of his arms clasped around her waist.

'Ready?' She half inclined her head.

'Just about,' he grinned.

She revved the engine and they were off, the rush of breeze warm on her face as they cut through the streets of Sorrento and reached the coast road that led to Amalfi.

She knew it by heart. Every twist, every turn, each and every bend. For a while she forgot that Sam was clinging to her as she absorbed the all too familiar sights and brought him on a journey that was breathtaking in its beauty and mapped forever in her heart. To the right lay the blue, boundless sea, the sparkling sun cutting a silvery trail through the infinite swell of the Golfo di Salerno. On the left side of the road, the jagged, mountainous face rose steeply and sharply. The road to Amalfi twisted and turned as it clung to the cliff face, suspended high above sea level, defying gravity. At some parts along the heart-stopping journey there was just a low wall separating the zigzag road from the sheer drop below and Abby smiled when she felt Sam's grip tightening. She knew the road so well that he had no need to be anxious.

Eventually she pulled into a viewing spot above the village of Positano. There were half a dozen coaches stalled, giving tourists a photo opportunity and time to catch their breath. Abby cut the engine and motioned to Sam to get off before she slid off the saddle herself.

'Do you come here often?' he quipped, removing his helmet.

'Sometimes.'

Sometimes? There was no way to explain that she was here, always, in spirit.

'That is one helluva spectacular journey,' he said. 'It's just bloody amazing. And *you* never cease to amaze me, Abby, a little slip of a thing driving like a pro on those roads.'

'I'm used to it,' she shrugged, letting his words lift her a little. 'C'mon, there's a great view of Positano from here.'

She led the way across to a path cut high into the cliff and down a few steps to a viewing platform. From there they could admire the lapis lazuli sea dotted with tiny white boats and miniature trails, and far below to the left, the town of Positano, row upon row of terracotta-topped buildings that tumbled down from the mountains, hugged the cliffs tenaciously and barely stopped short of falling into the sea.

They stood for a while in the heat of the day, admiring the spectacular view.

'I love it here,' she admitted. It was *Sam*, after all. She was safe with him. Had always been safe with him.

'Why? In what way?'

She hesitated, regretting her sudden confidences. 'It's just somewhere I love to come from time to time.'

'Why here and not some of the other beauty spots in the world?'

'Once upon a time, Positano was a small fishing village,' Abby continued, ignoring his question along with the slight chill that ran through her. 'Now it's a chic holiday resort. And we're going in for coffee.'

He looked back across to the sheer cliff face and down to the tumble of the village, clinging valiantly to the edge of the land where the mountains slanted down to the sea. 'You mean we're going down there, as in driving down?'

'Of course. The road descends so gradually you won't even notice. Look, if the tour buses can negotiate it, think how much easier it is for a scooter.'

'You've just made me feel a helluva lot better,' Sam teased. He put his arm around her as they strolled back to Abby's scooter, and she automatically slid her arm around his waist. Like old times, she reflected, the good old days when she and Sam were best mates, when he hugged her close and kissed her all better.

'So what are your plans if you're not going to stay in Sorrento? Or have you any more missions in life, like deep-sea diving in Mauritius or hanging out in Antarctica?' Sam asked as they sat sipping coffee outside a tiny sidewalk cafe. She had brought him away from the noisy main road and up a narrow side street. From inside the cafe came the clatter of crockery and the pitch of a high, excited voice issuing instructions in a stream of Italian. Outside on the warm flagstone path, a small black cat lay curled asleep in the sun.

'I've nothing like that planned right now,' she admitted.

'You should come back to Ireland, you know, pay us all a visit.'

'Elaine was always inviting me over. Mum has the family home on short leases so it's there for me if I ever want to go back.'

'So what's stopping you? There's nothing to keep you away, surely.'

'I'm not sure how welcome I'd be,' she hedged.

'Don't be ridiculous. I'd welcome you with open arms. I could even try and contact Elaine if you want. I might be able to put in a good word for you,' his eyes twinkled. 'Hey, Mark will be forty in August. I might persuade him to come home for a party. Jeez, that's a great idea. We could all get together and have some kind of reunion bash. You, me, Mark, Elaine, Paula. What d'you think?'

'I don't think Paula would be too impressed,' she said, referring to Elaine's older sister. 'She never had much time for me. I still remember the time Elaine and I tried to play Cupid and fix her up with Mark. We were thirteen going on thirty-three and thought we knew everything.'

Sam laughed. 'I don't know how Paula stuck the pair of you, the way you drove her demented. And whether Mark fancied her or not, he had no chance the way you two interfered. The night before he high-tailed it off to the States he told me he couldn't wait to see the back of Mayberry Lane.'

'Yeah, I felt really guilty about that,' Abby mused. In her childhood, Mark Ryan had always been a rather distant figure to Abby. Politely self-contained in a manner that bright and breezy Sam couldn't begin to imitate, he'd always been in the background of her childhood years, yet funnily enough, she'd feared the loss of his approval far more than Paula's incandescent rage. Even now, a lifetime later, Abby still recalled the pricking of her conscience when she'd fretted that her adolescent meddling had sent him fleeing.

'Surely that's all water under the bridge,' Sam said. 'I suppose Paula's up to her neck in domestic bliss and babies.'

'No, I met her at Elaine's wedding and she's strictly a

career person. She's all blonde and elegant and ever so sophisticated, and from what I gather, she doesn't really share her private life with Elaine. She runs her own recruitment agency in Dublin and it's supposed to be mega successful.'

'I'll bet it is. She always took life a lot more seriously than you and Elaine. Really, Abby, you should come home. See it as the next expedition, if you like. You should come back and say hello to all your old pals. Make it up with Elaine.'

Or make it up with Sam? The thought hung like a gossamer thread in the air. She smiled at him. 'Dunno, Sam. Too much time has gone by.'

'What's time got to do with it?' He reached over and squeezed her hand. His eyes were warm and friendly and she looked away, finding it difficult to meet them. She saw the glitter of a thin silver chain at his throat and realised that in all her years growing up, she'd never fully appreciated him, never mind how attractive he was.

Long after she'd kissed him goodbye outside his hotel and his plane had lifted into the skies over Naples airport, Abby sat on her balcony and felt the comfort of Sam's arms around her.

The following morning she checked her calendar, with its picturesque photographs of Italy depicting various months of the year, the month of May flaunting the panorama of the Marina Grande in Sorrento, with June and July showing equally sensational images. She heard his voice in her ear urging her to come home as she flicked through the months and tried to visualise herself returning for a party. It was three months to August and a lot could happen in that time, she reflected. It had only taken a few short weeks for her life to alter completely.

Her heart contracted when she came to the month of August, for it showed the town of Positano by night, and it reminded her of a mouth she longed to feel on hers, and another voice, equally insistent, urging her to stay.

PAULA

5

A week after Abby kissed Sam goodbye in Sorrento, Paula Stevens awoke on the morning of her thirty-eighth birthday, and for a long, enticing moment was tempted to be kind to herself. Why couldn't she take the morning off, lounge around in her velour robe, sip coffee and juice and laze in front of daytime television? She could flick through the newspapers at leisure and then go for a pleasant stroll.

But some habits were impossible to break. That kind of a day was alien to her and belonged to a different kind of life, not the life of Paula Stevens, who was far too driven putting Dublin's most elitist recruitment firm up there in lights.

So instead of being kind to herself, Paula slid out of her king-sized bed shortly before her alarm clock was due to beep at six twenty-five. She stepped into her sensor power shower and twirled around under body jets adjusted to her favourite temperature, then swathed herself in a thick Egyptian cotton towel. Out in the gleaming kitchen of her dockland penthouse apartment at Hanover Quay, she sipped cool boiled water with a slice of lemon. She opened the blind, barely noticing the sparkle of the nearby River Liffey, glad that it was a bright, dry morning.

Paula turned from the window and stubbed her toe on an empty wine bottle, sending it spinning around the Scandinavian pine floor while shockwaves bounced through her foot. She picked up the offending bottle, brought it out to her press in the hall and had to restrain her temptation to fling it into the overflowing recycling bin. She positioned it gingerly on top of the pile and gave it a baleful glance.

In her bedroom she pulled on plain white panties and a matching bra. She dried her pale blonde hair and pinned it back in a diamante clip while the smoothie-maker was blending precise quantities of bananas, kiwi and natural yoghurt for her breakfast. A crisp white Marc Jacobs shirt and black Chanel suit completed her office ensemble. You couldn't go wrong with black teamed with a fresh white shirt, and she'd picked up three suits and a dozen shirts last February in Saks Fifth Avenue during a weekend shopping blitz in New York.

Paula checked her glossy image in the mirror and told herself that no one would ever guess her life had completely disintegrated just over three years ago. Thank God it was all behind her, she shuddered, accidentally squirting a spray of perfume into the air instead of on her pulse spot. In throwing all her energies into her career, she'd managed to get over the heartbreaking pain, the gut-wrenching hurt and the anguish. Since then she'd locked her guilty secret away along with her emotions and nowadays, her career was her life. Best of all, she smiled to herself as she plucked her car keys out of her Fendi, it was totally under her control. By ten past seven, Paula was firing up her Jaguar and accelerating out of her designated parking spot en route to her office in Smithfield.

'How many enquiries this morning?' Paula asked Kate, her business manager, when she brought in Paula's black coffee at ten-thirty and they had a quick briefing.

'Over a dozen and rising,' Kate said.

Without fail, Monday morning brought a flood of emails and phone calls, the majority of which were urgent pleas from employers looking for temporary staff to fill in for post-weekend no-shows. 'Why can't people wake up to the fact that I'm not into contingency recruitment?' Paula said. 'It would serve those employers better to instigate sufficient disciplinary procedures to prevent staff absences in the first place. They're certainly not the quality clients I want to retain on our portfolios.'

'The temp market is very lucrative,' Kate pointed out. 'And your name is becoming known, which is surely all for the better.'

'Yes, but we're a specialised unit for the financial sector. I've spent the last three years defining our business strategy and raising our profile so that we'll be recognised as delivering only the highest calibre of staff to our blue chip client list. If Johnny Bloggs needs a data entry operator or a mediocre receptionist who'll fill in while his secretary recovers from a weekend hangover, he's come to the wrong place.' Paula stopped for breath and smiled at Kate. 'And that's my little grumble over for the day.'

Her private line buzzed and she recognised her sister's phone number on the caller display. With a nod, Kate withdrew when Paula lifted the phone.

The voice at the other end sang, 'Happy birthday to you, happy birthday to *you* . . .'

Paula frowned and tapped the desk impatiently with a pencil. 'Thanks Elaine, this is all I need.'

'Get you at a bad time, did I?' Her younger sister's voice was upbeat and unapologetic. 'Thought you'd be having your coffee by now and it was safe to phone.'

'I am and it is,' she said crisply, 'but I don't want to know about today, thanks very much.'

'Spoilsport. It's your *birthday*, you should be feeling a little special. Will I read out your birthday horoscope?'

'No, thanks. I've far more important things on my mind.'

'Like?'

'Elaine, I really don't have time for a chat. I'll talk to you later this evening.'

'Surely you're going out tonight?'

'I've no plans other than an early night. I've another busy day ahead of me tomorrow.'

'Aw. I'd come up to Dublin to meet you myself, only Ruth is sick.'

'Poor thing,' Paula's voice softened as she visualised her little niece. 'Give her my best love.'

'She has an ear infection and it's terrible to witness her fretting when she's not well, and you feel useless. But seriously,' Elaine continued in an assertive tone of voice, 'you should give yourself a break and go out on the town. Birthdays come but once a year and deserve to be celebrated.'

'Celebrated? Some hope,' Paula said. 'It's all right for you, but in terms of birthdays, I've nothing to celebrate. In two years' time I'll be forty. *Forty!* And I'm living in an age-obsessed society where the emphasis is on all things youthful. If I want to stamp my mark, I just have a couple of years left before I'm considered over the hill.'

'All very noble, but what's the point in running your own company if you can't take your birthday off? Just as well I posted a card to your office. And it's not because I'm psychic. I guessed you'd be there. You're far too conscientious.'

'What's wrong with that?'

'You should chill out and laugh at life a little more. You're too hard on yourself. At least try and go home at a reasonable hour.'

After the call, Paula picked up the luminescent pink birthday card Elaine had posted to her office. *Kisses from Ruth in case you don't get home until your special day is almost over. xxx* The kisses were so irregular that Paula guessed her sister had been guiding Ruth's tiny fist across the page. On impulse she placed it at the corner of her immaculate desk, even though it looked totally out of place. There was no doubt that Paula Stevens, the shy, scholarly girl from Mayberry Lane, had come a long way. She had a clear vision for the recruitment company she'd set up three years ago. Kate had been appointed to the role of business manager after Paula had poached her from one of her rival companies. In her late forties and with a wealth of experience, loyal, trustworthy Kate was very valuable to Paula.

'I need someone I can trust, with good interpersonal skills to manage day-to-day operations,' she'd said to the elegant lady with the neat mahogany hair when she'd met her for lunch in the Morrison Hotel. She'd sensed straight away that Kate was a natural people person, skills Paula felt she was sadly lacking.

Kate had smiled warmly. 'I'd love to come and work for you. To be honest, it's just the kind of new and exciting challenge I need after my rather messy divorce,' she'd shrugged and looked rueful.

So Kate had had her heart damaged, much as she had, Paula realised as she gave her new business manager a brief, sympathetic smile. But unlike Paula, who had shamefully locked that episode away, Kate wasn't afraid to admit it. Although she doubted very much if Kate had behaved half as foolishly as Paula.

'I can promise you challenge and excitement,' Paula went on smoothly. 'I have an ambitious mission statement, and I'm not afraid to climb into the ring with any of my competitors.'

Now Stevens Recruitment was based in an imposing suite of offices in a fashionable block in Smithfield. Paula had fifteen staff from whom she expected the optimum in terms of commitment, motivation and loyalty, and whom she rewarded appropriately with excellent fringe benefits and a fulfilling career path. Staff who were ecstatic to be offered a contract with the dynamic, exclusive Stevens and who quickly realised that if their sophisticated boss with the penetrating blue eyes was ambition personified, then Kate was the warm, human face of Stevens, managing the staff with a wise and sensible hands-on style.

Not so long ago, Paula would have been intimidated by a haughty receptionist sitting poised at an immaculate desk. Sometimes she found it hard to believe that she now had such a receptionist to keep any unwanted visitors at bay, a receptionist who was, comfortingly enough, slightly in awe of Paula. Her signature logo with the huge curving S was emblazoned on the outer wall of her office suite and on the nameplate outside the entrance to the building. It was incorporated into the cobalt blue uniforms worn by her staff, as well as her stationery and website. It was the emblem of success, for Stevens was going to be a *huge* success.

They said everything in life had an opposite, a corresponding antithesis. Paula might have scoffed at Elaine's proposed reading of her horoscope, but she secretly hoped there was such a thing as yin and yang, positive and negative, darkness and light, for surely she was due a big, bright success to make up for the equally big, dark chapter in her life.

On the morning of her birthday, she was interviewing applicants on the shortlist for one of her newest clients, a global financial firm that was seeking a fund manager to assist in heading up their Dublin base. The applicants had already been screened by Emer, her most senior consultant who had drawn up the shortlist, but from what Paula could see, none of them met the precise business requirements of her client.

Her final applicant that morning was a presentable Dublin

man in his early thirties who sensed he'd blown it halfway through the interview.

'I'm not giving you the right answers, am I?' Brian said bluntly. 'Look, I know I have the potential to do this job. I just need a chance to prove myself.'

She allowed for a certain amount of nerves, as most people were intimidated on being brought into the inner sanctum of her office. It was one thing to survive Emer's sharp interviewing skills, but Paula was another matter. Most candidates didn't know what to make of her, never mind her office. With its dramatic views of Dublin city discreetly veiled by voile drapes and Japanese-crafted maple and silver furniture, including a squashy nutmeg sofa by the window, it exuded power and success. As well as that, Paula usually dispensed with their CVs; after all, Emer rigorously covered that ground, and the fact that she had nothing at all, not even a blank page, on the enormous maple desk in front of her often put applicants off if it didn't faze them completely.

Paula sat back in her leather chair. 'That might be the case,' she said, spreading her neatly manicured fingers in a conciliatory gesture, 'but I have my reputation to consider, Brian. I can only recommend someone if they possess all the qualifications desired, and you have a gap in relation to hedge fund experience. You see, my client's needs are paramount. I have to ensure that I surpass their expectations, or at the minimum give them the highest-quality outcome in terms of intellectual capital acquisition.'

He rose to his feet.

'I'll retain your details on our database,' she said, also rising fluidly to her feet and extending her hand. 'We may be able to assist you in the future with your next career move.'

Brian was looking at her rather oddly and Paula realised too late that she'd kicked off her towering heels. She deliberately chose sky-high heels because she felt she needed the addition of authoritative inches to her five-foot, three-inch frame. Trouble was, maintaining her balance even from the lift in the underground car park to her office was a daily challenge. She'd purchased this particular pair of Manolo Blahniks in the heat of the moment. Now the skyscraper stilettos lay out of reach under her desk and she realised to her embarrassment that she stood almost five inches shorter than when Brian had first entered her office.

He swiftly concealed his surprise with a polite expression. 'I'd prefer if Stevens didn't keep my details,' he said, ignoring her outstretched hand. 'I know I'd be an excellent candidate for this job, but you won't give me the opportunity to prove it. I don't even see my CV on your desk, so how do I know I've been given proper consideration?'

'I can assure you I'm perfectly au fait with the relevant details of your experience,' Paula said, enraged at being challenged and already at a disadvantage in her stocking feet. 'However, in the circumstances, I won't be initiating any further communication with you.'

In spite of her mask of professionalism, Paula felt a pang of dismay as he shrugged his shoulders and strode out of her office. In a sense, she was playing God with other people's lives and careers. Brian might well have gone on to make a great success of the job. She had a gut feeling that he'd make a success of whatever he set out to do, but she couldn't trust her female intuition, considering how badly it had let her down before; so badly, in fact, that her personal life had been destroyed.

However, she'd learned her lesson and since then romance had been strictly off her game plan. But the prospect of having children was a different matter.

The minute she'd seen tiny Ruth nestling in her sister's arms, she'd known she wanted a baby of her own. Not so long ago, her latest birthday might have meant that time was running out for babies, but nowadays there were ways around that, thanks to advances in reproductive medicine. Only recently she'd pounced on an article outlining new developments in the whole process of putting fertility on ice and she'd had made a mental note to explore it further. Best of all, in these enlightened times, you didn't even need a man, never mind a relationship, in order to enjoy the motherhood experience. It was all about choice, and these days, thankfully, women got to choose.

There was a sudden commotion outside her office just before lunch. The door opened and Kate swept in looking unusually flustered.

'Paula, I apologise for this intrusion,' Kate began. 'There's a gentleman outside who insists on talking to you. He has no appointment or—'

'In that case he has no business with me.'

'He says it's personal.'

'Personal?' She felt a stab of anxiety.

'Yes, he—' Kate was forced to step aside as a tall, blond man sauntered into Paula's office and into her carefully-controlled life.

He was indeed a ghost from the past, but not the one she'd feared, and that fact alone restored her breathing. But it was a scant reprieve, for he was someone who caused her mind to catapult back to a place where she'd grown up and a time when her quiet, shy reserve had been no match for the careless devilry of her sister and Abby, her friend, and Sam, the boy down the road.

She might have come a long way from Mayberry Lane, but for all her success, none of that essential part of her had changed, Paula ruefully realised as she gave him a swift, all-encompassing glance and rose to her feet.

6

'I'd scarcely have recognised you,' he said with an amused smile.

'Excuse me?'

'You look different. So this is Paula Stevens, all grown up.'

He neared her desk, invading her space. She might have been bemused with a slight sense of shock and her adrenaline was still all over the place, but Paula had reacted quickly enough to shove her feet into her Manolos before she'd stood up, the better to confront him.

'What's more,' he tipped his head to one side and looked at her quizzically, 'I think you've gotten taller as well.'

'Sam? Sam Ryan? What on earth are you doing here? It's all right, Kate,' she nodded. 'I'll take care of this.'

'Sure?' The expression on Kate's face was a picture and Paula felt a stab of annoyance. Her inviolate office had never been breached like this. She didn't want her worlds to collide. One of the reasons she valued her job so much and appreciated the ordered sanctuary of her office environment was the fact that it was an entirely separate entity to her disastrous personal life.

'Yes, Kate, this is just an old neighbour of mine,' she said smoothly.

'Hey, less of the old,' Sam quipped as Kate withdrew.

'A cheeky old neighbour,' Paula said, looking at him meaningfully, unconsciously falling back into the casual disdain with which she'd treated all her younger sister's friends.

'Can I sit down?' Sam asked.

Paula indicated the chair in front of her desk. 'You're scarcely here on business,' she said, pulling the edges of her Chanel jacket together but feeling as though she was pulling her professional self together. She subsided into her chair, somehow grateful for the yards of polished maple between them. Then she raked a cool, observant eye over him, much in the way she sized up her job-seekers.

Sam sat back in his seat, looking totally relaxed and in control. The only thing he had in common with her intimidated candidates was his pristine dark suit, silvery tie and excellent appearance. Mid-thirties, she swiftly calculated, and twelve years since she'd had a conversation with him, for it was twelve years since she'd moved away from Mayberry Lane into her first, minuscule city centre apartment. The unruly shock of blond hair she remembered was now fashionably trimmed. In fact, the friend of Elaine's that she'd given a cursory nod to many a time had matured rather sexily.

Then her thoughts drifted to his older brother.

Mark. Not as tall as Sam, dark-haired and more sensitive by nature compared to Sam's extrovert athleticism. It was longer again since she'd spoken to him. It seemed like a lifetime ago since he'd taken himself off, rather hurriedly, to the States and she wondered briefly how his life had turned out.

'You know, I've gone by this building plenty of times,' Sam said, 'but I never realised you were the brains behind Stevens.'

Paula lifted her eyebrows. 'And when did you manage to make that connection?'

'Just today. When I looked at the nameplate this morning

as I was going by, it suddenly clicked that in all probability, this was your baby. Although I've been meaning to look you up.'

'You have?' she said, unable to mask her incredulity.

'Yeah, I bumped into Abby recently, in Sorrento of all places – Abby Lacey?'

'Abby, yes, who could forget Abby.' Paula had a vision of a slender, waif-like teenager with an impish grin on her oval face and an indifferent toss of her long, dark hair. Abby and Elaine, giggling together, swapping secrets, making mischief and playing basketball with Sam at the end of the lane.

'I haven't seen her in years,' Sam said. 'She told me about your successful recruitment agency. That's how I put two and two together. Jeez, you've a bloody great view.' Sam abruptly rose to his feet and strode across to the plate glass window. He pulled aside the softly-draped voile to stare at the grey-blue panorama of Dublin city.

'We're on the fifth floor,' Paula pointed out unnecessarily.

'Beats working in the dungeons of the law courts,' Sam said with his back to her.

'Is that your baby?' she asked in imitation of his casual slang. 'Though you were studying law, weren't you?' She had a recollection of seeing Sam hurrying down Mayberry Lane in the mornings, a bulging satchel on his back, and more often than not, calling into Abby's on the way home from college.

'Yep, I'm gainfully employed quite a lot of the time, but I also have interests in the world of music as well.' He let the drapes fall back into place, moved away from the window and sat down on the squashy sofa. 'Don't tell me,' he grinned. 'I bet this is your casting couch!'

'Sam Ryan! You're still an outrageous rascal and you haven't changed a bit.' Torn between annoyance and exasperation, Paula couldn't help but smile.

'No, thank God.' He rose from the sofa and nodded at the door in the corner. 'Your private interrogation room?'

'My private facilities,' she told him, trusting he wouldn't ask to use the bathroom in mischievous little boy fashion. Her en suite was sacrosanct.

'And what are all those?' he asked, nodding at the series of framed scrolls along the wall above Paula's desk.

'My qualifications,' she said, disgusted to realise that she felt embarrassed by her display of scholarly achievements.

He gave an appreciative whistle.

'What brings you here?' she said, wondering how soon she could get rid of him. She didn't want him crowding her office, crowding her mind with memories. Mayberry Lane was another part of her past, and her past was something she was doing her best to forget.

She felt a measure of relief when he sat down on the chair in front of her desk. Her relief was short-lived, however, when he suddenly reached forward and plucked her pink birthday card from the spot beside her laptop. Unashamedly, he read Elaine's greeting and quirked an eyebrow. 'Birthday, huh?'

'No. Yes. It's – look, Sam, you shouldn't even be here.' She dropped all pretence of patience. 'I've a full day's work to do.'

'I'm sure you have. No one gets to be as successful as you are without putting in twelve-hour days. And you're even hard at it on your birthday.' He gave her a sympathetic grin.

She shrugged. 'It's not important.'

'Nonsense, of course it is. Hey, have you had your lunch yet?'

'No, I'm just going to—'

'Let me guess, a quick tuna wrap at the desk?'

She frowned. 'Well yes, but—'

He shook his head. 'Uh-uh, not today. Today, Ms Stevens, you're coming out to lunch. Number one, it's your birthday, and number two, I'm making up for all the tricks and leg-pulling you had to put up with at the hands of the wicked Abby and Elaine.'

'*And* you,' she pointed out a little acerbically.

'I was only following orders,' he said with mock innocence.

'Hah!'

'Well, are you on for lunch or what?' He stood up and jiggled loose change in his jacket pocket. 'I want to talk about something with you.'

'What would you want to discuss with me? I haven't seen you in years.'

'Come out to lunch and you'll find out,' he grinned.

'I don't go out to lunch. I always have it at my desk.'

'Surely a high-powered tycoon like you occasionally swans off to expensive, tax-deductible business lunches.'

'I don't have time for any of those fringe benefits,' Paula told him.

'Not even for the cool bottle of Chablis I'd like to share with you?'

'Definitely no alcohol in the middle of the day.'

'You might look more sophisticated, but behind it all you're still the same old diligent Paula.'

'And that, Sam,' she smiled sweetly, swallowing her annoyance, 'is precisely how I got where I am today. And if you don't mind,' she tapped her silver pen lightly against the glass of her watch, 'my schedule is tight. I have an information checkpoint with my business manager first thing this afternoon.'

'Information checkpoint? Don't tell me – the latest buzz word for meeting.'

She raised her eyebrows in her most imperious Ms Stevens expression, the one she'd developed to strike terror into anyone who crossed her.

It had the desired effect on Sam. 'Okay.' He threw up his hands and backed away. 'I know when I'm not wanted.'

'Look, Sam,' she said, feeling somewhat chastened, 'it's nothing personal. I'm just very busy.'

'Sure. Perhaps some other time?'

'Yes, if you insist.'

'Maybe later in the week then? I'd like to talk to you about something. This time I promise I'll go by the rules and make an appointment.'

She was so relieved to be rid of him that she readily agreed.

Lunch was black coffee and a tuna and sweetcorn salad at her desk while she scrolled through some e-publications on the net. Straight after lunch, Kate popped in to discuss the presentation Paula planned to make to two clients she was hoping to poach from a rival recruitment firm.

'It will really be a coup when I manage to convert them,' she told Kate as she called up the relevant details on her laptop. 'It might be a bit of a challenge, but I'm confident we can win them over. Our placement figures speak for themselves – make sure they're up-to-date and absolutely correct, won't you? I'll mail the presentation across to you and you can fine tune things with Ursula.'

'Ursula's left,' Kate pointed out.

Paula frowned. 'Damn, I'd forgotten. Remind me again who has taken over her administrative duties?'

'We'd agreed that Sadie was best placed to take over, but actually, Paula, she asked to have a word with me just before lunch and she's also tendered her resignation, effective in four weeks' time.'

Paula felt a sliver of anxiety. 'What? That's rather a loss, isn't it? Ursula and now Sadie? What's going on? The last thing I need is to have my key staff headhunted by one of my rivals!'

'Ursula's gone to work for an insurance company, but I'm not sure what Sadie's plans are.'

'Sadie's been with me since the beginning. This won't do. I'll have to speak to her. My schedule is jammed for this afternoon, so why don't you arrange for her to meet with me at, let me see . . .' Paula clicked her keyboard and checked her calendar. 'Say five o'clock – no, make it five-thirty?'

When the meeting was over, Kate phoned through to Paula and told her that five-thirty didn't suit Sadie.

'And why on earth not?' Paula demanded.

'I didn't ask her,' Kate said quietly. 'Look, Paula, she's only contracted to work up to five-thirty.'

'But she's often worked beyond that. Surely she can see that this is important? This is her whole career we're talking about.' Paula felt tension flickering in her stomach.

Kate's voice was smooth. 'Then maybe that's all the more reason to arrange a suitable time when neither of you will be rushing to get away.'

Paula was tempted to say that she wasn't in a rush to get anywhere. She almost pointed out that even though it was her birthday, there were no pressing engagements, no reasons for her to be rushing home to get glammed up for a night on the town. No going out to dinner. No form of celebrations whatsoever. But she bit back the reply. Her rapport with Kate, although relaxed and friendly, was strictly on a business footing.

'In that case, I'll see her at two o'clock tomorrow,' she said.

By the time Paula was nosing her Jaguar out onto the sun-drenched quays in the direction of home, rush-hour traffic had long since subsided and the bustling streets were full of revellers out for the evening. A line of taxis snaked slowly along the bus lanes, disgorging happy, laughing people. Lovers were everywhere – strolling arm in arm along the boardwalk, standing close together at traffic lights, holding hands as they darted together through the crowds on their way to a show or a film.

Once upon a time . . .

Paula pressed the accelerator and sped through the lights at O'Connell Bridge. It didn't matter that she wasn't out there and it didn't bother her that this was her third birthday alone. Once upon a time, she'd listened to promises of wedding rings and commitment, wrapped in the arms of her lover. She'd spent other birthdays enjoying luxury weekend retreats, being wined and dined in chic restaurants. She'd woken up to find roses on her pillow and petals in the bath. But she'd spent those birthdays in blissful ignorance of the anguish that lay ahead.

Paula realised she was gripping the steering wheel so tightly that the joints in her fingers objected and she made herself relax. Tonight she was quite happy to be going home alone and putting her feet up. She loved her elegant, comfortable apartment decorated in neutral tones of beige and cream, with the luxury taupe sofas and cream rugs on the lacquered floor. She'd spent a small fortune having the spacious interior professionally made over the previous year and she appreciated the cool sumptuousness of it all. She'd skip the gym, shove a pizza in the oven, open a bottle of that special reserve wine she'd been saving and put on one of her favourite laugh-a-minute DVDs. *Legally Blonde*, perhaps, or *Love Actually*, or one of her all-time favourites, *Clueless*.

No one, but no one, regarding her across her powerful, sexy desk would ever guess that hard-as-nails Ms Stevens's guilty pleasure was her continually expanding collection of chick flick DVDs. Guaranteed to lighten her mood and take her far away from the loneliness of life at the top, never mind life without a man, they'd brought her through many a solitary evening. Occasionally, as she caught herself in mid-laugh or wiped away a sudden tear, she knew there was a different Paula Stevens in there struggling to get out; a more sensitive, emotional woman who, for her own peace of mind, was best kept firmly under wraps.

She swept down towards Hanover Quay and home. At least her birthday hadn't gone completely unnoticed. She'd had a lunch invitation that she'd turned down, she reminded herself, recalling Sam and his totally unexpected appearance in her office.

Sam Ryan. A blast from the past. Memories of another era indeed, an era when everything she did was safe and predictable, with her future all carefully calculated and mapped out in front of her.

Or so she had thought.

7

Sadie McNamara sat in front of Paula's desk. In her late twenties, she'd been with Paula for three years, which made her one of the stalwarts of her consulting staff. Paula remembered the day she'd interviewed Sadie for the job. Stevens had been in its infancy, and she recalled the younger girl's passionate enthusiasm and go-getting personality. Now all that eager enthusiasm had vanished. Sadie couldn't quite meet her eye and Paula felt a sharp sense of disappointment.

'Is there any particular reason why you want to leave?' Paula asked, hoping she would get this right. Staff relations weren't her strong point, which was why she relied so heavily on Kate.

'I feel that I need a fresh challenge,' Sadie said.

'I'm sure we could accommodate you in that respect,' Paula went on. 'There will be plenty of opportunities for career progression and promotion within Stevens as the company develops. I'm hoping to attract some new clientele and I'd be happy for you to manage their accounts. And if it's a question of your salary,' Paula paused for effect, 'I can assure you that your remuneration package will be up for consideration along with your annual appraisal in a couple of months' time. Believe me, Sadie, one of my principles is to ensure that high-performing consultants such as you can enjoy an accelerated career path within the company.' Paula finished on a triumphant note and smiled encouragingly at Sadie.

She was thrown off balance to realise that Sadie looked unimpressed. 'No, this isn't about the money,' she shook her head.

Paula hesitated fractionally. Money was usually the bottom line with ambitious twenty-somethings, wasn't it? 'Look, Sadie,' she smiled. 'I – *we* – still have a lot of work to do to put this company firmly at the cutting edge. I was hoping to retain you for at least a couple of more years. So far you've really proven yourself to be loyal and committed and a valuable asset to the team. Is there anything I can do to make you reconsider your decision?'

Sadie was silent.

Paula squashed her impatience and tried another approach. 'Where are you hoping to take your career? Are you by any chance joining another recruitment firm?'

'God, no.'

Paula frowned. 'Surely the field of recruitment isn't all that unattractive?'

'No, it's not that. The thing is, Paula, I . . .' Sadie looked as though she'd rather be anywhere else and Paula instinctively knew she wasn't going to like this. She might appear calm on the outside, but she felt a ball of tension in her stomach as Sadie gave her an apologetic look and told her that she wasn't yet thirty years of age, but already she felt burnt out.

'Burnt *out*?'

'Yes. I can't continue any longer at the level at which I've been operating,' Sadie told her. 'Another few months in Stevens, and I won't have a relationship left.'

'A relationship?' Paula laughed dismissively. 'And what does your private life have to do with your career?'

'It's just – I need my life back. There have been far too many nights when I've had to work late at the drop of a hat, or weekends taken up with recruitment fairs. Even my holidays last year had to fit around the demands of the job and I was lucky to manage a week away with my boyfriend.'

'Your boyfriend? So a week on a Spanish beach is more important than your job?'

'No, it's not just that, it's everything. I've missed concerts and turned up late at restaurants and lost out on weekends away on account of Stevens and I want a better work–life balance. I want marriage and babies in the not too distant future. That's why I'm handing in my notice.'

Paula was silent as she absorbed Sadie's words. Restaurants. Concerts. *Marriage and babies*. She felt as though she'd been personally snubbed. Not a trace of her agitation showed, however, as she sat back in her chair and regarded Sadie thoughtfully. 'I was convinced that the younger generation would be more goal-orientated, certainly more competitive, and perhaps even snapping at my heels,' she said icily. 'You do realise that your twenties and thirties are your prime years to establish your career? You'll never have quite the same energy again. If you want to get ahead, a certain amount of sacrifice is required. I intend to take Stevens up to the next level. I was hoping to have you on board. However, in view of what you've said . . .' She paused, a rush of adrenaline causing Ms Paula Gung-ho Stevens to jump in all guns blazing and make a split-second decision that she instantly regretted. 'If you're really that unhappy working for me, I'm releasing you from your contract with immediate effect.'

She felt a certain amount of bittersweet power when Sadie's face paled.

Paula sensed the change in the atmosphere over the next few days. Whenever she stepped out of her office, she was acutely aware of hurriedly broken-off conversations, eyes suddenly absorbed in computer screens and a general air of tension.

'This won't do at all,' she said to Kate when she brought in her coffee on Thursday morning.

'No indeed. It's uncomfortable for everyone.'

'I'm more concerned that job candidates presenting for interview will surely sense the general air of malaise and our reputation will suffer.'

'Sadie was very popular,' Kate pointed out. 'Some of the girls are unhappy with the way she left.'

'Too bad.' Paula hid a niggle of dismay. She couldn't afford to be sensitive. 'It was Sadie's decision to opt out. She wasn't fired. I have a business to run and targets to meet. *And* monthly salaries to pay. Have we had any suitable applications for our own vacancies?'

'Yes, there are eight candidates coming in next week.'

'Refer them to Emer and then I'll interview the shortlist myself,' Paula told her.

'Oh, and Mr Ryan phoned, looking for a late evening appointment with you.'

'Mr Ryan?' Paula frowned. She still held a mental picture of Sam striding into her office and causing ripples of disturbance in the calm order of her working life. Much to her irritation, she'd found herself replaying his visit at odd moments in the day, recalling the amused gleam in his eye, the set of his shoulders and the way he'd carried himself as he marched across to her window to admire the view. Other times, she uncomfortably recalled the snappy way she'd dismissed him and refused his lunch invitation. 'Tell him this evening is the only time that I'm available,' she said to Kate. Hopefully the short notice wouldn't put him off. The sooner he said what he had to say and was out of her head, the better. As the afternoon went by and she answered emails and listened to her voicemail, she was conscious of being slightly tense when she thought of seeing him again and decided that the atmosphere in the office must be getting to her.

When Kate ushered him in just before she left for the evening, Sam was wearing a crisp dark brown suit and refused to sit down.

'I'm not one of your job-seekers facing a grilling across that obstacle course,' he said, nodding at her desk. 'I'm taking you out for a drink. You can call it a belated birthday drink if you like, or an old neighbourly get-together.'

'And supposing I don't choose to go out?'

'Why ever not?'

He looked so hurt and offended that she asked herself why ever not indeed?

Paula had all but forgotten that the Dublin weekend whirl usually started on Thursday nights and that the nearby pubs would be doing a roaring trade. Sam's broad shoulders were most convenient for pushing through the noisy crowd and she gratefully squeezed through the gap he made, grimly maintaining her balance on her skyscraper heels. He found a corner away from the crush of bodies and the huge plasma screen.

'I'll have a mineral water,' she said. 'I'm driving.'

He made a face. 'Pity. Couldn't you leave the car for once and get a taxi?' he said.

She shook her head and watched him push his way back to the bar. Why the hell was she was so damn inflexible? This wasn't the office, but even out for a drink with an old neighbour, she was the same old diligent, serious Paula. It wouldn't be a mortal sin to loosen up a little, enjoy a couple of white wines and hail a taxi home.

He returned with their drinks and sat down beside her. It was then, as their fingers brushed and their eyes met when he handed her a bottle and a glass with ice, that it struck her that she hadn't been out with a man in a long time. She was used to negotiating with men around a conference room table or lording it over them across an interview desk, but she'd forgotten what it was like to be sitting close to a man in the noisy, convivial atmosphere of a pub, having his undivided attention, sharing conversation and laughter.

Paula was slightly appalled to find herself checking Sam out and she hurriedly pulled herself together. She was just shattered after a tough week in the office and was overreacting. Besides being the boy next door, Sam Ryan was younger than her. He had brought her out for a drink because he wanted to discuss something with her. Otherwise she wouldn't be there.

'Cheers anyway,' he tipped his pint glass to hers and she felt the full blast of his warm smile.

'Cheers, Sam,' she said, meeting his eyes again and feeling distinctly ruffled. 'What did you want to discuss?' she asked, belatedly realising that her tone of voice was ridiculously formal.

'Well, Abby . . . and Mark . . .'

Abby. On Mayberry Lane it had always been Sam and Abby, Abby and Sam. Indeed, it had been a mantra of Elaine's, as she'd scarcely spoken of one without the other in the same breath. Then Abby had flown off on her quest to see the world, leaving Sam behind. Having met her recently in Sorrento, Sam obviously wanted to put things right between them. All this flew through her mind in the nanosecond that she watched him raise his glass to his lips and for the first time noticed the contours of his mouth.

He thunked his glass back down on the wooden table. 'What's up?'

Paula felt hot, as though she'd suddenly stripped off in front of him. 'Nothing,' she swiftly replied, deliberately focusing her gaze on the middle of his face in order to avoid his eyes, not to mention his mouth. 'Tell me about Abby.'

'She's working as a wedding planner in Sorrento, believe

it or not. I told her to come back to Ireland, take some time out and make up with Elaine.'

'I didn't know she'd fallen out with my sister. Although since Elaine's had Ruth, her whole world, her every conversation, in fact her whole focus revolves around Ruth. I don't blame her, though, because my little niece is just gorgeous.'

'You sound a little envious.'

'Do I?' Paula laughed. To her own ears it sounded forced and she dismissed the twinge of resentment she'd felt as she'd first caught sight of Elaine holding tiny little Ruth. 'No, thanks. At the moment all my energy is going into Stevens.'

'That's not good either,' Sam lightly admonished, then continued, 'I still can't picture the mad cap Elaine married, never mind with a little one of her own. Anyway, about Abby . . .' he lapsed into a thoughtful silence.

Paula sipped her chilled water and waited.

'There was something, I dunno, something fragile about her.'

'Fragile? Abby Lacey?'

'Yeah. I can't put my finger on it. Oh, she talked about all the places she's seen and the travelling she's done, but behind the smiles, she wasn't the sparky self that I remember. And what the hell is she doing planning weddings anyway? Abby was never a fan of weddings. I think a trip home would do her the world of good.'

Paula felt irritated. He'd brought her out to talk about Abby, to use her as a sounding board to discuss the possibility of getting Abby back home. And maybe if he enticed her home and the circumstances were right, no doubt Sam was hoping that Abby wouldn't be going off again. Maybe he was looking for some advice from a feminine perspective. She was surprised to find that she, successful company founder and director, felt – well, there was no other word for it, she thought, other than slightly at a loss. She might have qualifications coming out of her ears, but there was no point whatsoever in coming to her for female advice.

'. . . and that's where it comes to Mark,' Sam was saying. 'I just wanted to ask you if you'd have a problem with that.'

'Sorry, you've lost me,' Paula apologised. She was embarrassed to realise that she hadn't heard a word he'd said.

'He'll be forty in August and I thought it would be a good excuse for a reunion of sorts.'

'Is he still in America?'

'Yeah, San Francisco. If I could persuade him home, maybe for some kind of party, get Abby over from Italy, and yourself and Elaine,' he shrugged. 'It's just an idea. We'd have a bloody great night out, maybe a couple of nights. It would do Abby good to touch base with her friends. And I'd like to see Mark back to his roots for a while as well. How does that sound to you? I know there was something with you and Mark . . . ?'

Sam was looking at her with a measure of concern and Paula felt suddenly warmed with his attention. He was sitting so close that she could feel some kind of energy emanating from his body, see the dark pupils in his hazel eyes, eyes that were regarding her intently. She had the odd thought that if eyes were the windows of the soul, then Sam's soul was kind and affectionate, definitely roguish, but full of humour and intelligence. Not like her soul. Oh no, Paula Stevens's soul was sour and blackened, bitter and well and truly screwed up.

'No worries, Sam, I've moved on since the days of Mayberry Lane, so I've no problem seeing Mark again,' she said smoothly.

'Cheers. That's that sorted. Shall we have another drink? I'd love to find out how exactly you ended up at the helm of such a prestigious company, with a kick-ass receptionist, a suite of offices straight out of *Star Trek* and a set of uniformed staff who put the fear of God into me.'

Paula found herself laughing at Sam's image of her business. 'And that's just for starters,' she retorted. Her mind raced ahead as she swiftly edited whole chunks of her life and selected only conversational topics that were safe to take out in front of Sam.

'Let me guess,' he grinned. 'You probably have a Merc or two stashed away, a villa in Madeira and live in a split-level bungalow with views of Dublin Bay.'

'How about a Jag and a penthouse apartment with views of the docks?' she tossed.

A second drink led to a third, and Paula found herself relaxing and enjoying their evening, sketching the bare facts of how she ended up as the MD of Stevens – college, various positions in the banking, accountancy and recruitment sector, networking and flying up the ladder until she'd decided that the time was right to strike out on her own, and with her specialised background knowledge, set up her own recruitment company.

'Hey, Paula, I'm not asking you to recite your CV off by heart,' he joked. 'You've got the job. Tell me about the rest of your life.'

'You wouldn't want to hear the other stuff, believe me,' she told him.

There must have been something in her face that told him not to go there, for he switched subjects and began to talk about his career. She listened while he spoke of his work as a barrister in the law courts. He specialised in family law and balanced that with playing music part-time.

'They seem a total contradiction,' she said.

'I guess they do,' his white teeth gleamed. 'I always liked

messing with a guitar, but you can thank Mark for getting
me really involved. And now that my law career is established,
I pick and choose my casework because I need to do
something different and creative outside the rigid constraints
and frustrations of the courtroom. My life doesn't revolve
around my legal files, I'm glad to say. Otherwise I'd be a
cynical bore.'

She sensed that he, too, was putting a slick snapshot
together without delving too deeply into personal motives.
In a sense, she knew little about his personal life by the time
the night was over, but she could have painted a picture of
him, so aware was she of his physical presence.

She watched his eyes as he spoke and was mesmerised
by the way he used his hands and could well imagine those
long, lean fingers plucking the strings of a guitar or mandolin.
She noticed the way his mouth curved into a warm smile
and although she was sorry when the evening came to an
end, she had a funny sense of relief because she was
uncomfortable with the direction of her thoughts.

He insisted on leaving her back to her car.

'Of course, it's really only an excuse to see the Jag,' he
joked as they left the pub. The night was mellow, the pungent
scent of fruit hung in the air from the nearby Smithfield
markets and the streets were quiet with occasional passersby.

Paula tripped on the cobblestones as they crossed the road
and Sam looked at her in alarm.

'Hey, are you okay? How the hell can you walk in those
things anyway?'

She grimaced. 'I can't. Not really.'

'Don't tell me they're part of the ammunition?'

'Well, to be honest, yes, they are.'

'Here, you ninny, hang onto me.'

'Okay, thanks.'

Anyone glancing at them would have assumed they were

a couple, she realised as she clung to Sam's arm. She allowed herself to consider this for a moment or two, briefly imagining a scenario when she was going home with Sam after an evening out together. It was rather scary to realise that the idea didn't seem all that preposterous. There was something honest and open about this grown-up Sam, something convivial and refreshing that she found appealing.

Bloody hell, that was the polite version. She inwardly admitted that her gut instinct was really screaming something else, something she'd noticed the minute he'd set foot in her office. Now that he'd matured, Mark Ryan's younger brother was gut-wrenchingly sexy. Lurking behind the amused smile and the expressive way he moved his hands was a highly beddable Sam. She had a vision of his mouth coming down on hers, her hands reaching up and threading through his hair, their clothes being in the way, and she had to blink hard and bring herself back to the dimly-lit foyer of the office block, the night security giving the cool Ms Stevens a polite nod of recognition, the whine of the lift as it brought them down to the echoing grey chill of an almost deserted car park.

Sam was suitably impressed with her gleaming cream Jaguar and on impulse she offered him a lift home.

'No, thanks,' he said. 'I couldn't drag you all the way out to Malahide.'

'It wouldn't take long,' she said, surprising herself with her offer, as she wasn't usually so forthcoming. She balanced herself against the door of the car as she chucked off her stilettos, flexed her toes and pulled on her flat-heeled driving shoes. She was aware that she was letting him see her with some kind of guard down, and exhilarated that she noticed his eyes connecting with her legs as she changed her shoes.

'Tell you what, you can drop me on the quays near the Dart station,' he suggested. 'It's on your way home and it will give me a chance to have a blast in this.'

She felt a definite sexual charge as he sat close beside her in the cream leather seats and all too soon they arrived at Custom House Quay. She restrained a quiver of regret as he unbuckled his seat belt and opened the passenger door. She should have asserted herself and insisted on dropping him out to Malahide. Besides being curious to see where he lived, he might, just might, have asked her in for coffee.

Coffee? Yeah . . .

'Hey,' he hesitated and turned to face her. 'I've had a good time tonight.'

'Have you?' She considered this for a moment, and then, feeling as though she was putting a small but important part of herself out there, admitted, 'So have I.'

'Really?'

'Yes, really.'

'Then we might do it again? I still owe you that birthday drink.'

'Sure, Sam.'

When he leaned across and lightly brushed her cheek with his mouth, Paula's face burned and she imagined what it would be like to kiss him properly. She watched as he climbed out of the car and strolled off into the dusky evening. When he turned to give her a casual wave, she let out the clutch, beeped the horn and accelerated away. She switched on her music and drove home with the sound cranked up, feeling as though she was sixteen all over again as Nelly Furtado echoed around the car and streamed out through the gap in her open window.

She awoke during the night and tossed and turned in the quiet of the dark and shadowy small hours, feeling hot and cold as she recalled every detail of her evening with Sam. What had she been thinking of? Surely she'd learned her lesson the hard way? She was older and wiser now, with no room in her life for even a mild flirtation. In any event, starved of masculine attention, she was surely blowing a handsome bloke and a couple of drinks all out of proportion.

Early the following morning, Paula went over to her bookcase in the split-level living area and took out a slim volume of Yeats's poetry. Ignoring the written dedication, she skimmed through the pages until a small photograph fluttered out. She looked at the happy couple, arms entwined, barefoot on a beach against the panorama of white-capped waves and curving blue-grey mountain slopes splashed with gorse-clad valleys.

He'd set the camera shutter and rushed back to her side, barely making it on time. Even then, little had she realised that it was going to be the last photograph of the two of them together. The laughter in her eyes held no knowledge of what lay ahead in terms of heartbreak and distress. For soon after the photograph was taken, they were history and her world was shattered. She kept it on purpose to remind herself of the extent of her hurt and how resolutely she'd vowed never to get involved again.

8

'Do you feel like having a visitor?'

'Do I what?' Elaine chirped down the phone. 'How soon can you come? Hopefully now, this instant!'

Paula didn't hesitate. 'This afternoon. Or would Colin mind?'

'Of course he wouldn't mind, don't be ridiculous. But aren't you in the office today?'

'I am, but I'm leaving soon.'

'Halleluijah! It's about time you had a normal Saturday like everyone else. I keep telling you, you're the boss. Why should you—'

'Elaine, if you're going to lecture me, I'll change my mind.'

'Right. Just get your ass down here. I'll put Colin on babysitting notice and you and I are going out – you'll stay over, won't you?'

'That's the idea.'

'Ruth can't wait to see you and neither can I.'

It had been a month since she'd seen her sister and baby Ruth, Paula calculated, and emailed photos of her adorable niece weren't the same as holding that warm, cuddly bundle in her arms. It was a bright Saturday afternoon when she took the road out of the city centre and down to Wicklow and she had the gratifying feeling of leaving everything behind, even if it was just for one night.

She'd gone into the office as usual that morning, intent on going through the details of the job applicants for Stevens that she'd be interviewing the following week while everything was quiet, but for once the silent phones and banks of empty desks outside her office had unsettled her. All her staff, with the exception of Kate, had gone to a farewell lunch with Sadie on Friday. Kate had quietly informed her that there'd been some kind of collection for her, but for once, Paula hadn't been approached to sign her good luck card or contribute towards her gift vouchers. As her staff noisily commandeered a large table in a nearby restaurant, Paula had her usual sandwich at her desk while she caught up with her business reading and tried to tell herself that such trivial matters weren't worthy of her consideration.

'It might be an idea to bring forward some of the appraisals,' she'd said to Kate. 'And I'm looking at the possibility of having a corporate night out. I can't afford to lose any further core talent at the moment.'

'You've lost four key staff since Christmas,' Kate had quietly pointed out.

'And discontented employees are not performing at their optimum,' Paula had said, 'or giving off good vibes to prospective clients and job-seekers.'

Nor were they happy, she'd silently thought.

As for Sam Ryan . . . She'd found herself on Friday, in between all the drama with her employees, foolishly jumping whenever her phone rang, which was silly and stupid as he didn't even have her private number, her mobile or email. The only way he could contact her was through Kate and the main office number or by dropping by in person. When half past five came, she found herself recalling the minute details of the previous evening with him, much as a silly, infatuated teenager would do. She'd been so annoyed with

herself that she'd gone straight home and spent a punishing
hour in the gym.

A night in the company of her bubbly, outgoing sister was
just what she needed.

Paula dropped her overnight case in the tiled hallway and
crunched back down Elaine's gravel driveway. To the left,
the hills lifted away, swathes of emerald green gently curving
to meet the crisp blue of the sky. It was a far cry from the
urban jungle she had left behind, and for a moment she
paused long enough to breathe in the relaxing scent of
newly-mown grass and to wish it was as easy to drop all the
baggage and leave everything else behind. Then she reached
into the boot of her Jaguar and lifted out a cardboard container
with half a dozen bottles of wine and a large carrier bag full
of summery outfits for Ruth.

'What's all this?' Elaine asked.

'I dropped into Cornelscourt and picked up a few goodies
on the way down,' Paula explained.

'You're far too kind.'

'Not at all. I'll be drinking some of that wine and I couldn't
resist the cute little outfits for Ruth. Allow me to indulge
my little poppet.'

Elaine gave her a warm hug and ushered her into the
spacious dormer bungalow situated just outside Wicklow
town.

Growing up, they hadn't been all that close, the six-year
age gap as well as their different personalities not lending
to much in the way of sisterly togetherness or shared
confidences. Paula had been the quiet one, the responsible,
introspective and ambitious older sister who had been slightly
appalled and often impatient with her younger sister's
disregard for all things in authority. Shunning college, Elaine
had gone straight to work in a noisy, overstocked city centre

boutique and thrown herself and her lively talents wholeheartedly into the job and the compulsory, edgy nightlife.

Over the years she'd been regularly promoted, and before she was thirty she had progressed to managing an exclusive designer label outlet in Powerscourt Centre. Along the way, she'd also discovered how to dress properly and make her bubbly style work for her, how to flatter her fair complexion with the correct make-up and how to be selective about her social life. Then she'd met Colin at a party and the gradual transformation from spirited teenager to glamorous, confident woman had been complete. Marriage to Colin was followed by relocating to Wicklow and a move from the designer outlet in Powerscourt Centre to a similar one in south County Dublin. Then she'd given birth to Ruth. Now, at thirty-two years of age, Elaine's vocabulary revolved around Ruth and was peppered with references to bottle feeds, Farrow and Ball neutrals and the all-important Mothercare.

Everything had changed after that. Somehow the arrival of Elaine's little daughter had brought the two sisters closer, altering their relationship completely. And although Paula wasn't suddenly brimming with sisterly confidences, nowadays the two women were a lot friendlier and more relaxed in each other's company.

'Ruth's fast asleep,' Elaine said, anticipating Paula's question as they headed down to the kitchen where a tasty aroma of roast lamb was filtering around. 'You can see her later, as I've no intentions of disturbing my peace!'

Elaine bent to check the oven and lifted out the bottles of wine Paula had brought, her eyes widening appreciatively as she stacked them in the wine rack. 'Yum, yum! You're far too extravagant. And you remembered Colin's favourite!'

'And where is your lovely husband?'

'He's out doing the garden. *And* all prepared to babysit

tonight so that you and I can kick up our heels. Within reason, of course, as I can't go overboard with Ruth.' Elaine stopped and grinned, then threw her sister a worried look. 'God, Paula, am I gone all dull and boring and mumsie now?'

'Not at all,' Paula smiled. 'It's just that Ruth is practically your only topic of conversation.'

Elaine groaned. 'I know, it's totally astonishing how much your whole world can revolve around a tiny little scrap. I never imagined how much Ruth would change my whole life. For the better, I must add. I just hope you won't be too bored with the humdrum domesticity of a weekend in the country. It's a far cry from the glittering lights of Dublin, never mind,' she paused and gave her sister a slightly mocking smile, 'the successful and scintillating world of Stevens.'

Paula pulled out a chair and sat down at the scrubbed pine table. She rested her elbows on the table and was tempted to admit that the world of Stevens wasn't so shiny at the moment. Elaine's warm, fragrant kitchen was scattered with baby paraphernalia and from the back lawn of the house came the rhythmic whine of a petrol mower. It was an ambience full of ordinary homeliness that spelled out warmth, comfort and security.

It plunged her back to her childhood.

She saw herself sitting at the table in the kitchen of their house in Mayberry Lane, fingering the gold stars in her copybook; gold stars to make her mummy happy, her lovely mummy who was tired and worn-looking with the cross new baby who cried during the night and kept her awake and who was crotchety and windy during the day, Paula heard her mummy tell her neighbours. She didn't quite understand how a baby could be windy like the breeze outside on the lane or why everyone said it was great for her to have a little sister. All she knew was that she could make her mummy smile and look happy when she showed her the gold stars in her copybook. The more stars she had, the happier her mum was, it seemed. And it was nice being the teacher's pet and mummy's good little girl.

Habits that had been ingrained as a child and impossible to break.

Her mother had been well into her forties by the time Elaine had been born, Paula mused as the fragment of memory now shifted into a slightly different perspective. She'd been a slightly older mum, past her first flush of youth, and had less energy to cope with the demands of a small baby. Both of their parents were now dead, but somehow the safe and secure home life they'd given their two daughters was being recreated on instinct by Elaine.

'Maybe I want to get away from scintillating Dublin for the weekend,' Paula said. 'Tell you what – if it's not too early for you, let's open a bottle of wine.'

Colin strolled in from the garden, greeting Paula warmly on his way to the shower. Ruth was cuddled and fed, bathed and sung to. Paula inhaled the sweet baby scent of her niece, marvelled at how much she'd grown and watched the way Ruth's trusting and adoring eyes followed Elaine around the room. To have a child of your own, she reflected, was simply wonderful. Elaine was so lucky. For once in her life, she felt outdone by her younger sister. But in due course, thanks to modern medicine, she'd have a lovely baby of her own. Although if she left it much longer, Paula mused, she'd be in her forties by the time that monumental event was initiated and the process would be that much more difficult.

Elaine served the roast lamb followed by banoffi, and through it all, at the back of her mind, Paula realised that she hadn't left the city behind after all, for the prospect of talking about Sam and telling Elaine what had happened filled her with an annoying kind of anticipation.

Later that evening, in the pub, it was difficult to mention his name without sounding too proprietal, to sound nonchalant as she told Elaine about his visit to her office and the subsequent trip to the pub. And it was uncomfortable to realise that the sound of his name on her lips gave her a peculiar thrill.

Elaine's eyes sparkled with recollection. 'Sam Ryan! I haven't seen him in years! The last time I saw him was at his mum's funeral – Mark was home for that, of course, but you were on holidays in France.'

'Was I?'

'Yes, and Abby was somewhere on the other side of the world. Although even if she'd been near enough, I doubt if she would have come home.'

'Why not?' She was greedy for the details. Much to her chagrin, minute facts about Elaine's friends that would have been beneath her notice once upon a time now seemed to be weighty with a new significance.

'She didn't really want to face Sam again.'

'I thought they were very keen on each other – two peas in a pod?' Paula injected her voice with what she hoped was the right degree of casual nosiness. She couldn't bring herself to admit to Elaine that she found Sam sexy and fanciable. Apart from the fact that Paula was still trying to deny the effect he was having on her, one confidence might lead to another and Paula's love life might be questioned. Even now, more than three years down the line, it was a matter of pride with her that Elaine would never learn how disastrously things had turned out for her clever big sister and how stupidly she'd behaved, never mind how hurt she'd been in the process.

Elaine shook her head. 'Abby was the love of Sam's life, but she never felt the same way about him.' She signalled the bar girl for more drinks. 'Anyway, I'm out to enjoy myself tonight,' she said. 'Not to go back over ancient, boring history.'

'Yes, you're right,' Paula shrugged. 'Thing is, Sam's trying to organise something for Mark's fortieth. In Dublin. He has the idea that we'll all get together and have a reunion.'

'Wow! That would be some crazy bash. Are you on for seeing Mark again?'

'After all this time? It makes no difference to me.'

'Your old flame?' Elaine's voice was teasing.

'He was never my old flame,' Paula snorted. 'Mark was always far too arrogant for my liking.'

'Arrogant? Never. He was just shy, Paula. And very suspicious of me and Abby. Maybe you'll finally get together at last after all our failed attempts.'

'Elaine, cut it out. You're being ridiculous.'

'The reunion won't happen anyway, because I can't see Abby coming home from Italy.'

'Sam had the impression that she's not so full of the joys. Also that you pair weren't talking?'

'That's right. We had – oh, I dunno, some kind of falling out after Christmas.'

'You and Abby? You never told me about it.'

'She had stopped emailing, but I didn't notice so much because I was busy with Ruth,' Elaine said. 'Then she said she couldn't come home for Ruth's christening because she was too busy. Too busy, my eye. There can't be that many weddings in Italy in January. I gave her plenty of notice, she could have got time off *and* she could have stayed with us. Then I phoned her to see if anything was the matter, and she was very short with me and said everything was fine. I told her I wasn't so happy, 'cos it was important to me that my old pal saw my cute little baby.'

'I'm sure it was.'

'Then she said if I was really her old pal that I'd respect

her decision . . .' Elaine's voice trailed away. 'She spent Christmas with Lia, but she couldn't come to Dublin to see my baby.'

Lia. Paula recalled the diminutive red-haired figure with the light, amber eyes who'd drifted up and down the lane dressed like a free-spirited hippie but who strictly kept to herself.

'From what you've said, Abby will scarcely come home just for a party,' Paula said. 'But look at Lia. I still find it incredible the way she managed to turn her life around. She totally spoiled Abby and always seemed airy-fairy to me, but behind it all, she must have tremendous discipline.'

'She sure does. You don't reach her levels of success without hard work. Anyway, I haven't been in contact with Abby since. The weeks went by, I was busy, the christening came and went and it's been over four months now. I'm surprised she even mentioned it to Sam, I didn't think it bothered her that much. And you're right, I can't see her coming home after all this time.'

Paula ordered more drinks and let her sister's voice flow over her head. She didn't need to be reminded of Abby Lacey, Sam's former girlfriend, who couldn't come home for Ruth's christening. Growing up, the impish, exasperating friend of Elaine's had been a thorn in her side.

And Sam Ryan didn't get a look in on her frame of reference. She'd made the firm decision three years ago never to get involved with a man again. Now she had other, far weightier concerns. Her staff retention rates for one, and the constant yet absorbing challenge of evaluating the most cost-effective ways of sourcing top-calibre candidates. Maybe at times she was a little distant from her staff, but thankfully she had Kate on hand to keep things running smoothly.

Still, for the first time ever, in all the times she'd visited

Elaine, Colin and the baby, she felt a hollow sense of loss when she kissed them goodbye. It was difficult to plant a final kiss on Ruth's soft cheek and to disentangle her chubby arms from their warm embrace around her neck. The sight of the three of them framed in her rear-view mirror as they stood in the doorway and waved goodbye made her accelerate rather sharply as she whisked out of the driveway and took the road for Dublin and her luxurious but empty Hanover Quay apartment.

The interviews the following week were a disaster. Paula couldn't concentrate properly, let alone come to a decision, and she did something she'd never had to do before. Of the five shortlisted applicants for her company vacancies, she selected three for a further interview, giving them the false impression that the initial interview with her had merely been a preliminary one.

The following day, she told Kate to offer overtime to her staff to make sure the monthly targets were met in the absence of Ursula and Sadie. She was surprised to see her business manager still at her computer, her dark head glued to the screen and her desk awash with files, when she left to go home at half past eight on Wednesday evening.

'Kate? Thought you'd have finished by now.'

'So did I,' Kate said a little guardedly. 'There wasn't anyone available for overtime this evening, so I'm just getting some stuff cleared.'

Paula frowned. 'I appreciate that you're helping me out of a tight spot, but I certainly don't want you to feel obliged to pick up the slack if no one else is prepared to help out.'

'No problem,' Kate said.

'Any particular reason why no one volunteered to work late? Or have they all got wildly exciting social lives?'

Kate shrugged. 'I can't answer that, Paula.'

'Never mind,' Paula said impatiently. 'I'm locking up now. Those figures can wait until tomorrow.'

She drove home, unable to identify why she was going through that week devoid of her usual energy or why she felt that everything was flat and uninteresting and empty of colour. Funnily enough, at odd times she found herself recalling Elaine's face shining with maternal pride as she tucked her tiny daughter up in her cot.

Then at half past five on Friday evening, the stagnant place she'd found herself in all week dissolved around her as Sam walked into her office. And she knew – bloody hell, she only had to look at him standing in the doorway to know why everything had seemed dull, uninteresting and fudgy all week, because now, suddenly, everything was alive and exciting. Even the air she breathed was fresh and clear and invigorating.

She was tempted to demand how he'd managed to slip past Kate or what he thought he was doing there without an appointment in the first place, but she was so annoyed with her reaction that the words stuck in her throat. Sam forestalled anything else by marching right up to her desk.

Paula jumped to her feet, forgetting about the stilettos kicked under the table, and he shook his head and laughed in amusement as he leaned over her desk.

'That's more like it,' he said. 'Glad to see you're getting rid of the ammunition.' He straightened up. 'I was going to say I'd called in to discuss more plans for the reunion bash, but I haven't. Not really. This time it's just an excuse to bring you out for a drink. A belated birthday drink, if you like, or a chance to see some life outside of the office. And may I have your car keys? You're not getting away with it this time.'

She was eternally glad that the office was empty, because

the Paula Stevens who was most definitely finished with men felt as though she was free-falling into dangerous space as she took hold of Sam's arm and went out the door.

LIA

9

The make-up girl was chatty.

'You have such beautiful skin,' she enthused as she dipped an enormous brush into some kind of russet-shaded blusher and stroked it over Lia's cheekbones.

Lia's expressive eyes darkened and she tried to keep a straight face as she stared at her reflection in the brilliantly-lit mirror. She scarcely recognised herself. She looked like a painted clown – worse, some kind of Pierrot doll, all daubed and tinted for glorious effect. It was all necessary, of course, for the draining glare of television studio lights. On screen, she assured herself, she would look perfectly normal. Lia Lacey, bright, attractive, articulate and far, far younger than her forty-nine years.

'It's so fine and delicate and typically Irish, almost alabaster,' the make-up girl continued. She was barely twenty, far too thin and wearing silly scraps of clothes, but there was something about her innocent enthusiasm that reminded Lia of Abby, so she softened her response and found herself being unexpectedly frank.

'You're too complimentary,' Lia chuckled. 'Let's be honest – you really mean pale and colourless.' She paused and made a tentative face at her reflection, wary that she might put a crack in her multi-layered foundation and ruin the girl's expert artwork. 'What's more, it's freckly. Although you've done a great job in camouflaging those horrid things.'

'Oh, but I think your freckles are lovely – they add character and they're so refreshingly authentic.'

Lia didn't reply. She shot her reflection a rueful glance. *Refreshingly authentic* was not how she'd been described all those years ago in the rough and tumble of the schoolyard. The make-up girl rummaged in her brimming box of cosmetics and out of the tons of colourful ammunition selected a thin, dark pencil. Lia watched in the mirror in resigned acquiescence as she began to make swift strokes across her eyebrows, transforming them into wide, curving arches that made Lia look alert and alive.

'Your skin is flawless,' the make-up girl said. 'I bet you keep your face well screened from the killer sun.'

'I've no choice,' Lia laughed. 'Otherwise I'd resemble a boiled lobster.'

'You must have an excellent skincare regime. I suppose you use all the right products.'

'Sure I do. Nothing like a plastering of good old Pond's cold cream,' Lia found herself admitting. 'My all-time secret is that it works equally well the morning after the night before.'

The make-up girl giggled. 'Do you know, for someone so famous, you're really down to earth.'

She'd heard this before, Lia mused, as though people were suddenly elevated to a different plane once they were in the public eye, or mutated by a chemical reaction into a different species of being. Well, in a way she had been, hadn't she? She'd achieved a lifetime's ambition and made herself a little famous in the process, and in some respects her life had changed beyond recognition. Sometimes she was even a stranger to herself, Lia privately admitted, her eyes examining her artificial reflection.

'Why, what did you expect?' she asked.

'I dunno. Some authors are pushy and full of themselves,

although I suppose the Irish authors in general are warmer and friendlier.'

Lia didn't feel quite as warm and friendly twenty minutes later when Rachel, the television presenter and star of *Lunchtime with Rachel*, started asking her a series of ridiculous questions that could have come straight out of *Hello!*.

'Now Lia,' Rachel sat forward on the sofa, thus showing an impressive amount of boob, and directed a huge fake smile in the direction of the bank of nearby cameras, 'I know you have a really good website, but all your fans are dying to know a little more about what's *really* going on in your life right now.'

'Ask away,' Lia smiled, doing her best to ignore the hot, bright spotlights and trying not to work out if Rachel's boobs were as false as her smile. Expecting to be asked about her forthcoming signing schedules for her latest bestseller, *Death on Friday*, she mentally ran through them: London first, of course, then Oxford, Bath, Birmingham and Liverpool, and then a trip to Scotland which would be both work and pleasure as she intended taking some time out up there. Gary, her publicist, had suggested a trip across to Dublin, but Lia had refused. She hoped that Rachel wouldn't question her about the omission of her home town.

Rachel shuffled her papers. 'Let me see . . .' she paused, looking, Lia thought, as though she was trying to come to an earth-shattering decision. 'We have an *amazing* number of questions that have been texted and emailed to us since we went on air just over an hour ago and announced your appearance. You're certainly very popular.' Rachel put down her papers and listened intently to her earpiece. 'Okay, Lia, here goes. First one up: what colour is your bathroom and do you have a Jacuzzi bath?'

'My *bathroom?*'

'Yes, your bathroom.' Rachel smiled beatifically at the bank of cameras.

'Well, it's – I suppose some kind of greeny colour. And yes, I have a Jacuzzi bath.' She directed a mystified look at the camera and the invisible viewers, as though trying to fathom the logic of the question.

'Out for a meal, what is your favourite starter?'

Lia shrugged. 'Smoked salmon, I guess.'

'A fan from Birmingham wants to know what the worst fashion mistake you ever made is.'

'I'd have to think about that one,' Lia paused. 'My biggest mistake was matching outfits to my colouring, but now I don't care one way or the other.' She casually dismissed the turquoise stretch-fit Versace dress that moulded her slim figure.

'Is it true that the stress has been removed from coordinating your wardrobe because you have a personal stylist in Harrods?'

'Oh, I have a personal stylist in all my favourite stores,' Lia said expansively, lying through her teeth. What the hell kinds of questions were these anyway? She was scarcely a candidate for *Big Brother* or some other brainless reality trash.

'I guess that comes with your celebrity standing,' Rachel flashed another megawatt smile, a perfect advertisement for expensive dental surgery.

'Yes, it does,' Lia smiled an equally potent smile.

'Next question – your favourite handbag?' Rachel enthused. 'Prada or Gucci?'

'Neither, actually,' Lia paused. She hadn't exactly expected a deep, stimulating discussion, but this was ridiculous. She couldn't prevent the gleam in her amber eyes as she adopted a confidential tone and leaned forward in the manner of someone about to release a state secret. No doubt Rachel and her legion of fans were waiting for her to confess to being on the waiting list for a Hermès Birkin. She was tempted, sorely tempted, but for once, a spark of the old Lia Lacey gleamed as she admitted, 'My favourite at the moment is a Selfridges canvas shopper. It brings me everywhere.'

'How ... how fascinating,' Rachel said, clearly a little flummoxed. She frowned as she listened again to her earpiece. 'Next up, what's your all-time favourite movie?'

'*E.T.*' It slipped out automatically. Lia only realised she'd said the words aloud when Rachel responded with a puzzled glance.

'*E.T.*? Isn't that kind of a kid's film?'

'No, not at all.' And could I have the next question please, Lia fretted, preferably about the feng shui aspect of my hall door or something equally frivolous.

Rachel looked confused, as though Lia wasn't supposed to deviate from her carefully researched notes. 'We thought you would have gone for something like *The Silence of the Lambs*. Why *E.T.*?'

Lia paused. Why, indeed. How the hell had she slipped up like that? The past was well and truly over. Yet with a flash of remembrance, she was glued to her cinema seat while Abby munched popcorn and Lia tried to stop the tears from pouring down her cheeks as she watched the closing credits roll up the screen and listened to the transporting music. Abby must have been about seven at the time. Lia hadn't wanted to frighten her little daughter with her crying, and she'd struggled to hide her face and compose herself as they joined the shuffling queue exiting the darkened auditorium. They'd bumped into a then teenage and pimply Mark Ryan in the brightly lit foyer outside and she'd been mortified to realise that he'd noticed her red-rimmed eyes. Nor was there any quick escape, for as luck would have it, they were all on the same bus home.

'*E.T.* carries a fundamental message for everyone,' Lia said, firmly squashing the memory. 'Love conquers all. In a nutshell, that's what life is all about.'

She realised too late that she'd given the presenter a juicy opening line for her next question. Rachel abandoned her papers and without reference to her earpiece, she smiled at Lia, this time her row of gleaming teeth resembling those of a man-eating shark about to pounce. 'For someone with such a fundamental belief, you're very secretive about your love life,' she said. 'You rarely get caught out by the paparazzi in any . . . compromising situation. Except, recently, with Piers Morgan?'

'We just happened to be at a book launch and I had dirt in my contact lens,' Lia said airily. 'Maybe he was standing pretty close as he tried to fix it, but the gossip columnists who managed to turn it into a torrid sexual encounter must have a very limited imagination.'

'So you're not having an affair with him?'

'Definitely not. And just to set the record straight, neither have I slept with Ralph Fiennes or Daniel Craig.'

'Hmm . . .' Rachel looked a little crestfallen. The ratings would have skyrocketed, Lia mused, if she'd wangled a confession from her. 'What about lunching with Brad Pitt in Bentley's in Piccadilly?' Rachel asked. 'That must have been thrilling.'

'It was thrilling in so far as he was discussing options for two of my novels for his company, Plan B.'

'Gosh. Really? Did you find him attractive?'

Not half as attractive as the ballpark figure he was tossing around. 'Of course I did. The man smoulders sexual magnetism.' The unseen audience could take what they liked out of that, Lia thought as she batted her reinforced eyelashes at the cameras.

'And is there anyone in your life right now? Anyone special?'

'I dare say my fans would find far more interest in what goes on between the covers of my books than the covers of my bed. Surely it would be more engaging to discuss the plot behind my latest novel rather than the boring incidentals of my private life?'

'That's where you're so *wrong*, Lia,' Rachel trilled. 'These are the days of reality celebs and people out there – our audience, your fan base – well, they're just *so* hungry for the intimate minutiae that make up a famous person's life. People find it fascinating. And you can't deny the rumours that you eat men for breakfast.'

'Nonetheless,' Lia smiled for the camera with what she hoped was a seductive smile, 'my private life is just that – private.'

'At least tell the *Lunchtime with Rachel* viewers if it's true that you never married? And that you raised your daughter—' she hurriedly consulted her notes, 'Abby? Single-handedly? And then became an instantaneous bestselling author?' With each question, Rachel's tone of voice gradually rose and gathered momentum until she finally reached a crescendo. 'What an inspiration!'

'No, I never married,' Lia said smoothly. 'As for raising Abby, it was scarcely a solo effort. It's no secret that I had her when I was seventeen years of age and that her father wasn't around, but I had the wonderful support of my mother, without whom I'd never have managed.'

'Her father wasn't around?' Rachel looked suitably sympathetic and repeated the words slowly in an effort to derive maximum impact. 'If I recall from my notes, he was an explorer who went off on his adventures before he knew you were expecting his baby?'

Lia's stomach heaved. 'That's correct.'

'And you never tried to contact him?'

'No. Communication was a lot more difficult in those days. We're talking about the nineteen seventies.' Heedless of the fans supposedly glued to the other side of the cameras, she fixed Rachel with a killer glare that said don't attempt to pursue this line of questioning. Thank God Abby was firmly ensconced in Sorrento and that there was no danger she'd be watching this silly show.

'How romantic,' Rachel sighed. Lia smiled sweetly. 'We just have time for a couple more questions.'

Lia struggled to look interested for the benefit of her fans. Her favourite breakfast cereal, perhaps, or shade of lip gloss – pink, purple or cerise?

'What is your mobile ring tone?'

Lia felt the smile tugging at the corner of her mouth. 'I don't have a mobile.'

'You don't *have* one?'

'No. I value my privacy and I've managed quite well without one thus far.'

'Oh, I see.' Rachel looked perplexed, as though Lia was surely some kind of dinosaur. She recovered her composure fairly quickly, however, and scrabbled her papers together with an air of brisk importance. 'And last but not least,' Rachel paused, looking very intent as she listened to her earpiece, 'on a desert island, Lia, and given the choice, would you opt for a manicure or pedicure or an aromatherapy back massage?'

'None of those, actually,' Lia swallowed her frustration and smiled a fake, dreamy smile at the camera. 'I'd far rather have Brad Pitt.'

10

'What the hell was that all about?'

'Lia, calm down. You were fabulous.'

'I was never put through such a rubbishy interview in all my life,' Lia fumed. 'It was so ridiculous it made me want to puke. I eat men for breakfast! You never know, Gary, you could be next on the menu!'

There was a short silence at the other end of the phone. 'Look, Lia,' Gary, her publicist, adopted a conciliatory tone of voice. 'It was lunchtime television; light and easy. Don't forget that nowadays you're competing with the shortest attention span on record, and the intimate details of a hundred and one other celebrities.'

'But I'm a writer, not a celebrity.' Lia's tone was softer, as she was sorry for snapping at him. Gary was relatively new to the job. Her previous publicist had retired and was now soaking up the sun in the Bahamas. In his early thirties, Gary was full of the brash confidence of youth and with a brazen enthusiasm for all his pet projects, he was eager to propel Lia further and further into the media stratosphere.

'Yes, of course you're a writer first and foremost,' he said, 'but in order to move shedloads of books, you have to act the part and put in a public appearance every now and again. It's been several weeks since you were on prime time television. You're lucky they jumped at the chance at having you on *Lunchtime with Rachel*. Celebrities are falling over themselves to get on that show.'

'You mean people actually *want* to be interviewed as though they were some kind of grade A bimbo?'

'You're exaggerating, Lia. It was light and entertaining, nothing more. It's all about putting yourself out there, and I guarantee that it'll shift you up a notch or two in the bestseller lists. You're doing really great, but in this cut-throat business you can't afford to rest on your laurels. You need to be visible to your fans. Surely you had some kind of idea of what the programme would be like? Haven't you ever watched *Lunchtime with Rachel*?'

'If I was a man, I'd never have been asked those silly questions. I think I'll cast Rachel as a villain in my next novel and have her die of saccharin poisoning.'

'I'll pretend I didn't hear that.'

'Then after all that, I had to sit in the cab all the way home with my face cemented with a thick layer of gunge. Yuk!'

'Maybe so, but you looked really great on the screen. Anyway, I really phoned you to talk about your book tour.'

'What about it?'

'I want to ask you if Dublin is really off the agenda. Your Irish fan base would love the opportunity to meet you. Lia Lacey, back to her roots after all these years, to where it all began. It would be a cracker. You're a huge success story, Lia, and your Irish fans would love inclusion at some level, whether it's book signings or talks, radio or television. I've made a few initial enquiries and if we planned for mid-autumn, we could get both *The Late Late Show* and *Tubridy*.'

Lia held the cordless phone in her hand as she leaned across her desk. God bless Gary, with his boundless optimism. Using the platinum pen held between her fingers, she proceeded to flick over the pages of the Italian desk calendar Abby had given her at Christmas. Before the row. The month of May flaunted an uplifting panorama of the Marina Grande in Sorrento, and June and July showed inspiring views of ports and marinas along the Amalfi coast. Lia had highlighted a lot of the dates in green, indicating her tours, book signings and appearances.

She flicked over August and September, which boasted equally breathtaking images of Positano and Capri and then coming to October, she paused.

She'd spent the previous October and November in a whirlwind of book tours, readings and charity bashes in the Antipodes, travelling through Australia and New Zealand, wryly observing that she could have met up with Abby, only Abby was by then in South Africa. This year, those months were clear. Not that it made any difference.

'I told you before, Gary, no Dublin. I've no intentions of returning home. Not even for *The Late Late*. Not for anything. I'm more interested in staying put and getting on with book eight.'

'You'd manage it, Lia. I've seen the way you operate when you're up against a deadline.'

'Well, you can send me to Timbuktu if you like, or even Outer Mongolia, but Dublin is definitely off limits.'

Lia put down the phone, clicked the save button on her Word document and went to the kitchen of her apartment. Was this it? Was this what it was all about? Stupid questions on a dizzy, lunchtime talk show that hours later still left a bad taste in her mouth, then pressure from Gary to revisit old haunts that were best forgotten?

She poured coffee into a chunky mug Abby had given her and told herself to relax. She was overreacting. Her life now was everything she'd ever dreamed of. Okay, maybe at times it involved a little compromise on her part, but above all she was enjoying it.

Moving to London after her mother's death and Abby's departure to see the world had proved to be a stepping stone to her deepest ambition. Thanks to her mother's legacy, she'd been able to devote herself to writing full-time. And that, in addition to all the hours she'd spent slaving away in her bedroom in Mayberry Lane, serving her apprenticeship, so to speak, as well as the instant success formula she'd found with her swiftly-paced crime novels, had handsomely paid off.

It was amazing in a way to think that something she wrote in the privacy of her own apartment found its way onto bookshelves all over the world. Funny also to think that stuff she created out of her own head was referred to in jacket blurbs and reviews as 'tight, chilling prose, villainous characters and complex, gritty plotlines against a backdrop of a fast, energetic London'.

Sometimes it felt as though she was moving around in a dream. Her life was full, busy, successful. At times it was glamorous and exciting. During the day, Lia Lacey the writer still found it comfy and relaxing to put on a tracksuit and wear her thick glasses while she worked at the laptop in the writing room of her London apartment in Sadlier Square, her desk positioned by long sash windows where she had a view out onto the small park around which the Georgian Sadlier Square was built. During the day she snacked on fruit and sipped mineral water and coffee and usually went around without a shred of make-up. In the evenings, Lia Lacey donned the carefully-cultivated image of the successful crime novelist and she dressed up, put in her contacts, went to places, sipped champagne and laughed, and did things she used to read about other people doing in glossy magazines.

Mingling with the glitterati as well as the literati, she found it sobering at times to realise that she couldn't cope without

Olga, her faithful hairdresser who performed miracles on her hair. Once upon a time, Lia's hair had been a carrot-shaded tangle down to her waist. Now with carefully blended highlights and lowlights, it was a neat, sassy, Titian-shaded bob. Never one to have much interest in cosmetics, Lia also depended on Sonia, her much-trusted make-up consultant who advised on facials and the correct foundation for her fair skin and whatever seasonal shadings were best suited to her colouring, and whose miracle fingers brought out Lia's striking bone structure and wide, amber eyes.

It was a scintillating life. And thankfully, it was light years away from the days of Mayberry Lane. Returning to Dublin wasn't on her agenda. Not now, not ever.

So she was thrown off balance when she returned to her desk with her coffee, logged onto her email and read that Abby, who up to now had insisted she was happily content in Sorrento, was now asking questions about the house in Mayberry Lane.

'If I ever did decide to return home, what's the situation with the lease on the house? I know you said it would always be there for me, but I realise that may not be as straightforward as it sounds.'

Return home? Lia's coffee grew cold and her heart stilled as she read and reread Abby's deceptively breezy email. There was no reference to the row they'd had at Christmas or the few terse phone calls and emails they'd since exchanged, no mention of how Abby felt or any explanation as to why she was making these enquiries. Lia took off her glasses and closed her eyes and her writing room in pastel shades of cream and lilac disappeared from view. Like a kaleidoscope of shifting images, her mind filled with pictures of Abby.

She saw her daughter skipping up Mayberry Lane with

her friends on a summer's evening and bursting through the back door of the house, thrusting a bunch of daisies at her mother, her dark hair falling like folds of velvet around her shoulders, her greeny-blue eyes huge with delight and surprise.

Abby at her Irish dancing class, a born natural with her ringlets flying, her footsteps quick and light.

Then there was the teenage Abby, with coltish, suntanned legs and wrists poking out of her sleeves, reaching gracefully to throw a basketball with a perfectly curving arc into a makeshift net as Sam Ryan, Abby's permanent shadow, looked on and whistled in approval. She heard her daughter's clear, musical laughter echoing across the summery evening and remembered the way her heart had lifted with joy for the perfect beauty of that moment.

More poignantly, she saw herself tucking a five-year-old Abby into bed and taking her into her arms and telling her exciting stories about Alejandro. Later on, Lia didn't have to look very far to guess why Abby was so restless and intent on flitting around the world. She'd nurtured those dreams herself, with her exciting tales about a globetrotting, adventurous father, magical stories that had sent Abby to sleep throughout her childhood years.

Then she'd brought a twelve-year-old Abby to Scotland to tell her the truth about Alejandro.

Only, of course, she'd baulked at the last minute and hadn't told her everything.

11

Abby was sick on the boat. Sick with giddy excitement. Up to now, Lia had usually brought her on holidays in Ireland, renting a house along with her mother, Anne Lacey, on the south or the east coast where Abby played to her heart's content on wide sandy beaches. So a trip to Scotland had filled Abby with excitement, especially when she heard they were going on the boat *and* train.

'That's a very long journey,' Anne Lacey pointed out when Lia made her plans. 'An overnight ferry to Liverpool and then rail to Glasgow? Look, I've a nest egg put aside for a rainy day, I can easily pay for your plane fares.'

'No way, Mum, you've done enough for me. I need to do this myself.'

'You sound just like your daughter, wilful and independent!'

'I want to do it like this and I have to tell her the truth about Alejandro before she's any older. I know I've walked myself into this mess with my fairytales, but I have to come clean. I'd like to show her where I met him. And the journey will be fun for Abby and a big adventure in itself.'

That's what Lia told her mother, but she, too, had an urge right there and then to get away from Mayberry Lane. A long journey, with the feeling that she was putting physical miles between herself and the lane, was just what she needed. And travelling on the boat, retracing the fateful steps she'd taken thirteen years ago, would be a kind of catharsis in itself.

Anne smiled. 'I just hope you don't get into trouble with her.'

Far from having trouble with Abby, her daughter viewed the whole expedition with an infectious enthusiasm that somehow engaged with Lia and it eased the journey for her across the Irish Sea. Abby gripped the rail tightly as the boat departed from the North Wall in Dublin, watching the ever-widening boat trail between dry land and the stern as if it was some kind of magic. The chilly, salt-laden breeze whipped her dark hair and reddened her cheeks, but for a long time there was no moving her away from her spot by the rail.

She loved the bunk beds in their cabin and declared that it was like being in a boarding school in one of her favourite books. The soft drinks and small packages of biscuits wrapped in cellophane that Lia bought were a novelty and a wonderful midnight feast. She laughed and giggled in her top bunk, and in the bottom bunk where Lia was trying in vain to sleep, Abby's upside-down face and streaming hair appeared so often in the gap between them that Lia eventually had to urge her to settle down.

She was glad, though, that Abby was fidgety and distracting, for it was impossible for Lia to sleep as memories crowded in thick and fast. The last time she'd travelled on a boat like this, she'd been journeying back to Dublin, vulnerable and distressed, her heart broken after bidding a tearful farewell to Alejandro, another farewell after the death of her father only five months previously. She'd found her way to the crowded bar, and despite being underage, she'd been served Bacardi and Coke.

It was all so long ago, Lia firmly told herself as she shut out the memories and cuddled into her pillow. She listened to Abby's giggles and told herself it was more than time she put the past firmly behind her.

The rail journey to Glasgow was just as exciting for Abby. She was entranced by the distance they covered, the names in an atlas suddenly becoming real, the countryside flying by the window, and she was fascinated with the ebb and flow of the bustling passengers humping all manner of cases and backpacks decorated with tags and travel stickers. She was swept up with the strangeness of all the sights and sounds, from the disembodied railway station announcements to the lilt of different voices.

'It's all so strange. We're in a foreign country, aren't we?' she said when they stopped for a short while at a major junction and she brought Abby out to the platform shop. 'Even the sweets are different,' Abby announced, making her careful selection and having to repeat herself twice to the lady behind the counter.

Eventually, her tired, worn-out daughter slept on the provincial bus that brought them from Glasgow out to Loch Lomond. Lia sat undisturbed and felt her spirits rise as she looked for landmarks in the countryside she hadn't visited in thirteen years. The details were different, new houses and hotels, yet the overall landscape was familiar and it tugged at her heart.

They stayed for a week in a family-run guesthouse, and Abby never lost her sense of excitement, bouncing out of bed full of energy every morning for whatever each day would bring. Lia brought her on picnics and bus trips around the lakeshore and up into the heathery lower slopes of the mountains, and she saw it all again through her daughter's fascinated eyes – the breadth of the unfathomable water, the deep clefts of green valleys between towering, purply mountain slopes and the colour and shadings of the breathtaking landscape as, rim upon rim, the mountains serrated the skyline in a joyous upsurge. For the first time since Abby was born, she felt a sliver of peace at some deep level in her soul.

Then one afternoon, as they sat in their favourite picnic spot, Lia plucked a piece of scented white heather for luck and talked to her about Alejandro.

Abby listened to her faltering words as Lia began to explain that she'd made up things about Alejandro that weren't quite true. For starters, he'd never been a voyager out to conquer the world. Then Abby said, in a matter-of-fact voice, 'I kind of guessed that already. I would have heard about him on the news or something. Or he would have sent you postcards.'

'I need you to understand why I made up all those stories and why I wanted you to think you had a dad that was different. You see, Abby, when you were small, I thought it was more exciting for you to have a father out adventuring around the world in South America and Africa.'

'The Far East, the South Pole,' Abby recited.

'Yes, well, I wanted you to feel more exotic than the other girls in school whose fathers weren't around because they'd run out on their marriage or deliberately abandoned their daughter.'

'So who exactly was Alejandro?' Abby asked.

'He was eighteen and from Madrid and was backpacking with his friends. I met him here, in Loch Lomond, when I stayed in the youth hostel. I was sixteen and I was here with my school friend Jane and her older sister and her friend. The four of us came across on the boat and train just like you and I did.'

'And Nana let you go?'

'I was allowed to go because my father had died after a battle with cancer the previous January and Mum thought it would do me good to get away for a while. On our first night, I met Alejandro and thought he was wonderful.'

She thought he was nothing short of Adonis himself, and couldn't believe it when she caught his interest. He loved the novelty of her pale Irish beauty, her alabaster skin and her fiery hair. Even her freckles. They spent the whole two weeks together. The June weather was unexpectedly warm and it was all so exciting and heart-stopping for Lia.

'. . . so after the holiday, when I found out I was pregnant, it was brilliant and scary,' she said, staring out across the shadowed valleys as she groped for words, choosing them very carefully for the benefit of her twelve-year-old daughter so as not to hurt her. 'Brilliant to think I was going to have a baby of my own, but scary also. And Abby, always remember that you were never abandoned by your father. He didn't know about you. You see . . .' Once again she paused, twisting the heather between her fingers, finding herself unable to continue.

'So you never told Alejandro?' Abby piped up.

Lia put her arm around Abby and hugged her close. 'For all our togetherness, we knew it was really only a lovely holiday romance. Like fireworks that blaze for an instant before fading away. We were so young and our worlds were so totally different that we didn't stand a chance and the romance would have burnt itself out quickly enough. Do you understand?'

'Yes. Honestly, Mum, it's okay, I do understand.'

'As well as that, Alejandro dreamed of travelling the world and of stepping foot on all the continents, but he was due to start college in Madrid and then take his place in the family business . . . My mother was delighted with you, though,' Lia swiftly continued, dropping a kiss on her hair. 'You gave her a reason for living after my father's death. She was thrilled to look after you while I went out to work.'

'Do I have to tell my friends the truth now?' Abby asked anxiously. 'Like Elaine and Sam?'

'You don't have to tell them anything at all,' Lia said with a smile. 'I brought you here to this special place where I met him, just to tell you and to help you understand.'

'Well, it's going to be our secret,' Abby said stoutly. 'And if they ever ask me about my dad, I'll just say I still don't know where he is, so that's kind of the truth, isn't it?'

'Yes, love, it certainly is,' Lia agreed.

Abby never mentioned her father much after that, but looking back, there was no doubt in Lia's mind that her magical bedtime stories about an adventuring Alejandro, along with the excitement of Abby's first trip away, had ignited some kind of restless spark in her daughter.

'I'm going to study languages. I'll need them for when I go travelling,' she heard a sixteen-year-old Abby say. 'Don't expect me to settle down in Dublin, Mum, I've far more exciting stuff to do first.'

And around the time of her twenty-first birthday, she stood in the kitchen, hitched up her slim-hipped jeans and said, 'I think Sam Ryan has high hopes for the two of us, but it's not going to be. I'm off to travel the world as soon as I've enough dosh saved up. I want to go places and see things and live, really live.'

Clear as anything, Lia heard her own voice. 'Well, Abby, you have to follow your star.' She felt a flash of sympathy for Sam, but it paled into nothing compared to her own heartbreak as she thought of losing her beautiful, darling daughter to the big wide world. Then Abby gave her a mischievous grin and said that she might even come across Alejandro on her travels.

Lia swallowed hard. She'd been waiting for this, had always dreaded this moment, and in the dark nights of her soul had known that if Abby began any kind of search, Lia would have to tell her the real, unvarnished truth, the truth she couldn't even face herself, let alone articulate. She forced herself to ask, 'Do you really want to go looking for him?'

To her immense relief, Abby laughed. 'Not at all. I know

you were madly in love with him once upon a time, but your young Lothario is probably fat and middle-aged and in his second or third marriage by now. I'd rather keep my exotic memories.'

'And so would I,' Lia said.

The day that Lia waved her daughter away at Dublin airport, the huge lump in her throat choked her. Abby's first port of call was Sydney, Australia, travelling with two of her college pals who were just as eager to spread their wings, and Lia had to remind herself that it was all her fault that her daughter was heading off, intent on conquering the world.

Yet in another sense she was glad that Abby made the break, because along with her mother's legacy, it enabled Lia to put some space between herself and the secrets and shadows of Mayberry Lane. Three months after Abby left, Lia sold her little Fiat, packed her most treasured books and music and filled the attic in Mayberry Lane with everything else. At forty-one years of age, she relocated to London to the start of a new life.

In between years in Australia and time spent in America, Europe and the Far East, Abby thankfully spent plenty of time with her, recharging her batteries and working for funds for her next excursion. Lia admired endless photographs and listened to Abby's tales of her adventures, and she exchanged news of her own successes. She brought her daughter shopping in Knightsbridge, treated her to foie gras and champagne and showed her off to celebrities at book launches, chic cocktail parties and exclusive premieres.

Very occasionally, when she needed to get away from the busyness of London, Lia travelled back to Loch Lomond to savour some peace and solitude, immersing herself in the natural, primitive beauty of her surroundings and touching base with her soul at some level. The guesthouse where she'd stayed with Abby was long gone, likewise the hostel where she'd stayed in another lifetime. Nowadays she relaxed in a quiet, exclusive hotel. She might have walked the same hills and valleys as she had all those years ago with a young and vibrant Alejandro, but otherwise, the past had ceased to exist.

Until the row at Christmas.

12

Her usually effervescent daughter had been quiet and subdued when she arrived in London for Christmas. She looked thinner and tired, and her hair – merciful God, her long, lustrous hair – was chopped into a short, waif-like style that defied even Lia's wonderful powers of description and thankfully rendered her speechless.

Because she'd been on the other side of the world, Lia hadn't seen Abby since the previous September. As Lia was preparing to head off to Australia and the Antipodes on an ambitious two-month book tour, Abby was packing for South Africa for a month-long camping expedition with a group of like-minded travellers. It never ceased to amaze her that Abby would choose to join a group of strangers to travel with, but Abby insisted it was great fun and there was usually a mixed group, couples and singletons, and always someone around her own age to relate to.

Lia had been more than surprised when Abby had emailed after the expedition to say she was now in Italy, had found a job as a wedding planner in Sorrento and was staying there for the foreseeable future.

'I'm only here for a few days,' Abby said on Christmas Eve when she arrived in Sadlier Square and humped her case into the spare bedroom. 'I'm going back to Italy for the New Year.'

'No matter, it's wonderful to have you here for Christmas,' Lia told her.

Man trouble, Lia decided. Something major had upset

Abby, had put a haunted look in her eyes and had driven her to have her hair chopped in what was obviously a drastic attempt to reinvent herself with a new, implacable-looking image.

'Do you like my hair?' Abby asked with a belligerent look on her face.

'Yes, it's quite nice.'

Abby ruffled her fingers though the jagged edges. 'I felt I needed a change of style,' she said, the closed-up look on her face stalling any further questions.

It could only be a man. To hell with him. How dare he upset her daughter to such a degree, she raged silently. She could cheerfully kill him.

Christmas Day was spent peacefully, almost, Lia thought later, like the calm before the storm. For once, Lia did most of the talking, discussing her marvellous two-month tour and showing Abby her photographs, asking for her help in downloading them from her camera to her laptop. The following couple of days were wet and windy so there was no venturing very far. Abby was quiet and spent a lot of her time curled up on the deep sofa pulled up in front of Lia's Venetian fireplace, her defiant head of hair stuck in a paperback novel, and then, with no idea of where the consequences would lead, Lia had given her the draft of *Midday Execution*, her next novel, to read.

Afterwards she thought that if she could go back to that moment in time, Abby relaxing by the fire, the rain sliding down the windowpanes, the Art Deco lamps glowing softly against the grey December evening, she would have summoned a cab and whisked her daughter out into the glittering city lights, to a captivating West End show or dinner in the Ritz. Anything to avoid the scene that followed.

Abby fingered the manuscript. 'Yes, I'd love to have a quick glance,' she said, carefully placing the bundle of A4 sheets on the coffee table, her lack of interest painfully obvious to Lia.

'Abby, is anything the matter?' Lia couldn't help asking, knowing full well that there was no real point in pressing the issue. Her daughter wouldn't talk unless she felt like it.

Abby merely shrugged. 'Why do you ask?'

'It's just, well, you haven't been yourself,' Lia hesitated. The look on Abby's face made her feel she was about to trample all over a delicate flower in a pair of hobnailed boots, but she couldn't keep up the pretence any longer. 'Are you happy in Sorrento?' she asked gently, thinking that it might be easier to approach the subject in a roundabout way. 'I was surprised to hear you've decided to settle there for a while. And a wedding planner. What made you take that up?'

'Why shouldn't I be a wedding planner?'

'I thought you were destined for different things.'

'There's nothing wrong with my job.'

'I'm not knocking what you do for a living, I'm just surprised at your decision.'

'Jesus, Mum, you're the last person to talk about what's right for me.'

'Maybe so, but it seems to me that something's wrong in your life. It is a man? Because if it is, believe me, he's not worth it.'

Abby's face looked pained.

Lia said, her voice a little gentler, 'Look, love, whoever he is, just forget about him. If someone has upset you, he doesn't deserve you and you're better off without him. If I thought any man had upset my darling daughter, I wouldn't like to think of what I'd do if I got my hands on him. Believe me, honey, you're worth far more than a hurtful love affair.'

'I'm perfectly fine, Mum.' The closed look was back on her face.

'Come on, Abby. You've been going around looking as

though the end of the world has come. There's no need to put up a front or pretend with me.'

'Pretend?' Abby suddenly turned on her. 'You of all people can't lecture me on pretence. You're the one who's spent most of your life in the land of make-believe!'

'That's not fair,' Lia recoiled.

'Well you have, haven't you? Take my father, for starters.'

'What about him?'

'Alejandro was never a hero voyager out to explore the world, was he? You weaved a whole fantasy around him when I was small.'

Lia's heart sank. 'Look, Abby, we've gone through all this already. I explained it all to you when you were twelve.'

'I can understand a makey-up story to stop a little girl from feeling unwanted and insecure. And when you told me what happened, I stayed quiet about it; I felt it was our secret. So I was as much to blame as you for keeping up the pretence, although everybody on Mayberry Lane sussed out the truth eventually.'

Lia felt her face draining of colour. 'What do you mean?'

'Sam told me, oh, years ago that they all knew my dad was probably just an ordinary bloke who didn't want to know about me. I set him straight. Do you know, Mum, you did such a good job that when I went away I was half expecting to find someone who looked like Alejandro, or who thought I resembled him.'

Lia felt weak. 'Does all this matter any more, Abby?'

'Then why are you keeping it up? I mean, whatever about a story to keep a young child happy, but Mum, what on earth possessed you to mention it on the television and in newspapers? Talk about a big fat lie! Even your fans all think it's such a romantic tale.'

Lia felt cold. 'Abby – hell, look, I was caught on the hop. It all happened so fast, the first interview coming straight on the heels of the first book deal, my head was somewhere else. I was dazzled and thrilled, and when I was asked about my child, my background, I just found the words slipping out unconsciously.'

'You mean you couldn't admit to discovering you were pregnant at sixteen, straight after your first holiday fling?'

'It wasn't just a casual holiday fling. Anyway, that's my problem. I don't need to explain myself to you over thirty years later. And I really don't know how we got talking about all this anyway. Why are you bringing it all up now?'

'I've been thinking about you and Alejandro recently and I was wondering if you'd ever . . . if you'd ever got over him.'

'Got *over* him? What do you mean?'

'All these years, there hasn't been anyone else, has there? Not seriously anyway. Do you still feel bitter that he's not in your life? Or that you were left holding the baby all those years ago?'

'What makes you think I'm still hurt and bitter?'

'You just about told me so when you said no man was worth it. I sometimes wonder if you still feel kind of cold and stony-hearted inside.'

'Cold and stony-hearted? Abby! What the hell brought this on?'

'Well to be honest, it kind of comes out in your writing. It's hard-edged and thrilling and cold. Your heroine detectives have balls of steel and crappy love lives, and your men are sad bastards or just plain evil. Do you think this is part of some hidden angst coming out in your writing?'

'I don't get you.'

'I always had the idea that your novels should be adventurous and soulful and layered with . . .' Abby hesitated, 'well, inspiration and redemption, as opposed to murder and rape and death.'

'I'll bear that in mind when I run out of ideas and

decide to change genres,' Lia said lightly. In spite of her reluctance to continue this conversation, she found herself asking, 'When did I ever give you the impression I was pining for your father?'

'I'm just trying to figure some things out and . . . get a handle on life. You were pregnant at sixteen. I can empathise with that. Did my father break your heart so completely that you never trusted another man? Or are you still in love with him after all these years?'

Abby looked pained and vulnerable, her aquamarine eyes huge in her pale face, and Lia thought of her daughter's unusual restraint and jumped to a conclusion. 'Don't tell me *you're* pregnant?'

Abby gave a short laugh. 'No way! I'm not even . . . seeing anyone right now. I know we talked of Alejandro many times, and my childhood was wonderful because I had you and Nana Lacey, but I was just wondering how you coped without him in your life.'

'I coped because I was busy with you and my job, and my mother and the house in Mayberry Lane.'

'Why no other relationships though? Why did you never marry?' Abby pressed. 'Was my father all that brilliant that nobody else came close? Or did you find it impossible to fall in love all over again?'

Abby was asking questions she'd never asked before. Lia cast around in her mind for something suitable to change the topic of conversation, to throw her daughter off the scent, to get away from dangerous memories that clawed at the back of her mind, but anxiety clouded her brain, making it impossible to think straight. 'You're being ridiculous, Abby. I don't understand the purpose of all these questions.'

Abby looked defeated. 'I told you, I'm just trying to work a few things out.'

'What is your problem?' Lia went on the attack. 'Has someone done the dirt on you? Forget him, I say. Take off the blinkers. Though maybe you're right on one score. If I'm hard and bitter, it's from experience. Because there's no such thing as everlasting love, not really. Lust, yes. Mutual co-dependence, definitely. But hearts and flowers and drippy romance? Forget it. It's only for losers. That's why I can't understand . . .'

'Understand what?'

'Why you've taken up as a wedding planner. And in a commercial tourist resort, of all places, after all your high-flying dreams.' Lia gave a short laugh. 'You can't very well accuse me of not being true to myself when you've so obviously turned your back on your own dreams.'

'There's nothing wrong with my job, and by the way, have you ever been to Sorrento?'

'No, not yet.'

'Then you don't know what you're talking about.'

'Is he keeping you stuck there, whoever he is? In that case, you'd be far better moving on and forgetting about him. Wise up, Abby. Please don't throw yourself away on someone who's not worth it.'

Abby was silent.

She sounded cold and hard, she knew, but she needed to be with Abby, Lia told herself. The last thing she wanted was to see her daughter down in the dumps and pining over a man. It was far better to jerk her out of her apathy, even if it was painful in the process.

'Come on, Abby.'

Abby jumped to her feet. 'You haven't a clue what you're talking about. I'm not listening to any more of this,' she cried. 'Maybe I'm not in a good place right now, but at least I'm not all resentful and angry inside like you.'

Lia finally snapped. 'Of course *I've* never been in love. *Or* felt desire!'

'Not from the way you're talking. You got knocked up by

a young guy on your first holiday with your friends and you can't even bring yourself to tell the truth to your fans, 'cos you've never got over it, have you?'

Lia was appalled at the sight of Abby, her flashing eyes and don't-touch-me prickly hairstyle, her mouth opening and closing in her white face. 'How dare you talk to me like this!'

'Don't worry, I've nothing else to say and I've no intentions of hanging around here either.'

Then Lia's heart plummeted soundlessly as the slam of Abby's bedroom door reverberated throughout the London apartment.

The shouts of children playing in the small park outside brought Lia back to her writing room with the bookshelves and cream leather armchairs, the music centre, tumbling ivy plants and curving beech desk. She gazed around at the high, stuccoed ceilings and original fireplace and the framed book jackets on the wall, and it took her a minute to gather herself together.

She hadn't seen Abby since then and communication between them had been reduced to a couple of cautious emails and stiff phone calls, Lia trying and failing to find some way to get through the defensive front Abby was obviously putting up. Lia blamed nobody but herself. Somehow she'd got it all wrong. Her daughter had obviously been hurting badly and instead of showing some sympathy, Lia had more or less told her to snap out of it, thinking it was the best approach, and in return, Abby was firmly keeping her at arm's length.

Now for some reason known only to herself, Abby was talking about Mayberry Lane. Reading between the lines, Lia had the oddest feeling that Abby was looking for permission to return home, even though Abby had never before looked for permission for anything. Used to churning out hundreds of words on a daily basis, Lia found herself hesitating over the simplest of sentences as she composed a reply to her daughter.

'The house is there for you whenever you want,' Lia slowly typed, her fingers shaking on the keys, but her tone was as light and casual as Abby's, much as though she was describing the weather instead of a major decision on Abby's part. 'If you ever decide to go home, I can contact the management company and set things in motion as regards the lease, and as it happens, it's up at the end of June . . .' Harmless, straightforward facts, Lia mused as she slowly composed the email, her fingers picking out bland words and deliberately avoiding the questions she most wanted to ask Abby in case she pushed her further away.

Had someone broken her heart? Was Abby prepared to absolve her mother for saying all the wrong things? And what had happened in Sorrento to make Abby think of home? She finished the impersonal email and clicked send, watching the confirmation message flash across her screen. Then she went out to the kitchen with her mug of cold coffee and poured it down the kitchen sink.

Abby's words still rang in her head because they'd wounded her deeply, for she was living a lie as much as her daughter was. There was the Lia Lacey who dressed up in glitzy designer labels and mingled with celebrities in the evenings, who donned a cloak of nonchalance when her beguiling looks and clothes were admired, who tinkled with laughter and sat in bookstores and smilingly autographed piles of carefully-contrived, cold-bloodedly plotted books for her eager fans.

Yet behind the scenes, beyond the glittering image and nebulous sheen of fame, she was the same flesh and blood Lia Lacey that she'd always been. The same likes and dislikes, much the same values, hopes and dreams, the same old haunts and fears that occasionally flickered at the back of her mind, and even the same desires, she privately admitted, despite the passage of years.

That last bit had hurt, when Abby had scoffed about her bitter resentment. Because she knew all about lost loves and secret desires. Oh yes, she did. She'd also tasted bitter disappointment and struggled to come to terms with it, putting it firmly behind her. But Abby had it wrong, for it hadn't been Alejandro. The smiling Spanish guy she'd met all those years ago had merely awakened her passions. Someone else had brought desire to a different level, but he'd proved to be fickle and disloyal.

As far as Lia was concerned, the past and all its disillusions belonged to a distant time and place that didn't exist any more.

13

No matter how discreetly Paula tried to ease them through the opening, the wine bottles made a fiendishly noisy clatter as they smashed against the insides of the recycling bin.

Paula prickled with embarrassment and glared at her enormous pile of empties still awaiting demolition. She seemed to have been there for an inordinate amount of time and it would be all too easy for a passerby to assume that she was some kind of alcoholic. She tried to squeeze in three bottles at a time to speed up the process and get the hell away, but she wasn't very successful. Then she ended up forcing a half smile at the middle-aged man shoving bottles into the adjoining bin. She easily had four times as much as him and was tempted to pass a jocular comment about the mad party she'd held the night before, or the fact that her huge collection dated back to last Christmas and she'd been far too busy to clean up her carbon footprint.

As if.

And since when did Paula Stevens worry about justifying her alcohol consumption to a stranger? She fired another bottle through the aperture with a vengeance that resulted in a satisfying crash. She wouldn't normally have had so many empties, she fumed, only for a man called Sam Ryan. It had been one week and two days since he'd called to her office to take her out for a belated birthday drink, and she hadn't heard from him since.

Problem was, he'd kissed her so thoroughly at the end

of the evening that despite her best intentions and all the
anguish she'd finally come through, it had left her wanting
more.

Their night out still had the power to make her smile at odd,
inopportune moments.

Sam had cheekily confiscated her car keys, dropping them
into his pocket, and told her she could get a taxi into work
the following morning. 'We're having a meal along with that
bottle of wine,' he said as they took the lift to the ground
floor. Paula was too surprised to reply as he went on to say
he'd already made a reservation. He mentioned one of
Dublin's most exclusive restaurants and at the back of her
mind she wondered how he'd managed to pull that at such
short notice. Out loud she said, 'But I'm not dressed,'
immediately regretting her choice of words, for his eyes
sparked and slowly ran the length of her body. She felt her
skin flash with heat in the narrow lift.

He flashed a mischievous smile. 'I could have sworn you
were fully dressed.'

She decided to shut up. If she'd had some warning she
would have showered and freshened up in her private
bathroom and loosened her hair from the French knot it was
scrupulously tweaked into. Her Chanel suit would take her
from the office to any kind of engagement, but given the
chance, she would have swapped her prim white shirt for a
softer cami top. However, there was no way she could have
asked Sam to wait, no way she could have coped with him
and his lethal charge of testosterone prowling around the
confines of her office while she ducked into her en suite to
undress, shower and change.

Sam was full of relaxed authority in a black suit and a
silvery tie. Armani, she guessed. He'd probably come straight
from the law courts. She could just imagine him in action,

an impressive figure with his long-limbed height, incisive and articulate as he held forth in the closing stages of a case or succinctly wrapped up an argument.

A far cry from the Sam Ryan of old, the rangy-looking student, expert basketball player *and* boyfriend of Abby. Some instinct for self-preservation told her that all she needed to keep in focus was the boyfriend of Abby part, but that went flying out the window as she faced him across the table and wondered what to do with her hands.

'Do you know – forgive me,' he said, fiddling with the cutlery and throwing her a sheepish glance with his hazel eyes. 'I've practically hijacked you here and taken for granted that you're free and available to come out with me.'

Her mind raced. How come he'd taken it for granted? Was she wearing some kind of sad singleton label? And why was she worrying?

She twiddled with her napkin, folding and unfolding it. 'The way it is, Sam, I'm far too busy with the demands of Stevens to have time for any, ah, extracurricular activities.' She threw him a bland smile and congratulated herself. Her reply covered a multitude, didn't it?

'Yes, Abby more or less said as much.'

'Abby?'

'Yes, she met you at Elaine's wedding?'

'That's right, she did.' To hell with Abby Lacey. She didn't want to be reminded of her, not with Sam oozing pure gorgeousness as he sat across the table from her. He'd removed his jacket and his shirt was equally as crisp and white as hers. His cufflinks gleamed as he moved his hands expressively. She watched the way his lean fingers held the menu. Long, square-tipped fingers. Perfect for guitar-playing. As well as other things . . . Her face flushed as her thoughts ran amok.

He lifted an enquiring eyebrow. 'And I suppose some men

find a powerful, entrepreneurial woman like you a major threat to their egos?'

'Maybe so.' She forced herself to meet his gaze head on. 'Others, however, find it rather a challenge.'

'No doubt they do.' Sam relaxed back in his seat and his mouth twitched at the corners, and she had the feeling that he was highly amused with rather than challenged by her veneer of calculated composure.

He ordered champagne cocktails. 'We've a lot to celebrate.' He touched his glass to hers and said, 'To the success of Stevens.'

'Cheers.'

'To your birthday.'

'Skip that one.'

'Nonsense. It's always something to celebrate. Next up, old friends meeting after so many years.'

'Friends?'

'Sure, although we were scarcely bosom pals. I suppose to you I was the snotty-nosed kid down the road. Hey, maybe I still fall into that category,' he grinned.

'Not quite.' She flashed him a keen appraising glance over the rim of her glass.

He gave her an equally penetrating look. 'I dare say you were far too busy with your schoolbooks to pay me, Abby and Elaine any attention.'

'There were times when I was a bit jealous, actually,' Paula found herself admitting. She put down her glass and for a long moment she stared at the candle flame flickering on the table. Then she raised her eyes to his and said, 'The three of you were such good mates and always having a laugh, sometimes at my expense,' she smiled in remembrance. 'I used to get all bossy and on my high horse, but there were times when I envied you all your camaraderie.'

'Shucks, Paula, don't tell me that. We all thought you were

a dedicated bookworm who constantly looked down your nose at us. Even Elaine used to be wary of your reaction when she was taking the piss with you.'

'That didn't prevent her from pulling out all the stops – between fake college reports, hiding my lecture notes, watering down my perfume and fabricating letters from a dating agency ... as well as all the messing about with Mark. There were times when I could have strangled her. But behind it all, I was a little jealous.' Paula was glad of the distraction as the waitress arrived with her starter of home-cured salmon. God knows what else she'd admit to under his friendly scrutiny. Sam was obviously expert at wrangling information from reluctant witnesses. Or else he was just plain easy to talk to.

Sam had ordered seafood antipasti and he took a couple of bites before saying, 'Elaine used to moan that she had a very hard act to follow. As far as we were concerned, you were up there in a league of your own. You know she was always being compared most unfavourably with you in the classroom?'

'Obviously she survived all that,' Paula said. 'She's very happy and her little girl is gorgeous. She's made a terrific success of her life.'

'Is that success?' he asked, his eyes suddenly serious. 'A happy marriage and a child of your own?'

She didn't need to think twice. 'It could be, Sam, but obviously not for me,' she said dismissively. 'Marriage isn't part of my life plan. I've far bigger fish to fry. I'm determined to put Stevens on the map and I have a strategic action plan to carry me through the next five years.'

If her action plan impressed him, he didn't show it, merely looking at her enquiringly as he asked, surprising her with his directness, 'Wouldn't you like to have kids?'

'You make certain choices, don't you?' she said, fudging the issue. She instinctively knew that he'd never approve of her tentative plans to control her own fertility. No man liked to think he wouldn't be part of the equation.

'So you've no unfulfilled ambitions?' he asked.

'None whatsoever.'

'I know what my choice would be,' he said as he looked at her thoughtfully. 'I'd love a couple of kiddies, a boy to play basketball with and a cute little princess of a girl.'

She had a sudden picture of Sam playing tag with his son and swinging a little daughter onto his broad shoulders, the two of them scrambling to sit on his knee. They'd be golden-haired, lively and happy-go-lucky, just like their dad. She felt a sudden inexplicable pang that shook her to the core. 'Is there any reason why that hasn't happened yet? Or why you never got married?' she blurted. Then, recovering herself and throwing her hands up in surrender, she said, 'Apologies, Sam, that was far too personal. Pretend I never spoke.'

'It's okay,' he grinned. 'There's no major secret as to why I'm unattached. Even though I'm thirty-five next birthday, I guess it just hasn't happened for me yet. Anyway, this is your treat. I'm not going to spoil it with the boring details of my life. Now, Ms Stevens, when you're not planning your next strategic move,' he asked, his voice rich with amusement, 'what do you get up to in your spare time? I take it a high-flying executive does allow herself some me time?'

Paula was tempted to admit it was all work and no play, but instead, as their starters were cleared away and their mains arrived, John Dory for her and rib-eye steak for him, along with the bottle of wine Sam had promised, she found herself talking up the gym in the apartment block where she lived, her walks along Dun Laoghaire pier, books she enjoyed and the contemporary music she listened to. Naturally enough, she left out her collection of DVDs, but it was all solitary stuff, she realised, and it scarcely added up to an exciting life.

Hang on – she was at the helm of Stevens, wasn't she? What could be more exciting than that? And at least her career was dependable and under her control. Nor would it ever ravage her heart.

The evening slid by and she found herself relaxing, even enjoying her conversation with Sam and admitting her total ignorance when it came to Irish trad music. There were no hidden undercurrents with him; what you saw was what you got. Looking at him laughing across the table, it was obvious he was comfortable in his own skin and full of common decency, and that alone made her unwind. As well as that, he was attentive and undemanding, with a light-hearted attitude to life that belied the heavy responsibilities of his day job.

'You don't take life too seriously, Sam,' she said.

'When you spend your days disentangling obscure points of family law, you tend to appreciate your down time and uncomplicated life,' he told her. 'I don't discuss my casework for obvious reasons,' he smiled ruefully, 'but sometimes it bothers me and I love it when the good guy wins, male or female. Especially when there are kids involved. And when things go wrong, well, I won't even go there. Anyway, moving on, can I tempt you with dessert?'

Sensitive too, she thought, behind that upbeat exterior.

She passed on dessert, but Sam tucked into a generous helping of tiramisu and when he saw her eyeing it appreciatively, he asked for an extra spoon.

'Go on, have some. I won't finish it and I can see your big greedy eyes feasting on it,' he joked, passing his plate across the table.

'Greedy? Thanks a bunch,' she retorted, a huge smile on her face. Nonetheless, she pushed her spoon into the untouched side of his tiramisu, feeling like a kid again. When she saw his eyes settle on her mouth as she raised the spoon to her lips, she practically choked on the cool mouthful.

He saw her home in a taxi, even though it was out of his way. He walked her up towards her apartment block and she stood there rather awkwardly, feeling at an acute loss, the rules of the dating game rusty and alien to her.

Dating? That hadn't been a date. No way. Dating was off her life plan.

As though he sensed her hesitation, Sam laughed softly. 'Come here, let's say goodnight properly.'

Sam's going to kiss me and I very much want him to, the thought sparkled just as he pulled her into the shadows of the nearby shrubbery, out of view of passersby, and into his arms. Afterwards, there was no forgetting the crackle of electricity as their mouths met and he kissed her most thoroughly, the hard strength of his chest as she steadied herself against it and the overwhelming pleasure of being in his arms.

He drew away and stared at her curiously for a long moment. He flicked her cheek lightly and said, 'That was a lovely surprise.' Then he kissed her again.

Eventually they stopped and looked at each other.

'Well, goodnight,' Paula said, stepping back and summoning her composure. She had the overwhelming need to escape, to get away from this attractive man, before—

Before? Before he disturbed her peace of mind.

''Night,' he said, then squeezed her hand and backed away towards the pavement, his arm raised in farewell.

'Sam?'

'Yes?' There was an unmistakeable flash of optimism in his face that caught her breath.

'My car keys . . .'

'Of course,' he grinned. He stood a few feet away from her, plucked them out of his pocket and threw them into the air. 'Catch!'

She deftly caught them in her hands.

'Not bad,' he chuckled. He backed down the path again, hands in his pockets, and only at the last minute did he wave, turn away from her and head up the road.

She hadn't seen him since.

Paula was hugely relieved when she fired the last offensive bottle into the recycling bin. She dumped her empty crates into the boot of her Jaguar feeling as though she'd received some kind of munificent absolution after a much-delayed and embarrassing confession. Then she gunned the accelerator and shot out of the recycling centre car park. The next time, she vowed, she wouldn't wait until she'd amassed such a humiliating amount of bottles.

She squashed the critical voice that said she shouldn't be drinking so much in the first place. She'd been so stressed lately that *of course* she'd had to relax with a glass or two of her favourite *vino* each evening. And she was stressed because for the first time since the age of sixteen, she was suffering like an anxiety-ridden teenager and she didn't like it one bit. It was even affecting her in the office, and she'd been more driven than usual that week, snapping at Kate and almost causing a rift in their relaxed yet businesslike camaraderie. For Paula was finding that at the most inappropriate moments, she was imagining what it would be like to sleep with Sam Ryan.

She pressed a switch and blasted music. A week and two days was no length of time. Even so, she reasoned, it had only been a casual birthday treat between old friends. Last night, as an empty Saturday evening had stretched into a long boring night, she'd ended up drinking a whole bottle of Sauv Blanc. Alone.

She preferred it that way, didn't she? Having had her heart fragmented into a million pieces, it was safer all around to keep her emotions in check and to stay away from men.

Especially someone like Sam, who was already a huge threat to her firm resolutions. But there was no making sense of her sudden yearning or the empty, unsettling spot that had appeared in the busy fabric of her life.

14

'*Buon giorno*, Abby,' Rosita smiled when Abby strolled into the agency office on Monday morning to collect her paperwork. 'But you look tired! Where is the friendly sparkle that we all love to see?' Rosita was darkly Italian in a lustrous way, her eyes danced with merriment and she loved her travel agency work so much that she never failed to enthuse Abby.

'Dunno.' Abby pulled out a chair and slumped down at a spare desk. After a minute, she reached forward to switch on a fan. She put her elbows on the table, cupped her chin in her hands, felt the cool air ripple around her face and smiled a lopsided smile at Rosita. 'It must be the heat.'

'This heat? *Non capisco!*' Rosita looked puzzled. 'You should be used to it by now! I'd say you just had a busy weekend.'

Abby remained silent. Apart from going out for a meal with other reps and wedding planners from the agency on Saturday night and a desultory stroll around the small boutiques that peppered the quaint back streets of Sorrento, she'd skulked around her apartment, not even venturing as far as the Amalfi coast.

'I think you will need lots of energy for your brides this week,' Rosita said.

'Yeah, three days in a row.' Abby pulled her files towards her. 'Three Irish Bridezillas. I wonder what last-minute panic attacks this lot will indulge in.'

'Abby! This is not like you. What has happened to our calm Irish girl?'

'Oh, nothing.' She made herself smile, appalled at her sudden cynicism. 'Just that Lisa from Kilkenny has phoned to say she's having a nervous breakdown because she can't decide between a medieval or a modern background for her soft-focus photographs. Her fiancé is threatening to call off the whole thing.'

'Problems, problems!'

'And Gemma from Cavan wants to do away with the canopy for her vineyard hilltop ceremony. She hasn't a clue how baking hot the sun can be. She's bound to faint.'

'Don't worry, I know you can sort it all out with your big, soothing smile!'

But her big, soothing smile was wearing thin. Only last week, she'd been tempted to retort to hysterical Isabel from Limerick that it wasn't doomsday itself if the best man lost his carefully-drafted speech notes at the airport during the pre-flight booze-up, or if the groom's mother wrinkled her patrician nose at the specially-prepared lemon wedding cake and hissed that the spumante was corked. Which of course it wasn't. The groomsmen were knocking it back like water.

Her sudden irritability had nothing to do with Sam Ryan's surprising reappearance in her life and his sarky comments about her job, she told herself. She was tired and cranky because her night-time shadows were getting worse.

Even though the long midsummer evenings now shortened the dark night and dawn arrived with a cheeky punctuality at an unearthly hour in the morning, there were still long, empty hours to get through, those night-time hours when light breezes that drifted from the scented lemon grove and stole through the gaps in her shutters whispered in her ears and censured her for everything that had gone wrong.

She'd never loved anyone the way she'd loved him. But she only had herself to blame for the way it had ended. How could she have been so heedless, so reckless with that love?

Yet no matter how often she thought the night would go on forever, there came, without fail, the soft glow of light in the east. In the mornings when she pulled back the shutters, Abby stepped out onto her warm, sunny balcony and raised her face to the curving hills.

Ti amo . . . ti penso sempre . . .

She would never forget him. This was where she now belonged, held captive by the memory of his voice and the sound of promises exchanged as sunshine bounced with an even clearer, brighter whiteness against the pillars of the Cloisters of the Franciscan monastery.

Since his visit, though, and in an effort to get through those night-time hours, Abby found herself thinking more and more of Sam. She recalled the warm feel of his arms around her and the affection in his eyes, and spinning back in time, the way his secure presence had coloured most of her childhood and adolescence.

They'd sat out many an evening on the dry-stone wall in front of his house under the shade of the laburnum tree, sometimes joined by Elaine, other times just the two of them sharing their dreams and laughing at the world.

Best mates, he often said.

Friends forever, her usual reply.

He taught her basketball to take her mind off exams. He strummed a guitar in an imitation of her favourite pop group, Duran Duran. On one much laughed-about occasion, he resuscitated her when she choked on her one and only attempt at smoking a cigarette.

Sam was the first to go to college, heading off for the daily commute into Dublin city centre, discovering girlfriends

along with his legal studies, but he stayed good friends with
Abby. They revised together late into the night for their
college exams. They casually fell in and out of love with
other people, Abby slagging Sam about his girlfriends but
brazenly using him for advice on the male of the species
and vice versa. On more than one occasion, Sam provided
a comforting shoulder for Abby to cry on and kissed her all
better, until she discovered that the very same safety and
security Sam provided was threatening to suffocate her. On
her twenty-first birthday, Sam admitted that he was in love
with her, had always loved her.

She was between boyfriends and he took her out to
lunch, splurging his hard-earned student income on a
restaurant in Dublin city centre in addition to a silver locket
that he'd wrapped in a pretty red box. Afterwards they
strolled in St Stephen's Green. It was the end of March
and the small park was burgeoning with signs of spring.
Abby was chatting about going out with her college mates
that coming weekend when Sam stopped in his tracks and
turned her to face him.

'Can I tell you something?' he said, interrupting her stream
of chatter.

'Sure.'

He put his hands on her shoulders and drew her close.
'I don't know how to say this, Abby, but I'm finding it hard
to think of you off gallivanting this weekend. Ah, hell, why
should I pretend any longer? I'm insanely jealous of the lads
you meet in college. I'm jealous of all of the blokes you've
been out with over the past couple of years.'

'No you're not, Sam, don't talk rubbish,' she said, feeling
a cold chill slip down her spine.

'It's not rubbish. I hope that some day we'll get married.
You're my best mate, Abby. Surely you know that I love you?'

She felt the tips of his fingers in her scalp as he ran his

hands through her hair and smoothed it back from her face. 'What about all those girlfriends of yours?'

'They don't mean anything to me. I'm just waiting for you to see me in a new light.'

'Sam – God.' She was aghast, awkward and confused. Her hand lay clenched in the pocket of her jacket where the little red box was scorching her fingers. 'This is the last thing I expected. You're more like a brother to me. And you know I've got plans of my own,' she tried to explain. 'I've talked to you about them many times, my plans to travel and see the world and explore everything there is to explore.'

'But you surely don't mean all that. It's only castles in the air, some kind of teenage fantasy.'

She slowly shook her head, the lovely lunch they'd enjoyed now sitting like a rock in her stomach.

'At least give me some hope,' he asked. His blond hair gleamed like pale corn in the spring sunshine and she was achingly aware of his vulnerability at that moment. She couldn't bear the look on his face and tried to be gentle.

'Sam, why do you think I'm studying languages? There's a whole exciting world out there. I want to see it, feel it and taste it before I do any kind of settling down. And then, well, who knows?' The last throwaway remark was silly, brittle and stupid, she knew, apart from downright cowardly, but designed to ease things a little.

He didn't really believe her. He thought he could make her fall in love with him. They stayed friends, Sam determined to change her mind, Abby desperately sorry for crushing his dreams. She spent the next couple of years completing her degree in languages and then she began working to save some funds for her travels. On the eve of her twenty-fourth birthday, her much-loved grandmother died, leaving a wealth of warm memories and a sad spot in her heart, as well as a small legacy for Abby to help her on her way.

Before she left Ireland, Sam asked her to marry him again, and with her point blank refusal, he told her she'd broken his heart.

It was only now, Abby thought as she opened her patio shutters on a sparkling Saturday morning in June, that she had some idea of how much her rejection must have hurt him. Yet still he'd emailed her since he'd returned to Dublin, reminding her about the party and hoping she'd come home. She took a cup of creamy coffee and a fresh brioche out to her balcony and was thankful that Sam seemed prepared to let bygones be bygones.

The following week, Abby lost patience with Monica from Galway. The bride was in floods the day before her wedding because the monogrammed napkins she'd brought from the wedding stationers in Ireland were scripted in gold instead of silver.

'How could they have made this stupid mistake?' she stormed. 'Everything, the whole theme of my wedding, is *silver.* Silver invitations, silver menus, silver ribbons around the flowers, the balloons *and* the limousine. These are going to look ridiculous! Why didn't I double check? But it was all such a last-minute rush. What will everyone think? I'm going to look such a fool.'

'Look, no one will really notice,' Abby began in a conciliatory tone of voice. This was one problem she couldn't fix in a jiffy.

'Of *course* they will!' Monica raged. 'I want my wedding day to be perfect.'

'It will be perfect if you're marrying the man you love,' Abby pointed out, feeling inexplicably hollow and jaded. 'Surely that's what it's all about? Not some kind of extravagant performance to impress your family and friends.'

'Don't be facetious. Of *course* I have to impress them.

That's the whole point. That's why we're putting on such a lavish show. Get real, Abby. This whole bash is costing me an absolute fortune. For one day in my life, I want to be the princess in my very own dream fairytale and it has to be perfect. What's wrong with that?'

'Fairytale?' Abby's voice trembled. 'Surely your wedding day is far more important and meaningful than just one day in a makey-up *fairytale*?'

It was the nearest she'd ever come to slapping a bride across the face. Abby left the bride's hotel as soon as she could lest she gave in to temptation. She stalked across the Piazza Tasso, heedless of the hooting traffic, and in her agitated state the sun's glare was merciless on her shoulders. She went back to her apartment, Monica's words going around and around in her head.

Get real, Abby. She felt as though she'd been jolted out of something. Is this what her Sorrento lifestyle was all about? By absorbing herself in the frothy and frivolous and helping to give brides the best wedding day possible, she thought she was making up in some way for the loss in her own life and obtaining some absolution for her guilt. But in reality, by pandering to her brides' every need, every trivial request, she was helping – no, *encouraging* – spoiled brides to play the lead role in their own makey-up fairytale and letting them get away with murder when the silliest thing went wrong, which was a million miles away from the true meaning of marriage and commitment. Beguiled with images of white silk and promises, she was keeping herself frozen in a kind of dream fantasy, perhaps even surpassing her mother when it came to living an illusion.

That evening, her usual trip around the Amalfi coast and the deep blue expanse of the Golfo di Salerno failed to soothe her. She gripped the railings at the viewing platform high above the village of Positano and gazed out to the sea.

In the heat of the evening, Abby felt an unexpected longing for the soft Irish summer breeze and the sweet scent of the air after a shower of rain. She wanted the feel of a dry-stone wall under her hands, the taste of a cool breeze on her face and teasing her hair, but most of all to recapture the feeling that she was young and invincible with the world at her feet, where she had a loyal Sam by her side, kissing it all better.

As for love? Was it possible to forget the last few months and find love again? All of a sudden, Sam Ryan seemed solid and real and infinitely attractive. He'd never married. *I guess no one would have me*, he'd said. She'd told him all those years ago that she wanted to travel before she settled down. Was Sam, by any chance, still waiting? Had fate brought them together because it was time for her to forget about Raffaele and move on?

Raffaele. How could six short weeks have changed her life so irrevocably?

Abby took a long, slow breath as she stared across to the grey-green mountains above the medley of the sugar-cubed, tumbling village. She looked down below to the scatter of white toy-like sailboats crawling across the fathomless sea. She threw her questions out into the vault of sky and sea and listened hard to hear the whispers on the incoming breeze, but now they were guarding her secrets and they remained just as blank and silent as the deep swell of ocean far below.

15

'If you'd tilt your head to the right just a little ...' the photographer urged. His camera flashed. 'Now angle to the left. Don't look so petrified, I promise the camera won't bite!'

His comment backfired on Paula, who frowned in the moment that the shutter activated.

'No, sorry. This won't do at all.' It was the photographer's turn to frown as he squinted at the dials and buttons on his powerful-looking camera. He was young and enthusiastic and full of a fresh vitality she'd found herself envying. He hadn't been the least bit intimidated by Paula's imposing office. He'd breezed in that Monday afternoon and announced that his name was Philip and said that it was his job to capture her on film. He'd unpacked tons of impressive equipment with an air of busy importance, chosen the best spot to take advantage of the lighting in her office, whooshed back her filmy curtains and begun to click away. She could have pinpointed the moment when some of his enthusiasm had waned and disillusionment set in.

It wasn't her fault, though, if she felt stiff and uncomfortable and her poses weren't quite what he'd expected. She had the unnerving feeling that the camera lens was beyond her control, was some sort of invasion of her privacy, and she wished with all her heart that she had asserted herself and insisted that the magazine accept a couple of her file portraits.

Philip lifted his camera with renewed determination and

threw her an easy grin. 'Just relax,' he encouraged. 'It's not an interview. You've already had the hundred and one questions. This is the nice part where you get to look pretty for the camera.'

Paula bristled. 'I thought I was supposed to come across as businesslike.'

'There's nothing wrong with a smile,' Philip said. 'You don't want to look too stern and daunting, do you? It might scare off prospective customers.'

He laughed at his own joke and it took a major effort for Paula to hold her facial expression in check. When she'd arrived at the office that morning, she'd totally forgotten about the article and the phone interview that had been scheduled. Luckily Kate had reminded her in plenty of time, but she'd found the phone interview a huge effort. It hadn't helped that she was rattled from the effects of a hangover and still angry with herself for allowing Sam to unsettle her. The friendly but sharp-as-nails journalist fired off a volley of questions on a wide range of topics that Paula had answered just as sharply, but it had left her slightly dazed and wondering what exactly she'd said, never mind implied. In addition to her tips for success, issues such as the existence of the glass ceiling, the demands of family and motherhood, the role of fatherhood and an optimum work–life balance had all come under the journalist's skilful scrutiny. Paula was only too aware that journalists were notorious for reading between the lines and putting their own slant on things, maybe highlighting certain points with rather more emphasis than was originally intended in order to embellish an article.

But a double spread in *Business Tomorrow* was not something you'd lightly refuse, Paula considered, especially when she was being profiled, naturally, as the exciting new face on a very select list of up-and-coming entrepreneurs.

'Look, I think the problem lies with the desk. Let's think outside the box for a minute. Why don't you come around from behind that forbidding fortress and sit here on the edge,' Philip suggested, beckoning her out and patting the front of her desk. 'Pretend you're laughing at me, pretend I'm Bart Simpson, or better again Johnny Depp, whatever floats your boat. But let me have a nice, easy, relaxed pose. I'll run the shots by you before we decide which ones to use. And I guarantee that you'll prefer the friendlier versions.'

Paula allowed herself to be led around to the front of her desk, where she perched carefully on the edge and smiled dutifully for the camera. At least at this angle he would surely get in some of her framed qualifications.

'Come on, you can do better than that. Take off your company hat, forget about the budget forecasts and think happy thoughts. That's more like it.' He began to snap with fresh determination, swivelling his camera in all directions. 'Just a couple more . . . and even bigger and better happy thoughts, here we go . . .'

At last, Philip declared that he had more than enough shots to work with and Paula sighed with relief.

'That's some view out the window,' he said as he began to pack away his equipment. 'I don't suppose you have a balcony? A nice shot of you leaning against it and staring down at the city would look good – you know, on top of the world, on top of your game, that sort of thing.'

Paula was surprised that she was so easily persuaded to lead him across to the patio door at the side that gave onto a tiny private balcony overlooking the thrumming grey city, with its cars and buses and the steely tracks of the Luas glinting down beneath. The wind caught at tendrils of her hair, freeing them from her huge clip, and when she tried to tidy them, even more blonde strands broke free.

'Leave it,' Philip admonished. 'Just a couple of shots, that's all. Now another big friendly smile . . .'

The photographer was as good as his word. The following day, he emailed contact sheets of all the photographs to Paula. She sat in silence as she stared at a series of images on the screen.

She was appalled to realise that in the first few shots, far from looking astute and businesslike, she looked downright forbidding and slightly anxious. Was this how she presented herself as she sat behind her desk? She liked to think that she was at the helm of everything and fully in control, but she didn't look it. It was a cold, sobering moment for her.

But the later shots told a story of their own. She looked happier, more carefree, even sexier, especially in the final poses where she was half turned towards the camera while standing on her balcony above the city, with soft tendrils of her hair floating in the breeze. Her slightly aquiline nose and the curved angle of her cheek and chin combined with the look in her darkly-lashed eyes to give her an air of provocative sensuality. She scarcely recognised herself in these startling new images of Paula Stevens. A vibrant, attractive Paula Stevens.

Philip had asked her to think happy thoughts. Unconsciously, she'd found herself focusing her mind on mental pictures of Sam strumming his guitar, catching her eye and smiling at her, the touch of his hand on her arm as he guided her down the street, the electric feel of his mouth, Sam playing tag with his children.

Never in her wildest dreams had she expected such surprising results.

The camera never lies, she thought in a welter of anxiety as she scrolled through the images one more time. No matter how hard she fought to resist, there was no denying that even thinking of that man made her feel sexy.

He'd finally phoned that morning, after two long weeks. His call had come through on the main switch and he'd been passed to Kate, who in turn had informed Paula that he was on the line.

'Take a message please,' Paula had instructed, feeling incredibly nervous all of a sudden and utterly relieved that she was in the private sanctuary of her office and that there were no witnesses to her suddenly hot face.

So far, though, she hadn't phoned him back. Paula stared for a long moment at the final, sexy image of herself before closing the file. She'd had her share of love and promises, had tasted excitement and thrills, but it had ended in disaster. She couldn't afford to get hurt again. So how could she phone him back when even the thought of Sam turned her into someone she was desperately afraid to be?

16

Lia had to ask the middle-aged lady in the third row to repeat the question.

She smiled at Lia expectantly. 'I'd like to know how long it takes you to write a book? On average?'

It was a straightforward question she should have caught the first time around and which, thankfully, she could have answered in her sleep. 'About a year in total,' Lia told her in her best novelist voice, which meant injecting it with a confidential tone as though to include them in the ravishing secrets of her success. 'That includes research and redrafting.'

She felt like adding that you could tack on all the long, lean years she'd been soldiering away in the bedroom in Mayberry Lane, piling up hated rejections slips until she'd come to London and stumbled onto a winning formula. But the packed audience didn't really want to know about a long, hard grind. What they wanted to hear was instant success stories, instant fame, the glamorous side of the writing life and all its glittering accessories.

A flurry of hands. More eager questions.

'Ladies and gentlemen, we just have time for one or two more. Lia's been very patient and we've already gone way over time.' Wendy, the store manager, checked her watch. 'Could we have that nice handsome man in the sixth row? Yes, you, and don't act so surprised! You know you're the spit of George Clooney.'

A ripple of laughter went around the assembly and Lia

automatically refreshed her smile as she beamed at the gathering. She usually loved bookstore events, meeting her reading public and having a discussion on all sorts of writing-related topics. It was her love of books and telling stories, after all, that had led her to this path in life. And if she was perfectly honest, she got a kick out of the aura of glitter and magic that was attached to being a successful author. So normally, she enjoyed it all, but tonight she didn't know how the hell she had got through the last hour.

This evening, she was the much-feted guest of honour at a large Birmingham bookstore. The store was crammed. Wendy had delightedly informed her that the event had booked out in a matter of hours when it was announced that Lia would be visiting the store as part of her publicity tour for *Death on Friday*. She'd been spirited up onto the small raised stage as though she was none other than the queen herself, swept off her feet with an enormous bouquet of flowers and nearly blinded with a huge flurry of camera flashes. She had a pain in her wrist from the stacks of books she'd signed.

Olga had styled her hair that morning before she'd flown up from London and Sonia had referred her to a sister beauty parlour in Birmingham for her make-up. So between her sexed-up hair and glamorous high-octane face, and in her sapphire blue Balenciaga dress and matching peep-toed platforms, she looked every inch the part.

She smiled flirtatiously at the nice handsome man in the sixth row. Hmm. He did look a bit like Clooney all right, but tonight it failed to have the usual impact on her.

'Do you do all of your research in advance of writing the book?' he asked.

'Yes, most of it,' she said. 'Of course, there's always a certain amount of revision which can be done at the editing stage. But I would normally spend about three months purely researching my subject matter before I even start chapter one.'

'Are you in need of any research assistants, Ms Lacey?' he asked hopefully, causing another ripple of laughter.

'Why don't we discuss that afterwards,' Lia smiled.

'Excuse me, Ms Lacey, but is your female protagonist in *Death on Friday* purely fictional?' a strident female voice asked. 'I think a lot of us could empathise with her. I'd say there's quite a few of us here who can only dream of doing damage to a man's—'

'Yes, well, we're keeping things light and easy tonight,' Wendy smoothly interjected. 'Let's keep those gory details between the covers of the book!'

'Does it take you long to come up with ideas?'

'Do you ever write in longhand? Don't they say it's more immediate?'

Lia answered in turn, feeling suddenly jaded. She wished she was tucked up fast asleep in her hotel room. But there wasn't even the refuge of her hotel bedroom at the end of the event, she inwardly wept, and her face pained with the effort of a forced smile as Wendy closed the proceedings. Wendy and her staff who had helped co-ordinate the evening were bringing her out for a meal along with six of their valued customers, six customers who'd had to enter a hugely subscribed competition for the opportunity to dine with their favourite author.

Lia was duly relieved of her veritable forest of flowers and the magnum of champagne that the store had presented to her. 'We'll send them to your hotel,' they said, and she wished she could put her foot down and insist on going back to the Radisson with them. Instead she was escorted down the staircase and borne out into the mellow Birmingham night as though she were some kind of valuable trophy.

It was only when she was seated at a round table in a

posh restaurant, a table gleaming with silverware and candles and proudly sporting buckets of chilled Bollinger, that she realised that the George Clooney clone who was interested in assisting with her research was seated beside her. Any other night it would have sent a frisson of excitement up her spine, and it wouldn't have been out of the question to consider asking him to her hotel room – discreetly, of course. Now and again, Lia enjoyed the release of sex with an interesting-looking man as part and parcel of her new lifestyle, but tonight she couldn't entertain it whatsoever, no matter how sexy he looked. For behind the fake smiles she bestowed on the audience and the falsely effervescent conversation, her mind was churning over the same painful thing.

Abby had emailed. She *was* going home. Only it wasn't just for a casual break between her travels, as Lia had initially thought.

Abby was going home to catch up with old friends. Sam Ryan was planning a fortieth party for his brother Mark, who was returning from the States, and there was going to be some kind of reunion. The email had caused Lia to be sleepless long into the night. Thoughts of Abby back in Dublin was one thing, but rediscovering old friends, stirring up the past and perhaps even talking about Alejandro filled her with an apprehension that she couldn't shake.

She had the inexplicable feeling that something, somewhere, was about to shift, some fault line under the smooth surface of her life was about to fracture, and she had no idea what the consequences might be.

17

'I have a proven track record within agency recruitment in Ireland and I believe I can make a huge contribution to Stevens,' Madeline Jones enthused.

Madeline was a last-minute applicant for a vacancy in Stevens and she knew her stuff. Paula concentrated on the thirty-three-year-old sitting in front of her and tried to ignore the fact that she didn't like her. Madeline was confident. She was highly qualified. She had a good appearance and a pleasant manner and speaking voice. Her references were excellent. She could see her fitting into Stevens and being an asset to the company. Of all the shortlisted applicants, Madeline best suited the profile of the job. Except for one minor detail.

She was pregnant.

Madeline smiled hopefully across the desk. Her chic power suit was carefully tailored to accommodate her growing baby. Five to six months, Paula guessed, swiftly averting her eyes. She'd be working in Stevens for about three months before she'd be bunking off on maternity leave. Before that, there would be time off required for antenatal classes, and then an absence of at least six months, and all the time Paula would have to hire temporary staff to cover for Madeline and keep her position open.

Quite a tall order for a newly-emerging company, no matter how stellar it was.

'Have you any supporting information you wish to contribute?' Paula said.

Madeline smiled again. 'I hope my pregnancy won't be viewed as a barrier. I intend to remain at work as long as I can, and naturally, I'll be returning as soon as my period of maternity leave is finished.'

Yes, and then your little baby will always come first, Paula thought silently.

'The fact that you're pregnant is irrelevant,' Paula lied. 'Stevens employs its people strictly on a non-discriminatory basis. My company is committed to a policy of equal opportunity in both recruitment and employment practices in adherence to legislation set out in the employment equality Acts.'

'Oh, I didn't for one minute assume that I'd be treated unfairly,' Madeline smiled. 'I just wanted you to have my personal assurance that it would make no difference to my level of commitment to the job.'

Maybe Madeline genuinely thought that now, Paula considered, but the reality would be far different. She only had to think of Elaine and Ruth to know that if her baby sneezed, Madeline would down tools. Therefore Madeline couldn't commit to the job with the same degree as an unattached, childless person.

In addition to that, there was something about Madeline that had put Paula on edge from the minute she'd entered her office. She questioned her further about her learning curve to date, her mind only half on the answers. As she turned the feeling over in her mind, she eventually realised that she was jealous. The girl across the desk was blooming. Maybe her career path needed an overhaul – she'd certainly never be sitting on Paula's side of the desk – but she would soon have something that was infinitely precious. A little baby to call her own.

She had a sudden vision of Elaine's luminous face as she cuddled a newborn Ruth, the delicate feel of her small niece's skin and her fluttering matchstick fingers topped with tiny, pearly nails. She heard Sam's voice as he spoke about his little son or daughter. Hold on, Paula sharply pulled herself up; this was not her usual thought pattern. Pregnant women and babies did not fill her with unfulfilled longings. She brought the interview to a close, although not too speedily in case Madeline suspected unfair treatment, even giving her longer than usual to ask any pertinent questions.

'You can expect to hear from us within a week.' Paula was relieved to be finally shaking hands, knowing in her heart of hearts that even though Madeline was the most qualified for the vacancy in Stevens, she would not be offering her the job.

The following day, Paula called a meeting with Emer. Her senior consultant was skilled and experienced. However, instead of discussing the applicants with her and inviting her views, Paula announced that she'd chosen Andrew McCann as the most suitable candidate to fill the vacancy left by Sadie. He was thirty and ambitious, and with a blinkered focus on results, there was no fear of him looking for time off.

'Please draft up the usual contract, Emer, and arrange to have it couriered out to him. I'll phone him in the meantime and ask him to start as soon as possible.' She needed him on board as of yesterday and was prepared to offer him enough incentive to ensure he didn't feel obliged to work out the notice required by his present firm, information that could only be alluded to across a telephone line and not in writing.

'And you can shred the other applications,' Paula added, feeling the need to rid the office of any trace of Madeline Jones.

'Don't you want to hold them on file?' Emer asked.

'No. Please issue standard rejection letters.' She swivelled to her laptop, indicating that the conversation was at an end, even though she still had to fill the vacancy left by Ursula. If Emer was surprised with her decision, she didn't show it. She wouldn't dare accuse me of discrimination, Paula thought blackly, even though she *was* guilty.

She told herself that behind her desk she was beyond the reach of anyone. And she could forget about photographs that told a different story and niggled at the back of her mind. Then the following evening she found Sam waiting for her outside her apartment block when she walked up from the car park.

He was casually dressed and sexier than ever in stonewashed jeans and a Nike T-shirt, and she was alarmed at the surge of energy and adrenaline that slammed into her at the sight of him. It was a sunny evening and his blond hair gleamed in the light. She had the sudden urge to touch it and see how it would feel under her fingers. Someone nearby was having a barbecue, for the pungent scent carried on the air and it made her think of shared laughter and conversation and long evenings melting into hazy twilights.

'Sam? What are you doing here?'

'I'm doing a gig for tourists in a hotel up the road in about fifteen minutes,' he said, glancing at his watch, 'and I thought you might be interested in coming along?'

'So you just happened to be passing?' Instant deflation. He hadn't been patiently waiting for her to come home. He'd been in the neighbourhood and had probably remembered at the last minute that a certain Paula Stevens lived in the vicinity. That was all. She cursed her quickening heartbeat, told herself she was a fool of the highest order when it came to the opposite sex, and strove for calm.

'Not quite like that,' he grinned. 'I didn't just think of you on the off chance. I was in court all afternoon, so I didn't have time to make any calls – which you probably wouldn't have returned anyway,' he said, shooting her a meaningful look.

So far, he'd left three messages, which she'd ignored. Even Kate was becoming curious. Paula was tempted to retaliate by pointing out he'd taken his time about contacting her after their meal, but thankfully the words stuck in her throat.

'Look, Paula, I've been down in Cork on business, I just got back this week. This evening, I got delayed in court and had to rush over here. Even now, I'm pushed for time. I couldn't have waited much longer.'

'I'm sorry to say that your waiting has been in vain,' Paula said on the spur of the moment.

He looked confused. 'What's that?'

Already challenged in her flat driving shoes – why the hell had he found her in those? – Paula straightened her back and took a deep breath. She felt a peculiar ache as she said, 'Look, Sam, thanks for the invitation, but I don't think there's much point.'

He frowned. 'Not much point in a spot of music and dancing?'

Dancing? A vision of dancing with Sam filled her mind and her stomach somersaulted with anxiety. She'd danced with someone else before, wrapped in his arms under a star-lit sky, and her dreams had turned to dust.

'I like music and dancing of course, but my life is busy. My job takes up all my time and energy and the bottom line is that I just don't want to get involved in anything else.'

He quirked an eyebrow and his hazel eyes gleamed. 'Jeez, Paula, I'm flattered to think that you might have considered me as involvement material.'

Her face flushed. The sooner she got this man out of her life, the better.

'It's just that – come on, Sam, you know what I mean.'

'I don't. But unfortunately I don't have the time to tease out the exact ramifications because I should be tuning up right now.'

He was gone. Before she had time to gather her wits, never mind her breath, he had stalked off into the balmy evening.

Involvement material. How *dare* he, she seethed as she thrust a ready-made meal into the microwave. She kicked off her horrid flat shoes and opened a bottle of wine, heedless to the fact that her newly-refreshed supply was rapidly dwindling. She poured a glass and walked into her bedroom in her stocking feet. She deserved a drink after a demanding day at the office and needed to unwind after seeing Sam so unexpectedly. And what exactly was wrong with her, she fumed, that his reappearance in her life coincided with all her critical faculties being suspended?

She took a long gulp of wine before she undressed and went into the shower. She poured another glass, just to have with her healthy alternative meal. Besides, a glass or two helped her to relax and it was the only thing that prevented her from spending the night wallowing in thoughts of Sam playing music to a laughing, chatting crowd in a nearby hotel and the fact that she could have been dancing in his arms.

She put on her *Love Actually* DVD and found herself laughing and crying in turn.

Later that evening, she switched on her laptop and surfed the net searching for articles on fertility issues. Paula refilled her glass of wine more than once as she read about refinements in freezing eggs, the pros and cons of baby banks and the different possibilities of delaying motherhood thanks to constantly improving success rates in various techniques. Some of the facts and figures weren't quite what she'd expected, and some of the cold, invasive procedures made her heart lurch. She absorbed the information slowly, finding it difficult to digest the concept of anti-freeze chemicals being added to her microscopic eggs and the whole procedure around egg harvesting, including the necessary invasive scans. And as for the psychological impact on a child who'd have to be told it was once stored in deep-freeze . . . ?

Apart, of course, from possible guardianship and custody issues further down the line.

In addition to all this, Paula found it impossible to reconcile the hard factual information outlined on various internet sites with the vision she held of a radiant Elaine announcing her pregnancy. Then there was the likelihood of multiple births . . . God. As if one baby at a time wasn't enough.

But she found the answer to one of her problems. She pounced on the fact that her declining fertility levels were quite possibly creating havoc with her hormones. No doubt this was clouding her usually sharp analytical mind and causing her to see Sam Ryan through rose-coloured glasses. And that was the only reason she found him so attractive, she sighed with relief. No wonder nonsensical thoughts of having sex, and babies, perhaps even *his* babies, were hovering at the edge of her mind. And it was no surprise then that someone like Madeline Jones filled her with unadulterated envy. There was no point whatsoever in beating herself up on account of her brainless confusion. Thankfully, there was a perfectly logical explanation for it all. It was cold comfort nonetheless as she logged off the net.

Paula awoke the next morning, her mind clear and sharp despite the fact that she'd guzzled almost a full bottle of wine the night before. For the first time in days she felt a sense of energy. She hummed to herself as she went down to the car park. It was only as she edged her Jaguar out into early morning traffic that she recalled her dream of the night before and almost rear-ended the car in front. In her agitation, she leaned on the horn and was totally heedless to the upraised finger from the driver.

For in the dream, Sam was making love to her. In soft-focus images, and slowly and deliciously, he was kissing every curve of her body. Equally slowly and deliciously, her treacherous body was responding, as she saw herself running her hands through that blond hair and trailing her fingers southwards.

Paula felt hot as she swung down towards Smithfield, her eyes grimly peeled for the traffic on all sides. She reminded herself that there was nothing wrong with her beyond the loud ticking of her biological clock coupled with the fact that it had been a long time since she'd had sex – three and a half years, to be precise.

She jammed on the brakes as her chaotic thoughts fused together in a sudden flash of realisation. It was all so simple, really, so simple that she couldn't understand why it had taken her so long to make the connection. She didn't want emotional involvement. It messed up everything. All she really needed to slake her desires was sex with Sam. A few nights of lusty, no-strings sex would indulge her deepest cravings and soothe her frazzled nerves.

And if she became pregnant . . . well, so?

For in addition to her scintillating career, she wanted the satisfaction of a baby of her own. Yes, she'd certainly be tweaking her life programme a little in accelerating her plans for motherhood, but her scattered thoughts somehow arranged themselves into a rational, coherent argument as she drove down the ramp into the car park.

Becoming pregnant with Sam's baby would be far more advantageous than freezing her eggs, where unknown risks were still attached. It would save her from going down the grim, clinical trail of artificial insemination. There was no reason, after all, why she couldn't manage Stevens along with a baby. She didn't need months of maternity leave – hadn't she heard of other MDs who barely took two or three weeks away from their desks? Or who planned their pregnancies around the Christmas holidays? After the baby was born, she could afford to pay for the very best childcare, including a night nanny, to allow her to keep enough energy for Stevens. So there was no reason whatsoever why she couldn't have the maternal satisfaction enjoyed by Elaine and countless other women around the globe.

And Sam, or anyone else for that matter, didn't even have to know the baby was his, she swiftly calculated. For all anyone knew, she could easily have any number of lovers on the go.

All these thoughts neatly arranged themselves in Paula's head as she swung into her reserved parking space. Okay, she'd be taking a calculated risk. And the likes of Elaine, never mind Sam, would be horrified at her plan. *If* they ever suspected.

Deep down inside, she wasn't a cold, unfeeling monster, Paula told herself. That was the problem. Deep down inside she was all too vulnerable, weak and gullible. She'd learned the hard way that if she opened the door to her heart she would be lost, so emotional ties with men were a no-go area. But thankfully in these enlightened times, that didn't mean she had to go without the baby.

She felt full of renewed purpose as she sat behind her desk. It didn't take her long to scroll through her memos to find the messages that Kate had sent her containing Sam's phone number.

She just had to get Sam into bed.

18

'Hi, Mum!'

'Hello, Abby!' Lia sighed with relief at the sound of her daughter's voice. She was sitting at her desk in a Juicy Couture tracksuit trawling through copyedits for *Midday Execution* when the phone rang. Her daughter sounded warm and friendly, unlike the stiff, don't-talk-to-me tone of the brief emails they'd recently exchanged.

Abby chatted about the weather and mentioned that she'd seen Lia's latest bestseller in Naples, then said, 'Thing is, Mum, I just need to check the arrangements for the house.'

Her relief somewhat short-lived, Lia stared out through the window and focused on the lush green trees bordering Sadlier Square. Blooming with sun-kissed leaves, they filtered the bright, noonday light and provided welcome shadow on the park lawns beneath. Normally the vista of the park uplifted her, but now she felt heavy inside.

She'd been waiting for this call. She'd told herself that there was no need to panic, no need to feel under any kind of threat. She could pretend that Abby was heading off to South America or some far-flung location. It should make no difference to the daily routine of Lia's life.

And it was just as well that whatever had been keeping Abby in Italy and put shadows in her eyes had finally released its tenacious hold.

'How long do you think you'll be home for, Abby?'

'It could be for good, I don't know just yet.'

'Whatever. I'm really glad you caught me now before I head off to Scotland.'

'Scotland? At this time of the year?'

'Yes, I'm heading off at the end of the week and I'll be touring up there for a couple of weeks, the usual round in Glasgow and Edinburgh,' Lia told her. 'Bookshops and charity benefits and a couple of literary events.'

'So it's just book stuff?'

'Well, I'm going to spend a few days in total seclusion in Loch Lomond. No disturbances of any kind, I hope.'

There was a long pause.

'Abby? Are you still there?'

Abby's voice, when it came, was very faint. 'So you're okay about me going back home?'

'Of course, love.' She was tempted to ask why a party was luring her back home after all these years trotting around the globe, but instead she pulled over her desk calendar, which boasted June's spectacular picture of the panoramic port of Amalfi, and discussed arrangements for the house and Abby's expected timescale.

'Mum?'

'Yes?'

'Do you think I'm doing the right thing?'

Lia faltered. It was the first in years that Abby had asked her such a question. 'Like I said before, love, you have to follow your star, whatever it is, and if that includes going home, then so be it.'

'I think it might be.' Now Abby's voice sounded vulnerable and unsure.

It *might* be? Blasted, wretched phones. Lia took off her glasses and closed her eyes briefly as she formed a picture of her daughter. What she really needed was to hug Abby tight, then look her in the eye and try to figure out what exactly was bothering her. Although she'd had that chance at Christmas, hadn't she, and she'd blown it, Lia recalled, feeling swamped with guilt. Man problems, she'd guessed. To hell with them.

'Look, why don't you come to London on your way?' she suggested brightly. 'I'll be back from Scotland in three weeks and we could have a few days together.'

'If you don't mind, I think I'll pass on London this time.'

'Whatever you like.' Lia tried to sound upbeat when in reality all she felt was a numbing helplessness. 'I'll email you with all the details and arrangements about the house. God, it'll seem funny with you being there. There's lots of stuff stored in the attic. If you need anything replaced, I'll gladly foot the bill, although the management company did a lot of refurbishing for me last year between tenants, so it should be okay.'

When Lia eventually put down the phone, she emailed her favourite luxury retreat in Scotland and booked her usual suite for a few days. She looked around her peaceful writing room and sighed aloud. What she also needed was someone to talk things over with, to share things with. A friend, a lover. She might have plenty of acquaintances who she ran into on her social circuit and occasional men friends who were doubtlessly attracted to her aura of glamour and with whom she sometimes enjoyed the release of fast and anonymous sex, but there was no one special in her life she could share her worries with. And right there and then, she felt that loss very keenly.

Lia had never been one for having a wide circle of friends, though. She'd lost touch with her few schoolmates when Abby was born. Back in the 1970s, in a small village in Dublin, there was still a social stigma attached to being a seventeen-year-old single mum. But when a horrified Lia had nervously broken the news of her pregnancy to her mother, Anne Lacey had merely hugged her and said,

'All life is precious, no matter the circumstances, but my daughter's baby will be infinitely more precious by far.'

But Lia's schoolmates had drifted away. They'd moved on to bigger and better things, to universities and careers, whereas when Abby was three months old, Lia had got a job in Value Centre, a large supermarket chain in Dublin, leaving Abby at home in the care of her mum. The years began to slip by – Abby was three, seven, ten – and encouraged by her mother, Lia went for a promotion in work, picked up the threads of a social life again, learned to drive and sometimes went out with the gang from Value Centre. But she rarely went out on exclusive dates, spending many an evening hammering away on a battered Smith Corona typewriter, dreaming of the day she'd see her book lining bookshelves up and down the country.

Once and once only she'd found someone whose heart had thrummed to the same rhythm as her own, whose soul seemed like the other half of hers, but she'd been left bruised, battered and totally disillusioned. So although there were occasional men on the scene, it was strictly light and casual, for Lia, proud, private and battle-scarred, firmly kept her distance.

19

Paula's hands were shaking so much as she adjusted the front of her La Perla tulle and lace bra that she was furious with herself. She took what she hoped was a deep, calming breath. She wiggled her body in front of the bedroom mirror and looked at her reflection with a critical, objective eye.

Porn star. Definitely.

With a muttered oath, she tried to view herself in a gentler light.

There was no reason to feel nervous. The black bra, clinched around her cleavage, beautifully enhanced an enticing amount of creamy boob. Likewise her matching lace panties sexily moulded the contours of her bum. With her slender limbs slathered in Clarins fake tan, she was the perfect package, from the gloss of her shiny blonde hair down to her pedicured toenails.

The matching underwear was far sultrier than what she usually wore and had cost more than what she'd once earned in a week, but so what, as the hackneyed advertisement declared, she was worth it.

Sam was worth it.

For this was all for him. This was part and parcel of her action plan to get him into bed and she was determined to get it right. But it had been so long since she'd been to bed with a man that she was scared stiff. Almost as scared as some of her trembling candidates, the thought struck, and she felt a sudden flicker of empathy for them. She tried to imagine Sam hooking a finger under her barely-there panties and slowly gliding them off, his eyes silently locked on hers as she fell back against the pillows . . .

God.

She ignored the spasm in her insides and forced a smile at her reflection, trying to copy the sultry, seductive image she'd portrayed in the magazine shots, but her mega-glossed lips felt wobbly and she realised to her chagrin that not only did she look stiff and awkward, but terror plainly showed in the depths of her hugely exaggerated, darkly-flecked eyes.

The phone pealed and Paula jumped out of her skin.

Sam was cancelling. He'd changed his mind. He'd something better to do besides going for dinner with Paula. She dived into the kitchen, her pedicured feet cold on the tiles, shivering a little in her underwear in spite of the bright July evening. She grabbed the cordless handset, barely registering the displayed number in her agitation.

'Hello, stranger.'

'Oh, Elaine. Hi. What's up?'

'Should anything have to be up for me to phone you?'

'No, not at all.'

'Would you like to come down for dinner tomorrow? We haven't seen you in a while.'

'I'm afraid I can't.' Paula was hesitant. 'Thing is . . .'

'Don't tell me it's work again.'

Paula was grateful to jump on the ready excuse. 'Yes, well, there's a recruitment fair on tomorrow and I have to be there.'

'Pity,' Elaine sighed. 'I wish you weren't married to your job. That's the second invitation you've turned down recently. Ruth's missing her auntie and I'm dying for a chinwag. Wait 'til I tell you what she did today . . .'

Paula threw a frantic glance at the clock. Sam was collecting her in thirty minutes and she wasn't anywhere near ready.

She still had to finish her make-up and come to a decision on what to wear once and for all.

'Elaine, look, I'm missing little Ruth too and I'd love to hear everything, but I'll have to pass on that right now because I'm on my way out and don't have time to talk.'

'Oooh. A Saturday night out? Big date on?'

'Yes – no. I'm actually bringing out some of my staff, they'll be working tomorrow, you see . . .' Paula's voice trailed away. How could she have turned into such a blatant liar? Was this another undesirable behavioural trait she was suddenly picking up? Along with indecision, gripping anxiety, mood swings and complete loss of control over her emotions? And where the hell was cool, calm, collected Ms Stevens and her methodically plotted, carefully calculated action plan in all this?

And for all the lies she was telling, she had played it badly. Part of her original plan had entailed inventing men friends, and lots of them, hadn't it, so that when she eventually became pregnant, Elaine would have quite legitimately lost track of her sister's many amours.

God. This was crazy.

'Aw, Paula, trust you to be networking on a Saturday night. For a moment I was hoping you'd be in for a bit of romance. I just hope it's all worth it for you.'

Elaine sounded disappointed and Paula laughed a tinny, hollow laugh. 'I hope it's worth it too,' she said, her meaning quite different to that of her sister's.

Twenty minutes later, she was ready. Paula took a last glance in the mirror as her intercom buzzed. She looked seductive and alluring, her slithery Karen Millen cornflower blue dress a welcome change from her crisp black and white office ensemble, her eyes exotic and seriously magnified with the help of Wonder Length mascara.

She might look like a glamour goddess on the outside,

but inside, she felt like a glass fairy on top of the Christmas tree, all fake and glittery and ready to shatter.

'Is this where you bring your high-performing staff to reward them? Or do you bring them here to test their nerves as part of an employee psycho, whatever it is, therapy test?' Sam murmured, his hazel eyes inscrutable as he stared at her across the snowy white tablecloth.

Her heart dropped. 'Psychometric,' she said automatically. 'Is that what it seems like to you?' she countered defensively. 'I thought you'd like it here.'

'Of course I do. I think it's a fascinating dining experiment. It's not every day I have the privilege of being served as though I'm the Emperor of Japan,' he grinned, throwing her off balance.

Paula bit her lip. She had to agree that it was over the top. The maître d' and his staff were so obsequious that it was alarming. When she'd booked a table in Dublin's newest Michelin-starred restaurant, she'd no idea it would be full of movers and shakers who were desperately anxious to be seen in the right place and who laughed and talked far too loudly. And as Sam had pointed out, the restaurant itself was full of pretension in the form of gigantic leather-bound menus describing all sorts of impossible fusions, a formidable and overpriced wine list that she'd regarded in total disbelief and staff who were just short of curtseying every time they fidgeted.

Even as she caught Sam's eye, he put his hand firmly over his glass of wine to prevent an overzealous waiter from swooping forward and topping it up by approximately two centimetres.

She'd got it wrong.

But then, she'd got everything with Sam Ryan wrong. It

was her fifth date with him, and although she hadn't yet admitted it to herself, deep down inside she knew her coldly calculated plan that had been put together in a blaze of enthusiasm in the clear morning light became utterly preposterous the first night she'd gone out with him. The idea of having sex with him and using him to provide unwitting donor sperm for the baby she hoped to have was one thing after a warm, fuzzy, lingering dream, but the first time she'd seen him in the flesh after she'd finally made contact with him, she'd taken one look at all six feet of his gorgeous masculinity and felt as though she'd been flung into a whirling vortex.

It would be extremely difficult, if not impossible, to sleep with Sam and remain emotionally detached.

She'd played it safe by asking him to a show in the Olympia, so stricken with nerves at the nearness of him sitting beside her that she hadn't a clue what was happening on the stage and she found it an effort to applaud in the right places. She'd been relieved when he'd seen her into a taxi and she'd vehemently refused to allow him to escort her home. Then she'd spent the rest of the night staring at the bedroom ceiling.

In return, Sam had invited her to the opening of an exhibition of abstract art in Molesworth Street. She'd never been to an exhibition of abstract art before, but rather than admit her shameful ignorance, she'd googled to familiarise herself with a few arty phrases to throw into the conversation. There was a lot of standing around and sipping wine in awkward little groups, and Paula had gazed in fake reverence at the canvases, acutely aware of Sam at her elbow, ravishing in black tie. Even though it made no sense to her, she somehow managed to trot out a few intelligent-sounding phrases about deconstruction and loose compositions, spatial illusions and futuristic visions of the depiction of the frailty of humanity in all its forms. Then she was afraid she'd overdone it, because she caught Sam looking at her in puzzled surprise.

The exhibition had been followed by a monologue in Vicar Street, then opera in the Gaiety, both of which had been an endurance test for Paula. Being with Sam was eating her up at some level. She chatted to him and laughed at his jokes and revelled in his goodnight kisses, but all the while she felt anxious and on edge, conscious that she was playing a part, acting like a fraud, and all the time secretly horrified at the audacious plan she'd concocted.

Tonight, she was hoping that he'd voice his usual offer to see her home in a taxi. This time, instead of refusing him and travelling home alone, she was going to invite him back to her apartment. It was time to put the next part of her plan into action.

For since when had Paula Stevens ever shied away from a challenge?

It would be difficult, perhaps, but *not* impossible to go to bed with him and remain detached. Earlier that day, she'd rephrased it into a more positive statement, for the sooner she had sex with him, the better. Then she could stop feeling like the greatest jittery wreck of all time and get him out of her head.

'This isn't doing it for me,' Sam said.

Startled out of her reverie, Paula thought she'd misheard. She watched in horror as he crumpled his napkin and flung it across the table. He forestalled the waiter's attempt to place a fresh napkin across his lap.

'Look, Paula, we could sit here half the night playing silly games with the waiting staff, eating ridiculous concoctions that pass for designer food and talking about nothing in particular, but it's, I dunno, it's just not me.'

Paula had to wait a few moments for her heartbeat to

settle. Her fingers trembled as she picked up her wineglass and took a slow sip. So much for the lead-up to the great seduction scene. Her flirty glances across a candlelit table, practised in advance in front of her bedroom mirror, were obviously going nowhere. When she put her glass down, the contents were swiftly replenished by the minute amount of wine she'd just consumed.

'See?' Sam threw out his hands. 'I don't know about you, but I feel as though I'm in a shop window or something. No insult intended to you, Paula, but I don't understand the philosophy here. It's not my kind of scene. Anyway,' he leaned across the table and looked as though he'd just arrived at some kind of decision, 'I can't pretend any more.'

'Pretend? What on earth are you pretending?' she hissed back at him, conscious of a flurry of interest at the next table. A creeping dismay was liquefying her whole body, as she couldn't figure how she'd got it all so horribly wrong. Far from her grand plans to invite him into her bed, it sounded as though Sam didn't want to see her again.

'Everything. I have to confess that I've gone out with you these past couple of weeks under false pretences.' Sam's face looked so open and honest that it was a contradiction.

'What do you mean?' she asked icily.

'Well, number one, I don't particularly like abstract art. Two, I'm not a great opera fan, and three, monologues drive me scatty. As for food, give me a big juicy steak any day of the week, or a plateful of cabbage and bacon.' He looked at her steadily with his hazel eyes and reached across the table to clasp her hand. 'But Paula, please, no insult intended.'

She felt weak. 'I suggest we get the bill and quit while we're ahead.'

'Hold on, don't pick me up wrong. I loved the company,

but I just didn't care for the stuffy, boring places we went to.'

'*What?*'

The entire restaurant turned and stared.

With a huge grin on his face, Sam rose to his feet. 'Come on, we're out of here.'

He shoved some notes onto the table, disregarding Paula's entreaties that she wanted to get the bill. Ignoring the livid face of the maître d', Sam held her hand as they threaded through the tables, hesitating only briefly to ensure she was coping all right on her high heels. Then they were out in the humid evening air.

'Sam? What's going on?'

'Sorry for springing that on you, but I badly needed a breath of fresh air, in every sense of the word.'

'I'm sorry too, Sam. Obviously I don't come up to scratch.'

'Come here, you ninny.'

He pulled her close to him, and right there on the street outside the restaurant, he kissed her.

'That'll give them something to think about,' he laughed, holding her shoulders and turning her around to catch the impression of disembodied faces staring at them through the weave of greenery lining the windowsill of the restaurant.

'How dare you!' Paula exploded with anxiety and wrenched away from him. 'I don't understand what's going on in your head. I'm going home.'

'Hold on, Paula, don't go, not yet. Just listen to what I have to say. Please.'

It was the note of honesty in his voice that stopped her from stepping forward and summoning a taxi. That, and the scorching on her lips after his kiss.

'Go on.'

'I just think that you, me – look, what we've been doing is all wrong.'

'Really?' Her tone was icy.

'In the nicest possible way. The things we've been doing, places we've gone ... you haven't seen the true me, the original Sam Ryan.'

'So it was all a façade, in other words.'

'Not quite. Let's go somewhere we can talk.'

'I thought you wanted some fresh air.'

'I do. It's a muggy kind of night in more ways than one. Let's go for a walk.'

'A walk?' She laughed at the absurdity of it. 'I can't get very far in these heels.'

Sam looked down at her navy skyscrapers and smiled. 'Trust me, you won't need them where we're going. Look, Paula, I really want to talk to you somewhere I can hear the sound of my own voice and not be ogled by wannabe celebs who think I'm Brian O'Driscoll's brother, or have a super-attentive waiter who interrupts me every five seconds because he's terrified of losing his job.'

Paula smiled in spite of everything. 'Come to think of it, you do look a bit like Bod. But it's okay, I won't hold it against you. You're on. We'll go for a walk. So where are you bringing me that I don't need the heels?'

20

In the pearly grey evening, Sandymount Strand was dotted with strollers and dog walkers, couples and lovers. To the west, the sky was folding into a pink and violet dusk, and in the east, pewter-grey clouds scrambled on the horizon. Beneath it all, the steely, ruffled sea was a silent, pulsing beat. The cooling breeze blowing in off the sea helped to take the humidity out of the air.

Paula didn't care if they looked all that unusual. For once in her life, she was so bemused by the sudden turn of events that she didn't care if she was strolling along on the strand in her carefully-pedicured bare feet or if her Karen Millen dress wasn't exactly beach-walking attire. Sam had peeled off his jacket and was holding it slung over his shoulder. She had taken off her killer heels and they dangled glitteringly from her free hand. She dismissed the thought that she'd walked barefoot on a beach with a man before, just before it had come to an ill-fated end. The night was turning out to be very different from her expectations, yet she was content to go with the flow. She thought, with a giddy excitement, that they resembled a pair of students – lovers, perhaps? – returning from the Trinity Ball the morning after the night before.

They strolled in silence for a while, not in any particular rush to get to the end of the beach, Paula enjoying the feeling of Sam walking beside her, her free hand tucked into his, and the taste of the fresh, tangy air on her lips. It was so far removed from the starched and stuffy rigmarole in the restaurant that she gave a sudden laugh.

'Does that mean you're not annoyed with me?' he asked, slowing his pace.

'I'm not sure yet,' she said, unwilling to condone his behaviour. She'd never before allowed a man to take her out of a restaurant halfway through her meal. 'It all depends on your explanations. I mean, Sam! You don't like monologues, operas aren't your cup of tea and if I recall, you didn't even enjoy the art exhibition! And it was *your* idea to bring me there.'

'I suppose I was trying to impress you. I mean, what do high-flying entrepreneurs with five-year, iron-cast strategic plans do in their spare time?'

'They have very little spare time.'

'Yeah, well, I thought that you might turn up your nose at popcorn and the movies, or expect more than a run-of-the-mill play.'

'So it was all for my benefit?'

'Kind of. I ended up pretending to be interested. Don't get me wrong, I'm sure the paintings were brilliant if you're into that rubbish and the opera was special – although it's not my favourite, too melancholy for my liking – but the monologue left me absolutely cold. And the ridiculous carry-on in the restaurant was the last straw. So there, true confessions.' He flashed a grin.

'I see. Did you get anything at all out of our dates?' she asked in a small voice.

She felt his arm curling around her shoulder. 'Course I did. I was with you, wasn't I? And I'm not a completely uncultured bastard.'

'I never said you were.'

'No, you're far too polite. God knows what you're really contemplating behind those big, blue, intellectual eyes of yours. Sam Ryan, the complete philistine.'

She laughed outright because it was so different to what she secretly thought. At the same time, she squirmed a little at the idea that to Sam, her eyes looked intellectual. Bookish, highbrow and studious were labels she'd suffered under for most of her life, so that even now with Sam, they were still following her around.

They turned slowly and began to retrace their steps.

'Sorry, Paula, are you managing okay without your stilts?'

'These stilts, I'll have you know, not only set me back a small fortune, but are supposed to be sexy.' Paula smiled disingenuously at him in an attempt to make light of her comment.

'Sexy?' He halted. 'Did you wear them on purpose?' There was something in his eyes that made her catch her breath.

The energy between them shifted. Maybe he was aware that she was suddenly uncomfortable, maybe he sensed the stirring of something different, for he said in a tone that was deliberately light and friendly, 'What do you say we go grab a beer?'

She could have said she wasn't really into that, or that grabbing a beer wasn't exactly Ms Stevens's favourite pastime and was a million miles away from the hushed, sobering ambience of the restaurant, but the whole evening had gone so topsy-turvy that she readily agreed.

They got a taxi to a small pub near her apartment. The lounge was heaving with regulars, so they sat outside on two aluminium chairs and balanced their beer on the rickety table between them.

'This table has certainly seen better days,' he said. Sam bent down and jammed a beer mat under a leg to balance it. 'Is that better? Look, Paula, sorry about all this, it's a bit of a come-down from your fancy restaurant, I guess.'

Afterwards, Paula pinpointed that instant as the moment she began to fall in love with Sam. There was nothing spectacular about it, no flashing lights or shooting stars. It was all so shockingly simple that she was taken completely unaware. There was something in the movement of his body, in the angle of his head and his attentiveness as he adjusted the beer mat under the table, and then his eyes full of friendly concern as he straightened up before throwing her a sexy smile, that she felt something break over her head and slip like the warm, benign wash of a wave all over her body.

'Forget the fancy restaurant,' she said, picking up a beer mat and peeling away the layers, intently aware that her heart had stopped beating for a moment, leaving her suspended in some kind of hiatus before clanking up again to a slightly different beat. She would think about that later, much later, when she had time and space to examine it. She rested her elbows on the table and cupped her chin in her hands. 'Tell me, then, what you really like to do, Sam Ryan.'

'Irish music, and playing the guitar or mandolin. I like the rhythm of it all, the sheer life-affirming energy. Football. I like rugby and basketball, not that I get much chance to play and I'd never drag you unwillingly to a match. I enjoy getting stuck into thrillers as opposed to barristers' notes. I like sitting like this in the evening air, with you, having a pint in a local pub that sticks to its roots and hasn't been remodelled to resemble a space-age barn. I enjoyed our walk along the beach. Hmm, let's see . . . I don't like stuffy pretension in any shape or form, as I see enough of it in the dungeons of the Courts, and I don't like,' he smiled, 'going to a totally incomprehensible play just because it's supposed to be the in thing to do.'

'And yet you dragged me there.'

He shrugged and gave her a playful grin. 'I thought it was what you expected.'

'And the exhibition?'

'God, I could do better in my sleep. If I'd have sussed that out in advance, I'd never have brought you. Although, hold on, you seemed to like it. You were certainly knowledgeable enough.'

Paula smiled. She ran her finger around the rim of her glass before looking up at him. 'Guess it's my turn to confess. Truth is, I've never been to an exhibition quite like that before and I only pretended to like it because you seemed to. Mind you, I could happily spend the day in the National Gallery, but I'm not in the least bit knowledgeable about what passes for so-called abstract art these days. And I looked up some stuff on the internet just to impress you.'

Sam roared with laughter. His eyes met hers and it was such a hearty, genuine laugh that something warm clicked in Paula's head, some kind of connection that made her feel as though an electric current had switched on and was humming inside. She swallowed too much beer in one go, almost choked and had to apologise.

'Right. Let's start all over again,' he said. 'What do you say we strike those last few dates and begin again?' he said. 'Agreed?'

'Agreed,' Paula said solemnly, helplessly feeling as though she was crossing an invisible border, a border she had told herself she'd never cross again. She had no option, though, not with Sam looking at her like that across the rickety table and the way she suddenly felt reborn.

As if the night hadn't already delivered up enough surprises and unexpected developments, as they strolled home in the direction of Paula's apartment, the muggy night air was rent with a flash of light and a peal of thunder, and just as Paula realised what was about to happen, the heavens opened and the rain lashed down.

They ran. Paula once more whipped off her heels and

held tightly to Sam as they scurried along the streets, running through the sheets of rain, breathless and laughing. Sam tore off his jacket and threw it around her shoulders and became totally soaked in the process. They burst through the door of her apartment block and arrived in the foyer in a heaving tangle of sodden hair and drenched clothing.

'This is mad. Come up and get dry,' Paula said, her feet flapping wetly on the tiled floor.

There was no question of playing the sultry seductress and inviting Sam back to her place with appropriate flirty glances. All that went out the window. They dashed into the lift and Paula burst out laughing when she saw their saturated reflections in the mirror, her carefully applied mascara halfway down her cheeks. She caught Sam's eye in the mirror and he was laughing too, his hair stuck to his head. Looking at her messy reflection, it was amazing to think that she felt so light and happy. She pushed open the door to her apartment, incredibly amused at the realisation that a slightly different Paula Stevens was returning now this evening. A different Paula to the one who had fondly pictured bringing Sam back for the great seduction scene, who had strategically placed scented candles and flowers and prepared background music, checked out her selection of drinks and smoothed fresh linen onto her bed.

She'd never expected to return like this, soaked and saturated and make-up streaked, yet aware that a glimmer of something new had opened in her life.

'Two drowned rats,' Sam smiled. He shook his head and sent some raindrops flying and Paula squealed.

'Hey, as if I'm not wet enough.'

'Yes, you're soaked to the skin.'

Her Karen Millen dress, carefully smoothed down over breasts and hips earlier that evening, was now clinging wetly to every curve in her body. Underneath that, her expensive, sexy underwear that she'd fondly pictured being carefully removed by Sam was stuck like glue to her skin. And it was impossible to miss the sudden charge in his eyes as he looked at her.

Paula shivered. She led the way into her kitchen, where she grabbed some tissue and tried to repair her face.

'Hope you don't catch cold over this,' he said.

'Nor you.' She forced the words out through her chattering teeth. Sam's shirt was equally glued to his chest, his trousers blackly sodden.

Then they both spoke at once.

'I can throw them in the dryer . . .' she said.

'I think the only solution is a bath . . .' he said.

There was a silence.

Then, 'A bath?'

'Yes, Paula, it's the tried and trusted solution when you get a wetting like this. Damp clothing can take a lot of heat out of your body. Don't worry, I'm not about to seduce you. You can go first and I'll have a look around this amazing apartment. Then when I'm in the bath, you can throw my clothes into the dryer. Sorted?'

'Sorted except for one thing.' Paula bit her lip and felt as though she was about to step over the edge and dive into space.

'What's that?'

'My bath is quite generous and takes a lot of water. I think, em, there's only enough for one bath. And I'm kind of worried about your wet clothing. I don't want you getting double pneumonia while you wait, so why don't we share . . . ?'

She dared herself to meet his eyes, swooning at the look in them.

Nothing mattered. Nothing in the world mattered any more

except for the feel of Sam's hands on her body and the touch of his breath on her cheek as he peeled off all her clothes. She moved her hands and legs to make it easy for him. The dress slid down and the sodden underwear peeled away from her curves, leaving her achingly vulnerable, while her damp, pearly skin quivered in expectation. Sam's eyes were locked onto her body as he flung off his own clothes haphazardly and kicked them into a pile in the corner of her bathroom. She couldn't take her eyes off the taut strength of him, his broad chest, his body tapering down to powerful hips, the size . . . oh, God.

He caught her staring at him and he grinned. And in that moment Sam looked incredibly beautiful. Her body flashed with heat as he lifted her into the hot, foamy water and got in beside her. Her large claw-footed bath held the two of them and they sat with the scented water up to their chins. Paula's breath was squeezed as she felt the long, hard nakedness of his thigh against hers.

This was crazy. Her carefully-laid plans had been blown into smithereens, yet this was exactly where she wanted to be. Naked in the bath with Sam, and he equally naked beside her. Feeling fuzzy and floaty and sick with desire.

'Are you warming up yet?' he asked.

'Getting there.'

'Good. Can't have you getting pleurisy, or worse.'

I've already caught something far, far worse than pleurisy, she panicked. And how on earth could they be even *having* this conversation?

'Nice bathroom,' he observed.

'I had it remodelled last year,' she told him, her voice tight as she struggled to concentrate on his face and not his nakedness. 'I wanted it to be a place of total relaxation. One of my favourite chill-outs is a long soak in the bath.'

'*Chill-out*?' He quirked an eyebrow and Paula laughed.

'You know what I mean. The room is wired up to my music centre and you can also adjust the lighting.' She reached out a hand and briefly dried it on a nearby towel, then picked up a remote control. The overhead lighting was instantly muted and tiny coloured bulbs set into the tiled floor sprang on, creating a fairytale atmosphere. Paula pressed another button and the room filled with an instrumental version of a love song. She turned back to find Sam staring at her.

'It's lovely, very effective. But I don't feel relaxed at the moment.'

'Don't you?'

The air crackled with sexual tension.

Sam said, his voice hoarse, 'How could I when I'm sitting naked in a bath with you? Paula, it's only been a few dates, but right now, I want you. If you don't feel the same, I think I'd better get the hell out of this bath. And fast.'

'I'd like . . . but I'm nervous,' she blurted. 'I'm only just getting to know you. And I'm kind of . . .' her face flooded with scarlet embarrassment but she had to say it. 'Out of practice.'

If anything, his eyes were even more intent. 'Paula,' he said, 'why don't I start by washing your back and we'll see how we get on?'

By the time Sam had washed and tickled every inch of her skin using her soft, natural sponge sprinkled with drops of her favourite bath essence, Paula was weak with need. He'd devoted great care and attention to sponging her breasts and the tops of her thighs, ducking his head and going under the water so that it slopped over the edge of the bath. Paula squirmed and begged for mercy, her nipples on fire, her insides aching with desire, but he merely shook his head and said she'd have to wait.

The water had cooled by the time he was finished, so Paula let some out and filled the bath again. Then Sam handed her the sponge.

'Your turn,' he said.

She smiled. 'I can't wait to torture you just as much as you've tortured me.'

Sam was groaning and breathing raggedly long before she was finished soaping him. She sat back in the warm water, eyes glinting, feeling weak with need and suddenly strong at the same time. 'Do you give in?'

'Come here.'

They moved together in a flurry of wet hair, wet limbs and slopping water, mouth seeking hot mouth, bodies pressed together. After several long, satisfying kisses, Sam got out of the bath and she looked at his hard, glistening body as he went over to his clothes, rummaged in the pocket and took out a condom. Somewhere she registered the gratifying fact that he had come prepared. Somewhere else, a tiny voice told her that there would be no baby-making tonight. But this had nothing to do with hormones or baby-making or carefully concocted plans for motherhood, never mind past hurts. This was above and beyond all that and had everything to do with pure, undiluted need.

Sam climbed back into the bath and she felt a painful spasm of desire as his hands cupped her buttocks and pulled her towards him. She thought she was going to faint as she felt him enter her. He teased her with short, rapid strokes before he finally answered her desperate whimpers and plunged all the way.

Paula gasped. Something flared inside her, something beyond the unbearable pleasure of Sam filling her up. She didn't think she'd ever felt so close to another human being before; so connected, so alive, so real, so *wanted*.

'Paula,' he murmured hoarsely.

She couldn't talk.

'Look at me,' he said.

Then she stared into his eyes, looked into his soul and

held on to him, arms twined around his neck, as he moved deliciously slowly, and the sweet, fraught tension built up and up and up before the ripples crashed into a bright, white, blinding flash. She heard herself cry out. Then Sam, still holding her gaze, exploded inside her.

She'd never before had such an erotically intimate experience.

Later, they climbed out of the bath, all of Paula's limbs trembling, her insides molten. They wrapped each other in enormous fluffy bathrobes. Sam plugged in her hair dryer and gently dried her hair, his massaging fingers sending shockwaves all the way down to her toes. She turned on muted lighting and lit her scented candles. She fetched wine and they lay together on her big wide bed with the smooth linen sheets, making love over and over, and she clung to him, feeling weak with need and helpless with longing as the night slowly waned and the streaming rain outside eventually dwindled to a soft, gentle spill.

21

Abby's darkened reflection stared back at her from the kitchen window.

She'd forgotten how quiet it was on the lane at night and how dark. The inky void outside was broken only by a welcome spark of light that flickered intermittently through waving branches of trees from what used to be the Stevens' house.

She'd arrived home two days ago. She'd stared down at the Italian landscape receding further and further away as the plane had banked in the skies above Naples. She'd watched as it fell away into a miniature toy town landscape, until stretched cotton clouds had obliterated her view. Then she'd lain back in her seat and closed her eyes.

It was all history now, Raffaele as well as her Sorrento existence. Her relationship with Raffaele had been far too brief, but her refuge in Sorrento had gone on too long. Once she'd finally begun to realise that her life there had been a fantasy ideal, she'd put together in order to cope with her frozen hurt, her ghosts and her guilt, it had been easy to book her flight home.

She'd landed in Dublin airport and jumped into a taxi to pick up the keys from the management company as Lia had arranged. Then the taxi had taken her out to the house on Mayberry Lane. Abby had unlatched the gate and walked up the tree-lined driveway, and for the first time since she'd left Sorrento, she felt a wave of uncertainty.

Her childhood home seemed older, faded and slightly

reduced. Taking a deep breath, she'd let herself into the house. Once inside, some residue of excitement brought her giddily through the familiar rooms, alternately smiling and laughing and sometimes feeling the prick of tears as memories surged.

Lia had arranged for the house to be cleaned and polished and some of the furnishings had been replaced only last year, so the house was warm and welcoming. There was a vase of tiger lilies on the side table in the living room, spilling their scent into the room, and a bowl of fresh fruit on the pine dresser in the kitchen. Lia had even arranged for a bottle of champagne to be ready and waiting in chilled splendour in the fridge and Abby smiled at her mother's extravagance.

Her mum's room, tucked under the eaves of the house, held no memory of her. It was neat and tidy and the closet was empty. Her desk, its surface clean, was still in place by the window, but the second-hand typewriter she'd begun her writing career with, along with boxes of notes, was cleared away.

Her grandmother's room was equally clean and tidy and now an anonymous guest bedroom. Abby's heart had lurched for a moment as she stood on the threshold and the image of her kindly grandmother swam in front of her.

On her first evening back, she'd taken a deep breath and strolled up to the end of the lane along a path so familiar that she could have drawn every crack and crevice and tumble of cow parsley in her sleep. The dry-stone wall was the same, and even the laburnum tree was throwing its shade across the garden, but the gate was tied up with rope and the lawn scattered with the brightly coloured toys of young children. She half expected to see the tall figure of Sam loping across the grass in the fitful sunshine, but even as she hesitated, she heard the whine of a lawnmower coming from the rear garden and two small girls came scrambling from around the side of the house and started to wrestle over a small pink pram.

Abby turned away, feeling a catch in her throat as she passed the spot on the wall where she used to sit with Sam. She was tempted to put her hand out, to reach across and touch the smooth hollow where her hips had neatly fitted, as if to lay some claim to it, to span the gap between then and now and return to the girl who'd sat there, the girl with all the fiery, idealistic dreams of adolescence.

Now she turned from the darkness outside the window into the welcoming light of the cosy, rustic-style room.

She'd come home to reconnect with the Abby Lacey who'd sat on the wall and felt that the world was a magical place just waiting to be explored. She needed to rediscover the Abby who'd lost sight of herself in recent months, and where better than Mayberry Lane and with the prospect of Sam's company? And maybe his love?

Kind, affectionate Sam. If anyone was to melt her chilled heart and chase away the shadows, it was surely him. To think he'd told her he loved her. He'd even asked her to marry him. To think she'd turned her back on all that tenderness and affection. She longed for it now, to feel cherished and loved and to be held and kissed instead of the numbness that chilled her day and night.

And she owed it to Sam to make up for the hurt she'd caused him all those years ago. She now knew just how cruel that must have felt.

Abby's head swam and she gripped the back of a chair for balance. She hadn't contacted him yet. She just needed a little time to adjust to being back in Mayberry Lane and let the familiar security of it all wind itself around her and bring her back to a time when life had been happy and innocent and perfect.

★   ★   ★

'Lia, pet, I was surprised when you phoned. We don't usually see you in July,' Florence said.

'No, indeed,' Lia smiled as she signed the Glenlyon Lodge guest book with a flourish. 'Although it's nearly a year since I've been here.'

'Doesn't time fly! Did you fancy a wee break?'

'Yes,' Lia admitted. 'I've just come from a busy week of engagements in Glasgow and Edinburgh before that, so I'm looking forward to a few days of peace.'

Her tours of Edinburgh and Glasgow, normally the most enjoyable experiences as she liked meeting her Scottish fans, had been fraught with undercurrents of tension as she counted the days and then the hours to Abby's arrival home, clinging to the fervent hope that by some miracle she might change her mind at the last minute.

But she didn't.

'Och, you'll get that, I promise. We've some new spa treatments you might like to think about. And if I catch a whiff of excitable fans, I'll scoot them off. We'll no' let anyone disturb you!'

'Thanks, Florence!'

Florence's husband, Hamish, took Lia's bags up to her usual suite, asking her courteously if there was anything she needed.

Lia looked around her comfortable bedroom. The wide four-poster bed had the old-fashioned quilt turned down on soft white sheets and mounds of snowy pillows. All of a sudden she couldn't wait to sink into it, but it was early yet, not quite six o'clock. 'A large gin and tonic would be lovely, please.'

'Will be up in a minute. And your usual table in the dining room is reserved for you this evening. The chef recommends the brown trout caught in the loch this morning.'

Lia smiled at the tall, redheaded Scotsman. 'Sounds perfect. You really know how to pamper me.'

'Aye, it's what we're here for,' he said. He returned a few moments later with a chilled glass for Lia. As soon as the door had closed behind him, she sat down on the window seat and took a long sip, the ice cubes rattling against the rim of the glass and refreshingly cold against her lips.

She looked out at the tumble of fields and the surrounding mountain range. She'd discovered the luxurious retreat quite by accident. On the edge of Loch Lomond, the small hotel was owned and run by Hamish and Florence Maclean. The decor was sumptuous, the food incredible, the selection of spa treatments designed to pamper even the tensest executive. Outside you could walk for miles, right through the gardens to the nearby woods, then to the edge of the loch and along the foothills of the towering mountains.

It was the retreat where Lia sought to renew herself, where she touched base with the girl behind the façade of glitzy crime novelist, where she came for a soothing few days at regular intervals in her busy life. Gary, her publicist, Clarissa, her editor, Marcus, her agent, even Abby all knew better than to disturb her here.

The dining room was almost full by the time Lia came downstairs that evening, barely noticing the ripple of interest that followed her progress as she glided across the room.

Dining alone didn't bother her. It was the one thing that most solitary travellers balked at, but Lia was quite relaxed and comfortable at her usual table in the corner, observing those around her. Hamish made a show of handing her the wine list, and as usual Lia smiled and waved it to one side and asked him to surprise her. It was their habitual carry-on, Hamish producing with splendid aplomb his finest selection of Pinot Noirs or Chablis, or perhaps something new and unusual to tempt Lia's taste buds.

This time he chose a bottle of German Riesling, and Lia

raised her glass, took a sip and rolled it around in her mouth before pronouncing it perfect. 'You always manage to get it right, dear Hamish.'

'Have you any plans for tomorrow?' he asked.

'Oh, out for a long endorphin-inducing walk, until my legs give out! Then a couple of hours in the spa.'

'Mind how you go,' he said. 'I know it's July, but the weather forecast isn't too favourable, so don't go rock climbing or abseiling.'

Lia laughed. 'Don't worry, I've no intention of doing anything that strenuous. I'll leave those exploits to the young and lively.'

But the following day, the rain came down in torrents and Lia went straight to the holistic wellness centre attached to the lodge. She spent time unwinding in the thermal spa, then closed her eyes and gave herself up to the sensual pleasure of a full body aromatherapy massage, drifting away into a warm cocoon of slumber as the therapist gently kneaded her back and shoulder blades. She followed that with a light lunch and then relaxed with a seaweed facial. Afterwards, her treatments complete, she lay on a lounger listening to tranquil music in the relaxation suite, feeling blissfully detached from everything.

This was why she had come. It was exactly what she needed – time out to surround herself with some kind of calm buffer against the practical reality of Abby going home. There were bound to be emails and phone calls from Dublin, bits of news and gossip, talk of parties and reunions, and Lia needed to be well armed in order to be able to cope with them and keep her composure. If she could conjure up this feeling of fuzzy detachment at will, it would help her to survive any consequences.

She eventually strolled back towards her room, still muffled in her terry robe, her mind and body wrapped in tranquil peace.

There was something else she had come to do, though, while she was away from London. Lia went over to her laptop bag and took a DVD out of the side pocket. She'd recorded the programme some months ago, but hadn't had the guts to watch it yet, nor did she want it to invade the privacy of her London apartment. Now in the relative anonymity of her hotel bedroom and enfolded with a peaceful indifference, she switched on her laptop and slotted in the disk.

She was silent as she absorbed the screen and the image of the man with the seductive eyes. He hadn't changed all that much, any more than her feelings had. She watched the recording twice, telling herself that her heart was sufficiently hardened so that nothing about him could hurt it now.

When she went downstairs for her meal that evening, the commotion in the entrance hall startled her.

'What's up?' she asked Florence as Hamish strode by in full mountaineering regalia and joined two other similarly dressed men who were clearly anxious as they waited for him in the porch.

Florence's face was creased with concern. 'There's been an accident up on Ben Lomond. Hamish is going out with the mountain rescue. God only knows what they'll find.'

Lia snapped out of her veneer of tranquillity as something icy slithered down her spine.

'An accident? What kind of accident?'

'We don't know what's happened. Someone has fallen and could be injured, or worse. That's the second incident in the space of a few months. Some poor tourist, no doubt, with no regard for the weather warnings. Or no respect for the cruel might of the mountain.'

'How dreadful.' Lia shook her head, her calm shattered as she imagined the frantic rescue scene. She hated to hear of tragedy and disasters, and in an instant, the peaceful serenity she'd carefully built up had been stripped away, leaving her bothered and dismayed. 'Why can't people heed the warnings? What makes them behave so irresponsibly with their own lives?'

'Hush, now, don't go upsetting yourself. It's the lure of the mountains. It just seems to reach out to some people and draw them in.'

'God knows what kind of horror those tourists are going through up on that mountain.' Lia wrung her hands. 'The shock and the distress, the feeling of being totally helpless . . . how awful for them.'

'Och, Lia, you've gone pale. Don't let your vivid imagination gallop away,' Florence said stoutly.

Imagination? I wish, Lia thought ruefully. Fear and terror tasted the same, no matter the circumstances.

'Hamish and the men will do a good job,' Florence continued. 'It's not like years ago, when there were no mobile phones or helicopters full of high-tech equipment ready to scramble at a moment's notice.'

'Yes, I suppose you're right.' Lia gave a half smile.

She was immensely relieved the following morning to hear that the injured tourist had been safely airlifted and was now comfortable in a Glasgow hospital bed. The next day she flew back to London, trying to gather her serenity around her once more. That night, she made a phone call and ended up in a plush hotel bedroom with a south London surgeon.

He was good, skilful and practised, yet as usual, the sex was coldly impersonal. Even though she felt a measure of physical release, sometimes Lia hated the way she availed of it as an antidote to her loneliness and her crushed, unforgiving heart.

22

'Hello? Abby? That's the second time you've tuned out.'

Abby jumped. 'Sorry, I'm just remembering stuff. I guess it's with being home and all that.'

Elaine grinned. 'Okay, I forgive you. Just as I forgive you everything else.'

'Like not coming home for Ruth's christening,' Abby recited as she leaned against the worktop.

They'd been through this already. Abby had apologised profusely, although she'd stopped short of revealing the truth as to why she'd stayed away, for Raffaele and her guilty secrets were well and truly buried. Now she was back to the happy, carefree Abby and not the frozen, hurt Abby who might invite sympathy, or worse, some kind of pity, or make things strained or embarrassing, even between friends.

'Not keeping in touch as often as you should have . . .'

'Not, let me see . . .' Abby wrinkled her nose.

'There's nothing else to apologise for. You love Ruth to bits and that's total redemption in my book.' Elaine finished decorating the top of her luscious-looking pavlova and placed it carefully in the fridge. 'That's for after our lunch.'

'Are you trying to do permanent damage to my waistline?'

Elaine chuckled as she poured coffee beans into her cafetière and took two Avoca mugs out of her Shaker press. 'At least you have a waistline. Listening to all your adventures, I can't believe you still look the same. Although,' she said, tilting her head to one side, 'I still can't get used to your hair. If you flattened it down a bit you'd look remarkably like Audrey Hepburn.'

Abby ran a hand through her short black spikes. 'I'm sure this gave Mum a heart attack, but bless her, she didn't say a word. It's grown since I saw her at Christmas.'

'Jeez, if that's the case, you must have had it scalped. What possessed you to change it so drastically?'

Abby shrugged noncommittally. 'I just felt like it.'

Elaine threw her a thoughtful look. 'Come on, we'll bring our coffee through to the sunroom until lunch is ready.'

Abby relaxed in the padded cane sofa in the sunroom adjoining the kitchen and felt some of the tension slide away from her limbs. She'd seen Elaine on and off throughout the years, before Colin arrived on the scene. Her friend had flown out to visit her, bunking on sofas or fold-up beds or whatever she could sleep on in Abby's temporary accommodation, the two friends chatting endlessly into the night and causing mayhem and mischief in Sydney nightclubs and Boston bars.

Abby had emailed her the previous Sunday night, telling her she was back in the country but asking Elaine to keep that piece of news to herself for now. Sure enough, much as Abby had hoped for, Elaine had immediately phoned with an invitation to her home. She'd even offered to collect Abby at the train station at lunchtime on Tuesday, correctly guessing she'd no transport of her own just yet. She'd been waiting when Abby came through, with her chubby-cheeked daughter fast asleep in her baby seat of her Volkswagen, and she'd thrown her arms around her friend in a welcoming hug. Abby had fallen in love with Ruth immediately and had admired Elaine's modern and comfortable home. She'd even fed Ruth her baby yoghurt and helped tuck her up for her mid-day nap.

Her friend had moved on. She radiated the warm fulfilment

of marriage and motherhood. It was obvious she was totally happy in her beautiful home with Colin and adorable baby Ruth. Today she looked elegant in a mint green floaty dress and gold sandals. Her hair was stylishly sleek. At first Abby had felt as though she was stuck in a time warp, awkwardly recreating the happy-go-lucky girl who'd swapped clothes and make-up with Elaine, but in a short space of time, they'd seamlessly picked up the threads of their friendship again.

'Right, Abby,' Elaine said, 'spill the beans. Surely you realise that your homecoming is radioactive gossip? So why the secrecy and who exactly did you not want me to tell?'

'I didn't want Sam to find out yet. I wasn't sure if you were in touch with him recently? I met him over in Italy. He's trying to arrange a reunion for Mark's birthday.'

'Yeah, he tracked Paula down in Dublin and told her about it. Asked her if she'd have any objections on account of Mark, which she hasn't.'

'And how is Paula nowadays?'

'Great. Her business is thriving.'

'Good for her.'

'There's not much in her life, though, in the way of romance. I'd really love to see her with someone, and I think – no, I *know* – there was a love interest a couple of years ago, but she kept it quiet. You know Paula, she's so private, and then I guess it fizzled out or something. That was when she started Stevens.'

'She always was an overachiever.'

Elaine pulled a face. 'Not like me! Although I'm delighted to say we're getting on great these days. Ever since I had Ruth, in fact. One of the best things that has come out of Ruth is that I really feel I have a sister now and it means a lot to me. It's as though having a little niece has brought out a different side to her. I'll never forget her face when she came to visit me in the hospital. She was so emotional that I thought she was going to cry. My big, aloof sister, who always seemed as tough as old boots, actually had tears in her eyes. That's why I'd love to see her with a man and maybe a kiddie or two.'

'You never know,' Abby said.

'Hey, we're getting off the hot, juicy topic. What on earth finally persuaded you to come back to dear old Ireland? Don't tell me it was a party for someone you haven't seen in years. And why the hell don't you want Sam to know?'

'I didn't just come home for the party,' Abby hesitated. 'You can laugh all you like, but I think I have feelings for Sam.' It was the only way to describe the sense of warmth that crept around her icy heart when she thought of him. And it meant so much to have some kind of tender feeling that she welcomed it immensely.

'You *what*?' Elaine's cup slipped from her grasp and clattered to the floor, the remnants of her coffee splashing in a star-shaped design on the tiles.

'Yeah. When I bumped into him in Italy, it was like . . . I dunno, afterwards I kept thinking about him and it was though I was really seeing him for the first time.'

'Jeez. You and Sam? I don't believe you! You and *Sam*?'

Abby nodded and dug her nails into the palm of her hand. *Please don't laugh*, she silently prayed. *Please don't look at me as though I've suddenly sprouted two heads. Please give me some support in this.*

'Abby! Never in a million years!' Elaine jumped to her feet and gave Abby a quick hug. 'After everything that guy did to try and keep you here . . . Does Sam know how you feel?' she asked, sitting down beside her. 'Does he still feel the same way about you? I know you were the love of his life once upon a time.'

The questions were pouring out of Elaine. Abby held up her hand. 'That's the thing, I don't know. When I met him, oh, a couple of months ago now, he didn't have any ties, or so he said.'

'He's scarcely fallen for someone else in those few short weeks. God, Abby, I can't believe it!'

'I'm as shocked you are. I was taken by surprise when I bumped into him. We both were, and it was kind of awkward in the beginning. You should have seen his face!'

'Yeah, he told Paula there was something – that maybe you weren't yourself or . . . I dunno exactly.'

'Did he?' Abby said, lost in thought for a moment. Not herself? Was that really what Sam had thought? No matter. In a way he'd been right. More proof that he knew her so well, if she needed any. 'I've spent the last few weeks thinking about him, and remembering all sorts of little things about him,' she continued, wondering why she felt on the defensive. 'I guess I'm only now realising that I didn't really appreciate what I had at the time. It was great to see the world and go places and do things and be free and easy, but at the end of the day, it's the people in your life who count the most, family, friends, and I guess I took a long time to find that out.'

Abby felt shaky. It was the first time she'd voiced the actual words, the first time she'd heard herself say them aloud, and it helped to reinforce something inside her. Although it didn't need to be reinforced. She *was* doing the right thing.

'I trust I count as one of those friends?'

'Of course, Elaine. I made friends on my travels, and I still email some of them, but we were mostly ships that pass in the night.'

'And no steamy love affairs along the way?'

Abby swallowed as a sliver of pain caught her chest. Steamy love affair? That didn't come anywhere near describing the passion she'd tasted with every fibre of her being or the desire that had swept her off her feet. But that was all over and finished, and it was about time she moved on. Her destiny lay with Sam, for hadn't he come to her rescue just when she needed him most? 'Nothing that lasted, no.'

'Well you scarcely did without sex for the last few years! Or is that why Sam seems so attractive?' Elaine grinned wickedly.

'No, Elaine, it's not just sex. Although that's quite attractive too,' Abby said. She wanted Sam to take things further than just a goodnight kiss. She needed him to hold her as close as he could. She also wanted to make up for her hurtful rejection of him.

'Sex with Sam? I can't believe it. What happened to cause this change of mind?'

'I think I've finally grown up. I'd love for me and Sam to have all this.' She waved her hand expansively around Elaine's sunroom.

'And when are you going to see him and tell him this momentous news?'

Abby smiled faintly. 'I can't very well just make a huge declaration and expect an instant response. I'll have to take it carefully. I want him to know it's for good this time.'

'Well, you certainly can't mess him about,' Elaine advised as she slowly rose to her feet. 'You did leave him high and dry all those years ago. He was very upset after you left.'

'Was he?'

'Of course. The poor chap went into an awful depression. I tried to talk to you about him when I went out to visit you in Australia, remember? But you didn't want to know.'

'Didn't I?' Abby felt stricken. How could she have been so negligent with Sam's feelings?

'No, Abby, you didn't.' Elaine bent to mop her spilled coffee with a paper napkin, chucking it in the bin before returning to her seat, and Abby had the feeling that Elaine was striving for patience.

'Was I an awful cold-hearted bitch?'

Elaine hesitated. 'Look, Abby, yes and no. But I couldn't very well take any sides. You were both my friends. You had your mind made up to travel, but Sam chose not to believe you, and that made you exasperated. You thought that a clean break was best, so you weren't even going to keep in touch with him. But you have to be very sure that this is what you want now.'

'Yes, it is what I want.' Abby lifted her chin. 'I want Sam back in my life again. But I just don't know how to go about it. I'm even feeling shy at the thought of seeing him again.'

'Abby Lacey, *shy*?'

'Shy, excitable, shaky . . .'

'Heavens, maybe you're in love with him after all. God Almighty, I'd love to see his face when he realises you're home.'

In the end, it was Elaine's idea. She would host Sunday lunch in her home, ostensibly so that they could have a get together in advance of Mark's fortieth, but it was really a chance for Abby to meet up casually, like, with Sam and surprise him.

'Can you bear to wait a couple of weeks, Abby? This weekend we're visiting Colin's parents.'

'That's fine. Great.' It would give her more time to get back to her bright, breezy self and to work out the best approach to Sam.

'I'll phone Paula next week and ask her to bring Sam down. She has his contact details,' Elaine said, warming more and more to the idea. 'I won't breathe a word about your return. The more I think about it, the more excited I feel about the special moment when Sam Ryan finds out that the girl of his dreams has come home at long last!'

23

On Wednesday morning, Paula stared at the next PowerPoint slide in her maximum-impact presentation, desperately trying to ignore the pompous stuffiness of the room, her challenging Christian Louboutin heels and, worse, the seismic pounding in her muzzy head.

'At Stevens,' she enunciated as clearly as possible, maintaining rigorous eye contact with the three men scrutinizing her performance, 'our thorough candidate screening and expert market knowledge, combined with an understanding of your specific recruitment requirements, can help you to optimise your business performance through people.'

'How can you prove to us that you have an in-depth understanding of our business?' The man in the grey suit asked.

She felt her stomach lurch and was appalled to realise that she felt like telling him to shut the hell up. A handsome man, and smug with it, he'd been eyeballing her from the start, looking mildly amused as she introduced herself, lounging back in his seat with a cynical look on his face and cross-examining her every time she stopped to draw breath. She knew the type. Male arrogance seeped out of every pore in his body. Women should be at home, no doubt baking and cleaning and cooking. He was married too, she noticed. God help his wife.

She should never have guzzled three huge glasses of wine last night, though. Not when she had this all-important pitch to deliver. Somehow or other, the Chateau whatever-it-was had gone down the wrong way, causing her to feel far more edgy than usual this morning. Or maybe, a little censor chirped, she had simply indulged in too much of it.

'You can be assured that our main strategy is to work in partnership with our clients,' she dutifully trotted out, her calm exterior belying the furious way she was casting about in her mind for her usual pitch. She took a sip of water and gathered her thoughts. 'Your goals are our goals, and our consultants posses the requisite sector-specific experience and will invest whatever time and resources are needed to solve your most critical business issue – your recruitment,' she said, wishing this was all over, that the three investment bankers she was confronting across the royal blue carpet of their solemn, stuffy conference room would decide that they'd heard enough to satisfy them. She'd originally thought that it would be a major feather in her cap to pull their business right from under the impertinent nose of her nearest rival. Now she was beginning to think it would be a major feather in her cap if she managed to emerge from the room unscathed.

'And what, Ms Stevens, makes you think we should drop our existing providers and engage Stevens to look after our people solutions?' The handsome bastard was up to his tricks again, but she had a standard answer to that question.

At long last, the inquisition came to an end.

'I think we've heard enough, Ms Stevens,' the chairman of the interrogation panel said. 'We'll obviously need time to reflect on what you've outlined and talk to our HR department before we have any further discussion. We may come back to you for some more detailed information before we proceed any further.'

'Of course,' Paula murmured. It was standard procedure.

She was just unutterably relieved to be finished. No more alcohol during the week, she swore as her trembling fingers powered down her laptop, no matter how badly she needed it to relax. And certainly not when she had an important engagement such as this, which required all her wits.

'Why don't you take a breather and have some coffee before you leave?' the chairman suggested with a kindly smile. 'I think you're more than due some refreshment.'

A cup of coffee was just what she needed, Paula thought, already tasting the caffeine charge on her lips. 'That would be lovely, thank you.'

Coffee and croissants were brought into the room, and although Paula's empty stomach was rumbling and she would have given anything to bite into a luscious fresh croissant, she refused. No sense in having flaky crumbs anywhere near her perfect Dior suit.

'You must have some set-up, to deliver all that you promise,' Grey Suit said.

Paula's heart sank. His tone might be chatty and conversational, and officially she was off stage, but she'd relaxed too soon. She couldn't even remember his name, as she'd been too flustered at the outset to take it in.

'I employ some of the most talented consultants in the industry,' she said airily. 'Your success is our success and that's very much dependent on the quality and potential of my people, and the pride, commitment and passion they bring to the job.'

'Passion?' His eyebrow rose. 'I'd guess you'd expect them to burn the midnight oil from time to time.'

'My team of consultants are eager, enthusiastic and resilient. If challenging working hours are required from time to time, I can assure you they are more than prepared.'

After the coffee, Grey Suit carried her laptop and insisted on escorting her down to her car. She felt she'd never get away. As he passed across her laptop, he remarked, 'I guess you choose your team very carefully in view of your challenging working hours.'

'Of course I do,' she replied coolly. 'I have a very precise selection process.'

'And I suppose that's why my expectant sister-in-law didn't get a look in?'

'Your sister-in-law?'

'Yes. A Mrs Madeline Jones. Although,' he went on silkily, 'I don't doubt your integrity and ethical conduct, Ms Stevens, when it comes to equal opportunities. Do you know that approximately ten per cent of complaints to the Equality Authority are around pregnancy-related discrimination?'

Paula's face flamed. 'I don't doubt that this conversation is most unethical, Mr . . .'

'Jones.'

Her legs were shaking so much when she slid behind the driving seat that she made several failed attempts to chuck off her Louboutins and scrunch her feet into her driving shoes. Then, as luck would have it, she had to reverse her Jaguar out of a tight parking spot and it took several attempts to swing clear, all the time aware of his eyes coolly observing her and the sweat pouring down her back.

She drove back to the office in tatters. There was nothing he could prove, she told herself. Absolutely nothing.

The most talented, committed, resilient consultants in the country were engaged in boisterous activity when Paula swung though the plate glass office door that was etched in her logo.

'What d'ya think?' She identified Maeve Breen's voice floating out across the floor, accompanied by a burst of laughter.

'I'd say he'll think all his birthdays have come at once!'

'Go for it, Maeve! Seduce him big time!'

As Paula stalked around the bank of desks, weeping with the pain of her killer heels as well as her angst and frustration, she spotted one of her consultants flaunting around a scrap of material that could scarcely be described as a dress. The rest of her female staff were crowded around her in a gaggle.

'What on earth's going on?' Paula's outraged tones carried the length of the office floor.

Everyone jerked their heads around and she got a certain satisfaction in noticing the guilty looks on most of the faces.

'I was just showing the girls my wedding outfit,' Maeve Breen trilled without a trace of apology.

Maeve Breen. Ursula's replacement and her newest junior consultant. Twenty-two years of age and bursting with shiny confidence. She'd told Paula she was going places and she'd start by exceeding her monthly targets. Paula had surprised herself by disregarding her usual strict criteria, recognising her determination and believing her enough to give her a three-month contract.

'Your *wedding* outfit?'

'Yes, Ms Stevens. I'm going to a wedding on Saturday and I just needed some expert advice from the team here. I was wondering, you know, if it was a bit risqué.' She waved the slinky number at Paula, a sliver of film that left nothing to the imagination.

'You're entitled to all the advice in the world, but not during my company time,' Paula frostily snapped. She headed down the floor to the sanctuary of her office aware of a thick, embarrassed silence emanating like a black fog from her staff. She closed her door, sat down at her desk and put her head in her hands.

She felt like staying there, in that position, forever more. Her life, which had been neatly tied up and safely boxed in just a few short weeks ago, was slowly and relentlessly sliding out of her control.

Any manager worth his or her salt would have commented pleasantly on Maeve's outfit and sent her staff back to their desks in a calm and harmonious manner. But not her. Not gung-ho Ms Stevens, who had leapt immediately into defensive mode like an insecure child, a juvenile whose interpersonal skills were so sadly lacking that she took herself much too seriously and was far too quick to jump to the defence. She was slipping up and making silly errors of judgement, all because of one man.

And as for what she'd blithely decided about Sam Ryan – difficult but not impossible to spend the night with him and remain detached?

Oh, yeah.

If anything in her life had been a serious error of judgement, that was a major example.

Why was she doing this to herself? She was losing control of her emotions again, even though she'd learned her lesson the hard way. In spite of her firm resolutions to avoid involvement, Sam was slowly but surely getting under her skin, leaving her defenceless in the face of his sexy attraction and wide open to hurt.

After the night he'd spent in her bed, not to mention her claw-footed bath, he'd asked to see her the following evening.

'I'm working late,' she said. She wasn't, but it was an automatic defence barrier.

'I see.' It was six in the morning and already bright when he was taking his leave, grabbing a taxi over to his apartment to freshen up before he had to go to into the Law Library.

She stood in her kitchen full of pearly light, wrapped in her dressing gown, aware that she felt like a stranger to herself and that every inch of her skin and every bone in her body was gloriously, beautifully and most dangerously humming with life. He gulped down coffee, put his mug in the sink, took her into his arms.

'Paula, I don't make a habit of one-night stands.' His voice vibrated against her mussed-up hair. 'Last night meant a lot to me and I want to see you again.'

'For more of the same?' she asked, resisting the temptation to melt into his embrace.

'Yes, of course, but not just bed.' He pushed her slightly away from him so that his stricken gaze could connect with her. 'Jeez, I don't mean it was *just* bed, far from it. I'd like to get to know you, every single thing about you. Big things and small things. What are your deepest thoughts? What would you grab first if your apartment went on fire? Things like the kind of books you read, your favourite holiday spot. I like your company . . . God, I'm getting this all wrong.' He shook his head in mock despair.

'Relax, I know what you mean, but as I said to you already, I'm not interested in involvement.'

'Paula, I don't have a big important-sounding plan to involve you in anything other than seeing how we get on, maybe do a few fun things like the movies, come to a gig with me, go for a picnic on a sunny day, catch some ceilidh dancing . . .'

She was silent for a moment and felt like kicking herself. Why did she always take things so seriously? Then in spite of herself, she smiled. 'I've two left feet, you know.'

'Great! That's means loads of personal tuition.'

And with that he kissed her, grabbed his wallet and mobile and rushed out the door.

Paula had stood in the kitchen after he'd left, looking at her smoothie-maker as though it was some kind of foreign instrument and not the purveyor of her breakfast every morning. She'd felt strangely bereft. Then again, she'd never expected to lose herself so thoroughly in Sam's arms and feel as though her soul was no longer hers but had taken flight from her body and was now held in abeyance somewhere else.

She'd never expected to struggle through the following days and nights feeling as though she was suspended in some kind of fragile, glittering bubble, to go in and out of Stevens and see everything in a different and peculiar light. Had she really chosen that sombre dark grey colour for the floor covering? Why were her staff uniforms so sharply tailored? Surely something soft and feminine would look better on the women? And why, oh why had she ordered such a stark, forbidding-looking desk for herself? It was the female equivalent, she thought hysterically, of a man buying a huge car to compensate for shortcomings in another department.

There had been no evidence of any shortcomings, however, the night she spent with Sam, and now her face flooded hotly as she remembered the way her body had responded to him, time and time again.

Deliberately she lifted her head and tried to focus on the cleanly-designed lines of her office, fearing that the very thing she had fought so hard to resist was happening. It was beyond her comprehension how she had so carelessly allowed Sam Ryan to infiltrate her heart. When he'd phoned her yesterday, having got her mobile number, she'd weakly agreed to see him the following Saturday night and already her nerves were eaten up.

She jumped when there was a quiet knock on her office door. It was Kate, who wisely passed no comment on the earlier scene but merely asked Paula how the pitch had gone that morning.

'It's hard to know,' Paula said. 'I'll hear from them next week. By the way, thanks for all the hard work on the presentation material. I could see they were impressed.'

'It wasn't just me,' Kate said.

'Could you issue a memo thanking everyone who was involved,' Paula asked.

'I certainly could, Paula, but . . .' Kate hesitated.

'Yes?'

'It might be more effective if it came directly from you.'

'Would it not look as though I'm just trying to butter everyone up after . . .' Paula shrugged.

'So?' Kate smiled. 'As the saying goes, you'll catch more flies with honey.'

Paula's lips twitched. Thank God for sane, sensible Kate. 'Is Maeve Breen serious about wearing that piece of fluffy nonsense to a wedding?'

'Apparently so. Looking at it, I felt suddenly old and very decrepit,' Kate dryly admitted.

So did I, Paula thought silently. I felt middle-aged for the first time in my life. And too old for the kind of fun and games that Sam wants to play.

All the same, she was ready and waiting for him the following Saturday evening when he called for her in a taxi. Once again, she'd taken time to get ready, choosing an antique white Philip Lim chiffon dress that complemented her blonde hair. Feeling like a teenager experimenting with make-up, she'd vastly glamorised her usual understated look by using MAC kohl to create a classic smoky look around her blue eyes, and she'd even defined her strawberry lips with heaps of extra gloss.

No bed tonight, though, she'd decided in advance. She couldn't start making a habit of losing herself in Sam's arms. It was too dangerous for her peace of mind.

He brought her to a pub on the outskirts of Dublin where they sat outside in the bright, soft evening light and watched the swift-flowing Liffey catch the dancing light as it flickered between the flower-decked banks.

'By the way, Mark's coming home next month,' Sam said. He swirled the contents of his pint glass, examining them as though they were of extreme importance.

'Oh?'

Then he looked at her and asked, his tone lightly enquiring, 'Would you be interested in seeing him again?'

'Sam, there was never anything between me and Mark.'

'Never? So I don't have to worry about brotherly competition?'

She looked at him in the pale evening light, his hazel eyes fastened on hers, the expression in them hard to gauge, and caught the hint of vulnerability about Sam that she hadn't noticed before. A vulnerability that she recognised simply because it was something she was all too familiar with herself.

Someone, somewhere had badly hurt him. He might appear to be much the same cheerful, upbeat Sam as the adolescent she'd met on the lane, but like her, he'd had his heart kicked over, and it always, without fail, left a trace.

'No, you don't have to worry about brotherly competition,' she said, reaching slightly to put her hand on his arm, surprised at her instinctive gesture, as she'd never considered herself much of a touchy-feely person. 'Will Mark be staying with you?' she asked.

'He will, actually. I, ahem, just hope it won't cramp our style.'

'Cramp our style? What on earth do you mean?'

'I was hoping you might want to visit my place, spend some time, maybe, um, stay over some time? Although the problem is, my bath is rather a tight squeeze for two people . . .' Now his voice was edgy, and all traces of the vulnerability gone. The look he gave her was loaded with desire.

Paula couldn't believe she was actually enjoying this conversation. And couldn't believe that at the mention of Sam's bath, a river of liquid craving coursed though her whole body. Had she seriously thought she could go out with Sam again and not want to go to bed with him?

'I'm good at solving problems,' she said, wondering how she was ever going to extricate herself from this one, swiftly deciding that she didn't want to think of that right now. She couldn't. All her analytical skills were taking a poor second place to her urgent physical need.

'So you've said. I wonder,' he asked, his fingers making lazy circles on the inside of her wrist, 'if you could come up with a comprehensive four-point action plan in the time it would take us to taxi out to Malahide?'

'Bloody hell, Sam, just how much money do you earn?'

He grinned. 'Rather a lot.'

'Well, I'm in the wrong business. Sorry, God, that was appallingly rude of me. I fervently apologise. I just never expected this.' Paula looked around his mansion of a house and let out a long, slow breath. She should have known she was in for something special the moment the electronic gates at the end of the driveway had silently opened for Sam.

'How long have you been living here?'

'Two years. Not bad for the snotty-nosed kid down the road.'

'Definitely not, and stop talking about yourself like that. I'm nearly afraid to ask what kind of car you have parked in the garage.' He'd already told her that he mostly used the Dart and Luas for getting in and out of town, but he did have transport for his equipment when he was doing a gig.

'I've a Mercedes estate. Plenty of room for storing my instruments.'

'And a palazzo in Italy, as well as a yacht and a few off-shore bank accounts.'

'Not guilty. And when you've finished gawping, you might recall why we're here.'

'Why are we here?'

He pulled her to him and pushed back the hair from the side of her neck. She felt the brush of a tender kiss in that sensitive spot below her ear. He said, 'Why don't I show you around first, and then we can decide which room you'd like to, um, start with? I trust you have your action plan all sorted?'

Her legs like jelly, her heart thumping, Paula followed as he showed her around the enormous, eclectic house he called home, their voices echoing around the strikingly vaulted interior, the mellow evening light slanting in at various angles through floor-to-ceiling windows.

'*Where* did you get those murals?'

'Ah. That's privileged information. Perhaps if you kiss me, I might share it.'

'Those bathroom tiles must have taken you months to source.'

'Yep, something like that.'

'You're spoiled with those stunning views of the bay.'

'Most rooms have an aspect onto it. It sealed the deal for me.'

'Argh! The kitchen of my dreams!' she gasped as she stood on the threshold and realised that she was enjoying herself immensely.

'You have to pay a forfeit to enter. Guess . . .'

'Just how many instruments do you have in this music room?'

'I'm afraid that's more privileged information. Come here.'

Then, as they continued their exploration between lingering kisses, they finally arrived at the sunroom on his rooftop terrace.

'Sam! You never told me you had a hot tub!'

'Didn't I?' The look he shot her was anything but innocent.

'How perfectly lovely. It's like a tropical oasis with all the plants and foliage. Don't tell me – the French doors . . . ?'

He pressed a switch on the wall. 'The doors slide back to give an uninterrupted view of the bay.'

'How fabulous.'

When he was finished showing her around, Sam cracked open champagne and handed her a fizzing John Rocha crystal flute.

'Now, Ms Stevens, welcome to my world.'

They decided to try out the hot tub first. It was a unanimous decision. Then they'd move on to his bedroom with the king-sized bed, silk sheets and deep leather headboard. Paula said she'd forgotten to bring a swimsuit. Sam said it was okay, there were plenty of towels and he promised not to look. She went into the changing room just off the terrace to undress and when she emerged, towel-clad, he was sitting in the tub, his hands over his face, the secluded terrace shadowy in the late evening.

'No peeping,' she reminded him as she dropped her towel in a fluid movement and dipped a toe into the water.

'Okay, no peeping,' he said, taking his hands away and staring at her in the dusky twilight, desire blazing in his eyes, and everything else dissolved.

24

Just over a week after Sam introduced Paula to the delights of his hot tub, Abby sat on Elaine's patio in her sunny back garden and took a large, fortifying gulp of wine.

'I feel terribly nervous,' she said, pulling at strands of her hair, suddenly unsure of herself. 'Maybe this isn't such a good idea.'

Elaine sloshed more Wolf Blass into Abby's glass. 'Nervous? The girl who climbed Machu Picchu? Give over.'

'That was different. That just took nerves of steel. I'm far more terrified of my feelings,' Abby admitted. More terrified, in truth, of the way her heart was starting to melt around the edges. In a way, life had been safer back in Italy when everything was numb.

'Jeez, Abby, since when have you been terrified of your feelings?'

'Sam might get a shock when he sees me, or think I've tricked him or something. I hope he doesn't react the way he did in Sorrento. He walked off, Elaine. Turned his back on me and marched away. Then later, he apologised. Said he'd just been so surprised.'

She couldn't cope if Sam turned away from her again and her heart was galloping so hard that she could scarcely breathe.

'Relax, Abby, stay cool. You're not going to be swearing undying love, are you? This is just a chance for us all to meet up in advance of the party for Mark and make a few plans. Then you can see how it goes. Anyway, he did ask you to come home, or so you said.'

'Yes, he did all right.'

'For years you were the girlfriend of his dreams. Just remember that. And it's not as if he has someone else on the scene.'

Abby popped a crisp into her mouth and almost spat it out, for in her present frame of mind the black pepper flavour tasted like sawdust. But there was no reason for her sudden anxiety. It was *Sam*, for God's sake. Her friend forever, the guy who'd loved her enough to want to marry her.

'Hey, I don't deserve all this.' Abby turned her attention to the table. Elaine was busy arranging salads and cold meats, fruits and cheeses, delectable baby potatoes and savoury quiches. There was banoffi and pavlova and gallons of Wolf Blass chilling in the fridge. 'You're far too good to me.'

'You're right, you don't deserve it. I'm just delighted to show off my culinary skills. Move over Nigella Lawson. I've come a long way from opening a tin of spaghetti hoops!'

'He has definitely no idea I'll be here?' Abby asked.

'Abby, relax! You've asked me that about a hundred times. Neither Sam nor Paula has any idea. She thinks she's just bringing Sam here for Sunday lunch and a chat, so that we can make some plans for Mark's party.'

'And Paula doesn't mind giving Sam a lift?'

'I think they're coming in his car, as it's more convenient. She was against the idea at first, until I said that if she didn't contact Sam and arrange to bring him here, I'd invite him all by himself. Then she caved in. Which was funny, because I've no way of contacting him and I can't understand how Paula didn't figure that one out for herself. However, it worked out okay and they should be here for two o'clock.'

Abby glanced at her watch. Half past one. Yet again, the

knot in her stomach twisted. She leaned back in her patio chair, out of the shade of the umbrella, and tilted her face to the Irish sun. There was no need to be on edge. Sam was her best mate who was going to kiss her and hold her and make everything better, just as he'd always done. All she had to do was act as if she was the Abby Lacey of years ago. Then everything would work out.

'Okay?'

'Yes, fine . . . no, Sam, I'm not fine.' Paula twisted her fingers in her lap.

The journey to Wicklow was proving to be far swifter that she'd anticipated. Sam's navy Mercedes was eating up the miles.

'I still can't understand why Elaine came up with that invitation out of the blue,' she said.

'It wasn't out of the blue. You've told her I'm organising a reunion bash of sorts. Good idea to have a get-together in advance. I'm quite looking forward to seeing Elaine again.'

'Yes, but – oh, I don't know,' Paula sighed. 'I couldn't believe it when she phoned me last Monday and asked me to bring you down to Wicklow.'

She felt Sam's sharp glance. 'Not that I meant – look,' she backtracked, 'I'd prefer if Elaine didn't know about us.'

'Us? Is there something going on here?' Sam quipped. 'Or do you think she'll figure out by looking at us that we spent half the night having torrid sex?'

'Sam! It's not a joke! I—'

'You're ashamed of me. The snotty-nosed kid from down the lane and the perfect little princess from—'

'Sam, please, I like to keep my private life just that, and it's too soon anyway.' She pulled up the front of her Jasper Conran top to hide her cleavage a little. She wasn't just being paranoid, she told herself. She was too nervous to feel sexy, too afraid of Elaine sensing the sparks flying between her and Sam. For it was all far too new and strange and different – and scary – to be picked up by Elaine and put under a microscope by her enthusiastic sister.

'Don't worry, I won't embarrass you.'

'You're not embarrassing me. *If* there's anything to tell Elaine, I'd far rather do it myself in my own time. Okay? So can we just leave it out for now?' In an attempt to hide her anxiety, she knew she sounded cool and formal and she felt Sam glance at her again as they whisked down through the motorway glen. It was her favourite part of the journey, where the blue vault of the sky peeped down between canopies of majestic trees, but she took no pleasure in the scenery and was sorry that she'd agreed to Elaine's lunch idea.

'If that's what you want. Fine. I'll say nothing to embarrass you. At least tell me if you enjoyed yourself last night,' Sam asked. 'Apart from the torrid sex.'

Paula smiled. 'It was great, marvellous fun, even though my legs were twisted sideways. Celtic Shade are terrific. And your music is brilliant, Sam.'

He'd brought her to a gig they were playing in an old-fashioned pub in the Dublin Mountains. He introduced her to the other band members, Dave and Rory, and she watched him from the sidelines as Celtic Shade played to the packed venue. Her heart sang with feelings she was afraid to identify. She saw a different side to him, the Sam Ryan who could make a guitar throb and echo in her heart, and watch her face as he plucked quivering notes on a soulful mandolin, and whip her up onto the energetic dance floor, catching her time and time again in the strong breadth of his arms. When he laughed with her, once again she felt a wave of love and desire rise up over her head.

Finally they left together, his arm on her shoulder guiding

her through the exit, and she felt caught up in a funny thrill of intimate belonging, as though they were united against everyone else, those who had watched him play and, almost, the rest of the world.

Afterwards they went back to her apartment. She caught his hands and kissed them and told him how skilful they were. He ran his hands up and down her body, his fingers making her writhe and gasp, and he laughed and said there was only one skill he was interested in. Then he drew off her clothes excruciatingly slowly and kissed all the delicate hollows of her body until she was weak and trembling and desperately aching for him. Just when she thought she could bear it no longer, he finally slid inside her. He stayed motionless for a long moment, smiling at her and watching her bite her lip, before starting to move slowly and surely, then faster and harder, bringing her to peak after peak of exquisite pleasure . . .

She didn't want Elaine to know. Not when it was all so precious and she didn't know where it was going, and not when she was still trying to recognise herself in the suddenly sensual woman who made long, lingering love to Sam, who teasingly slid out of his grasp in his hot tub, then slept with him between soft silk sheets and brazenly kissed him awake the following morning.

And she was ever so grateful that she'd kept her silence when they reached her sister's house.

It was unnaturally quiet when Elaine opened the hall door and welcomed them in, throwing a surprised, appraising glance at Sam before giving him a warm hug.

'Colin's brought Ruth out for a while to give us a chance to say hello in peace,' she explained as they walked down the hall. They turned into the kitchen, where a blast of sunshine flooded through huge picture windows. Paula's eyes were caught by the shimmering dance of velvety green hills rising up beyond the windows before she came aware of a figure standing motionless in the corner.

'Hi, guys! I'm back!'

She sensed Sam's head jerking up, heard his indrawn breath. Then a blast of icy coldness engulfed her, for in a flurry of slender limbs, a ripple of delighted laughter and a sudden gush of tears, Abby Lacey tore across the room and jumped into Sam's arms.

25

They were all talking at once, seated under the bright umbrella at Elaine's big table on her sunny patio. Even Ruth in her high chair was trying to make noises and banging her spoon delightedly off the lid of her dish. With another spoon, Paula fed her mashed banana, measuring out each mouthful in tiny bite-sized doses, concentrating grimly on the task of propelling the soft food in the dish to her niece's small pink mouth. Ruth smacked her lips. Paula wiped the trickle of saliva that ran down her dimpled chin. From time to time she glanced across at the vista of green she'd seen through the window and tried to figure out why it looked just the same.

'You should visit more often,' Colin said to her as he refilled her glass of wine. 'Ruth's behaving perfectly for you.'

She felt like crying at the note of kindness in her brother-in-law's voice, but suddenly everyone's attention was focused on Paula and the baby, the exact opposite of what she desired right then.

'It's a novelty for me to feed her,' she laughed, hoping her voice wouldn't crack and turn into a strangulated sob. She ran her pained eyes around the gathering at the table, managing to avoid Sam's face. So far, she hadn't looked him in the eyes. So far, she hadn't directed any conversation at him, but that didn't seem to matter, as Abby was doing enough talking for everyone.

Fun-and-games Abby Lacey, mischievous and cute,

especially now with that absurd, punky haircut, limbs attractively tanned from the warm Italian sun, compared to serious, stodgy, diligent Paula. There was no comparison at all. Abby wouldn't recognise a budget sheet, let alone a five-year plan, even if they jumped up and hit her in the face. Worse still, she looked like a rather adorable teenager in a stretchy pink T-shirt that contrasted rather beautifully with her raven hair, and a pair of grey, skinny cut-off jeans.

Going out with Sam over the last couple of weeks, Paula had somehow managed to forget all about the prospect of Abby coming home. Another incredible, ridiculous, monumental error of judgement, she inwardly wept.

Colin went around the table refilling everyone's glass, save for Sam, who was driving.

'Come on, tell us why you're really home,' he said when he reached Abby.

'I'm home for the party, of course,' she announced in bright, breathy tones, as though, Paula thought savagely, everyone was expected to applaud her marvellous achievement.

'Just the party?' She heard Sam's voice slicing through her consciousness. She tried to eat a wedge of tomato and almost choked on the slimy feel of it in her mouth.

'Maybe not,' Abby grinned at Sam and Paula realised to her horror that she was flirting with him. Her stomach knotted with jealousy.

'And you were the one who persuaded me to come home after all,' she smiled at Sam as if he was the only person there. Then she directed a huge smile at Paula. 'And thanks, Paula, for showing Sam the way down here today. I owe you one.'

She caught a quick glimpse of Sam's gaze as he shot her a bemused look across the table. But she didn't respond.

Instead Paula reverted to the coping mechanism she'd used down through the years when she found it difficult to rise above the teasing in the classroom or college lecture hall – she quietly withdrew into herself.

Conversation went on around her and she smiled mechanically and nodded her head as required, but she scarcely contributed. She was hotly aware of every time that Abby connected with Sam, whether it was a flirting smile or a shared memory, or the touch of her hand – tiny and fragile, of course – on his. As the afternoon wore on, Paula felt as though someone was slowly cutting out her insides with a rather blunt knife. From time to time she felt Sam's puzzled glances darting in her direction, as though he sensed her withdrawal and didn't understand it. She flashed him glinty little smiles in return.

She welcomed the chance to escape by moving inside to the kitchen and helping her sister stack the dirty crockery.

'You're very quiet,' Elaine said.

'Am I?' Her voice was high and bright as she scraped the remains of her salad into the bin.

'Isn't it brilliant that Abby's home at last?' Elaine nodded over her shoulder. By now Abby was sitting on the double swing, playing with baby Ruth in front of an admiring Sam. Their cute intimacy made Paula want to throw up. Trust Abby to manage her homecoming event as though it was the milestone of the century.

'I bet you never guessed.'

'Guessed what?'

'That this was all set-up as a way to get Abby back into the swing of things. That's why I asked you to bring Sam here today.'

'Oh. I see.'

'You *are* in a funny one. Everything all right in the scintillating world of Stevens?'

How did it always come back to her career? Elaine would never guess in a million years just how hurt, jealous and downright scared her older sister was feeling. How come all the paths in her life seemed to lead to her successful company, and not to the achy feelings in her heart for the attractive blond man who'd slept with her just last night, bringing her right to the edge, and was now throwing back his head and laughing traitorously at something Abby was saying?

And she had only herself to blame. She'd been too embarrassed and humiliated to confide in Elaine about her earlier heartbreak. Then she'd stayed quiet about Sam instead of admitting what was going on. Maybe if she'd shared confidences from the beginning, Elaine would have prevented this kind of scene.

On second thought, Paula realised with a spark of anxiety, it was just as well she'd stayed quiet about Sam. For all she knew, that bit of juicy gossip might have gone straight back to Abby, who'd no doubt laugh her head off at the idea of Paula Stevens and Sam Ryan together.

'When is Mark coming home?' She heard Abby ask through the open patio door.

'Around mid-August,' Sam replied.

'Then we'll all be together, the Mayberry Lane gang. Like old times.'

What kind of old times, Paula agonised. Times like Sam asking Abby to marry him?

After lunch, everyone moved inside. Her heart sank when Colin took out his guitar for Sam to play, for she knew more torture had to be endured before the day was over. Abby kicked off her sandals, and in her cut-off jeans, her bare feet looked like a child's as she sat on the floor with arms wrapped around her tanned legs, gazing up at Sam as though he was nothing short of Bono. Then they were all treated to the story of Sam playing the guitar at a wedding that Abby had helped to arrange.

She'd *never* have guessed.

Couldn't *believe* it when she saw Sam.

Paula viciously decided that she'd quite forgotten just how annoyingly chirpy and flighty Abby was. Almost over-eager today, over-enthusiastic, but bright and lively, and so very, very bubbly compared to the flat, dull fog Paula was wrapped in.

It was arranged that Sam would bring Abby home. She didn't know who suggested it, as she was beyond registering who said what. The evening came to a natural conclusion and she heard someone say it was only a small detour for him en route to Malahide. Someone else said he could drop Paula off first, after all she lived on the southside, and then bring Abby home, back up to Mayberry Lane. Paula heard all this as though through a painful haze.

'Is that okay with you, Paula?' Sam was beside her, looking at her with that familiar concern, his hand on her elbow, and she felt like fainting and sensed he was trying to rescue her from slipping away altogether on the whirling tide.

'Yes, I've no problem with that, Sam. None whatsoever.' Her voice was prim and she could see he wasn't happy with her answer, but tough shit.

In one sense it was just as well that it was finished now, she decided, her heart low as they cruised back to Dublin, Abby, naturally, having jumped into the front passenger seat beside Sam after having a fake heart attack when they finally left Elaine's and she laid eyes on his gleaming Mercedes. As if she'd never seen one before, Paula thought viciously.

'Oh my *Gawd*, Sam, is this your car? It's *fabulous!* Can't believe I'm going home in such style.

And to think I stuck you on the back of my scooter. Do you forgive me?'

'Did you hear that, Paula?' Her spiky head appeared in the gap between the front seats. 'I took Sam for a ride on my scooter over in Italy. He was hanging onto me far too tightly 'cos I don't think he trusted me on the hairpin bends. But I was fine, wasn't I, Sam?' She twisted back to face him again. 'Remember the time . . . ?'

Abby spent the whole journey back to Dublin chatting and giggling about all sorts of things, while in the back seat Paula grimly rehearsed nonchalant goodbyes and hoped her voice wouldn't falter at the crucial moment. She presumed that Sam would just drop her off outside her apartment block, and was ready with her casual farewells as they neared Dublin 4, but he pulled up a short distance away, turned off the ignition and slipped off his seat belt as she gathered her bag, struggled to climb out and hurried up the road, anxious to be gone.

'Back in a minute, Abby,' she heard him say.

26

Sam caught up with her further down the pavement. Taking her by the arm, he whirled her around to face him.

'Just what was that all about?' he asked, his jaw set.

'All what?'

'Don't play games, Paula. You've hardly acknowledged me all afternoon, then when you did happen to glance in my direction you looked at me as though I was a particularly nasty worm.'

He was angry. A far corner of her mind seized upon this information as though it could be of significance. But fuddled with an excess of white wine and hurt, she was unable to keep a grip.

'Take a walk, Sam,' she said, her voice shaking. 'I know I'm out of the picture now with your old girlfriend back on the scene.'

He looked thunderstruck. 'Abby? Come on, Paula, I had you credited with far more intelligence than that.'

It was the word 'intelligence' that did it, that sent her spiralling off.

'So that's what I am, is it? Intelligent, conscientious, all those boring, serious attributes? I'd be far more attractive, wouldn't I, if I'd been gallivanting all over the world, climbing sexy mountains and riding exotic waves in the Pacific.'

'I can't believe I'm hearing this.' Sam stepped back and his eyes raked her face. 'Have you really such little regard for me? Or yourself?'

It was only when he turned and strode off that she realised they were standing in broad daylight right outside the entrance to her apartment block and she was shaking and trembling in the warm summer evening as though she was freezing cold.

When she reached the sanctuary of her apartment, she switched off her mobile, kicked off her heels and spent two hours steadily working her way through another bottle of Sauv Blanc, agonising over visions of Sam and Abby in Mayberry Lane. Maybe he would bring her to Malahide and show off his hot tub. Maybe at this minute, he was welcoming her home in a very special way, in his vast bed with slinky sheets and leather headboard. After a while, she began to feel comfortably sozzled and the pain subsided a little.

Alcohol, the great cushion. Sometimes, even, her best friend.

She weaved her way across to the bookcase, took out her book of poetry and stared at the small photograph of the laughing couple on the beach. She'd been down this road before, a bitterly dangerous route she was only too familiar with. She'd put up with divided loyalties and given her heart away only to have it painfully trampled on. But this time she was aware of the perils and could read the warning signals well in advance.

Sam would never really be hers. Not when the love of his life was back on the scene. And she wasn't playing second fiddle. Not this time.

Abby awoke suddenly. The darkness was all-engulfing.

Something had disturbed her. A noise, perhaps? A rising wind? The flutter of the blind at her window? Perhaps it was the breeze rustling in the fir trees outside? She lay in her narrow childhood bed looking at old, familiar shapes as they slowly emerged from the shadowy darkness and tried to pinpoint the source of her disquiet.

All was quiet in the house, all hushed in the dead of the night. There was no sound coming from the house or the gardens. Not a creaking floorboard or even the sound of a car on the lane outside. Her window was firmly shut, so there was no chance her blind had been agitated by a stray wisp of wind. Nonetheless, her skin prickled with unease and a tight tension flared through her body, paralysing her limbs. She could taste it in her mouth, the heavy taste of fear, as well as the enormous fuzz of melancholy that seemed lodged in her throat.

She told herself it was okay, she was home in Mayberry Lane. She was safe now. With a huge effort, she reached out her hand into the thick cloak of darkness and picked up her mobile. She pressed a button and the tiny screen lit up with welcome light. It was half past two in the morning. She brought up her contacts and scrolled down to Sam's name.

He'd given her his mobile number when he'd dropped her home that evening. It had been very strange when he'd followed into the house, but he hadn't stayed long, telling her he was really pleased that she was home at last.

'When will I see you again?' She couldn't help the words slipping out.

'I'm playing in town next Saturday night at The Pier. It's supposed to be the hottest new venue, so if you'd like to come along . . .'

Next Saturday was almost a week away. She swallowed her disappointment, but it must have shown on her face.

'Hey, Abby, I'll be in Limerick most of next week on business.'

'Next Saturday night, so. I'll talk to Elaine, she might like a night out.'

'Great idea.'

Abby turned around and lay on her stomach and tried to forget the funny hollow feeling she'd had when Sam had said goodbye. As though there was something missing.

She'd even sensed it during lunch in Elaine's. She'd chatted brightly, perhaps overdoing it in a huge attempt to recapture the Abby Lacey of old. At some level she'd sensed that Sam was removed, distant even. It was in the way he looked at her and waited fractionally to laugh at her nonsensical jokes. When he'd said goodbye, he'd hesitated just briefly before he'd kissed her lightly on the forehead. Then he'd patted her arm in a comforting gesture that struck her as being apologetic.

Apologetic? *Sam?* She was just imagining it, she told herself. It was just that she was still a little disconnected from him. She left his number ready on her screen as she burrowed into her pillow and shut out the world with its ghosts and nightmares, and imagined instead the warmth of Sam's arms. If anything, she was the one who should be apologetic. She'd hurt him to bits, gaily swanning off across the world and leaving him to pick up the pieces of his broken heart. No wonder he was a little reserved with her.

She just had to make up for all the hurt she'd caused.

27

Lia asked for pink champagne.

'Pink champagne coming up,' Gary said, summoning the sommelier.

It was a bit early, she supposed, barely two o'clock, and champagne at two o'clock in the day meant she'd get no more writing done that evening, but who cared? She was celebrating, wasn't she? Celebrating yet another milestone. Sales for *Death on Friday* had gone through the roof. Wow. Bingo. All her dreams rolled into one. All those painstaking, lonesome hours coming right in the end.

All of a sudden, she wished Abby were here with her now, in the opulent splendour of the Ritz in Piccadilly, to share the moment. It was such a tremendous achievement, yet it meant little without someone of her own to share it with. She was lunching with Gary as Marcus, her agent, was in the Maldives and unavailable. Clarissa, her editor, was over in Japan and due home the following weekend. She would have preferred to wait a few days and include Clarissa, but Gary had insisted she meet up with him without delay as he had a proposition to put to her, and great and all as the occasion was, it felt kind of flat.

'Well done, Ms Lacey. May I say I'm a great fan of yours.' The waiter offered her warmest congratulations as he poured her a snipe.

'Goodness, call me Lia,' she insisted as she beamed her

widest, most successful novelist smile and took the glass he proffered with a perfectly manicured hand.

Funnily enough, she'd enjoyed many a celebratory moment without Abby around and her daughter's absence hadn't bothered her too much. Maybe it was because she'd been on the other side of the world. Maybe she was missing her now because she wasn't very far away. And Lia would have much preferred to have her here now, at her side, where she was safe.

Safe? Why safe?

Safe from the tentacles of the past, which were already, now, starting to shift. Abby had emailed yesterday, full of chat about Sam and the upcoming party. It was as though the intervening years had never been and the last thing Lia wanted was to be catapulted back in time.

'Excuse me, Ms Lacey. Pardon me for disturbing you, but it would mean so much to me and my wife if you'd just give me your autograph.' A sixtyish gentleman approached her table, proffering his diary. 'We love your books, all of them. Even though they rather keep us awake at night.'

Lia smiled graciously and swiftly penned a personal note in the man's diary.

'How kind of you,' he said as he backed away.

She felt like saying there was no need to be so grateful, that she was just ordinary behind it all, but that would dispel some of the mystique that surrounded her, sitting there in her sparkling Schiaparelli dress with her Titian hair strategically styled, gelled and sprayed to within an inch of its life, so she merely smiled as he left her table.

'Cheers, Lia,' Gary touched his glass to hers. 'You deserve every ounce of success.'

'Thanks, Gary. I often wonder, though . . .' she hesitated, unsure how to proceed, aware that she should be having this conversation firstly with her agent. She took a bracing gulp of fizzing champagne before continuing. 'I sometimes wonder, supposing I wasn't writing crime fiction?'

'What do you mean?'

'Perhaps a different genre. Something mythical, in the realms of fantasy, maybe with a clear message of redemption . . .'

Gary guffawed, almost choking on his champagne. 'I'll tell you one thing, Lia, we sure as hell wouldn't be sitting here now. You've a great talent for bringing out the worst horror imaginable in your books. I don't know how you do it. Some of your characters are so pure evil, *I'd* even be afraid of them in the dark of the night. And for a woman such as yourself, living an ordinary life in relative obscurity in Dublin, I don't know how the hell you can get so much terror and fright, never mind blood and gore, onto the page.'

It wasn't the first time this has been said to her and Lia gulped her champagne before trotting out her usual comment. 'Well naturally, I just let my imagination run riot.'

'Whatever it is, a lot of people out there can identify with it. And that's what you need to shift mega amounts of books, something to draw the reader in. Some people just love to be scared shitless. And you do it so well, you'd swear you had personal experience! Ha, ha.'

'Yes, well, they do say write about what you know,' she quipped, smiling blandly at Gary.

Gary laughed even louder. 'That's what I love about you, Lia, you've a great sense of humour and you're so down to earth. You've never got hung up on your own importance. I mean, someone else would have ignored that fan because he was interrupting their celebratory meal.'

'What good would that do me?' she asked, utterly relieved to change the subject. 'Anyway, my fans are all-important. They're the people who part with their hard-earned cash to buy my books. Why shouldn't I give them what they want? Isn't it all part of the package?'

Gary leaned across the table, looking serious all of a sudden. 'I was hoping you'd say that. Really hoping that that was still your attitude despite your stellar success.'

'I'd scarcely be a success if it weren't for my fans, would I? Catch twenty-two.'

'Which brings me neatly to my proposition.' Gary poured more champagne into her flute before dunking the bottle into the chilled bucket.

She never saw it coming. She was sipping bubbly champagne and nibbling on Dover sole, still wishing Abby was there, still mindful of another part of her head skittering around the possible consequences of Abby back in Mayberry Lane. She had to ask Gary to repeat himself. Twice. Caught up in his excitement, he didn't realise that he'd left her far behind.

'Thing is, Lia,' he was saying, 'the researchers consider it would be the hottest television imaginable. It would shoot the ratings right through the roof and keep you on top of the lists for months to come.'

'What ratings, Gary? I'm not really with you on this . . .'

'It can't do your profile any harm. In fact, it would be priceless publicity. I can just see the drama of it all.'

'Sorry, but what drama?'

'*Lunchtime with Rachel*, of course. Have you been listening to a word I said?' he grinned. 'Or are you as gobsmacked as I am? Lia, this will make you a megastar, a household name! Not just in the UK, but on the Continent! And America would love it. Think of the ratings. We won't be able to keep your books on the shelves after this.'

'Gary, could you start at the beginning?'

'It's simple but riveting. *Lunchtime with Rachel* want to go looking for Alejandro,' he said.

She caught the drift of his words through the pall of chilling disbelief that was slowly engulfing her.

Gary was into his stride. 'Alejandro, the intrepid explorer; Alejandro, your teenage lover who set out to conquer the world – he's a cult figure, isn't he? A legend in his own right. The bored housewives would love him to bits. You've no idea of the letters and texts that poured in after your television appearance. And then when they find him, *Lunchtime with Rachel* want to reunite you. On live television, of course, and with Abby. Imagine! Seeing her icon of a dad after all these years, the dad she never knew. So what if he's married now, etcetera? I'm sure his wife and family will see his relationship with you exactly as it was, a youthful fling, a different take on *Romeo and Juliet*, a—'

'Stop right there, Gary.' Lia raised a trembling hand and tried to speak through painful shards of glass that seemed to have suddenly lodged her throat. 'Sorry to disappoint you, but that is not going to happen. Never. Over my dead body.'

'Look, Lia, think about it for a minute. Don't go knocking it on the head before you've had time to fully consider it. The researchers have assured me of the utmost discretion. Nowadays, with technology being what it is, it should be relatively easy to trace your teenage lover. I'm only surprised he hasn't come looking for you, given your success. Of course, if there are major objections from his family, we'd have to work around those, but that's if he has one – perhaps you were his one and only love, which would be even better again, as your fans would love to see you back with your childhood sweetheart. And as for Abby, surely you'd like to see your daughter reunited at last with father?'

'Leave Abby out of this. Never mind his family, there's a major objection coming from me,' Lia said stonily.

She felt sick. Of all the intrusive, invasive, thoroughly revolting things to do in the name of television ratings!

And of all the nasty things to do to her in the name of publicity. Maybe Gary thought it was wonderful – a hero Alejandro, replete from all his explorations, getting back together with the woman he'd loved all those years ago. Abby meeting the legendary father she'd never known. It was the kind of stuff Hollywood movies were made of. And it would be electrifying virtual reality television.

If the story was true, of course.

'I'll see my solicitor about this,' she said in a chilly voice. 'This is not a runner, do you hear me? No. Way.'

Across the table, Gary was looking at her with disappointment etched all over his face. His days were numbered, Lia swiftly decided, if he seriously thought she'd agree to this preposterous idea. It was a nightmare, her worst nightmare. The voracious researchers were bound to discover that Alejandro had just been a rather ordinary Spanish guy all along. But she could live with that.

What terrified her, made her push her meal to one side with a trembling hand and knock back her champagne far too quickly, was the prospect of the awful truth coming out, the truth she'd hidden for thirty-two years.

Apart, that is, from the one person who'd been sworn to absolute secrecy. Although she still wasn't sure if her secret had been kept all these years . . .

28

Paula's fingers skittered across the keys of her laptop when Sam ducked through her office doorway on Monday evening, looking crisp and sexy.

'How did you get in?' she demanded, ready to explode after her heart-wrenching Sunday. 'The main door is locked.'

'Kate saw me waiting outside and took pity on me,' he grinned. 'I promised her you wouldn't give her the bullet.'

'You've no right to make such presumptions. How long were you waiting out there?'

'Long enough.'

'Then it must be obvious I'm very busy.' She looked at him imperiously.

He leaned back against the closed door with the broad, relaxed smile that flipped her stomach. 'I wouldn't dream of holding up your important deadlines or impeding your strategic targets, so I'll be as quick as I can. On one condition.'

'Yes?'

'You come out from behind that monstrosity of a desk and sit beside me on your sofa, where we can have a proper civilised conversation like two mature adults.'

Her leather sofa? 'No.'

'Scaredy cat,' he said, giving her a meaningful grin.

Paula swallowed.

'Right, so, I'm coming to you.' He swiftly pulled his chair around to Paula's side of the desk. The side of the desk where she brokered six-figure business deals, hired and fired, and kept herself aloof and apart. And safe. He was much too close for comfort. She caught the scent of him. Saw the flecks in his eyes.

'So this is the important side of the desk where it all happens,' he said, sitting back in his chair, his eyes scanning the office. 'This is some power base. It must make you feel very important. I don't know whether to be flattered or annoyed with your carry-on,' he went on in the same casual tone of voice. 'I didn't think even the multi-talented Paula Stevens had the ability to behave like a six-year-old. With all due respect to six-year-old girls.'

Paula raised a supercilious eyebrow. 'Forgive me, Sam, but when the guy I'm seeing spends a Sunday afternoon hanging onto every word out of his ex-girlfriend's mouth, I know when to call it quits.'

'So you're jealous.' His voice was rich with amusement and maddeningly sexy.

She felt like crying but covered it by sounding angry. 'From where I am, the girl you wanted to marry is back on the scene. Right? And frankly, Sam, this is where I duck out.'

'I was hoping you'd have calmed down enough to talk,' he said.

She stayed silent.

'Paula, you scarcely think Abby's return home is going to affect us.'

'Well, isn't it?'

Sam looked serious now, all bantering forgotten. 'What do you take me for? Do you really think these last few weeks have meant nothing to me? Or have you that low an opinion of me? Quite apart from yourself?'

She swallowed. 'I don't know what to think, beyond the fact that judging by yesterday afternoon, you and Abby look all set to pick up just exactly where you left off.'

'This is ridiculous,' he said testily. 'You're talking like a petulant teenager and not a successful, rational woman.'

A petulant teenager was exactly what she felt like and she could have wept with frustration. 'Looking at it from my angle, I consider I'm being perfectly rational. I felt excluded, Sam. It was nice while it lasted, but now that Abby's back, I quite understand if—'

She didn't get any further. Sam leaned across and stopped her with a kiss.

She yielded. Melted into his arms. Opened her mouth to his. Felt something that had constricted her throat since Sunday dissolve. Did all the things she had vowed not to do. Truth was, she was hungry for the taste of him, the nearness of him, the sheer bliss of being in his arms. When they eventually drew apart, he was looking at her with such a tender expression on his face that her heart contracted.

'Paula,' he said, his finger tracing the curve of her cheek, 'we have to talk about this somewhere I won't be tempted to kiss you every five seconds, or worse . . .' His finger slid down to the V neck of her white cotton shirt and into her cleavage, sending sparkly ricochets around her body.

'I don't think so.' With a huge effort of will, she pushed back her chair and widened the gap between them. 'I don't have time for fun and games. I have a business to run and far more important issues on my mind besides—'

'Us? The nights we slept together?'

'Especially the nights we slept together.'

'I don't believe you.'

She raised her shoulder in an eloquent gesture of dismissal.

'Paula, surely you understand that Abby and I are just good friends and nothing more?'

'That's not how she sees it. Elaine phoned me this afternoon, and according to her, Abby has come back on account of you.'

'I find that hard to believe. She was never interested in me in that way.'

'It must be flattering to your ego all the same,' Paula said acidly. 'She's had all sort of exciting adventures gadding around the world, yet she's come home to you.'

'I'll have to talk to her and set her straight,' he said.

'Do that.'

'I will.' He hesitated. 'I don't think Abby's quite herself. She's ... I dunno, too happy clappy, as if she's trying too hard to be a souped-up version of her old self.'

'You'd want to watch it, or you might find yourself trying too hard to ask her to marry you again.'

'Don't do this to us, Paula.' He shook his head. 'You must know that I want a whole lot more than friendship from you.'

When she didn't reply, he rose to his feet, disappointment on his face.

'I won't hold up your number-crunching decisions much longer. I'll be in Limerick for the rest of the week. Celtic Shade are playing on Saturday night in The Pier. It's that new pub on the canal.'

'I know where it is,' she said sharply.

'You're more than welcome.'

'Elaine and Abby have been invited?'

'Yes, and I'd love you to come.'

'I scarcely think my presence is required.'

He walked over to the door and turned to face her. 'You said you used to envy us our friendship. Don't shut yourself away and don't freeze me out,' he said, his eyes surprisingly warm. 'The Pier, Paula. Next Saturday. I'll be expecting you.'

The Pier. Next Saturday night. She felt full of fluttery nerves and asked herself if she had the guts to show up.

*   *   *

Abby sifted through rails in bright, glittery department stores packed with designer labels, gingerly fingered stuff she'd no intention of buying in exclusive laneway boutiques, and rummaged through high street cheap and cheerful racks for the budget conscious. Under her fingers, colours and fabrics glided across her vision, a cacophony of yellow and purple, pink and white. Then instinctively, her hands reached out and plucked a frothy white dress off the rails. She felt the shimmer of heat on her skin and caught the scent of fresh roses in her nostrils. There was the whisper of silk and the drift of a gossamer veil ...

'Can I help you?'

The words startled Abby. Her eyes flew to her reflection in the mirror. She was holding a white dress up against her jeans and T-shirt, and a sales assistant was hovering impatiently. Abby dropped the dress as though it was on fire.

'*Scusi*,' she apologised, bending to retrieve it.

The assistant was there before her, swooping to rescue the soft white cotton. 'No problem. Have you taken a fancy to this dress? You've been holding it up to yourself for ages.'

'Have I?' Ages? Funny, she seemed to have been in the boutique for just a few minutes. The sharply angled spotlights were hurting her eyes. They bounced off stark white-washed walls against which clothes rails in gleaming chrome flaunted an intimidating selection of colours and designs.

'You can try it on if you like.'

'No, it's okay,' Abby said. She felt slightly faint, as if she'd been breathing far too quickly and her lungs were galloping ahead of the rest of her. She turned around and walked out of the boutique.

Outside on the pavement, she stopped short. The July afternoon was slightly overcast. Abby shivered and stared at the blurry outlines of the street in surprise. Everything seemed odd; it was colder and greyer, with no familiar landmarks.

Her head was filled with a vision of sunny, hot Sorrento, with the narrow streets and alleyways, the rippling blue of the Bay of Naples, the burning sun and bright summery clothes. But this wasn't Sorrento, this was Dublin. Abby Lacey had finally moved on with her life.

She was home.

She walked slowing down the street, getting her bearings, her breathing gradually returning to normal. She was somewhere off Grafton Street and she'd been looking for an outfit to wear for Sam, an outfit for Saturday night. Only she couldn't seem to come to any sort of decision.

She took a break for coffee, sitting on a chair outside a bistro. Then she picked up her mobile.

'Elaine, I need help.'

'Hi, Abby, what's up?'

Her friend's cheerful voice gave her some kind of stability. 'Just what do you wear for going out on a Saturday night? Like, for music and dancing?'

'God, Abby, I can't really talk, I'm just about to feed Ruth her lunch.'

'Ruth?'

'Yeah, she's suddenly developed an enormous appetite. I can't get the food into her quickly enough.'

All of a sudden, she pictured Elaine sweeping a laughing baby into her arms. Of course. Ruth. Abby laughed at herself. She was doing far too good a job of remembering the way it used to be. She'd forgotten for a moment that her friend was married and a mother. All she'd recalled, as though she was rediscovering an important piece of information, was that Elaine knew all about fashion and style and could be relied on to give advice.

'Elaine, it'll just take a minute, please? I'm stuck. I forget all about going out on the razz in Dublin. Do I go designer jeans with a Topshop vest, or something more upmarket?

Maybe a bright cotton mini from BT2 and a sleeveless blouse? And what about my feet? Cork-soled wedges or heels?'

'Whatever you're comfortable in, Abby.'

'But that's just it. Supposing whatever I'm comfortable in is a bit too casual? I mean . . .' She wanted to looked groomed and stylish. Most of all she wanted to look right.

'Don't worry, you'll look good in whatever. Abby, you're the one who always set a style statement without worrying about anyone else or behaving like a fashion victim. I've gotta fly, Ruth's going ballistic.'

Abby could hear the thin wail of Ruth in the distance. Once upon a time, Elaine would have chatted on the phone to her for hours. 'If I pick up a few things, can I run it by you again?' she asked desperately. 'But I'll probably see you tomorrow night, won't I?'

'I'm staying in Paula's,' Elaine pointed out. Abby heard even louder sobs in the background. 'Look, Abby, I really have to go.'

'Elaine. Wait!'

The line had gone dead. Abby disconnected the call and focused on the hustle and bustle around her, observing Dublin's beautiful chic going about their usual Friday business of lunching and shopping, watching the way they modelled their clothes and flaunted huge carrier bags. It was as cosmopolitan as London.

London. Thanks to her indulgent mum, her wardrobe in Sadlier Square was bursting with designer labels that she showed off at book launches and cocktails events, and smart outfits suitable for office wear. If she visited her mum, she could bring home some of her wardrobe. She hadn't brought many clothes home from Italy, for at all other times it was second nature to lounge around in jeans and a T-shirt. She certainly had nothing that she could wear on Saturday night and feel confident in. Confident enough about getting closer to Sam.

For inside, although she was doing the right thing, she felt the tiniest blip of inadequacy now that she was home again on Sam's territory. Going back to the Abby Lacey of eight years ago was so strange that she felt like an imposter of sorts. She just needed more practice. She picked up her mobile again. Maybe Sam was back from Limerick by now.

'Yes?'

His voice sounded disembodied.

'Sam? You sound funny.'

'I'm on hands-free as I'm driving, Abby.'

'Driving home from Limerick?'

'Yeah.'

Abby stood up, threw some coins on the table and slid on her shoulder bag. With her mobile glued to her ear, she began to stroll down Grafton Street, chatting to Sam. She felt alive all of a sudden, part of his world again, picturing him in his sleek Mercedes with the countryside flashing by while her voice echoed around his car.

'It'll be fun on Saturday night,' she chatted. 'Elaine's coming up, so we'll have another mini reunion.' She didn't add the fact that Elaine planned to stay with Paula in case Abby brought Sam back to Mayberry Lane.

'I think Paula may be coming along also,' he said.

'Really?'

'Yes, I've asked her to join us.'

Abby giggled. 'Good idea. She might need some warm-up practice for Mark's party.'

There was a silence. She thought that Sam had been disconnected until he said, 'Abby, I'd like to see you, just the two of us, so that we can have a decent chat. Soon.'

Her heart lifted. 'I'd like that too. How about Sunday? I could cook for you?' It would be the perfect excuse, she realised, to get him to stay over with her after Saturday night at The Pier.

'I'm not sure about Sunday.' He hesitated and for a moment she tried to guess what else could be occupying his Sunday. She put her hand up to her hair, forgetting for a moment that it was cut short, and ran her fingers through the spiky edges. 'Next week,' he said. 'Say Monday evening?'

'So is that a date, then? Monday for dinner at, say, seven thirty?'

'That's a date.'

Abby stuck her mobile into her bag and watched a couple strolling by arm in arm. The girl was wearing a beautifully-cut jade green dress that swung to the knees. Something like that would be perfect for Saturday night, Abby decided, imagining herself strolling along in Sam's arms in the not too distant future. For dinner in her house on Monday evening, she could buy the crinkly white top she'd admired in Monsoon. It would go with the Armani jeans she'd bought in Naples.

And she'd need some sexy new underwear, she decided, turning back up the street in the direction of La Senza, for thankfully life was beginning again for her after all those months she'd spent frozen in time.

29

It was a serious mistake to go shopping when your decision-making skills were in meltdown, Paula fretted. In the compelling energy of the city-centre boutique, the stretchy blue top and short cotton skirt looked as though they'd knock six years off her age and ten pounds off her figure. In the bedroom of her apartment, she looked like a desperate phoney.

By the time Elaine arrived that evening, dressed in floaty lemon and in a flutter of excitement at the prospect of a night out on the town, Paula had bolstered herself with a large glass of wine and looked coolly glamorous in a soft cotton Moschino top, pink Dolce & Gabbana trousers and lashings of make-up.

They strolled into the city centre and met Abby, the younger girl emerging from their meeting point in a swirl of energy. Paula's heart missed a beat when she pounced on top of Elaine, greeting her as though she hadn't seen her in years. Almost immediately, Paula realised that Sam hadn't talked to her, for Abby's eyes looked at her much as they'd looked at her the previous Sunday. Much as they'd always looked at her, with that mixture of tongue-in-cheek wariness. They went for cocktails in Cocoon, Abby chatting about clothes and shoes, Elaine boasting about Ruth's new tooth, and at nine o'clock, they got a taxi together out to The Pier.

'Sam told me they'd be on stage just after nine o'clock,'

Abby said proprietally as the climbed into the taxi on Dawson Street.

Paula hated herself for wondering how she knew.

The Pier on Saturday night was thrumming with life. The newest Dublin hot spot, all lacquered wood, chrome and glass, never mind death-defying angles, was spread over three floors. The ground floor served food, the first floor had a small stage for music and cabaret acts, and there was a semi-circular raised mezzanine that formed the third floor.

All life was here, Paula thought, in the form of the beautiful people. Throwing confident shapes, showing off size-zero waists in their belly-revealing tops, flinging back manes of richly-coloured hair, wafting round in clouds of designer perfume and air kisses, pouting lips smiling to reveal perfect teeth. Most of them were a decade younger than she was. She cynically decided that some of them must have been paid to be here, just to look alluring and inject a dose of hard-edged glamour into the venue.

She sat at a table up on the mezzanine. From here, she had a perfect view of Celtic Shade and a perfect view of Abby and Elaine dancing on the tiny floor in front of the group. Abby, whirling around in a black top and burnt orange skirt, ever so light on her feet in spite of her sparkly heels. She was a natural dancer, of course, something else to be included on a long list of fluffy and engaging attributes, Paula thought sourly.

From the stage, Sam had seen them arrive. He threw a long glance in their direction and Paula could have sworn he smiled at her, although looking around her now at all the bright young things gazing at him, many of them probably fancied that he smiled exclusively at them. He was wearing stonewashed jeans and a black shirt. He looked devastating, and out on stage playing his guitar he resembled a handsome stranger. Paula found it inconceivable to think that she'd recently shared the intimacy of his bed, not to mention his hot tub.

'Sam's absolutely brilliant! He's so talented,' Abby said, scraping back a chair and sitting down.

Paula hadn't noticed that the band had slowed down the tempo, and Abby and Elaine had reclaimed their seats.

'Yeah, imagine he's ended up like this.' Elaine put her bottle of beer to her lips and took a long slug. 'It must be great to do something you really enjoy and get paid for it.'

'And then to hold down the day job as well. *And* in the law courts.'

'He can choose the cases he wants to accept, so it's not necessarily full-time,' Paula deliberately joined in. She wasn't going to sit all night and listen to Abby waffling on, but she felt her voice sounded stilted and forced as opposed to Abby's light, breezy tones.

'You don't say.' Abby gave her a cool look with those huge aquamarine eyes as though to say it was really none of Paula's business.

'Hey, didn't you find out everything about him when he dropped you home on Sunday?' Elaine asked.

Paula froze. The last thing she'd expected was an in-depth account of whatever had luridly transpired between Abby and Sam on Sunday. Nonetheless, she sat on high alert, greedy to hear.

'No, we've plenty of time to fill in the details,' Abby said, waving a small tanned hand dismissively. Her slender wrist was encircled with a pretty turquoise bracelet, Paula noticed. 'Sam didn't hang around too much. He had to go home to read up on some stuff for the next day. I showed him around the house and we went out into the back garden for a bit.'

'A bit?' Elaine chortled. 'A bit of what? It must have been dark by then . . .'

Abby smiled impishly. No one could do impish quite like Abby, Paula decided blackly.

'Never you mind,' Abby shook her head. 'Oh, listen, I love this song!' And she turned around and stared down at Sam, enraptured.

Elaine laughed and shook her head. 'I think, Abby, that you're falling in love with him all over again.'

'Can you blame me?' Abby grinned, looking like a teenager idolising her favourite pop star. 'To think he was here all this time, waiting for me.'

Paula choked on her Courvoisier and Baileys. Somehow wine wasn't giving her the kick she needed tonight, so she'd opted for something with a higher alcohol content. She felt Abby's concerned eyes on her. 'Paula! You okay?'

She tried to talk above the constriction in her throat. 'The drink, I guess it went down the wrong way.'

'All we need to do, Paula, is fix you up with Mark,' Abby said gleefully.

'What?'

'You know, when he comes home.'

'Don't be ridiculous,' Paula said coldly.

'Paula, there's no need to be shy with us,' Abby persisted.

'There never was a "Mark and me". Get it?' Paula snapped. She picked up her bag and stalked off to the ladies, despite the jaw-dropping stares from Elaine and Abby that followed her out and scorched her right between the shoulder blades.

When she returned to the table, the first thing she noticed was the absence of music and the increased swell of conversation and laughter. Celtic Shade were taking a break. Then she noticed that Abby was missing. Elaine was sitting alone and busy with her mobile.

'Paula, I'm just texting Colin to check on Ruth.' She looked up at her sister worriedly. 'Look, I'm sorry about—'

'Forget it.' Paula forced a smile as she sat down. Her

little show of temper had scarcely been Elaine's fault. It had been a huge mistake to come out like this. She must have been desperate to think that she could socialise with Abby without feeling awkward and on edge. And Sam so near and yet so far away. Abby was pushing all the wrong buttons and Paula was furious that she'd allowed the younger girl to upset her and that she'd put herself into this ignominious position in the first place.

Her eyes flew down to the stage where Celtic Shade had been playing, and she saw the tall figure of Sam standing with his back to her, chatting to Rory, who played the flute and keyboard. Paula's anxious eyes scythed through the crowds but there was no sign of Abby. It was only when Sam turned around that she felt a bolt of distress cut through her. Abby was snuggled into the shelter of his body, angled with her back pressed against his chest, fitting neatly into his broad frame. Sam's arms were draped around her shoulders and she was hanging onto them as though to glue herself securely in place.

Paula didn't have to feign a headache. The pain shooting through her head was making her nauseous.

'Elaine, I'm heading off,' she said, wondering if she'd make it to the exit without bringing up the contents of her stomach.

'So early? The night has scarcely begun. I really hope Abby didn't upset you about Mark.'

'No, I have a headache. Bad week in the office and all that,' she gabbled. 'You stay as long as you want. You have a spare key, haven't you?'

'Sure. I promise I'll be quiet. I won't be too late. It all depends on how early Abby and Sam go off together. They won't want me around,' Elaine grinned.

Paula painted a smile on her face. 'See you tomorrow.'

Her limbs felt stiff as she teetered out into the cool night air and collapsed into a taxi. Some part of her vaguely wondered what Sam would think when he looked up to see her gone. No matter. It was clear he was busily occupied with Abby. She went home, utterly relieved to reach the sanctuary of her apartment. She felt like a robot as she removed her make-up, grimly telling herself not to dare cry while she checked her clean face in the mirror. She stepped into her sensor shower, feeling ridiculously grateful for the soothing comfort of the jets sluicing her body.

Then she took one of the sleeping tablets that she kept for emergencies. Otherwise she'd have lain awake all night long.

30

The carton of orange juice slipped from Abby's careless fingers. It thunked onto the floor, disgorging a pungent stream of bright liquid that ran unimpeded across the tiles. She tore off a handful of kitchen roll, dropped to her knees and began to mop. Seconds later, the kitchen filled with the acrid scent of burnt toast.

Abby let rip a stream of angry Italian.

She plucked the offending toast between the tips of her smarting fingers and dropped it hurriedly into the bin. She hugged her pink terry robe tighter around herself, reached into the fridge for a yoghurt and went into the front room. She picked up the remote control, turned on the television and swiftly flicked through the channels. Then she curled up on the sofa, comforted herself with Sunday morning cartoons and the taste of strawberry yoghurt and tried to work out why things hadn't gone the way she'd expected the night before.

She'd danced her heart out on the floor, feeling as though her body was in a silvery spotlight as she imagined Sam's admiring eyes upon her. She'd joined him during the interval when Celtic Shade had taken a break, making a fuss of him, leaning back into the shelter of his chest and pulling his arms down around her in the way she used to do all those years ago. If she'd expected him to respond, she'd been sadly mistaken. Now, looking back, she had the impression that he'd been embarrassed by her display of familiarity.

Too much too soon, she decided. Or maybe Sam had simply grown out of public displays of affection. Besides playing with Celtic Shade at functions, he had a high-flying law career. That's what she needed to do, Abby decided as she gazed at the television. Try to connect with him on a different level.

And for all Elaine's grand plans to stay with Paula so that she'd be out of the way, Abby recalled with a sinking feeling that there had been no question of Sam spending the night in Mayberry Lane. At the end of the evening, he came over to their table carrying a pint of iced water. She felt a heightened excitement as he sat down, looking so gorgeous and sexy and with something so reassuring about his presence that she wanted to bask in it forever. How had she turned her back on him and waltzed away so glibly from everything he'd promised?

'Where's Paula?' he said.

'She's gone home,' Elaine told him. 'She said she had a headache.'

'Yeah,' Abby giggled, anxious to appear shiny and happy, 'right after I said I'd fix her up with Mark. I don't think she was impressed with me.' Abby made a face.

'She's tired and she just overreacted,' Elaine said.

'This probably isn't her scene anyway,' Abby shrugged. 'She's not exactly into wild Irish dancing! Sam, let me get you a drink. A proper one.'

She couldn't believe it when he said, 'No, thanks, my car's outside and I'm not going to hang about, I'm whacked. It's been one hell of a busy week. I'll leave you and Elaine to catch up on everything.'

'Don't forget, Monday evening at my house,' she reminded him.

'Oh, yeah, sure thing.'

Abby felt a huge pang in her chest when he gave both of
them a chaste kiss farewell. Her eyes followed his figure
threading through the crowds until she could see him no
longer.

She'd slept late on Sunday morning. Elaine's text to say
she was home in Wicklow had awoken her. She felt a pang
of envy for Elaine, with Colin, baby Ruth and her beautiful
home. Once upon a time, they would have got together for
a long leisurely brunch and had a postmortem on every little
detail of the night before.

Once upon a time, she'd never have felt as deflated as this
after a night out.

The cartoons came to an end and a sports programme
began. Outside, the slanting summer rain rapped against the
windowpane and dripped through the trees that fronted the
garden. Abby lay on the couch and stretched like a cat. She
wondered what Sam was busy with and how she was going
to fill in the time until Monday evening. And then she had
a brainwave. Her lethargy suddenly forgotten, she scrambled
to her feet. She slid out of her dressing gown as she stepped
into the shower. Afterwards she pulled on jeans and a grey
top and went up into the attic.

The attic was reached through a small door beside her
mum's bedroom. Abby crouched down, stepped through
into shadowy darkness and pulled the cord for the light
switch. Light sprang on, illuminating the jumbled shapes of
bags, boxes and crates piled together under the slanting eaves.
There was a faint musty smell and the sound of rain
drumming on the roof. Her mother had painstakingly stored
their belongings in the attic before she left for London and
everything was labelled.

There were two full plastic bags with Abby's winter
clothes. 'I'll scarcely need them in Australia,' she remembered

saying. It had been raining the day she'd packed for Australia. She smiled when she came across a cardboard box full of her stuff from college – lecture notes, A4 binders and books.

'You can dump all that,' she'd said, but her mum had clearly taken no notice. Or else it had been more convenient just to shove it into the attic.

She pulled back the flap of another box and drew a sharp breath as she was transported back in time. The box was full of all the favourite things she'd hoarded down through the years – old birthday cards, CDs, Valentine cards from Sam (mostly humorous), her collection of foreign stamps and her novelty pens. Abby smiled at an old Barbie doll with all the clothes removed. She'd never been one for dolls of any description.

And lastly, down at the bottom, a small, plastic figure of E.T.

Abby picked it up and held it in her hands, and the memory flashed of the evening when Mark Ryan from the bungalow at the end of the lane had knocked at the door.

It was just after they'd been to see *E.T.*, and Abby had laughed with him all the way home on the bus. Mark was dark-haired and his voice was funny and deep, like a man's. Now he was standing at the door with a small gift-wrapped package in his hand and her mother was waving it away and protesting.

Mark, however, held his ground in the face of her mum's disapproval and Abby stamped her foot until her mother eventually relented. Then Mark handed her mother the packaged gift, which she'd immediately passed to Abby. Abby had kept the E.T. figure with her teddies and dolls, eventually packing it away when she'd redecorated her bedroom into a teenage den. On impulse, she lobbed it out onto the landing to put on her dressing table. She moved another bag and there in front of her, safely stored in a heavy-duty box, was what she'd been seeking.

Her photo albums.

Brimming with memories of the way they were, she couldn't wait to show them to Sam.

31

Lia prayed that her solicitor would set her mind at ease when she phoned him on Monday morning. There had to be some way to prevent the nightmare scenario she'd been envisioning ever since her lunch in the Ritz with Gary.

John Holmes, her solicitor, was precise and to the point. One of the advantages of being a writer, Lia had found, was others' willingness to help her out with her research, no matter how silly or illogical her questions might be. It was a simple enough matter to thank John for taking her call and to explain that she was enquiring about the legal implications of tracing another person. She was relieved that he automatically assumed that Lia was phoning on a point of research, and equally proud of the way her voice didn't falter.

'There's no law prohibiting a person from attempting to trace anybody else,' John said, dashing her hopes. 'Any appropriately-licensed investigation bureau could conduct a search. In fact, anybody at all.'

Lia's heart sank. 'Really? Surely there are some kind of safeguards?'

'Searches conducted by investigators are usually carried out with the utmost discretion. Investigators are trained to be circumspect, at least in most cases. But there are many legitimate ways and means of finding the whereabouts of another person, if one is so inclined.'

'Just supposing . . .' Lia hesitated. 'What would you say

are the chances of finding someone after thirty years?' This
was out of his remit as a solicitor and there was definitely
a quaver in her voice. But John was the epitome of
professionalism. If he was in any way surprised at her query,
he certainly didn't show it and she thanked God for his
detached manner.

'Now that, my dear Lia, is extremely hard to guess,' John
said evenly.

'For example, how would an investigative bureau go about
it?'

'Obviously they'd need as much basic information as
possible. Name, date of birth, last known whereabouts, next
of kin.'

'And if they had very little information, what then?'

'It's impossible to gauge. Internet query tools have
revolutionised that whole area. Between a raft of online
records out there in the public domain, electoral rolls, etcetera,
it can be relatively easy compared to years ago. Some
companies boast that people can be traced within thirty
days, even with the minimum of information. Although if
someone is determined to disappear into the ether, it may
prove impossible to find them. If you need more detailed
information, I can certainly refer you to an expert in this
field for further advice.'

'No, John, that won't be necessary, thanks.'

They chatted further, John telling her he was off to Mexico
for his annual summer break at the start of August, Lia
struggling to maintain a normal tone of voice as she said
she was waiting until October to take a break in order to
suit her publishing deadlines.

'What, no summer holiday?'

'No, not this year.'

John chuckled. 'So there really is work involved. We stuffy
suits envy the writer's life. I thought successful scribes could

debunk for the whole summer and lounge around sipping cocktails aboard Mediterranean yachts.'

Lia smiled for the first time that day. She'd recently had such an offer. One of her male admirers was spending a month on the Med and she'd been invited to join the cruise party, but she'd turned him down. She was busy, yes, and she certainly couldn't afford a month off. She could have gone for a week, though, and the idea of frolicking on a sunlit deck in her bikini with a chilled cocktail within easy reach was tempting. But not tempting enough to absent herself from Sadlier Square while Abby was over in Dublin. And certainly not after the bombshell Gary had dropped.

She finished the call and stared out at the hazy rain blurring her view of the park. Thirty days. Even with the minimum of information. One never knew, she sighed, just what exactly life was about to throw up. Sometimes it was just as well.

She cast her mind back to interviews she'd given, trying to recall any details she would have let slip about Alejandro. Had she actually mentioned Madrid? What exactly had she said about Loch Lomond? God. Maybe she should sift though her press cuttings and television recordings just to see what leads she might have unintentionally given.

After a while, she roused herself sufficiently to put in her contacts and swap her tracksuit for a long flared skirt and her favourite Chloe top. She had a one-thirty luncheon engagement with Clarissa, her editor, in a restaurant in Kensington. *Midday Execution,* the draft of which had sparked the row with Abby the previous Christmas, was about to go to print. Now the preliminary draft of Lia's eighth book in as many years, *Imperfect Murder,* was up for discussion.

It was the last thing she felt like doing, but Clarissa had just flown back from Japan and wanted to see Lia as soon as possible, so Lia phoned her usual cab company and at one o'clock promptly, all dressed up and ready to go in spite of her heavy heart, she emerged from the apartment block into the drizzly July day.

'Lia, is anything the matter?'

'No, everything's fine,' Lia said, beaming widely.

Clarissa flashed her a look of concern before going on to discuss the characters in *Imperfect Murder*.

'You know this is just brilliantly plotted,' she began. 'I think it's your best so far. I couldn't put it down, I had to keep turning the pages. The plot is riveting,' Clarissa enthused. 'However . . .' she paused.

Lia broke up slivers of salmon with her fork without putting any into her mouth and waited. In her early forties, Clarissa was a senior editor in Gaynor-Munro, the worldwide publishing giant who had taken a chance on the unknown Lia and had seen that chance pay off handsomely. Clarissa had worked in the industry since she was twenty, but had absolutely no aspirations herself in regard to novel-writing.

'What, are you joking?' she'd often declared. 'Slaving away in isolation for months, sometimes years, then to have your precious book damned with faint praise or comprehensively slated by some point-scoring reviewer, and that's after it manages to stand out above the hundred or so scripts we see each week? No, thanks. I can think of better ways of inflicting torture on myself.'

Neither had she any compunction about dissecting a novel in the most constructive way, her editorial guidance strictly aimed at bringing out the best. Now she smiled at Lia across the table and told her that she was concerned because one of her characters, a villain named Jacob, was more evil than evil itself.

'In terms of the chill factor, it ranks up there with Stephen King,' she said. 'But I'm concerned about the fact that he has absolutely no redeeming factors.'

'I guess he's just an out-and-out baddie,' Lia said blandly, finally abandoning her food and sipping her mineral water.

Clarissa shook her head good naturedly. 'Lia! Be charitable. Show some mitigating circumstances, no matter how small. Could you at least give Jacob a rotten childhood or a bully for a father? I don't think anyone could be as corrupt as he is without some degree of emotional deprivation.' Then Clarissa came to a halt and regarded her with such shrewd eyes that Lia felt uncomfortable.

'Lia?' she hesitated. 'Are you sure everything is all right?' Clarissa's blue eyes blazed with concern and Lia felt something crack inside her.

'Oh to hell with it, there *is* something bothering me,' she admitted, her voice a little choked. 'I don't think I'm really up to a proper analysis of the script. Not today.' It was useless to pretend any further, and Clarissa was the closest thing she had to a friend.

'Why the hell didn't you tell me? We could have postponed. On second thought, Lia, lunch time or no lunch time, we deserve a treat so I'm going to order us both a Bellini. How does that sound? We can just chat for a while – that is, if you feel like it?'

'Thanks, Clarissa, I'd love to have a chat.'

The crack that Lia had felt was like the start of a dam bursting. By the time she had finished outlining the proposal that *Lunchtime with Rachel* had put to Gary, Clarissa's eyes were full of empathy.

'Unfortunately, Lia,' she said gently, 'I know you value your privacy and it sucks to high heaven, but you can't prevent them from going ahead in their quest to look for your old boyfriend. You can, of course, refuse to have anything

to do with it. That's your prerogative. Has Gary informed
the programme researchers of your feelings?'

'I'm sure he has by now,' Lia said miserably.

'Problem is,' Clarissa said, 'in these days, individual wishes,
never mind any display of sensitivity, are totally disregarded
in the race for the mega-buck, never mind the optimum
ratings. Look at it this way – what's the worst thing that
could happen? Is it really so horrendous if they go ahead
and manage to trace the dashing Alejandro?'

'Thing is, Clarissa, there are a couple of problems with
that . . .' Lia went on to tell Clarissa exactly what she'd told
a twelve-year-old Abby when she'd brought her to Scotland.

'But I think that's a lovely, romantic story,' Clarissa smiled.
'And so very understandable. It has all the ingredients of a
fantasy novel. I know you hate the thoughts of your privacy
being invaded, but no one could take issue with you for
embroidering the truth, Lia. Your daughter certainly didn't.
If anything, you showed remarkable grit and determination
in bringing up your daughter alone. And your fantastic story
was all for her benefit.'

Lia sipped her cocktail, hoping the bolstering effects would
kick in sooner rather than later. She'd only told Clarissa half
the story, much as she'd told Abby all those years ago. But
the rest of it was bound to come out piece by agonising
piece if the programme researchers were successful in tracing
Alejandro's whereabouts.

She didn't care if her fans found out about her big white
lies. So what if there was consternation because Lia Lacey
had hoodwinked her adoring public with a real-life fairytale
surpassing some of her novels for sheer creativity? She could
rise above the hullabaloo.

But her daughter was another matter entirely.

Lia was glad when Clarissa signalled for fresh drinks,
saying that she wasn't in a rush back to Gaynor-Munro.

It was far more convivial to be out for the afternoon in a busy Kensington restaurant sipping Bellinis rather than sitting at her desk watching her coffee go cold and feeling that the elegant walls in Sadlier Square were closing around her, in much the same manner as the murky past. For one thing was becoming very clear to her and it was easier to turn it over in her mind while she was out in company, rather than being at home alone obsessing about it.

She couldn't sit back and wait for her secrets to unfold without giving Abby some kind of advance warning. Her daughter was thirty-two years of age. She wasn't a twelve-year-old child any more but a grown woman who'd been all around the world. Like it or not, Lia was going to have to tell her the cold, hard truth.

32

Abby tweaked her dark spikes into a softer shape around her head. Her Armani jeans were a tiny bit loose, so her slender waist was clinched with a big silvery belt. Her white crinkle shirt showed off her tan and you could see right through to her lacy plunge bra.

She hoped they'd end up in bed. She'd never been to bed with Sam. Now it seemed the best idea in the world, to hold someone so close again and be held in return. Even thinking about it made her feel dizzy and elated. She and Raffaele were over, finished. She'd moved on. She'd come home to start a whole new life.

With Sam.

He was late.

She knew that without looking at her watch, because she'd been conscious of the minutes ticking by as soon as it went seven o'clock. Everything was prepared. She'd spread some old photographs along the mantelpiece in the living room. She'd shopped in Tesco and bought a ready-to-cook lasagne and the makings of a salad because she was far too nervous to cook. She'd bought so much that she'd staggered out of the huge supermarket and had to get a taxi home. She'd even changed the sheets on her bed and added extra pillows.

When she finally heard his car draw up outside, she took a deep breath before opening the door.

'I'm late, Abby, sorry.' Sam bent to kiss her cheek. He smelled of toothpaste and aftershave, but what affected her most was the freshly laundered scent of his denim shirt. She wanted to bury her face in it. Before she had a chance to relax into his body, he straightened up and handed her a bottle of wine and a bouquet of fragrant, long-stemmed lilies. He was taking up so much space in her small hallway that her heart was racing.

'I hope you like lasagne,' she babbled, leading the way to the kitchen, feeling strange and slightly out of her depth in the dynamics of this cosy domestic scene with this new confident and mature Sam.

This suddenly sexy Sam.

'Mmm. Smells wonderful.'

'I have salad as well,' she prattled on, listing her menu in a jokey, sing-song voice. She turned around to find him staring at her. 'Hey, sit down.'

He grinned. 'I'm just trying to get used to you again. It seems mad that you're home.'

'I'm sure it does.' She was going to take it nice and easy, Abby had decided. She had a lot of making up to do. 'Would you prefer red or white wine?'

'Neither. I'll just have a mineral water, as I'm driving.'

'Okay,' she grinned. Hopefully he'd change his mind about going home before the night was over.

'Mark has booked his flights,' he said as they chatted over their meal. 'I really didn't think I'd see him home. I can't believe I managed to persuade him.'

Abby passed him the bowl of dressed salad. 'How long is it since you've seen him?'

'Earlier this year. We were in London for the BAFTA awards.'

'Why didn't you meet up with Mum? I'm sure she'd love to have seen you both. You could have contacted her through her website.'

'We were only over in London for a couple of nights.'

'Pity. So have you finalised the plans for the celebrations?'

'As soon as Mark gets over his jet lag, the partying will start. I've booked a table in the Four Seasons for the Saturday night, then it's on to a night club after that and taxi back out to my place in Malahide. I've enough room for everyone to stay over. I'm having Sunday lunch there, a barbeque, and inviting more friends and family – a very late, relaxing lunch, I hasten to add.'

'Just how big is your house?'

'Big enough.'

'I'm dying to see it.' Abby paused, hoping for an exclusive invitation. When Sam didn't reply, she helped herself to crunchy bread and went on. 'Sounds like the makings of a great weekend.'

After their meal, he helped her clear the plates. It seemed so natural to be moving around the familiarity of the kitchen with him that it gladdened her heart. She took a bowl of fresh fruit and a carton of cream out of the fridge.

'No, thanks,' he said, 'I'll just stick to the coffee. I don't intend to delay you much longer.'

'Delay? You're not delaying me, Sam. Anything but.' Her hands shook a little as she replaced the fruit and cream and busied herself with the coffee.

'I want to talk to you about something,' he said. 'Tell me first, though, what are your plans? Are you just home for a couple of weeks?'

'A couple of weeks? No, Sam, I'm home for good.' She swung around to face him and her voice trailed away at the flicker of surprise in his eyes.

'I thought you were well and truly settled in Sorrento and that you loved your job,' he said.

'I thought it was time to move on.' At least that was the truth.

'How did you manage to end up there in the first place?'

'End up there?' Her hands gripped the coffeepot and she frantically wondered how much she could safely explain to justify her job to Sam. 'It was funny, really,' she began. 'Do you believe in serendipity?'

'Dunno. It all depends.'

Abby brought the coffee over to the table and sat down. 'You see, I was visiting Sorrento,' she said slowly, picking her words carefully and lacing her fingers around her mug. 'I went to have a look at the San Francesco Cloisters. I'd heard that the venue was used for weddings and was supposed to be beautiful. It *was* beautiful. There was a wedding taking place that day, so I hung around soaking it all up – it seemed so perfect and lovely, the clothes, music and flowers, the whole atmosphere. I started chatting to the wedding planner. She was English and moving on to Rome in a couple of weeks. They hadn't yet found a replacement for her, and her apartment would also be vacant. It all fell into place so neatly that it seemed to be the right thing to do,' Abby shrugged.

'I see.' Sam threw her an odd glance.

'After your visit . . .' Abby hesitated.

'After my visit – what?'

'I kind of realised I was living in a fantasy land. I mean, I think marriage is great and all that—'

'That's a change.'

'And mostly the brides were fine, but I began to realise that my job was meaningless. By and large, I was spending my time sorting out silly little problems that had nothing to do with the precious vows people were exchanging.'

'Precious vows?'

Abby met his startled glance and stretched her hand across the table to connect with his. 'I've changed, Sam,' she said resolutely. 'I missed you after you left. I kept thinking of us, and what we had, how much you meant to me. I'm truly sorry I hurt you the way I did.'

'Hurt?' Sam's glance was rueful. 'I don't think you've any idea of just how cut up I was at the time. But I got over it. Anyway, it's long past now, and there's something I need to tell you.'

'Believe me, I do have an idea,' she insisted. 'And I want to make it up with you.'

'Consider us friends again,' he said.

'Can we kiss and make up?'

'Well, if it makes you happy.'

In a flash, she was up and darting around the far side of the table. She stood behind Sam's chair and wound her arms around his neck. She nuzzled into him, inhaling his scent. Her lips were close to his face and she hesitated before kissing the side of his mouth. She was hoping he'd turn to face her, that he'd pull her into his lap and kiss her properly, opening her mouth with his, kissing her slowly and deeply in a way he'd never kissed her before. She squeezed her eyes shut and felt her lips brush the side of his mouth again, but to her disappointment, he didn't follow through.

Instead, he peeled her arms away from his neck and sat up straighter in his chair.

'Abby? What's this?'

She opened her eyes and stared into his. 'I told you, I want us to kiss and make up. Properly.'

'Consider it done, Abby.'

'I don't think you understand. It was only after you left that I began to realise how much you mean to me.'

'Abby, slow down.' He rose from his chair, giving her little option but to step back.

'No, listen to me.' Abby moved forward, threw her arms around him and nuzzled into his chest. 'I want to make up for everything,' she said, her voice distorted against the fabric of his shirt. 'I need you, Sam.'

'*Need* me?' He held her at arm's length. 'Since when has Abby Lacey ever needed anyone?'

'I know you find it hard to believe, but there's no reason why it can't be Sam and Abby back together. For good this time.'

'Abby, there's every reason why we can't be together. I'm not the guy I was eight years ago. I've done a helluva lot of growing up since then.'

'So have I.' She smiled her brightest smile. 'Surely you realise that I came home because of you?'

'Don't say things like that to me.'

He sounded cross. He just didn't understand. 'But it's true.' She gave him another dazzling smile. 'I never really appreciated what we had at the time, how much you loved me. Sam, you asked me to marry you *twice!* I must have been a right fool to walk away from all of that.'

'You weren't a fool. You were following your dream.'

'Maybe I got tired of gadding about. After you left me in Sorrento I kept thinking of you, thinking of the way we used to be together.'

He carefully extricated himself from her arms. 'Hey, Abby, pet, let's take a breather and slow this down. I guess you're looking at me through a soft-focus lens or something. I'm not the person I was.'

'No, you're even more fantastic than I remember.'

Sam laughed gently. 'Definitely the soft-focus lens!'

'I'm just seeing you in a new light,' she smiled, fidgeting with the buttons on her shirt. 'Remember, you asked me to do that years ago?'

Sam fell silent.

She put her head to one side and looked at him through her eyelashes. 'I think I've said enough for now,' she said softly. 'It'll take time for you to absorb everything. I know it must come as a surprise.'

'Abby, look, when you've settled down a bit and taken off the rose-coloured glasses, you'll ask yourself what the hell you saw in me and you'll know that you were right all those years ago to turn me down.'

She shook her head. 'I don't think so.'

'Listen, you and I were – are – good mates. But surely you know that that's as far as it will ever go between us? It wouldn't be fair of me to pretend otherwise.'

'I don't blame you for talking like that. I'd be talking like that too if you'd broken my heart the way I broke yours.'

'Abby, I'm not the guy who asked you to marry him. That guy took his head out of the sand and grew up a long time ago. This is a different me to the one you left behind.'

He seemed a little impatient and her heart faltered. 'Of course you're different. We're all older and wiser, for a start. You've been hurt, I've been hurt, but we can move on, us, together.'

'Who hurt you, Abby?'

How had she let that slip? 'Oh, you know,' she said shakily, avoiding his gaze. 'I guess we all get a little bruised along the way.'

Sam was silent for a long moment. And then he reached out and she went into his arms. She closed her eyes and absorbed the security of those arms around her, the familiar way her head fit into the curve of his neck, the muffled thud of his heartbeat.

Sam was talking and she heard him as if in a daze. 'I'm very fond of you, Abby, I always have been. I'm your friend and that will never change.'

He was talking about friendship. *Best mates*, he'd said to her. Then in the next breath, *Surely you know that I love you* . . .

'I'm sorry if you were bruised along the way,' he went on. 'I don't want to see you hurt or unhappy. But there's no going back for you and me. There'll be other boyfriends for you, Abby.'

After a while, she heard him say that he had to leave. She felt cold as he gently disentangled her arms. He asked her if she was okay and she mutely nodded her head. He asked her if she understood what he was saying and she nodded her head again. She felt his kiss on her forehead but was afraid to ask why he was avoiding her mouth. She saw him picking up his mobile and car keys and giving her a warm smile.

She followed him to the door and watched him jump into his car, checking the rear window as he reversed down the driveway, and wished she was going with him instead of being alone in the emptiness of the house. She stood and waved him off and the bright July evening, warm and mellow in lingering sunshine, was a total contradiction to how she felt inside.

33

'The way it is, Kate,' Paula said coolly on Tuesday morning, 'I've been reconsidering my initiative to engage with Gleeson-McMahon as prospective clients. I've come to the conclusion . . .' she searched around for inspiration, conscious that she sounded a little ridiculous, but tried to bury her dismal failure under a fudge of complex explanation, 'that, ah, the culture of their organisation is incompatible with the ethos of Stevens. Irrespective of what problem-solving approach we might take as regards their people solutions, it represents a challenge I'm unwilling to commit to at the moment.'

Kate was silent for a minute, then asked, 'Have you heard from them yet?'

'I have. They want to discuss a few issues with me in further detail.'

Paula's face reddened a little at the outright lie. Hopefully Kate hadn't copped it and had swallowed Paula's rather convoluted and gobbledegook fabrication. The stiff, formal note she'd received from her trio of investment bankers conveying a negative response to her pitch was now shredded into an unidentifiable mass of recyclable paper. She'd just had time to straighten her Dior jacket, pull herself together and compose a suitable explanation to offer Kate to cover up her abysmal failure before Kate arrived in with her ten-thirty coffee.

'Do you want me to draft a reply?' Kate offered.

'Not at all, I'll look after that myself,' Paula said casually, sitting back in her chair, much as though she wasn't going to bother Kate with such trivial concerns.

That's all it was, she told herself. A triviality. A lucky escape. Not, as she'd first viewed it, an abysmal failure, which compounded all her abysmal failures to date.

'How are we fixed for holiday cover this week?' she asked, straightening in her seat as the spectre of Ms Madeline Jones resurfaced on the horizon.

'Emer's on leave and her work has been reassigned among the rest of her team. She'll be back before Audrey takes her holidays. You know I'll be away the last two weeks in August?'

'Yes, remind me again about ten days beforehand so we can discuss, won't you?'

'How about yourself, Paula? Are you taking a break?'

'I've nothing planned right now, so I'll probably wait until September.'

She needed to get away from it all, Paula decided as Kate left her office. She hadn't had a break since her shopping blitz in New York the previous February. Suddenly restless, she rose from her desk and marched across to the window, staring out at the Dublin summer sunshine and the grey sprawl of the city below her. A few days' break in August suddenly sounded like heaven. So what if she missed this marvellous so-called reunion? She couldn't sit in the same room as Abby and Sam together without feeling nauseous.

Her head still throbbed with the sight of Abby in Sam's arms the previous Saturday night, although from what Elaine had said the following morning, things hadn't gone quite the way Abby had expected. Elaine had brought orange juice into Paula's room and had sat on the bed, chatting cheerfully about the night before she headed home to Wicklow. In spite of being groggy from the effects of her sleeping pill, Paula had felt a tiny lift, but she told herself that the more distance she put between herself and Sam and Abby, the better.

She wasn't going to put herself through an eternity of torture every time she thought of them together, no matter how innocent Sam declared it to be. Even though a little voice insisted that Sam was different, she dismissed it.

For she'd been there already. She'd played the role of the other woman and had ended up with her life in smithereens, and her self-esteem and self-respect at zilch. It had been a long, hard climb back out of that abyss, and a place she was determined never to revisit.

Later that evening, in the emptiness of her apartment, she sat watching *Clueless*. She'd made a supreme effort to stay off the wine for once and was sipping fruit juice when her doorbell buzzed.

'Hi, Paula.' Sam's voice came through the intercom.

'Yes?'

'I need to see you, to talk. Please.'

'Come up,' she said, activating the door release, needing to see him in spite of everything, wanting to give him every chance to put things right between them.

In the few minutes that it took Sam to take the lift up to the top floor, she dived around the apartment, straightening cushions, locking the closet door on her guilty collection of empty bottles and – *thank you, God* – remembering to flick off her DVD and stabbing the remote control just in the nick of time. Then she flew into her bedroom and sprayed herself with Elizabeth Arden perfume. A frenzied glance in the mirror – no time to change, but she looked fine in her blue shift dress – and she whipped out her clasp and let her pale blonde hair flow freely around her shoulders.

Ah yes, Paula decided angrily, she might have spent the last three years focused on her career, determined to deny her emotions, but some things never change. Behind it all, where men were concerned she was weak-willed and spineless, and where Sam was concerned, full of a hopeless, helpless, treacherous rush of desire. The sight of him filling her doorway, charcoal suit, tie removed, white shirt opened at the neck, sent her senses reeling.

'Hi,' he smiled, crooking an eyebrow and looking bashful and slightly unsure of her reaction. It made him all the more endearing. It was ten long nights since he'd slept with her. She knew because she'd counted every single one.

'Hi.'

'We need to talk,' he said, following her into the living room.

'We certainly do,' she said smartly. Then in an effort to remember her manners, 'Would you like coffee? Mineral water? Wine?'

'Just water, thanks.'

She went into her kitchen, opened the fridge and poured him a glass of water. When she returned to her living area he'd taken off his jacket and was sitting on the sofa. She sat opposite him and waited, struggling to look cool and calm.

Then Sam's eye was caught by something on her television screen and he frowned and cocked his head to one side as if to make sense of what he was viewing. It was only then that Paula became aware of the running commentary.

'. . . and the male of the species hunts down the female, lunging behind her in a typically predatory fashion, before preparing to inseminate her with . . .'

She threw a startled glace at the screen just in time to see two King Kong lookalikes copulating furiously.

'Paula! Is the mating habits of . . .' Sam turned his head the other way as he examined the screen, 'giant apes your normal television viewing?' He grinned with such friendly amusement that her heart flipped. She grabbed the remote control and put the television on standby.

'Right, Sam, you wanted to talk?'

'Yes, I saw Abby last night, and—'

'I hope you set her straight.'

He shook his head. 'I tried. Thing is, she wasn't taking it in.'

'You mean you weren't clear enough,' Paula said sarcastically. 'Did you tell her you were seeing me?'

'No, not exactly.'

She felt a stab of disappointment. 'In other words,' she drawled, 'you chickened out.'

'You didn't want to tell Elaine that we were seeing each other.'

'That was different,' she said. 'I was only getting to know you and my sister would have had me engaged, married and pregnant all in the one breath. She'd be analysing every little detail I might let drop in order to extract the maximum romantic factor.'

'And you had a problem with that?' He gave her a long, thoughtful look that she didn't want to analyse too closely.

When she didn't reply, he said, 'She'll find out soon enough when I tell Abby.'

'When, or if?' she asked tartly. 'I can't understand why you're allowing her to harbour false illusions. If they *are* false illusions.'

'Paula, the reason I didn't get around to telling Abby about us is because I think she's cut up about something.'

Her face felt tight. 'And you'd know, of course.'

'I've known Abby since she was about five. I've seen her though all sorts of ups and downs. Something has obviously gone wrong in her life and she has the absurd idea that we can go back to the way we were, which is totally crazy. And she'd know that if she was thinking clearly.'

From the sound of his voice and the expression on his face, it was all too easy to believe him. But Paula couldn't afford to listen to her heart. Not after the stupid mistake she'd made the last time. Then Sam's mobile beeped.

'Excuse me a minute.' He rummaged in his jacket pocket and took it out. He read the text message and threw Paula a rueful grin.

'Abby?' She silently acknowledged Abby Lacey's impeccable timing.

'Just saying thanks for last night. And don't look at me like that,' he said tersely. 'Nothing happened.' He put the phone back in his pocket without replying.

'This is all very moving,' she said, heedless of the honesty in his face. 'But you're putting your ex-girlfriend's needs before mine. You seem to have a big blind spot where she's concerned.'

'We're just friends,' he said evenly. 'I don't want her having any illusions any more than you do. I'll tell her about us when she's a little less needy and more settled. Okay?' He stood up and moved across, sitting on the arm of her chair, his fingers caressing the nape of her neck.

Paula closed her eyes and tried not to relax into the mesmeric touch of his fingers.

'Trust me,' he went on. 'You're very special. I want it to be right. And you're strong and resilient, whereas Abby . . .'

Strong? She didn't feel strong. She felt weak with need and longing and a little green thing called jealousy. It had been a mistake to allow him up, considering the way her body felt hollow with a raw, aching desire at just the sight of him and the sound of his voice.

'Right now Abby seems troubled. She hasn't got a decent job, never mind being at the helm of a successful company with cutting-edge staff and a high-class portfolio,' he was saying.

'And that makes it all right for you to juggle the two of us?' Her voice was acerbic as she twisted out of his grasp.

Why, oh why, did Stevens seem to define her whole way of living?

'You don't trust me, huh?'

'Why should I?' she snapped. She held his gaze and wrapped her arms across her chest, holding herself together. She ignored the vulnerable look in his face. 'You can't tell your ex-girlfriend about us. Could be you were only biding your time before she came home. Maybe,' she went on hotly, 'you were just getting in some practice.'

Sam stared at her for several moments. 'Ouch. You know how to hit low, don't you? I could take great offence at that remark.'

'You did tell me at the start that you were only interested in a few fun things. Isn't that right?'

'You're taking my comments out of context. I didn't want to scare you off. I've never met anyone like you before. I can't stop thinking about you, wanting you, desiring you . . .' he paused. 'I'm just asking you to be patient for a little while.'

She stood up. 'Go home,' she snapped. 'I've heard all that before, or should I say I was taken in by that kind of crap talk already and I'd rather walk away from it right now.'

'Paula, listen—'

'Are you listening to me? Because I'm asking you – no, *telling* you – to leave.'

They glared at each other. Then Sam stood up and picked up his jacket. 'If you're going to be so damned obtuse, I guess there isn't anything else I can say.'

'No, there isn't.'

He strode through the doorway to the hallway beyond without a backward glance. Then she heard the main door open and close. She bit down hard on her knuckle to stifle her cry. Agonising as it was, she was right to send him packing.

She moved jerkily across to her bookcase. She reached

for her book of poetry, for the small photograph that acted as her reminder, her talisman, the prompt that strengthened her resolve not to venture down that same old slippery slope.

For the man she'd been photographed with on the beach had taught her than men could lie with loving eyes and be masters of delusion. They could promise the sun, moon and stars with caressing hands and softly-spoken endearments. And clever Paula, of the shiny gold stars and glittering qualifications, could be taken in all too easily with false promises and illusions. She'd been so ashamed of herself that she'd never even confided in Elaine. It had been impossible to admit how foolish she'd been, even to her sister.

Paula was still staring at the image of the couple together, feeling empty and lost, when she was encircled from behind in a pair of warm arms, and the photo was plucked from her trembling fingers.

'Would you care to tell me about him, Paula?' Sam murmured.

34

There was no escaping the solid heat of his chest, for he was anchoring her securely to him. She twisted her head sideways and looked up at him, and her breath stopped at the expression in his eyes.

'I thought you were gone,' she said.

'I got as far as opening the hall door, but I couldn't go through,' he said. He dipped his head and nuzzled the side of her neck, brushing a tender kiss on her ear and another one on the side of her hot face. 'And now I'm rather glad I came back.'

'Why did you come back?'

'Something you said took a little while to register properly. Something about being taken in? I only heard the words "crap talk" at first and was so insulted that I failed to understand the full sense of what you said. So are you going to tell me what exactly happened that makes you so determined not to trust me?'

He guided her over to the sofa and held her close.

'I wasn't clear enough earlier,' he murmured. 'I didn't tell you that the day I called into your office, I thought I was just catching up on old times. Little did I know that Ms Paula Stevens was going to blow me right out of the water with her five-year plans and regal blue eyes and those ridiculous stilts she likes to wear.' His voice softened further. 'Although I like them too, the spiky heels, 'cos it means she has to hang onto me and stop pretending to be in charge of everything. You can't deny that there's something big happening between us.' His fingers traced her mouth. 'I want to give it a chance to grow. I don't want anything or anyone to mess it up, certainly not someone who means nothing to me beyond an old friendship. So will you tell me why you can't take me on trust?'

She hesitated.

'Maybe if I tell you first about Abby and me, would that help?'

'It depends on what you're going to say,' she said. *Please God, don't tell me you slept with her. I couldn't bear that.*

'Thing is, Paula, when I asked her to marry me I was young and foolish, and I found it hard to be rejected,' Sam told her. 'When I finally accepted it was over, it was a relief. To be honest, my ego was dented far more than my heart. Then I was angry with all the time I'd wasted running after her. In the end, it was Mark who sorted me out.'

'Mark?'

'Yeah. I went over to visit him in the States and spilled my guts one night over a few too many beers. The next day he brought me into his music studio and told me to wake up and get a new life, which thankfully I did.' Sam smiled self-deprecatingly. 'That's how I became more involved in music. By the time I came home from the States, Abby was history as far as I was concerned. I went on to have other relationships that fizzled out. And when I saw Abby in Italy, it was like catching up with a favourite, long-lost sister. I thought I was in love with her all those years ago, but looking back, it was equally as much a pig-headed ego trip on my part, trying to persuade her to stay. And I outgrew all of that a long time ago.'

'Pig-headed,' she smiled shakily. 'You said it first, Sam Ryan.'

Then she told him. Sitting on the sofa, in jerky sentences

and skimming over the sordid details, Paula told Sam about her affair, feeling a huge relief as she unburdened herself. It had lasted two long years, two years during which Paula had foolishly hung onto his every deceitful promise and stupidly believed every silken murmur from his treacherous lips in order to pacify her guilty conscience.

They'd met at a Christmas party in a large midlands hotel. The glittering function room was hot, packed and noisy, and the staff of the Dublin branch of the European recruitment agency where Paula held the position of chief business analyst were seated at a large, raucous, balloon-filled table right on the edge of the dance floor. There was a generous tab at the bar located just outside the function room that more than made up for the conveyor-belt meal being delayed. And for Paula, it helped to ease the sight of Richard Davis, the new guy heading up the IT department, making moves on Audrey Cronin, Paula's best friend and colleague.

At thirty-three, Paula had had a few relationships, but nothing lasting. She'd been attracted to Richard from the day he'd started and had hoped that the party might bring them together. Instead, it seemed that Audrey was moving in for the kill.

When Paula turned around from the bar having fetched her fourth – or was it her fifth? – vodka of the evening, she was already a little shaky on her gold Manolo Blahniks and a strong arm reached out to steady her, lifting her glass from her quivery fingers and setting it safely back on the bar. She looked up, straight into a pair of roguish blue eyes.

'Can't have you coming to grief so near the festive spirit,' he said in a warm Galway voice. 'You might not enjoy your plum pudding.'

'Oh, I always enjoy my pudding,' she said, suddenly emboldened as a result of all those vodkas on an empty stomach. His eyes looked her up and down, taking in her

silky black dress. Perfect bedroom eyes, she thought, eyes
that sparked with admiration, desire and hungry need. An
answering need that suddenly and recklessly swelled inside
her. It had as much to do with the look in his eyes and the
loneliness of the oncoming festive period as the sight of
Richard and Audrey laughing and chatting with their heads
close together.

She glanced at his strong wrist holding her hand captive
and he immediately released it, making her feel suddenly at
a loss. The party noise coming from the function room
unfurled like tidal waves around them and reminded Paula
just exactly where she was. 'I'd better go inside and join my
group, Mr . . . ?' she said.

'Alan,' he said. 'Alan Brady.' He lifted her hand again,
turned it over and planted a kiss on the delicate inside of
her wrist, setting her skin on fire. Then he handed her the
glass of vodka. 'Well, off you go, you pretty thing, into party
heaven.'

It might have all ended there, she agonised afterwards.
It could so easily have been nipped in the bud, finished
before it had begun and over before her heart had been
dragged through an internal combustion process that had
damaged it forever. Instead, she'd hesitated and lived to
regret her next few words as she'd twisted a strand of her
shoulder-length blonde hair, nodded her head in the
direction of the function room and asked, 'Aren't you going
inside?'

He laughed, his eyes wide with amusement, the fine lines
fanning from the corners telling her that he was a few years
older than her thirty-three. She noticed the slight sprinkling
of grey in his thick black hair. In his gloss of relaxed maturity,
his admiration seemed all the more heady.

'You couldn't drag me into that den of iniquity for
anything,' he said. 'What's the betting half your colleagues

will be rat-arsed before the food arrives, and I bet there'll be plenty of red faces on Monday back at the office, for God knows who'll smooch who between the mains and the dessert. And God knows,' his blue eyes flickered like a live electric cable, 'who'll sleep with who tonight.'

She took a sip of her drink and looked at him over her glass. 'Yes, who knows?'

She turned and went back to the party, feeling his keen glance following her as she threaded through the crowds. Audrey and Richard were engrossed in each other and oblivious to everyone else. She tried to guess whose bedroom they'd use, for that's where they were surely headed. Her starter tasted like sawdust, and even the ever-flowing wine failed to make her roast turkey and ham go down any easier. She told Audrey she was passing on dessert, fetched her bag and went back out to the bar.

He was still waiting and he laughed triumphantly when she saw her approach. He came up to her room, kissing her hungrily as he threaded one hand in her hair and slid down the zipper of her dress with the other. He stayed the night and it was by far the most frantic sex she'd ever had, born of an indefinable hunger inside her. It was also the start of a two-year affair that elevated her to the heights and plunged her down on the rocks of despair.

For Alan Brady omitted to tell her he was married until she was well and truly ensnared by the touch of his hands, and well and truly ready to believe him when he said he was married in name only, that he and his wife were just friends and it was only a matter of time before he left her.

'We were far too young when we got married. She was pregnant. I didn't really know what I was doing,' he'd admitted, his blue eyes contrite as he held her close in bed and stroked tantalising fingers around her aching nipples. 'I'd no idea what passion really meant until I met you.'

They had frantic weekends away in remote luxury hotels, all-night sex in her apartment, steamy holiday breaks in Ibiza and Paris. In between, though, Paula had spent many a lonely night with just a bottle of wine and a DVD for company, waiting for the day that Alan would be hers alone.

Back at the office, she worked harder and harder, developing a reputation for taking no prisoners. Audrey and Richard had a whirlwind romance and became engaged. Meanwhile, Alan promised marriage, children and happily every after, all in good time.

'As soon as the kids are old enough, I'll be out of there,' he said, pushing her back against the pillows in a Paris hotel where he was supposed to be on a business trip. 'Soon we'll be together, just the two of us.'

She hung by a thread to his promises, wanting to believe them, the sex between them roughly physical and far too addictive. She was unwilling to face the truth, to countenance how foolishly she was behaving, or how readily she'd been deceived. They'd spent what turned out to be their last weekend together in the hills of Donegal, where he'd taken the final photograph of the two of them on the beach.

'So what happened in the end?' Sam asked when she was finished sketching out the bare details, sitting on the sofa wrapped in his arms.

'We were in Donegal,' she said. 'He'd told his wife he was at a conference. Maybe she suspected something, I dunno. He was always very careful, even insisting on booking us into separate rooms. Probably afraid she might find his hotel bills or be checking on him or whatever. We'd gone to the beach in my car, I was driving, and when we returned to the hotel car park, he went in ahead of me as I was changing into my heels.'

Sam's mouth curved in such a fond, indulgent smile that Paula bit her lip.

'He was a few yards ahead of me as I went into the hotel, and who was waiting in the foyer only surprise, surprise, his heavily-pregnant wife. *And* his two children. They weren't the practically grown-up kids I'd been led to expect. They must have been about five or six. She threw her arms around him and the children were excited and calling him Daddy.' Paula's voice caught. 'And as I walked across the foyer, he looked right through me as though I didn't exist. I headed straight for the lift, got up to my room somehow, went home the following day and refused to take his calls. So it all ended in tears – my tears. I'll never forget how low I was, how much I hated myself. Afterwards, I moved across town to a new apartment, resigned my position, lost touch with Audrey and poured all my energies into Stevens in an attempt to move on and regain some self-respect.'

'So were you in love with him?'

Paula sighed. 'No. I thought I was, but it was just sex, really.'

Sam looked startled. 'Just sex?'

'Meaningless sex,' Paula sighed. 'I think I was swept away by the illicit excitement of it all.'

'Excitement, huh? So that's what you're really after?' he teased and flicked her chin. 'I knew there was another Paula Stevens in there somewhere. We'll have to see about that. So go on, tell me more.'

'It was the first time in my life – the only time – that I stepped out of line,' she said. 'Even the guilt seemed scarily different. But the relationship was empty of real feelings, not like—' she paused.

'Not like?' he prompted.

'Nothing like you,' she whispered. In response, his arms tightened around her. 'I just felt incredibly hurt and stupid afterwards. You've no idea how angry I felt with myself. I couldn't believe how badly I'd behaved, continuing to have sex with him after I discovered he was married. I couldn't understand how much I'd fallen for his lying words. My self-esteem was at an all-time low and I was fully to blame.'

'Paula, give over,' he said, brushing her hair away from her face. 'You're human, just like the rest of us. You took him at his word and you're scarcely to blame for that. If anyone was the villain of the piece, it was him. Sounds to me like you were angrier with your own behaviour than losing him.'

'I never even told Elaine the sordid story,' Paula went on. 'She knew there was someone in my life, but I felt so guilty that I pretended it was just casual. She's always looked up to me as her big sis and I couldn't bring myself to admit that I couldn't break free of him, even though I knew he was married. I didn't want to break free because I stupidly trusted him. I think I trusted him as a way of condoning my own behaviour. It was hard to admit that I'd got it so terribly wrong. After Alan, I felt I couldn't risk losing my head again, never mind my heart. So you see, that's why with Abby back on the scene I'd rather give you up completely than share you with anyone. And I don't do empty promises or illusions any more. Once down that crazy road was more than enough.'

Sam was silent. After a while he said, 'I'm really sorry for what happened. That bastard had no right to treat you like that, never mind his poor wife. At least you escaped from his clutches. But supposing I'd said that after Abby? That because of one bad experience, women were out of the picture?'

'Yes, but how would you feel if Alan was back on the scene again?' she countered, 'throwing his arms around me?'

'Come on, Paula, there's a world of a difference here,' he said. 'I never slept with Abby.'

Thank you, God.

'She's an old friend going back years, practically a sister

to me and she seems to be in a spot of bother right now. Whereas you had a two-year relationship that was all about sex.' His thumb gently traced the outline of her face as he said, 'I could feel insanely jealous, you know, but as far as I'm concerned, you and I are in a world apart from both of them. You're different. This is different. I've told you how I feel about you, Paula, and I meant every word, even,' he smiled, 'if you are a sex maniac with a preference for baths and hot tubs. I'm not complaining. I trust you. But can't you trust me? Even a little?'

Paula wavered. Her relationship with Alan had been an addictive, empty excitement. Being with Sam in the ordinary moments, laughing with him, exchanging smiles, sharing silly jokes, heartfelt beliefs and values, as well as being entwined with him in those deeply passionate moments, had brought warmth, colour and intensity to her life. He was tender, funny and thoughtful, as well as highly sensual. From the start, she'd sensed his honesty and common decency. A decency that was now compelling him to let his old girlfriend down as gently as possible. He could easily have been in Abby's arms tonight – even in her bed, she didn't doubt – but he'd chosen to come to her.

The rest was up to her.

Paula sighed and felt something yielding inside her. She reached across to clasp Sam's face between her hands, leaned over and kissed him.

August

Positano
Panorama Notturno

35

Lia flicked over her desk calendar and paused.

August. Already. It was here.

For this month, the calendar Abby had given her displayed a picture of Positano by night. The small village clinging valiantly to the sides of the sheer rugged cliff was all lit up. There were terraces upon terraces of yellow and gold shiny boxes, tinselly squares of houses tumbling like gaily wrapped presents under a Christmas tree, a symphony of bright, twinkling lights, held in the keeping of the slumbering, velvety folds of the midnight-blue mountain. The adjacent seashore was lit up with reflected light, and further beyond, the darkened ocean lapped quietly away to the hazy horizon.

Even given the choice camera angle and the possible application of airbrushing techniques, the scene was incredibly beautiful.

Then Lia frowned. She stared out the sash window onto Sadlier Square, where soft morning sunlight dappled the trees. She had the same niggling feeling in her head when her plot lines subconsciously knitted together. Guided by a strange instinct, she switched on her laptop and went into her documents, opening the folder labelled Abby's Adventures.

From the time Abby had set off to travel the world, she'd kept in touch via email. In all that time, Lia had carefully saved her daughter's pithy, frank, beautifully descriptive and downright funny accounts of her travels, the friends she had made and places she'd seen. At the back of her mind, Lia had always intended that one day she would print off hard copies, organise them into a file and give them to Abby as a keepsake of all that she'd done and seen.

Scrolling through them now and dipping into some of them, Lia was struck afresh at the quality of Abby's writing. Whether she was describing the sapphire blue Australian sky, begging children in Malaysia or the awesome strength of the Pacific Ocean, the words surged into life. Some of her descriptions were lavishly adorned and over-the-top, but no matter, Abby was clearly writing from her heart.

She'd emailed from Positano the previous November.

Lia had just arrived in Melbourne, Australia. She remembered how exhausted she'd been when she'd finally reached her hotel. A security alert at Perth airport had delayed her departing flight by hours. When she eventually got to her hotel room, she'd just given a cursory check to her emails, registering the fact that Abby had left South Africa and was now in Italy.

She remembered thinking that it was an unusual step for Abby, but she'd been far too fuddled at the time to give it much thought.

Now, months later, on a bright August morning, Lia opened the email.

'I'm here in a little village called Positano,' Abby had written. 'Not sure how long I'll be staying, I'll let you know.'

The email was abrupt and to the point, and quite devoid of all the little nuggets and observances that Abby usually imparted. And no mention whatsoever of the spectacular beauty of her surroundings. Lia looked at the scene on her calendar again. Given the magnificent, dramatic coastline, it was quite amazing that Abby had made no reference to it whatsoever. Not only amazing, but now, in retrospect, rather puzzling.

There had been no word from her for another three

weeks, by which time a jet-lagged Lia, tired out from a whirl of launches, charity benefits and cocktail parties, had arrived in Wellington, New Zealand. Abby's next email had taken her by complete surprise. Her daughter had announced that she was working as a wedding planner in Sorrento. She included descriptions of the Bay of Naples and the warren of busy, cobble-locked streets that crisscrossed the town. Then after that she'd arrived in London for Christmas, looking as though the bottom had dropped out of her world.

And just a few weeks ago she'd returned home to Dublin in a surprise move that had shaken Lia. Since then, Abby's emails and phone calls had been bright and breezy and full of gossip about Sam and Elaine. The one positive thing to come out of all this was that her daughter had sounded as though she was restored to her old bright and breezy self, so whatever or whoever had upset her, she had clearly bounced back.

It was just as well, and just in the nick of time, Lia sighed.

For her anxieties regarding emails and phone calls about the goings-on in Dublin as well as party preparations and reunion talks had paled into insignificance compared to the threat of her past life being revealed to serve as tacky television fodder for all and sundry. Of far greater concern, however, was the effect the revelations would have on Abby.

Only the previous day, Gary had told her that the *Lunchtime with Rachel* researchers intended to go ahead with their search for Alejandro, contrary to Lia's wishes.

'Naturally they'd prefer to have you on board,' he said.

'I want nothing at all to do with it,' she snapped. 'It's a gross invasion of my privacy.'

'Unfortunately, Lia, once you're in the public eye, you become public property. I've voiced your objections, but they're hoping you'll change your mind. And I'd better warn you, they might try to contact Abby directly.'

'Good God.'

'There's very little I can do to stop this voracious publicity machine,' Gary said. He sounded suitably chastened, Lia acknowledged. He might just manage to hang onto his job. 'If you like, I'll keep in contact with those involved, ostensibly in case you change your mind, but in reality to keep you updated with their progress.'

'My spy, in other words. You know, Gary, if you really want to earn your stripes, I could feed you with some false information to throw them off the scent. How about that?'

Gary laughed. 'If it's any consolation, without your cooperation the project will prove more difficult and costly for them. It'll also be time-consuming having to trawl through archives to glean the basic information that you could readily supply in a brief phone call.'

'That's some relief, I suppose.'

'Make no mistake though, Lia. They sound determined to bring this to a conclusion. If there's anything on your website you'd rather they didn't see, it might be an idea to have it removed.'

'No, I've already checked that out,' Lia said soberly. 'There's not much background info on that.'

'Okay. In the meantime, the best thing you can do is ignore the whole thing, keep on writing and know that I'll keep on top of developments.'

Keep on writing? She'd scarcely written a word since Gary had dropped his bombshell. The best thing she could do, Lia suddenly decided as she sat at her desk on that August morning, was to get Abby over to London as soon as possible. Now that she seemed restored to her normal self and was back amongst her lifelong friends, Abby should be well able to take the truth about her father. No matter if

Lia was terrified of her reaction – the sooner Abby was informed, the better. And neither was there any time to waste, with the prospect of enthusiastic researchers contacting her innocent, oblivious daughter hanging over Lia's head like the sword of Damocles.

Abby wasn't working yet, and from what Lia had gathered, the infamous reunion was planned for later in the month, so there was no reason why she couldn't book return flights for Abby for the coming weekend as a welcome home surprise.

She logged onto the internet and reached for her phone.

On Thursday morning, Paula flicked over the pages of the August edition of *Business Tomorrow* and her stomach knotted.

The photographs were sexy. What was it that sex and titillation had to be used as a commodity to sell everything these days? There was one of her sitting on the edge of her desk, legs crossed and skirt practically up to her thighs. The framed scrolls on the wall in the background looked contradictory. Unless, of course, you fancied that they boasted her qualifications in the area of carnal delights. When the photographer had emailed the contact sheets across, she'd been too busy examining her facial expression to notice her skirt. Otherwise she certainly would have asked him to delete that particular shot.

The main photograph in the article, taken on her balcony, depicted a sultry Ms Stevens between her pouting lips and the expression in her eyes. She had Sam to thank for that. Then as Paula read the text and absorbed the theme of the article, the warm fuzzy haze she'd been enveloped in since the previous night swiftly evaporated.

For the sexy photos were one thing, but the article was something else entirely.

Under the title of 'Women doing it for themselves', subtitled 'Paula Stevens – the new breed of twenty-first-century woman', the article painted a picture of the career-driven Ms Stevens, with her aggressive work ethic fuelling her determination to get to the top, her creative vision driving her plans for the future.

But in addition to fulsome praise of Paula for her sharp and enterprising tactics, buried in the heart of the article was the theme that Paula Stevens had no time for the opposite sex and regarded men with thinly-veiled contempt. As far as this stellar entrepreneur was concerned, the glass ceiling was a limitation imposed by men to keep women in check. Oh yes, men had their uses, and that was firmly in the procreation department. In time, this dynamic high flyer could soon be in the market for a father for her baby, but these days, thanks to modern medicine, who needed a relationship? Motherhood didn't have to mean a change in her single status. Hotshot, resourceful women like Ms Stevens were more than capable of managing the rest . . .

Not that Ms Stevens intended to let the call of motherhood versus career hold her back in her rush to triple her sky-rocketing turnover. There was no reason why she couldn't expedite the baby thing with her usual breathtaking efficiency when she calculated that it was prime time for her to indulge her maternal instincts and give birth. Paula Stevens epitomises the new breed of twenty-first-century woman, the journalist enthused. Smart, sassy, single by choice, and very much in charge of her own destiny.

She prayed to God that Sam never got his hands on this. Paula's face burned as she shoved the magazine into a drawer and slammed it shut. For the sake of her sanity, she would have to forget its existence.

He'd left her bed just before six that morning. She'd sat up wrapped in mounds of messy duvet and watched as he flung on his creased white shirt and kissed her goodbye before going home to shower and change in time for a day

in the courts. It was the second night in a row that he'd
stayed over, the second night in a row that they'd talked and
laughed and enjoyed glorious sex.

After her revelations about Alan, Paula felt as though
she'd been purged. Sam had watched as she ceremoniously
tore up the photograph and dumped the tiny pieces in the
bin. Then he'd whisked her into bed. He'd been more tender
than ever, as though to superimpose himself over the ghost
of her old lover. She'd felt like telling him there was no need,
but she'd revelled in it all the same. And if she looked pale
and tired this morning, the memory of Sam's strong thighs
flanking hers would surely sustain her throughout the day.

'Well done, Paula, great article,' Maeve piped up as Paula
passed through the office en route to a meeting with her
accountants. There were a few smiles thrown in her direction
as her staff acknowledged the publication before returning
their attention to their desks. All was well out on the floor
in Stevens and all would stay equally well in the rest of her
life, she fervently hoped.

Sam phoned her later that afternoon when she was back
in her office to explain that he had band practice that evening.
'We're having a session in a north county seaside venue on
Saturday night,' he went on. 'It's a twenty-fifth wedding
anniversary and it should be fun. Why don't you pack a bag
and stay with me for the weekend? I could pick you up on
Friday evening. I might even try to cook.'

'You? Cook? I have to see that!'

She didn't need a second invitation. The whole weekend.
Spending it in Sam's home. And Abby nowhere in the picture,
she realised gratefully. She was already planning her silky
Agent Provocateur underwear instead of her monthly targets
as she went into a meeting in the boardroom with Kate and
her senior consultants.

36

On Friday afternoon, Abby whooshed back the door of her floor-to-ceiling wardrobe in Sadlier Square and flicked through her clothes, pulling out trousers and tops, skirts, dresses and jackets.

'I'd forgotten about half of this stuff,' she called out to her mother. 'Just as well I brought over a big suitcase. I can take some of these back to Dublin.'

'So that's why you really jumped at my invitation,' Lia smiled, coming into the bedroom. 'You just needed to get your hands on some clothes.'

'I'd been thinking of coming over anyway,' Abby admitted. She replaced her red Karen Millen dress back on its hanger, turned from the wardrobe and watched her mother sit down on the edge of the bed. 'I haven't seen you since Christmas, after all. And by the way, Mum . . .' she paused for a moment and gathered her thoughts. 'I'm sorry for causing such a row and upsetting you. The things I said . . . I don't know what got into me.'

Even though their recent phone calls and emails had been warmer, she had to acknowledge it and get it out of the way. From the moment she'd arrived in Sadlier Square earlier that afternoon, her mum had seemed preoccupied. Anxious, no doubt, in case Abby went flying off the handle again, wondering what sort of mood her daughter would be in. Abby had been waiting for the right moment to say her few words and clear the air between them.

'Never mind the row, it's over and done with. I've forgotten about it. I was just concerned that you seemed very unhappy at the time. Was there anything you wanted to tell me about? Talk to me about, perhaps?'

Abby paused for a moment as something hovered on the edge of her mind. Deliberately she forced it away. There was no sense in going back in time and opening up old wounds or dredging up old hurts, not when they were locked away for good. Already she felt as though she'd put the past far behind her, thanks to her determination to put on her most positive, liveliest face.

'No, I'm fine, Mum. Everything's great. Don't worry, I'm not about to jump down your throat again,' she grinned. 'I suppose you could say I'm back to normal. And I've loads to tell you about Sam and Elaine *and* Dublin. I've even met hoity-toity Paula and believe it or not, Mum, she has something in common with you.'

Her mum frowned as she got up off the corner of the bed. 'And what might that be?'

'She's another Mayberry Lane woman who's successful beyond her dreams. Must be something in the air. And did you know about Mark and the BAFTA award? Sam was here in London with him. I told him they should have looked you up.'

Lia moved across to the door. 'We've the whole weekend to catch up,' she said. 'How about coming with me to a book launch tonight for one of my fellow authors from the same publishing house?'

'Free champagne?' Abby asked hopefully.

'Free champagne, nibbles, the works. It's very high-profile. I've Olga booked at six o'clock for my hair and she'll do something with yours if you like.'

'Will I finally get to meet Gary?'

'No, Gary won't be there. One of his colleagues is looking after the launch. Clarissa is coming though.'

'Good, I like Clarissa. She's a bit of a laugh.'

'So you're on for getting all glammed up and having a fun night out?'

'Yeah. We'll take London by storm!' Abby whirled around to the wardrobe again. 'Only problem is, Mum,' she flicked through a rail full of bustier-topped and spaghetti-strapped silk, 'I've so many glitzy dresses, I really don't know what to wear. Decisions, decisions!'

When she was finally ready, she stood in front of the bedroom mirror and asked herself what Sam would think of her sparkly Jenny Packham dress and Prada gold heels. Olga had streaked her dark hair with shots of blue to match the colour of the dress. She'd used loads of hair wax, teasing it into a soft, gamine style. Now Abby looked completely different – alluring and glamorous, all grown-up and sophisticated. It might be no harm to bring some of her glitzy clothes home. She could put on something special for Mark's party and let Sam see her new sparkling image.

He'd been really pleased when he'd heard she was going to London to catch up with her mother. She'd left a message on his mobile on Wednesday and he'd phoned her back at lunchtime on Thursday.

'I probably won't get to see you before I go,' she said.

'No, I've got band practice tonight.'

'Pity. I'm missing you already,' she ventured. 'I haven't seen you since Monday night. Actually, Sam, I haven't seen all that much of you since I came home.'

'Abby! And before that it was eight years. Don't tell me you were missing me when you were scaling Machu Picchu or plumbing the depths of Lake Whatever-it-was.'

'Titicaca,' she said automatically. 'And no, Sam, that was a different life. I've put all that adventuring behind me. Now that I'm back on Mayberry Lane, it seems strange not to have you nearby. It's kinda quiet and—' She'd been about to say too quiet at night but he'd interrupted her, sounding bright and breezy.

'Nothing stays the same, Abby. Just as well, I think. Life is all about change. Surely you've found that out by now.'

She felt like saying she didn't want things to be different, that she wanted everything to go back to the way it had been eight years ago, with Sam holding her close and asking her to marry him.

Now she fidgeted with her turquoise bracelet and looked at her reflection in the mirror. She ran a hand over the silky blue material, from the soft mounds of her high breasts to the slender swell of her hips. She wished he could see her now and tell her she was beautiful.

Gaynor-Munro knew how to do it in style, Abby decided, plucking another flute of champagne from the tray of a serving waiter. The event was being held in a Knightsbridge hotel, the drink was flowing and the finger-food was both unusual and delicious. The reception room was milling with celebrities and style.

Her mum was petite and slinky in emerald green, with her hair gleaming smoothly in a short, funky bob. She held court in the circulating crowd, accepting compliments, being air-kissed and plied with food and drink. She was pulled away and photographed with the author of the moment, with the hottest celebrity in town right now and with an Oscar-nominated movie star, and she pulled Abby along in her wake, careful to include her. Abby scarcely knew any of the beautiful women or attractive men that flocked to Lia. She smiled and nodded her head and sipped more champagne and felt ever so grateful when Clarissa bore down on her, dressed in satiny Dolce & Gabbana, and pulled her into her arms.

'Abby, pet, it's been far too long! Last time I saw you, you were getting ready for Africa!'

Africa. Abby scarcely skipped a beat. 'Clarissa! You look stunning.'

'So do you.' Clarissa put her head to one side, considering. 'And I like your short hair, it gives you an Audrey Hepburn appeal.'

'Yeah, so I've been told!'

It was difficult to be heard above the roar of conversation and laughter.

'It's grown since Christmas,' Lia said, almost shouting. 'You should have seen it then.'

'I thought you liked it, Mum?'

Lia's face flashed with confusion and Abby smiled and waved her hand dismissively. 'It's okay. Of course it was far too short. Even I knew that.'

'Let's find somewhere we can have a natter,' Clarissa suggested. 'I want to hear all about your travels, Abby.'

'We'll go outside to the foyer,' Lia said. 'At least we'll be able to hear ourselves think!'

'Just so long as we can bring our champagne . . .'

'And some of that lovely food . . .'

'What was it like, Abby, being a wedding planner?' Clarissa asked when they were seated outside in a thickly-carpeted foyer area, full of marble and gilt, armed with refilled glasses and a small platter of food between them. 'And in Italy, of all places! I can just imagine all those handsome Italian studs. Mmm. I bet they were all flocking around you, murmuring breathy *ti amo*s in that fabulously romantic language. It's a wonder you managed to tear yourself away!'

Abby didn't notice her drink slopping over the side of her glass until she felt a wet splash seeping through the material of her dress. Clarissa grabbed a napkin and handed it to her. 'Hey, watch the dress. Were the Italian men really all that distracting?'

The foyer shifted a little and Clarissa's face swam in front of Abby. She felt a heat on her face, a funny prickle on the back of her neck and a buzzing noise inside her head. Then she realised that her mother was talking.

'I dare say Abby could fill a book with all her bridal hysterics,' Lia said. 'I can just imagine the last-minute panic attacks she's had to contend with. Here, Abby, have some chicken,' she said calmly, passing the platter across.

'Bridal hysterics,' Clarissa echoed happily. 'Maybe that's a marketable prospect, hmm?'

Abby absently helped herself to a sliver of spicy chicken. She chewed on it, the flavour exploding in her mouth and bringing her back to the London hotel with a muted roar of conversation and warm air wafting from the open doorway down the hall. She didn't know what exactly had happened other than she had lost it for a moment. Now her mother was talking about brides and their hysterics as though she were an expert.

Abby took a slow breath. 'Yeah, I could fill a book,' she said. 'Only problem is, Clarissa, people wouldn't believe the half of it!'

'I could fill three or four books with all the emails Abby has sent me in the last few years,' Lia went on, once more passing the platter across to Abby.

'Hey, that's an idea. Let me think about that and get back to you.' Clarissa had a gleam in her eye.

'Sure thing,' Abby laughed. 'Never know, Mum, I could be leap-frogging you in the bestseller lists.'

Clarissa grabbed a passing waiter on this way to the reception room and ordered him to fill up all their champagne flutes, expressing mock horror that Ms Lacey's glass was empty. 'Cheers, everyone,' she went on when they were suitable replenished, 'and Abby, if your imagination or romantic tendencies are anything like your mother's,. you'd be doing okay.'

'Mum's books aren't romantic,' Abby scoffed. 'Even though I've told her she's missing a large part of her vocation.'

'I agree with you. You only have to think about Alejandro to realise that deep inside, Lia Lacey is a hopeless romantic at heart. Something she keeps well and truly buried beneath a layer of chilling suspense.'

'Yes, but—' Abby halted.

'It's okay, Abby,' Clarissa smiled kindly, 'Your mum has told me about your dad and the stories she made up.'

'You have, Mum?'

Her mother looked embarrassed. 'Yes, well, Abby – the thing is—'

'I told her it was such a romantic story that she need have no worries about her fans finding out,' Clarissa interjected. 'I mean, to have given you such a magical childhood figure for a dad, who could fault that?'

'Well, I dunno. Who could?' Abby asked. Her mother looked so uncomfortable that Abby's skin prickled. She seemed to be sinking back into her chair as though she wanted to vanish completely.

'I'm glad you have the same viewpoint as me,' Clarissa said. 'When the world at large finds out, courtesy of our great British reality television—'

'Excuse me?' Abby asked.

She was even more amazed when Clarissa's hand flew to her mouth. Her eyes were saucers of apology as she said, 'Oh dear, I've made a right faux pas, haven't I? You haven't told her yet, Lia, have you?'

'Told me what?'

'Go on, Clarissa,' Lia said. 'I was half hoping we might get around to this. Abby needs to know about this tacky television stunt and I'd really rather she heard it from you. I'm still too caught up in it to think straight.'

'Know what?'

37

Abby slept late the following morning.

After the book launch, they'd moved on to a London bar and once Abby had got over the idea of meeting Alejandro on live television, Clarissa and Abby had turned the whole thing into an outrageous joke, laughing and giggling and suggesting all sorts of far-fetched outcomes, including the prospect of Lia being proposed to thirty years later by a dashing Julio Iglesias lookalike. Even her mother had been unable to resist getting caught up in their nonsense, so much so that Abby and Lia had been overcome with laughter as they waited for a cab at two in the morning.

When Abby eventually appeared for breakfast in Lia's bathrobe, showered and smelling of Lia's Jo Malone Pomegranate Noir, her mother was deliberately brisk and cheerful, pouring orange juice and producing platefuls of scrambled eggs and toast and telling Abby to eat up, as she'd need all her strength for the shopping trip.

'What shopping trip?'

'The one I'm bringing you on in about thirty minutes or so. That gives you just enough time to eat breakfast and get dressed.'

'I'm fine for clothes. I'm bringing some of my stuff back to Dublin.'

'If you're going to be staying there for any length of time, you'll need some autumn jackets and decent shoes. Which I'm buying for you.'

'Look, Mum, I have enough money—'

'Not as much as I have, and besides, I want to spoil you a little.'

Saturday was spent in a whirlwind of shopping, lunching, more shopping, early evening drinks in Piccadilly, then a cab home to Sadlier Square, struggling laughingly with mounds of carrier bags, and a cab back out again for dinner to a busy Indian restaurant. Abby chatted about everything and anything and when their meal was finished, her mother asked Abby if she was happy in Dublin.

'I am, Mum. It's funny being back on the lane, with everyone moved on, but I'm glad I went home.'

'I don't want to pry, Abby, and you don't have to talk if you don't want to, but I gather things didn't go all that happily for you in Italy.'

Abby's heart thumped. 'How do you mean?'

'How shall I put it? I know we went over this already, but you didn't seem too happy at Christmas. Then last night, when Clarissa was asking you about Italy, I didn't have to look at your face to know you were a little rattled.' Her mother smiled indulgently and for a moment Abby was tempted.

But she'd locked it all away, hadn't she? She didn't want to talk about it or go down the painful route of resurrecting memories, bringing up stuff that was miles away from where she found herself now. Most of all, she didn't want her mother's sympathy. Any trace of tenderness would ravage her defences and wreck whatever façade she'd carefully put together.

Abby squared her shoulders. 'It's okay, Mum. There's nothing I want to talk about. I just know I made the right decision to go home. It's fun catching up with Elaine again. Best of all, I've made up with Sam.'

'Sam.' Her mother was silent for a moment. 'Are you and

Sam . . . ? Do you really think there might be something there after all these years?'

'I hope so,' Abby said, relieved to have diverted the topic of conversation. 'Oh, Mum, you should see him! He's so special to me as well as being really gorgeous. And you should hear him play the guitar. I can't really believe he was there all that time, waiting for me.'

Her mother frowned. 'I know he was mad about you but *waiting* for you, Abby? Are you sure?'

'Oh yeah, he was delighted to make it all up with me and thrilled I came home at last. It's early days yet, of course, but we're getting to know each other again.' Abby paused, 'Aren't you happy for me?' She didn't need her mother's validation, but it would be good all the same.

'Of course I'm happy for you, darling.'

'Why don't you come home for the party? I'd love you to be there. The house is a bit too quiet at night, so it would be great to have some company.'

'No, thanks, I'll leave the partying to all you young ones. Anyway, I don't want to cramp your style or get in the way with you and Sam.'

'You wouldn't be in the way. And a weekend wouldn't make that much difference, considering how long it's taken us to get together.'

'It'll take me a while to get used to the idea of you and Sam together.'

'Elaine couldn't believe it either. She was delighted. Let me tell you all about Sam, and Celtic Shade, and then there's little Ruth . . .'

It was late by the time they left the restaurant and hailed a cab back home.

'I've been talking far too much,' Abby yawned when they got back to the apartment.

'You'd lots of stuff to tell me,' her mother said.

'Yes, but we didn't discuss our plans for the famous television show.'

'No, thanks, Abby.'

'What's up, Mum? You still look unhappy about it. I don't care if they dig Alejandro up from wherever he is. Even if he was married ten times or has a harem and fifty children, so what? Hey, it might even be fun! Fifty half-brothers or sisters.'

'Abby!'

'We had a bit of a laugh last night with Clarissa, hadn't we?'

'Yes, I suppose.'

'Don't be worrying about me, Mum. It'll make no difference to me if he's found. Years ago, I'd have loved to have met my father,' Abby said dreamily. 'I often wondered if he'd have liked me, or if he'd suddenly turn up at the doorway in Mayberry Lane.'

'Really? I thought you were happy.'

'I was. But still, you can't help thinking what your father was like, or wondering what he might have thought of you. Once upon a time, it mattered to me, but not any more. The only thing I'm interested in is appearing on *Lunchtime with Rachel*!'

'Thanks a bunch!'

'Joke, joke. Look, Mum, it'll be a nine-day wonder. *If* they manage to trace him in the first place. I don't understand why you're all dead set against it.'

Her mother looked tense, and the same worry that Abby had spotted on her arrival in Sadlier Square was etched in her amber eyes.

'You really are unhappy about this, aren't you?' she said.

Lia sighed heavily. 'I think I'll have a nightcap. Will you join me?'

'Sure.' Abby followed her mother into the elegant sitting

room. Lia switched on her art deco lamps and took glasses and a bottle of brandy out of the cabinet. She motioned for Abby to join her on the sofa. 'Sit down, Abby, I need to talk to you about something important. I've been avoiding it all day, but I really can't put it off any longer.'

'What's going on?'

'I asked you over to London for a reason. And it's all to do with this farce of a television programme.'

'I told you, I don't care about that. We can just boycott it.'

'I'm afraid it's not quite as straightforward as that. If the television researchers manage to track down Alejandro, which they seem intent on doing, it's going to be highly embarrassing – no, even worse.'

'Mum, I'm sure most of your fans know you exaggerated him. They're scarcely expecting a swashbuckling Spanish Armada type complete with mountain gear or sailing boat to walk out of your past and into the glare of the studio lights.'

'You don't understand, Abby. I'm up against a major problem here. And it's with you, not the fans. I don't care about their reaction. I'm only concerned about you should the truth ever some out.'

'I told you, I'm not bothered if people find out that the romantic voyager didn't exist, as such.'

'No, Abby, it's . . . far worse than you think.'

Her mother seemed to be fighting for breath and Abby grew alarmed. Lia took a gulp of brandy before continuing, 'You see, darling, Alejandro from Madrid very much existed. Behind the façade of the carefree youth who was spending his last summer before university enjoying some travel, he was ambitious and clever, courteous and gentlemanly. He had dreams of travelling the world, but felt that they'd only ever be dreams because he was expected to join the family business.'

'You've told me this already. Are you still afraid of a scandal after all these years?'

'Well, it's a different scandal to what you might think,' her mother's voice shook.

'Like what?'

'You see, Abby – and darling, please don't hate me – but Alejandro was never your father.'

38

Paula opened her eyes to the blissful realisation that it was Sunday morning and she was lying naked between the sheets of Sam's bed, with Sam, just as naked, stretched out in slumber beside her. She lay in that languid state between deep sleep and gradual alertness for several satisfying moments, then turned on her side and studied Sam's profile, his face vulnerable in sleep, and a wave of tenderness and affection washed over her.

So far the weekend had been perfect.

Sam had collected her on Friday evening and she'd felt as though she was playing truant as she came down to the foyer in Hanover Quay with her Fendi weekender. Stevens was off the agenda until Monday. Neither was she going to expend any energy fretting about a silly magazine article that was best left buried in one of her office drawers. She'd also phoned Elaine just before she left her apartment, telling her not to expect to hear from her over the weekend as she'd be extremely busy.

'God, Paula, I wish you'd get a life,' Elaine had said. 'This is totally ridiculous. You're so obsessed with that job that it's wrong.'

It was slightly hilarious, Paula thought as she locked up, and vastly convenient right now, that Elaine had automatically assumed she was busy in Stevens. And not busy cranking up her love life and deepening her relationship with Sam. All that would soon change. The minute Sam talked to Abby, the cat would be out of the bag and she would have to deal with Elaine's mad enthusiasm.

Or would she? It all depended on whose side Elaine took, Paula realised, if it came down to that. But none of that mattered when she saw Sam waiting for her in the foyer. The warm sense of belonging that swept over her, coupled with the playful feeling of skiving off for the weekend, thrust everything out of her head.

Sam cooked on Friday evening, surprising her with a delicious chilli con carne.

'My talents are unlimited,' he boasted, impressing her with the carefully laid table, side salad and crunchy bread, fat creamy candles and background music. She felt thrilled to be involved in the ordinary intimacies of his life, to be here in his home sharing a Friday evening meal and a bottle of wine, admiring the view out of the window, the glimmering line of the sea in the distance and the pale blue of the evening sky, the weekend with all its promises just waiting to unfold.

Sam served Ben & Jerry's for dessert and poured the last of the wine into Paula's glass. She looked out the window at a seagull drifting in a lazy circle and gave a long, slow sigh.

'Yes, Paula?'

She smiled and took a sip of her wine. 'I'm just relaxing. This is lovely, Sam, really special. I'm finally unwinding after the hectic week in Stevens.'

'Good,' he looked pleased. 'I'll give you a body rub afterwards. That will really space you out.'

'A body rub?'

'Yeah, after the hot tub. You have brought your swim suit?'

'Actually, no, I forgot it.'

'That's very naughty of you, Paula,' he said in a husky voice. 'Looks like you're going to have to go without it. Again.'

'Oh dear,' she said as helpless desire fizzed along the edges of her languorous limbs.

Afterwards, Sam put on one of his favourite DVDs and she curled up beside him on the sofa wearing his navy robe, every bone in her body satiated beyond pleasure.

'*Twelve Angry Men* is a classic,' he said. 'Just listen to the dialogue.'

'I'd say it's your kind of film all right,' she said, quite prepared to watch even *Superman* if it meant snuggling into Sam like this on his sofa.

'I have to confess that I've amassed quite a collection of DVDs and I intend to watch every one of them with you.'

'I have a few favourites as well,' she said.

'Let me guess, *Wall Street?*'

'Not quite. I might surprise you with them some time.'

On Saturday, she accompanied him while he grocery shopped, turning it into a fun thing as she teased his haphazard route along the aisles and questioned his purchases, even slagging him over his brand of toothpaste. Later they picked up some Chinese takeaway and the weather was warm enough to eat out on his rooftop terrace, Paula finding her way around his kitchen as she fetched plates and cutlery and suggesting that she cook the following day.

The wedding anniversary party on Saturday night was a great success. She sat with Rory's wife and Dave's girlfriend and tapped her feet in time to the music, swept up in the rhythm of it all.

'I didn't see you out on the dance floor,' Sam said when he came over and sat beside her as Celtic Shade took a break.

'I need more tuition,' she smiled, relaxing into the arm he had slung across the back of her chair.

'Easily sorted,' he said. 'By the time I'm finished with you, you'll be an expert.'

It was after midnight when they cruised home along quiet country lanes and down the coast road. She was beginning to feel she belonged here, Paula thought, a quiet sense of satisfaction mingling with a rush of need as Sam took her hand and led her into the bedroom.

Now this morning, after a lazy breakfast, they were going for a walk along the curved, golden beach. Later they would have dinner together, courtesy of Paula's cooking, and Sam would bring her home that evening.

She'd never done anything like this with Alan, had never enjoyed the small, warm intimacies of domestic trivia. It had always been sex in her apartment or a trip away to an anonymous hotel. And it had always been fraught with tension that she'd mistaken for edgy desire, lust that she'd confused with love and a patchwork of lies and deceit, the true depth of which she'd been totally unaware of.

It was different with Sam, she thought, looking at his mouth relaxed in sleep. He'd drawn her into the whole of his life, sharing it with her with genuine warmth. Beside her, he finally stirred. He propped his head on his elbow and smiled down at her.

'Good morning, Ms Stevens, sleep well?'

'Very well, thank you.'

'Good.' He smoothed back her hair and traced her eyebrows and the curve of her mouth. Then he slowly peeled the sheets away from her body. 'Oh dear, what happened here?' he asked, his eyes raking the length of her nakedness.

'I don't know. I think some sex maniac took off all my clothes,' she said happily.

'I bet all your job applicants would be amazed at the wantonly sensual side of Ms Stevens,' he said. He bent his head and lightly tugged at her rosy nipples with his mouth, causing them to ripen. 'Now see what damage you've caused,' he went on, using his long legs to thrust the sheets free of his hard arousal.

'I have a remedy for that,' she grinned. She reached out and stroked him, then she suddenly slid on top, hearing his sharp intake of breath, feeling intense pleasure as she straddled him and took him deep inside her, letting him fill her up, moving slowly, now bending her face to tug his lips with hers, then letting her hair drift against his chest, moving swiftly until she heard herself cry out and felt him shuddering beneath her.

Afterwards, they lay together entwined, Paula's head nestling into the damp skin of Sam's chest, his hand playing with strands of her hair.

'That was a lovely wake-up call,' he murmured.

'Yes, it was.' Her voice was a whisper.

'There was only . . .'

'Only what?'

He twisted slightly away so that he could see her face properly. 'I hate to spoil the moment, Paula, but . . .'

'What?'

'I didn't get a chance to put on a condom.'

She took a deep breath. 'I know. It's okay, Sam, no harm done.'

'You sure?'

'Sure.'

'I do want kids when the time is right, but I don't like to take any chances.'

'Neither do I. Like to take chances. But it's fine.'

She'd known, in the split second that she'd eased down on him, that he was unprotected. Had known, too, that he was gone too far to think straight, let alone halt the proceedings. Neither could she stop, being swept away with desire. It had been the most natural thing in the world to follow all her instincts and make love to Sam like that.

There was no harm done on this occasion because she was in a safe part of her cycle. All the same, it wouldn't be fair to either her or Sam to risk a pregnancy, much as she might wish for it. How's that for a change of heart, she thought as she nuzzled into his chest. With the length of her body pressed against the warm heat of his, and the whole of the day sparkling ahead, she felt like a totally different person to the one who had coldly and calculatingly considered using Sam's sperm to fulfil her longing for a baby. If Sam was ever to be the father of her babies – and the idea was too perfect to bear – she'd want him there with her, all the way. Otherwise it would be unthinkable.

He mustn't ever, ever find out what she'd been planning at the outset of their relationship, she thought, feeling a sudden chill sweep through her.

He'd never forgive her.

39

On Monday evening, Abby wiped a solitary tear from her eye as the Dublin-bound jet thundered down the runway before breaking free of the tarmac and thrusting into the sky.

'Afraid of flying, are you, love?' The elderly passenger in the seat beside her asked. 'Don't worry, we'll be home in no time.'

Afraid of flying? She who'd gone through gazillions of boarding passes in the last few years? Abby felt her frozen face twist in the grimace of a smile. Not too friendly, she hoped, for she had no intentions of making idle chat across the Irish Sea, brief and all as the journey was. Just as well the elderly lady had no idea of the true reason for her tears, or that Abby felt as though every piece of her chest and rib cage, never mind her heart, was one enormous ache.

Her eyelids fluttered closed as the plane set course for Dublin.

'Having a nap, are you, dear?' the lady asked. 'I won't disturb you then.'

Abby forced another smile for the stranger's benefit and felt cross that she was bothering. 'I guess I'm tired after a busy weekend.'

'Say no more. I can just imagine you young ones out partying all night! I wish I could do it, but I haven't got your energy!'

Energy? Abby felt as though she was moving around in

some kind of blank slow-motion sequence that was totally devoid of any vitality. Apart from her heartache, the only piece of her that held a modicum of life was her head, filled as it was with fragments and images of the last couple of days.

She'd scarcely slept over the weekend, staying up most of the night on Saturday, shocked and stupefied as her mother told her the truth about her father in slow, halting sentences. Then up early on Sunday, stumbling into the kitchen, rubbing her tired eyes and wondering if it had all been a bad dream, a nightmare, quietly amazed to find her mother much as normal, calm and efficient as she moved around the kitchen, even pouring fruit juice for Abby as though there was nothing wrong, as though the foundations of Abby's childhood hadn't crashed away underneath her and would never be the same.

She'd hugged her mother and told her that she could never hate her for hiding the truth.

'At least I have you, Abby, and you're by far the best thing that ever happened to me. I'm glad you understand, because it was the only way to survive,' her mother said, hugging her back.

'I don't know how you can be so calm and cool,' Abby said.

'If I was sitting here now crying into my laptop, what good would that do?' Lia said patiently. 'The only person I'd be hurting is me. Look, Abby, I found out long ago that I have a duty to myself, to the very innermost essence of me, to make the best of things. Each of us is responsible for honouring our own lives.'

'It's just such a lot to take in. And so much stuff makes sense now, I'm shocked I never saw it before.'

'I'm rather glad you didn't.'

And on Monday morning, again feeling drained from lack of sleep, Abby recalled Christmas in Sadlier Square with a painful jolt. 'I'm really sorry about what I said to you at Christmas. God, when I think of what I hurled at you.'

Her mother smiled. 'No matter. You weren't to know.'

'Does anybody else know the truth?' When her mum didn't answer immediately, Abby spoke again. 'I'd hate it if someone else knew and I didn't. How about Gran, did she know?'

'No, Gran didn't know,' her mother said. 'She was still in mourning for my dad, so you see, it was easier to let on that Alejandro was your father.'

'Yeah, enough said.'

'She was very cross with me though,' her mum admitted. 'Afterwards, when you were small and she heard me inventing all those far-fetched stories around him. She said I was making a heap of trouble for myself.'

Later Abby asked, 'So what are you going to do if these crazy television people manage to find Alejandro? That could be a bit of a problem.'

'Don't I know! I do have something in mind,' her mother smiled enigmatically, a smile Abby remembered from her childhood days.

She'd wanted to stay on in London.

'I'm not going home,' she'd said earlier that afternoon. 'You can't make me. I'd rather stay with you for a while. Surely you can change my flight for later in the week?'

'Abby, I don't need minding,' her mother had smiled. 'Of course you're going home. I'm fine, really. I've lived with this for thirty-odd years, but I put it all behind me long ago. I'm not letting it have any impact on your plans. The only thing that counts is the here and now and the best thing you can do is get back to normal. Go back to Mayberry Lane. You said you were happy there, didn't you? So pack some glitzy clothes, go back to Sam and Elaine and get ready for the party.'

'I don't feel like the party now.'

'You're bound to feel upset by all of this and you've no idea how much I was dreading telling you, but I refuse to allow it to change anything. I'm asking you to be strong and put it behind you, just as I have. The past is in the past, darling, and we can do nothing about that. We must get on and make the best of our lives.'

'I guess you've invented a whole new life for yourself over here in London. I suppose you feel as though the old Lia Lacey never existed.'

'Sort of. But I'd far rather you went back to your friends and had some fun instead of hanging around here. Anyway, I've work to do, I'm way behind as it is. I can't seem to concentrate these days.'

And so her mother had insisted she catch her Monday evening flight, even travelling with her out as far as Heathrow. At the airport, Lia had thrown her arms around her. 'Just remember, Abby, I'm still me and you're still you, and I love you and am very proud of you. Nothing has changed. Not really.'

One thing was painfully clear, Abby decided as the plane began to lose height on its approach to Dublin. She and her mother were cut from the same cloth. Her mother had faced adversity and put it behind her, putting her best step forward and her best face to the world by acting as if it had never happened.

Just as she had been doing for the last few months.

In the house on Mayberry Lane, Abby hauled her case into her bedroom and tried to rid her mind of altered images of Lia, discovering she was pregnant at sixteen in desperate circumstances, trying to shield the truth from a bereaved Anne Lacey. How imperative it must have been for her mum, a born storyteller, to embellish her relationship with Alejandro. And how brave and courageous. Abby had been born just after her seventeenth birthday. And when Abby was small, she'd created an exciting image around Alejandro to make her little daughter feel cherished and extra special. Now the framework of her life had so totally changed that it was as though the ground had been swept from under her. So much had happened in the last few months, and even in the course of a weekend, that she felt like a stranger in her own life, a stranger who was suddenly without a centre of gravity or definition.

'I think it's best if I don't tell Sam about all of this,' she'd said to her mother somewhere in the early hours of Monday morning. 'At least not for now.'

'I'd rather you didn't,' Lia had said. 'We'll see how things turn out with this television stuff and we'll talk then. I'd prefer to have waited until after this whole party thing to tell you. I don't want to spoil any of your celebrations, but I couldn't afford to take the chance of you finding out by accident.'

'Spare the thought, Mum. In that case, I'd never have talked to you again.'

Meanwhile, the silence of the house pressed in on her. Restless and uneasy, she went back to her bedroom and began to unpack, sorting through new clothes her mother had insisted on buying for her and some of the outfits she'd brought from Sadlier Square. Casual clothes, work clothes and glitzy glad rags.

Work clothes. What she needed was a job of some kind, even part-time. There was no point in hanging around Mayberry Lane with time heavy on her hands and too many hours in which to think. A job would keep her occupied and give her some sense of fulfilment as well as money. And she had the expert right on her doorstep. Paula Stevens.

She would phone Elaine for her number, but it would be good to talk to Sam first and get his opinion. For the sooner

Sam realised that there was a lot more to Abby Lacey than merely a planner of fairytale weddings, the better.

There was no answer on his mobile, so she left a message, impatient for him to get back to her, wanting to hear the reassurance of his voice in the quiet of Mayberry Lane.

40

When Sam hadn't returned her call by midnight, Abby curled up in bed. The only way she could relax was to imagine what it would be like to have him beside her, holding her close, running his fingers through her hair and all over her body.

It was far too much to take in and she felt choked. Eventually, she slept.

When she awoke in the dark night-time hours, she automatically slipped out of bed and went over to the window. The curtains were heavy so she dragged them back, feeling around for the window catch. It took her a while to find it, but eventually she released the catch and opened the window. She shivered as cool night air swept over her face and body. She listened for the murmurs on the breeze, but all was eerily quiet and the darkness was thick and pervasive.

She closed her eyes and pictured the curving hills and imagined the warmth of the sun on her face. She felt a wave of hunger for the heat of his kisses, the warmth of his arms, the laughter flashing in his dark eyes and the all-encompassing feeling that she was wanted and loved.

Ti amo . . . Cara mia . . .

Abby's eyes flew open. She couldn't figure out if she'd actually heard the spoken words or if it had been her imagination taking flight. It took her a full, charged minute to realise that she was back home in Mayberry Lane and not on her balcony in Sorrento. Completely disorientated by now and sobbing, Abby closed the window and stumbled back to bed. She clicked on the lamp and checked her mobile once more. The silence was heavy. It seemed to stretch interminably, not just confined to her bedroom or the house or outside on Mayberry Lane, but spreading out far beyond, a thick, endless haze that she could reach out and touch. Frozen in something she couldn't define, she lay there stiffly and then, drifting in the air like a thin, whirling wraith, she caught the unmistakeable scent of lemons.

'Good news and bad news, Lia,' Gary said.

'Give me the good news first,' Lia said acerbically. 'I'm a great believer in looking on the bright side.'

'Sure. It seems there are no records or traces available of either you or Alejandro around the time you would have stayed in Loch Lomond.'

'Goodness me, what a surprise. Although I'm counting on these researchers being a little thick. Surely anyone with a sense of wit would realise that ancient paper records would scarcely have been lying most conveniently around and crying out to be examined. It was the mid-seventies, after all. Hang on a minute,' she said, feeling cold, 'how did they estimate what time I stayed there?'

'They figured that out from Abby's birthday.'

'Abby's birthday? But she was scarcely talking to them.'

'Her thirtieth birthday, when you brought her on a surprise trip to Paris. It was on your website in one of your news bulletins.'

'Shit. Would you mind having a close look at everything, all the bulletins, in case I've done any other damage?'

'I already did before I phoned you, but everything else is fine. And there's no harm done this time, Lia. There are no leads whatsoever coming from that particular origin.'

'But . . . ?'

'But the bad news is, it seems that the Spanish equivalent of our *Lunchtime with Rachel* is coming on board the bandwagon, which will speed things up at their end.'

'Bloody hell. That's all I need to hear this morning.'

'Why, what else is bothering you?'

Lia sighed. 'Oh, nothing much, Gary. Don't mind me. I guess I just need to conjure up some false trails so that you can send them off in the entirely wrong direction.'

'How about I suggest it might not have been Loch Lomond after all? If I said you were trying to sound romantic, but you really met in Glasgow, that might waste some further time.'

'Whatever you think, Gary. Or I could give you a false surname, or suddenly remember that Alejandro was going to study for the priesthood. God, this is getting so ridiculous, it can scarcely be happening.'

Ridiculous or not, it *was* happening. And the search for Alejandro was far from the only thing giving her cause for anxiety.

She'd no sooner finished the call when Clarissa phoned looking for the prelims for *Midday Execution*. The novel, due out before Christmas, was about to go to print, and Lia was late submitting her dedication and acknowledgements. 'You sound a bit off,' Clarissa said. 'I hope you're not secretly annoyed with me for spilling the beans about the television show to Abby last weekend.'

'Not at all,' Lia said, deliberately light. 'I was going to tell her myself. I just I got out of bed on the wrong side this morning. Bad sleep, you know.'

'I'm not surprised. But could I have them by Thursday, then? We do need to get it to the printers first thing next week.'

Lia closed her eyes and gripped the phone, 'Thursday. Sure. No prob.'

Work was impossible. Any kind of writing, editing or narrative composition, even a simple acknowledgement and dedication, required a supreme act of motivation, the level of which she simply could not attain because there was a fuzz of thick cotton wool inserted in her skull where her brain used to be.

She went out to the kitchen to make some coffee, only to realise that she was clean out of coffee and milk. Not surprising, considering she and Abby had gone through endless coffee over the weekend. Lia cursed as she eyed her deserted fridge and equally empty larder. She grabbed her purse and keys and stepping out into Sadlier Square, she hailed a cab to bring her to the nearest Sainsbury's. As she trudged around with her shopping basket, she tried to take her mind off visions that lurked in the corner of her mind and the picture of Abby going through to the departure area in Heathrow the previous Monday evening.

On instinct, she'd almost called her daughter back, told her to forget her flight and stay on in Sadlier Square for a few days. But that would have been selfish of her and it wouldn't have been fair to have Abby hanging around London, raking over haunting skeletons. It was far better, she had thought, for her daughter to get back to normal as soon as possible.

Problem was, the process of telling Abby and discussing what had happened had resurrected all the bad old memories for Lia, and now she felt on a knife-edge, as though her skeletons had infiltrated the safe haven of her apartment and cracked the veneer of her London life – the very thing she'd been determined to avoid.

As she hailed a cab to bring her home, she was also aware of a bubbling anger under the surface, an anger she'd never before experienced so keenly. It was as though the young, vulnerable sixteen-year-old girl had never completely slain her dragons. Although she'd never faced up to it, not properly. She'd chosen instead to hide behind a convenient smokescreen called Alejandro, almost believing her own made-up story in the process.

God. She still couldn't bear to remember it. Even now, Lia felt the blood drain from her face as she stared out the window of the cab bringing her home. The blurry London streetscape and trundling red buses were suddenly foreign to her.

'Hey, ma'am, don't forget your shopping!'

Startled, Lia looked at the cab driver who'd just deposited her at Sadlier Square. She'd emerged from the idling cab and paid her fare, leaving her plastic shopping bags full of basic groceries behind on the seat.

'Thank you,' she said, reaching back inside the door of the cab and chiding herself for being so careless. Her negligence wasn't surprising, though, for no matter what had happened all those years ago, by far the worst thing had been helplessly standing by as she broke the news to a white-faced Abby.

Now as she recalled her daughter's face, she felt even more distressed for not following her gut feeling at Heathrow airport the previous evening, for now her instincts screamed that she'd made a huge mistake in sending Abby back to Dublin so soon.

42

Abby broke some crusty bread between her fingers and looked at Sam with what she hoped was a flirtatious smile. 'So how come it took you so long to get back to me?' she asked, deliberately injecting a teasing tone into her voice. 'I thought you'd have time hanging on your hands with the courts adjourned for the summer recess.'

'Me?' Sam chortled. 'I never have spare time. I'm in the middle of negotiating with my accountants as to what exactly constitutes a tax-deductible expense. August is always the month I file my returns, and wading through a mountain of paperwork is always time-consuming. As well as that, Celtic Shade are expanding our repertoire, so that means more practice.'

'Okay, I take back what I said. Or should I say,' she put on a deep voice, 'I'm retracting my statement, Your Honour.'

Sam laughed. 'God, Abby, you could always get a job in the courts. Only you'd find it a total change from wedding planning.'

'That's what I wanted to meet up with you for. To discuss a job, or rather, my prospects.'

Wednesday afternoon sunshine sparked outside the Dublin city restaurant where she was lunching with Sam. He'd finally returned her call on Tuesday evening and suggested they meet for lunch the following day. When she looked across the table at him, all her night-time fears dissolved. Abby felt herself slide into the present moment and it was as though all her cares disappeared. He was so solid and real with his easy-going smile that she felt back to herself on some level. Even the way he'd greeted her, with a warm, reassuring hug and a tender kiss on her cheek, had been more than enough to dispel her ghosts. The restaurant was busy, the lunch was delicious, it was a bright day outside and Sam was friendly and attentive.

'Did you have a good weekend in London?' he asked, putting down his knife and fork.

Abby felt her mouth wobble while something deep and dark clutched at her insides, but with Sam sitting opposite her, it was easy to push it aside to another part of her mind and force a smile on her face. 'Yeah. Mum and I went to a book launch and the champers was flowing. We had some fun.'

'Living the high life, huh?'

'Of course. We went shopping as well and I brought home so many clothes that I've taken over *two* wardrobes in Mayberry Lane. So now I need to find a job to keep me occupied.'

'What were you thinking of? I'm sure your wedding experiences would be of benefit if you were to go into event management or something similar.'

'I'd really rather do something in the business executive line. Now that I'm back for good, I want to get onto the ladder of something decent, even if it's at one of the lower rungs. I've asked Elaine for Paula's number. I think I'll have a chat with her.'

'Paula?' Sam frowned and paused in the act of slicing a tomato, then threw her a cautious glance that made her feel uneasy. 'I'm not sure if she'd have anything suitable for you, Abby. She mostly brokers deals for senior management level in the financial sector.'

'Yeah, but she might be able to give me some tips, interview stuff, whatever. I am multi-lingual, after all, and I'm determined to get this right. I want a job that will make you proud of me,' she continued in a small voice.

Sam was silent and for a long moment Abby thought he'd forgotten where he was.

Then he said, 'I've always been proud of you, Abby, proud to call you my friend. Don't ever lose sight of that. But there's something I've, um, been meaning to talk to you about.'

'Like what?' This was déjà vu, Abby decided. She'd just gone through something similar with her mother. Surely Sam didn't have any devastating secrets?

He was talking again. '. . . to tell you, well, about Paula.'

'What do you mean?'

'Thing is, Abby, I've been seeing her. Seeing her a lot.'

Abby lifted the jug of water and poured some into her glass, focusing on the ice cubes clinking and jostling near the rim of the jug, determined not to let them splash into her glass. Then she put down the jug and looked calmly at Sam. 'Well of course you have, between lunching in Elaine's and the night out in The Pier, and now we'll have the reunion when Mark gets home.'

Sam reached across the table and took her hand in his. She was abnormally grateful for the warmth of it, and the strength of his grip.

'No, it's more than that, Abby. Paula and I have been going out, dating, for several weeks now. More or less, in fact, since I came home from Sorrento.'

Paula and I? Deep down inside, Abby knew it was imperative to keep a smile on her face. Sam didn't really know what he was saying. Or else she was taking a different meaning from his words. Naturally he'd seen Paula over the past few weeks. There had been lots of stuff going on. But hoity-toity Paula and her *Sam*? No way.

On Mayberry Lane, it had always been Sam and Abby.

Paula had been the clever clogs who looked down her nose at everyone else. On Mayberry Lane, Sam had asked Abby to marry him. *Twice.* Maybe he didn't really believe she was home for good. There had to be some way of impressing this on him.

She squeezed his hand. 'I'm home for good now, Sam. Maybe you find that hard to believe, but it's true.'

'I'm glad you're back in Dublin if it makes you happy.'

'I'm very happy. My only regret is that I took you so much for granted all those years ago. I'm really sorry I broke your heart.'

Sam had a funny look on his face. He took his hand away, pushed his plate of salad aside and sat up straighter in his chair. 'Abby, look, we've discussed this already. That's all ancient history now.'

'Good. That's what I wanted to hear.' She helped herself to another portion of nutty bread and somehow her knife gouged far too much butter out of the ramekin dish.

'So do you understand what I'm telling you? I'm dating Paula. We're seeing each other, as in going out together, and, um, to be honest, I'm very fond of her.'

'What about me, Sam? Are you still fond of me?'

'Of course. We go back a long way, don't we?'

'Friends forever?' she said, voicing Sam's usual phrase. And she held her breath and dug her nails into her palms until he replied, 'Best mates.'

'So what about my job prospects, then?'

'Are you okay about me and Paula? There was no easy way to say it, to tell you about us, but it isn't fair to leave you in the dark, with no idea of what's going on.'

What did he mean 'going on'? There couldn't be anything 'going on'. Not between Sam and Paula.

'I'm fine, Sam, honest. It's no prob. Do you think I should start to put my CV together before I talk to Paula?'

Sam's hand closed over hers once more. She wanted him

to hold it forever. 'Let me talk to Paula first. I'll see what she suggests and then I'll let you know.'

His voice was kind and Abby thought it was funny the way he talked of Paula and the familiar way he spoke her name, as though he knew her very well indeed, as though they belonged. Which was silly, really, for Sam had always belonged to her. Everyone knew that.

Even Paula.

43

Paula was expecting Sam for dinner. She hadn't seen him since Sunday night and they'd planned to have a quiet Wednesday evening meal in her apartment. Paula had toyed with the idea of showing off her collection of chick-flick DVDs. She'd envisaged them laughing together over *Legally Blonde*. She'd planned an easy menu that included luscious strawberries and softly-whipped cream for dessert.

She'd even imagined herself feeding him strawberries and letting him do very mischievous things with the cream.

But those plans had changed when Elaine had phoned her that morning. Now she was wearing an uncompromising black top and trousers and her hair was caught in a clasp, drawing it back severely from her face. Dinner, courtesy of Marks & Spencer, was heating in the oven, the strawberries forgotten.

All weekend, she'd felt as though Abby hadn't existed. There had been no phone calls, no texts, no Abby showing off on the dance floor or pulling Sam's arms around her and laying claim to him in a very public way. And why not? Because thanks to Elaine's phone call, she'd discovered that Abby had spent the weekend in London, conveniently out of the way. No wonder Sam had happily invited her to Malahide. He clearly hadn't bothered talking to her yet. Given the magical weekend they'd shared, surely he should have been more than anxious to set things straight?

Better again, from what Elaine had told her, Abby had

the bloody gall to think she could approach her for a job. Paula laughed mirthlessly. She'd already realised that things hadn't changed much from the time she'd lived on Mayberry Lane. Yet why, she chastised herself, did she revert to type and still feel she was no match for the careless devilry of Abby Lacey?

'What's up?' Sam asked. 'I know you said you were busy, but you look like you've had a lot more than just a hectic day at the office.'

Even this, the knowledge that he could read her face, that he already knew her so well, was a further tightening of the hurt. 'Oh, nothing much.'

'Yeah,' he looked at her. 'And I'm Santa Claus.'

Looking at him standing in front of her now, in the flesh, she felt ashamed of her fears and worries. She tried to sound nonchalant and hated the catch in her voice. 'I had a phone call from Elaine. Apparently Abby was away for the weekend, and now she's hoping I'll fix her up with a job?'

'Yes, she was over in London, visiting Lia—' Then he went on, reading her mind, 'Is that what's bugging you? Abby? You think I asked you to Malahide when the coast was clear? Before you jump to any more ridiculous conclusions, I met her for lunch today and I told her about us.'

'You did? Then why—'

She was about to ask how come word hadn't flashed back to Elaine or how come Elaine hadn't phoned her straight away to confirm this juicy gossip when Sam stood up and drew her into his arms, trapping her against his body, and despite everything, she felt herself yielding. It had been a long, lonely time since she'd kissed him goodbye last Sunday.

'Paula. Shut up. Don't reduce us to a silly squabble. I should be very cross with you for doubting me,' he said sombrely. 'What can I do to convince you that it's different with us? Although it does me good to see you getting uppity, because . . .' She knew by his tone of voice that he was smiling.

'Because what?' She was wavering.

'Because it means I've sneaked into that soft, vulnerable heart of yours.'

'Soft?'

'Yes, soft. See, I've discovered that the entire Ms Stevens ball-breaking thing is just a front. Lurking behind the formidable lady with the fortress desk, I've found a very passionate, sensual woman.' With an easy movement, he freed her hair from the clasp, sifting his fingers through it. It took all her discipline not to lift her mouth to his.

Could she trust him? She'd been led up the garden path before. Right here and now, she didn't know what to think.

She said, 'There's also a rational, sane woman in there who's not going to behave foolishly again.'

'I should hope not,' he said, nuzzling into her neck. 'I hope you're not going to be foolish enough to mess things up between us. I've told Mark about you. He said hello, by the way, but he knows he'll have to take his greedy eyes off you.'

'Mark's greedy eyes were never on me.'

'Wait until he sees you now.'

'Why, what will he see?' she asked, shivery feelings going down to her toes at the sensations coming from her neck.

'A vibrant, beautiful, sensual woman. God, Paula, even since Monday I've missed you . . .'

Later that night they were in bed together, breathless and replete, when his mobile rang, instantly shattering the mood between them. It had been dumped on the bedroom floor beside his cast-off trousers, and at first he ignored the increasing volume until it rang out. When it rang again she pulled away from him, aware somehow that it was Abby and equally aware of the cold rush of air when their bodies separated.

She could feel the nausea rising in her throat when he picked it up and answered it, throwing a helpless glance at her as though to say it wasn't his fault if his ex-girlfriend managed to contact him. Then as she watched, his face darkened from polite greeting to sharp concern. She heard him telling Abby he'd be there as soon as possible and she knew before he ended the call and gave her an apologetic look what he was going to say. She'd heard it all before, hadn't she?

'Sorry about this, but I have to go . . .'

'There's a problem at home . . .'

'I know you'll understand . . .'

'Make it up to you as soon as I can . . .'

Sam ran his fingers through his hair and looked so absurdly awkward that Paula was almost tempted to feel a little sympathy for him.

'Let me guess, you have to go,' she said.

His immediate relief was evident. 'Yes, well, that was Abby.'

'Really. I'd never have known.'

'Paula, please. There's some kind of problem. She sounds scared to bits and I don't know what's wrong.'

'But she needs you. Now. Even though it's . . .' she glanced at her clock, 'just after eleven?'

His face was a picture of chagrin and she could have wept.

'I could write this script in my sleep,' she said hoarsely.

'Please credit me with some intelligence. It's not what you think.'

She smiled wryly. 'No, it never is.'

'Why don't you come with me? I'd like you to come. Whatever's wrong with Abby, I don't particularly want to confront it by myself.' He was getting out of bed now, moving away from her and pulling on his clothes. She sat up and groped for the duvet, bundling it around her nakedness. For some reason her legs were shaking and she couldn't control the trembling of her knees despite the heat of the duvet.

'Oh, God, she might jump you. The spurned girlfriend. How could you cope with that?'

'She sounds in a panic. I don't know if she disturbed an intruder or what.' He was casting about for his jacket, searching for his car keys. Something icy trickled into her veins. She couldn't bear it if he left her now and went to Abby. She wanted to throw herself into his arms, much like a possessive juvenile, but instead she raised her eyebrows and said icily, 'Bullshit, Sam. I can't bear this kind of behaviour. If you leave now, you can say goodbye to me.'

He stared at her, his hazel eyes remote and puzzled. She recalled the weekend they'd just spent together, laughing, teasing, making love, shopping, holding hands as they strolled along the beach.

Then she saw Abby on the dance floor wrapped in Sam's arms, in her black top and the flaring burnt-orange skirt; saw her skipping up the lane towards him, and Sam catching her by the hands and swinging her around so that her tumbling dark hair fanned out all around her head and her warm, carefree laughter flowed across the air.

She couldn't go through all this again, the interminable hoping, holding her life in suspension while she waited for someone to be truly hers, feeling every atom of her self-respect draining away in the process. And it was all the worse, all the more painful and gut-wrenching, because she'd allowed Sam deep into her heart.

Caught in a vice grip of frozen pain and hurt, she heard him talking as though from a distance. 'Paula, you're the one who's talking bullshit. I've told you you're special to me. Can't you take my word for it? Abby's in some kind of trouble and she has no friends to call on except me. I'm just popping over to make sure she's safe. As soon as she's okay, I'll come back.'

'Off you go, then. Just don't come back here.'

'Paula, come on, that's a bit over the top.'

'Get lost. It's about as much over the top as you expecting me to believe it's all so innocent with you and Abby,' she snapped. Paula Stevens, full metal jacket, on the attack and going in hard, getting in there first with her wounding words. Feeling vulnerable and scared of her feelings and letting her mouth work furiously before her brain had a chance to engage.

44

Abby went around the house and switched on every single light, feeling weak with relief at the way the instant brightness banished the dark corners and cast out the murky night.

Better again, Sam was on his way. He'd dropped whatever he'd been doing to come to her rescue.

He'd left her at the corner of Grafton Street that lunchtime, asking her if she was okay, hugging her and kissing on her forehead.

'I'm great,' she'd told him brightly.

'What are you going to do now?'

'Shopping, of course. A girl's best friend!'

It was worth anything to see the light-hearted smile on his face, worth squashing the uneasiness tugging at a corner of her mind, the way she felt so out of sorts and the way her stomach had catapulted at the sound of Paula's name on his lips. 'And I want to get organised for my great relaunch into the working world,' she said. 'I brought some clothes back from London, but I need to check out what's happening in the Dublin employment scene and work out how to start putting together my CV. Let's face it, Sam, I can't afford to be a complete goof when I go job hunting. I need to sound as though I know what I'm talking about.'

So she'd waved him a cheery goodbye in spite of her heavy heart and watched him being swallowed up by the crowds. Then feeling lost somehow, she'd wandered aimlessly around department stores and boutiques, purchasing items she didn't really need, dropping into Boots to replenish her make-up and into Easons to purchase some magazines that she felt she should read to bring her up to date.

The evening gathered in rapidly, the sky low and brooding, and by half past eight it was quite dark in the garden outside. Abby flicked through her magazines, pouncing on one article and reading it carefully, allowing the implications of it to sift through her mind. Then she relaxed in a warm, soothing bath and went to bed early.

Something disturbed her. A fragment of a dream? The sound of her own sibilant murmurs? She wasn't quite sure. She got out of bed, stood at her bedroom window and stared out into the murky night. The darkness outside was thick and heavy and she thought she saw a movement in the shadow of the trees. Her head was light and swimmy and her bedroom in Mayberry Lane felt claustrophobic. She closed her eyes and even though there wasn't a breath of air, she found herself inhaling the citrus scent of lemons, a scent that plunged her back to Italy. She conjured up her balcony in Sorrento, scents of garlic drifting up from the nearby restaurant, the laughter and cries of the schoolchildren echoing in the air, the buzzing of the scooters. She felt the warm glow of the sun on her skin. Heard the sound of his voice . . .

Ti amo, bella Abby, amore mio . . .

Abby shook.

The big catastrophe was, he'd never actually stood on her balcony in Sorrento. He'd never been there with her to share the heat of the Italian sun. He'd told her all about his country. He'd talked about Sorrento, the Golfo di Salerno and the sheer-faced cliff road to Amalfi. He'd told her about the Cloisters. Most of all, he'd spoken to her lyrically of his native town of Positano, so much so that she'd felt an immediate sense of recognition when she'd arrived there.

Then, slowly and hesitantly, as though terrified to go there for fear of what she might feel or what it might evoke, she tried to remember Raffaele's face, but the image was dark and opaque and her eyes flew open as she realised with a sense of shock that she couldn't recall what he had looked like. All she could remember was the expression in his eyes, sparkling when he smiled, dark and steadfast when he drew her close and alive with desire when he looked at her mouth in that instant before he kissed her, and in the moment he roused from slumber to see her lying there beside him.

But she couldn't remember his face and she felt gripped with an icy terror. That was when she'd pressed the speed dial on her mobile and called Sam.

When she saw him standing in the light of the porch, tall and strong, his forehead creased with concern, she had to restrain herself from pitching forward into his arms.

'Are you okay?' he asked, stepping through into the hall and putting his hand on her arm. He moved on down towards the kitchen, his broad shoulders filling the narrow hallway. Abby gulped. Now that he was here, she felt safe again. All those chilly corners of her mind were suddenly warmed with his presence.

'You sounded rather panicky on the phone.' Sam stood on the threshold of the kitchen and threw her an anxious look. 'I thought someone was trying to break in.' His voice trailed away as he looked into the silent, empty kitchen. All the lights were blazing, much as they were all over the house.

Abby followed his gaze and focused on the vacant chairs sitting to attention around the spotless table. She had the odd thought that the kitchen looked empty and remote, as though it hadn't been used in quite a long time, even though she'd already been home a few weeks. Is that what she'd said? An intruder? She couldn't remember what exactly she'd said in order to summon him here, just that he'd replied that he'd get to her as soon as possible.

She followed him out to the kitchen and gestured helplessly towards the window. 'Yes, well, I wasn't sure. I thought I saw . . .'

'Was there someone outside? Someone trying to break in?'

'I'm not sure.' She hesitated, suddenly realising that Sam might call the police to check things out. 'I heard a noise,' she gabbled, 'outside in the shrubbery, but,' she pounced on the little white lie, 'it might have been a cat.'

'A cat?'

'After I phoned you, I thought I saw one scurrying down the drive . . .'

'I'll just have a check around then, shall I?'

'Thanks, I'd feel better if you did.'

It felt so right to see him there, to watch him splintering the cold silence as he checked windows and doors, went out into the night-time garden, then took the stairs two at a time to check the windows in the eaves. His presence cut right through the claustrophobic loneliness so much that she didn't want him to leave and have the house plunged into thick silence once more. She didn't want to be left alone with her black thoughts spiralling and her mind filled with the vision of that dark, opaque face.

Sam came down the stairs and stopped in the hallway. She intercepted his gaze as his eyes flickered to the hall door, as though preparing to leave, and then he looked at her a little sheepishly as he realised she'd caught him.

'I've checked around and everything's fine. There's nothing outside and all the windows and doors are secure. The house is alarmed, isn't it?'

'Yes.' Her throat was filling up, closing over. It was difficult to breathe and she took several shallow breaths. 'There's no mad rush home, is there? Why don't you have a cup of tea, or coffee?' It was only postponing the inevitable, putting off the moment when she faced the silence once more.

'No thanks, Abby.' He half turned towards the door. 'Are you sure you're okay?'

No, I'm not fine. Anything but. I don't want you to leave now, I don't want you to ever leave me again.

'Sam, I . . . look, please don't go. I need, well, don't just rush off, please.'

Something passed across his face. He looked at her as you might look at a tired and vulnerable child, with a hint of indulgent affection, and she couldn't bear it. Not when she needed him to kiss her and hold her tight and shore up the dark, lonely night. Then he said as he took out his phone, 'Just give me a minute.'

She understood he wanted to make his call without her hearing the conversation, and neither did she want to even think about who he might be calling at this late hour, so she went into the kitchen and lifted the kettle, gripping it painfully with her fingers.

Then almost immediately and to her immense relief, he followed her in.

'Okay, I'll have some tea.'

He swept away the chilly emptiness as he sat at the table. She sat opposite him, passing across milk and sugar, and she didn't realise that she'd been silently staring at him until he waggled his hand in front of her face.

'Hey, there! You're miles away!'

'Sorry,' she grinned. 'It's just so good to see you sitting there,' she blurted.

'Am I really that handsome?' he asked.

'Are you looking for a compliment?'

'I'm not that hard up.'

They were falling back into their adolescent banter, like

old times. She was finding herself again. Abby felt her heart
lift a little. She began to talk about Celtic Shade and his
music, chatting away as the hands of the clock crept towards
midnight and beyond. Then she talked about her shopping
trip in town after she'd left him that afternoon.

'Hang on a minute, there's something I must show you,'
she said, conscious now of the late hour, yet determined
to keep Sam hanging on for another few precious minutes.
She slid off her chair and went into the front room, returning
moments later with a glossy magazine. 'I bought some
business mags to get an idea of what's happening in the
Dublin commercial scene at the moment. I thought they
might give me some sound bites for putting my CV together.
But I was really surprised to see this.' She spread the
magazine across the table. Riffling through the pages, she
finally found what she was looking for and passed it across
to Sam.

'Paula seems to have made it, hasn't she?' Abby said.

Abby had felt so relieved when she'd stumbled across the
article that she'd read it twice. It was clear that Paula didn't
want a man in her life. The focused, disciplined girl Abby
had known growing up was only interested in putting Stevens
up there in glittering lights. Maybe she'd have a baby
somewhere along the way, but only when it was convenient.
So if Sam thought that Paula was interested in him, he was
mistaken.

She watched his face as he scanned the text and stared
at the photographs. Then he stood up, sliding his chair back
so hurriedly that it jarred against the floor tiles. 'If you're
sure you're okay, I'll head off.'

'I'd rather you stayed.' She hadn't meant to say it, to sound
so helpless, but the words slipped out of their own accord.

He gave her a bleak look. 'I don't think that's a good idea.'

'Why not? I need you, Sam,' she said, reaching out and

placing her hand tentatively on his arm. She ached to be held, to be gathered to him, to kiss and be kissed.

'*Need* me?' He gave a short, careless laugh that hurt her to the quick. 'Nonsense, Abby. You're the most independent person I know.'

'I'm not, not really,' she gulped, determined to make him understand. 'Since I came home, I'm seeing things differently. Remember years ago, you said you hoped I'd realise that you were the one for me? I'm realising that now and I just hope I'm not too late. I thought you'd be pleased to hear that I need you and *love* you—' She stopped short, the words she'd just said resounding in her mind.

Sam's face was full of affectionate concern, quite unlike the loving desire she longed to see. He was so close to her, and yet distant and removed like a stranger. She heard the echo of her own voice, telling him she loved him, and suddenly she swallowed hard and shook her head. It felt all wrong, it had sounded all wrong, and the ache in her arms and the chill in her heart became unbearable. Something came bubbling up inside of her, something from the buried depths that she couldn't stop, and she felt tears pouring down her cheeks. She just had time to register the shock flashing across Sam's face before he drew her into his arms.

Blindly, she fit her head into the curve between his shoulder and his neck, every part of her urging him to make her feel better. His arms comforted her like a benign blessing as she bawled her eyes out. After a while, she stopped and Sam held her at arm's length, his forehead touching hers in a gesture that she wanted to go on forever.

'Are you going to tell me what that was all about?'

'No, I . . .' she hiccupped, sudden exhaustion washing over her.

'Why don't we sit down for a minute?' His voice was gentle

and she allowed him to lead her into the front room, where he plumped up a cushion and sat her down on the sofa.

'Can I get you anything? A drink?'

'No, I'll be all right,' she said.

'All right? Abby, you were deeply upset. What's going on?'

She hesitated. With the curtains drawn, the room was cosy and welcoming, so much so that the dark night outside was irrelevant. Sam was beside her, holding her hand and ready to listen, even though she had dampened his shirt with her tears and was staring at him now with a blotched face. But talking was out. She couldn't begin to explain herself to Sam, not now, when she was feeling so disorientated, dazed and confused.

'Did something frighten you? Is that it?' he went on.

Yes it did, but it wasn't something I can explain. Not at the moment.

She latched onto his words. 'I guess I was a bit rattled. It's lonely here at night, and I'm finding it hard to get used to it, never mind the quietness of it all,' she gabbled. 'Then when I thought I saw something . . . I dunno, I guess it was just my imagination getting the better of me.'

His eyes searched hers. 'Don't tell me my adventurous Abby is afraid of the dark?'

She shook her head, more for her sake than his.

'Or else you have an incredible imagination, like your mum,' he continued, reaching out and ruffling her hair.

'Yeah, maybe,' she smiled. 'It takes a while to get used to the silence around here.'

'So you don't like being home alone?'

'Not really, no. I find it quiet, even spooky at times.' she said, speaking honestly.

'It's bound to seem quiet after all your travels. There's never been much excitement on Mayberry Lane, after all. But you shouldn't feel spooked. That's just your imagination working overtime.' He was beginning to look a little more reassured with her explanations. When he was satisfied that she was okay, he'd surely leave, and she felt susceptible to the peculiar vacuum inside her, to the rest of that disturbing night and somehow at a loss.

'Don't leave me,' she said, speaking without thinking. 'Please don't leave me tonight.'

He considered this for a few moments and said, 'I guess it won't do any harm if I bunk down here for a few hours and keep the spooks at bay.'

She told him that if he was staying, he might as well have a drink. He said just the one as he'd a busy day ahead of him tomorrow and needed a clear head. She fetched bottles of beer from the fridge and they talked about the silly things they'd done years ago to liven up life on Mayberry Lane. Afterwards he escorted her to her bedroom, made a joke as he checked under the bed, and kissed her goodnight on the forehead. He told her he'd sleep in her grandmother's old room, so he was nearby in case something rattled her again.

But she wasn't rattled in the night. She fell asleep the minute her head hit the pillow and it was twelve noon when she awoke the following morning. She pulled back the bedroom curtains to a brilliant August Thursday. The sun was high in the sky, the back garden an oasis of calm that sparkled in the sun's radiance.

Sam was gone. He'd scrawled a note on the back of a leaflet that had come through the letter box saying he'd talk to her later. She made coffee and sat by the kitchen window in her dressing gown, looking at the bright, vital day outside and the way everything seemed brand new, joyous and vibrant.

For a long, trembling moment she remembered that Raffaele would never again share the sunshine with her or wake up to the beauty of a fresh new morning. But it didn't bear thinking about, for it was too cruel to comprehend, so she went into the front room, switched on the television and blanked it away for now.

45

'What do you mean, there was no paper in the fax machine?' Paula demanded of Kate.

Two pink spots came and went in Kate's cheeks, signals that should have forewarned Paula. 'I mean just that,' Kate said. 'It appears we've been out of paper since yesterday afternoon.'

'That's fan-bloody-tastic. God knows what messages are waiting to get through. Why wasn't it spotted before now? Who's responsible? I can't believe something so ridiculously basic has been overlooked.'

'It's normally Maeve Breen's job, but I offered to monitor it as she's on leave this week.'

'What do you mean, she's on leave? She's only here a wet week.'

'Her sister is getting married in France and Maeve is doing bridesmaid. So she's been on leave since Tuesday.'

Paula's eyes glinted. 'I don't recall being informed of this when I took her on.'

'She came to me a couple of weeks ago about it and said she'd been too afraid to mention it to you in case it interfered with her being offered a position.'

'Too right,' Paula snapped. It was one thing to have her staff slightly in awe of her, but another to be equated to some kind of wicked witch. 'And you gave her permission to go off gallivanting to France, I suppose?'

'Paula, I am the floor manager, and it's within my remit.

I considered that her duties could be adequately covered for the few days in question.'

'Well you made an error of judgement there, didn't you?'

'I don't accept that I made an error of judgement. I did omit to check the fax machine. It was an oversight, but that was all.'

'That was *all*? God only knows what business we've lost on account of your slipshod oversight.'

'I'm sorry, but I can't accept being spoken to like this. If you're not happy with the way I'm discharging my duties, I can no longer continue to work for you.'

Paula swallowed. She focused on a spot on the wall and tried to breathe in slowly, the stark reality of Kate handing in her notice bringing her up short.

Damn and blast Sam Ryan. This was exactly what she'd feared – the see-saw of emotions, the blurry pain of playing second fiddle to an earlier love, feeling her heart being bruised all over again. Now thanks to her bubbling anxiety she was having a serious run-in with her much-respected business manager.

How had it come to this? At what point in time could she have called a halt to it all? Well, it had ground to a messy stop last night when he'd left her apartment to go to Abby. She'd told him to get lost when he'd phoned her later from Mayberry Lane. And she'd already discovered that Thursday morning that it was one thing dragging her broken heart into Stevens and inflicting it on those around her, but by far the worst thing to accept was the prospect of life without him.

'Kate, I apologise for speaking out of turn, it was wrong of me,' she said, struggling for calm and doing her best to placate her. 'Please let's not do or say anything foolish.'

Kate's eyebrows rose. 'It's not just me, Paula. To be honest, there have been rumblings of discontent among a lot of the staff. I'm doing my best to keep the peace, but I think you and I should sit down before I go on holidays and talk through a few issues.'

'Sure, Kate.' Paula ignored the sinking feeling in her heart as she drew up her calendar. 'Would tomorrow afternoon at four o'clock suit?'

'That's fine.'

At least Kate looked slightly mollified as she left the office, but it had been a close call. Paula's hands were shaking as she brought up her emails. But when Sam arrived in without warning just before lunch, dropping a magazine on her desk so that it slewed across the polished surface, she knew by the thunderous expression on his face that her hurt of the night before had been but a pale shadow of what was to come.

'I don't like being used,' he said in clipped tones.

Her insides plummeted and the walls of her office swam before her vision. 'Used? Sam – I – you're mistaken.'

'I don't think so. It's quite obvious that I turned up at a most convenient time in your life. Convenient for assisting you in your reproductive endeavours.'

'That's nonsense.'

The hostile look he threw at her was even more cutting than anger.

'Is it? It's all here in black and white, Paula. You can't deny it.'

'Look, you have it all wrong.'

'Then kindly illuminate me.'

'That article was put together *before* we—'

'Exactly. I now know what you had in mind when you decided to return my calls. The career entrepreneur who has no time for men in her life.'

'No.'

'Yes. It's obvious from last night that you don't trust

me, that you never have, that you probably don't trust any man on account of one crap experience. It's obvious that I've been used as a convenient baby-making machine. Maybe I should be flattered,' he sneered, 'but I'm not. I'm hurt. You gave me some grilling these last couple of weeks. And now you're looking for a handy excuse to get rid of me.'

'No, Sam.'

He ploughed on as though he hadn't even registered her voice. 'What about last weekend? Sunday morning? Was that part of your plan? Giving me no time to use protection?'

'Sam, please, I was carried away.' She fought for breath, her chest collapsing, hating the steely expression in his eyes.

'Bollocks. You used me to suit your ends. If – when – you'd eventually become pregnant, you probably didn't intend to even tell me about it. I know by the look on your face that I'm pretty close to the mark.'

'You have it all wrong. That article was put together weeks ago. Maybe I felt like that at the outset of our relationship, but—'

'Too right you did. About time you admitted it.'

'How dare you speak to me like this.'

'So far,' he glared at her, 'you haven't shown the smallest amount of trust in me. You've equated me with that jerk who took you for a ride. You slept with me to suit your own selfish plans. I was the idiot in the right place at the right time. More fool me.'

'This is all wrong. Look – look at the photos.' Her hand trembled as she rifled through the magazine. 'These were taken just after I met you. Before we started seeing each other. I was thinking of you when I smiled for the camera. What does that tell you?'

His eyes narrowed. 'You were probably thinking of the

lovely children I'd make. Imagining how my son or daughter would look.'

Her consternation, she knew, was reflected in her eyes.

'See?' he snapped.

'Sam, please, okay.' She struggled to take a calming breath. 'Maybe I had all that in my head at the beginning, but I soon realised how ridiculous the whole idea was. You've no idea how much you mean to me, how highly I think of you, how much I need to you to . . .'

'Yeah, sure. You don't need me, Paula, you only need a convenient stud.'

'Where did you get this anyway?'

'Does it matter?' he asked, poker faced.

'No, probably not.'

'Abby showed it to me. She bought this to help her fine-tune her CV.'

'Abby.' Paula gave a bitter laugh. 'How appropriate.'

'At least when she says she needs me, I know she means it.'

She watched him turn on his heel and march out of the office. He left the offending magazine on her desk and she picked it up with shaking fingers and fed it piece by ripped off piece into the steely jaws of her shredder.

After a while she rose to her feet, pulled on her jacket, grabbed her bag, car keys and phone. She said something to Kate to cover her sudden departure. She took the lift to the underground car park and was about to deactivate the alarm on her Jaguar when she realised that she wasn't in a fit state to drive anywhere. So she struggled up the ramp, hampered by her heels, made it out onto street level and staggered into the first available taxi to take her home.

46

Her head was pounding and her throat was dry. Her eyes felt gritty, as though someone had blown large quantities of sand into them. It was a struggle to open them, but she persevered.

It took Paula all of five minutes to register where she was. Her body felt stiff and cold. She was lying on her bed and the late evening shadow had fallen across the room. She gingerly stretched her body, realising that she had one shoe on and the other one was removed. Her skirt was twisted around her body, her shirt agape. She turned her head a little and the square of sky captured by the uncurtained window was a dark, molten grey glimmering with the reflection of phosphorous from the streetlamps. She was dimly aware of occasional traffic noises coming up from the road outside.

Even in the shadows, she could discern the shape of the empty wine bottle on the bedside locker. Somewhere above and beyond the pounding of her head, a phone was ringing insistently. Then Paula remembered. With a muttered groan she kicked off her remaining shoe and buried her head in the pillow.

After she'd struggled home from the office, she'd opened a bottle of fifteen per cent proof Chilean reserve. Several glasses later, her hangover had already begun to pound, so she'd taken two strong painkillers to counteract the pain. But nothing could counteract the pain in her chest, so she'd slumped on her bed in total despair and cried her eyes out. Exhausted, she must have fallen asleep.

When the phone began to ring again, she realised it was her mobile, which she'd left on the kitchen table, but she let it ring out, unable to gather enough energy to walk out to pick it up. She lay inert for a long time, held in the grip of sorrow and regret, her heart bleeding with the picture of Sam's face as he'd thrown up his hands in a despairing gesture and strode out of her office. Then she slid once more into a deep, dark sleep.

Eventually she roused herself and put one foot to the floor, followed by the other, and standing upright she stumbled out to the kitchen. She had to squint at her phone through half-closed eyes to see that there were four missed calls and three text messages. All from Elaine.

Bloody great. All she needed was her sister on her case. Glancing at the kitchen clock, she dialled Elaine's number, listening to the ringing at the other end as the phone pealed in Wicklow.

'Hello? Paula?' Elaine's voice was groggy. 'What on earth is wrong?'

'Why should anything be wrong?' Paula felt as though she was talking through sandpaper.

'Why should . . . ? Paula, are you okay?'

'Course I am.'

'Then why wasn't I able to contact you all afternoon, all evening? Why are you phoning me at three in the morning?'

'Three . . . ?' Paula looked at the clock again and realised to her horror that far from being eleven fifteen, as she'd thought, it was actually five minutes to three in the morning. Even though she was in the grip of a massive hangover, she felt as though she was drowning in a sea of embarrassment.

'God, Elaine, did I wake you?'

'Yes, you did, and don't dare tell me there's nothing wrong, you silly goose. What's up?' Elaine voice was soft and warm in spite of the late hour and Paula felt tears gathering once more behind her eyes.

She couldn't answer for several moments and tried in vain to control herself. From the sniffing and gulping noises, Elaine obviously guessed what was going on. She kept talking, telling Paula that she'd become concerned when she'd phoned the office that afternoon, and on getting no answer she'd let the call go through to the main office, whereupon Kate had told her that Paula had gone home before lunch and that she didn't really seem to be herself.

'Kate said that?' Paula's voice was dry and parched. She'd had words with Kate, hadn't she? On top of which Kate was bound to have witnessed Sam's thunderous march out of her office.

'Yes, she did. I asked her what she meant, but she wouldn't elaborate beyond telling me you'd left in rather a hurry and forgotten to log off your computer. So I'm coming up tomorrow night, rather, today night, as it's already Friday, and you can tell me all your troubles.'

'Honestly, there's no need. There's nothing to tell.'

'Jeez, Paula, quit pretending. You might be a big noise in the Dublin recruitment scene, but you're still my sister and it sounds as though you're in a spot of bother. So no arguments.'

After the call, Paula went into the bathroom and froze when she caught sight of herself in the mirror.

Her usually sleek, pale blonde hair hung in lank, clumpy tendrils around her head. Her face was blotchy and puffed, her nose swollen and roaring red. She could hardly make out her blue eyes because they were reduced to thin, purple slits.

Was this her? Is this what Sam had done? Reduced her to something out of a horror movie? The reflection in the mirror bore no resemblance whatsoever to Ms Paula Stevens, entrepreneur extraordinaire. Where had that woman disappeared to? She stared at her image in horror and then, like a fog clearing, the answer came in the form of a cold little voice.

Sam hadn't had a hand in this. She'd managed this all by herself without any help from him. And why? Why had she reduced herself to this? Truth was, deep down she cared so little for that clever, intelligent woman that she'd allowed her to disappear behind a bottle of Chilean red, Paula sadly realised. And she didn't need psychotherapy to know that it was her choice, and hers alone, as to whether she stayed there in that horrible dank place or did something about it.

The very first step was to switch on the faucets and gently rinse her swollen face. After that she felt a little better, so she stripped off her clothes and stepped into her shower, letting the warm, sluicing jets go to work on her tired, stale body, reviving and cleansing. She tipped her head back and felt the jets run down her face and massage her head. Then she wrapped herself in a velour robe and went out to the kitchen and methodically emptied the contents of her wine rack down the sink.

She felt more tears prick at the back of her eyes, but now they were tears of release and a kind of acceptance. Then she poured a large glass of blueberry juice, sat in her sitting room and watched the dawn break and the sun rise, mentally preparing herself for the day that lay ahead and practising thinking about Sam without bursting into tears.

She was sitting at her desk by half past seven, answering emails and responding to requests, checking her voicemail and fully composed by the time Kate arrived at eight o'clock. She went through the busy day, grateful for the discipline that allowed her to focus on Stevens and all its demands rather than the image of Sam's despairing face.

Kate followed her lead, and apart from a sympathetic glance when she brought in Paula's coffee, she gave no hint that she was aware of the turbulence in her boss's life. She surprised Kate by taking her out to lunch and instead of waiting until four o'clock to talk through some staff issues, she talked to her immediately after lunch, Paula finally agreeing to rethink her overtime policy and making back-up plans for Kate's holiday absence. Then she sent Kate home early to give her plenty of time to pack and relax before she headed off on her early-morning flight the following morning. Paula was shattered by the time she reached home that evening, just in time to shower and change before Elaine arrived.

'Where's Ruth?' she asked when Elaine breezed into the apartment, complete with a bouquet of flowers, a bag of goodies and a big hug.

'She's at home, of course, being spoiled by her daddy. I know I've been neglecting you lately, too wrapped up in my daughter, but tonight is for us, or should I say, for you. I'm staying over, if that's okay,' Elaine said, putting the flowers and goodies down on the kitchen table and ducking back out into the hallway to fetch her overnight case. 'You look like you could do with some company,' she went on, giving Paula no time to object. 'You look like you could do with a good night's sleep as well, but that's what happens when you go around phoning sisters at mad hours of the morning. Oh, and something else, Paula – I've no intentions of leaving until I'm satisfied that I've sorted out whatever is bothering you.'

For the first time in days, Paula couldn't help but smile. A surge of tenderness and affection for her sister washed over her. Elaine, with the benefit of her newly-acquired maternal instincts, obviously thought she could fix up Paula's problems much in the same organised manner that she looked out for her little daughter.

If only she knew.

She hesitated, vacillating between this new, motherly Elaine and the tearaway Elaine of yesterday who'd skipped up Mayberry Lane, thumbing her nose at her serious big sister.

'Thing is, sorting me out could prove to be rather difficult,' she said, her voice wobbling a little. 'I've made some pretty silly mistakes.'

'Come on, try me,' Elaine urged. 'Let it out, Paula.'

She swallowed hard and felt something melt inside her. Her pride? Dammit, she had none left. The last remnants of her stubbornness? Perhaps. Whatever it was, she felt a sudden urge to talk, to share, to open her heart to her sister. Taking a deep breath, she tucked strands of hair behind her ear and surrendered herself to Elaine's mercy. 'You've no idea how stupidly I've behaved, but right now I'm stuck fast in a messy triangle involving me, Abby and . . .' She could hardly say his name, it made her feel so ill. Tears sprang in her eyes and slid down her cheeks.

'Who, Paula? Tell me. It's okay,' Elaine reached out a comforting arm.

Paula gulped. 'You'd never guess, but it's Sam. Sam Ryan.'

She didn't have to say another word. It was as though Elaine immediately understood what had been going on. And this time, Elaine didn't thumb her nose up at her big sister. Instead, she gave Paula a look of tender concern as she pulled her into her arms.

47

At first Abby was delighted when Elaine phoned on Saturday afternoon to say she was dropping over for a visit. She decided she'd show Elaine the glittery heels and Jenny Packham dresses she'd brought home from London for the party. She'd already tried them on and felt like a different Abby Lacey. Elaine was bound to say she looked sexy and alluring. As sexy and alluring as Paula. Maybe they could even have a laugh at the idea of Paula and Sam together.

But none of this was happening.

Instead Elaine thought it was funny being back in the house on Mayberry Lane. She looked around almost dismissively and said she'd never expected to see Abby home again.

'I never thought you'd end up back here. Surely you find it a bit dull after all your exciting travels?' she asked.

Abby ignored her. 'Come and see what I've picked out for next Saturday night,' she said. She brought Elaine into her bedroom, the way she used to all those years ago when they were getting glammed up for the local discos and city centre clubs. 'Which do you think Sam would prefer? This blue slinky number or the silvery halter neck?'

If she'd expected Elaine to show some enthusiasm, never mind appreciation, she was mistaken. Elaine merely nodded her head. 'Whatever you prefer, they're both lovely. Colin's coming as well. He's heard so much about our crazy childhood that he's really looking forward to it.'

Abby swallowed her annoyance as Elaine sauntered out
of the bedroom and into the kitchen. 'Hey, guess what
happened on Wednesday night,' she began, anxious to put
herself and Sam into the same context.

'Did he stay over?' Elaine asked when Abby was finished
recounting the story of the supposed intruder and Sam's
swift response.

'He did.' For a long moment Abby was tempted to pretend
he'd shared her bed, but there was a knowing alertness in
Elaine's gaze that put her on edge and she heard herself say,
'He stayed in my grandmother's old bedroom.'

Abby made coffee and cut generous slices of cheesecake,
grateful to focus on something. Then she took out the photo
albums to show Elaine. She spread them out on the kitchen
table and Elaine pored over them, the memories springing
thick and fast. Elaine pounced on photographs of their last
day at school and shook her head indulgently.

'You couldn't wait to go to work and earn some money,'
Abby grinned. 'Whereas me, I went off to college and then
started to travel. Little did I know that I'd come back to
Sam.'

Elaine put down the photograph. 'Abby . . .' she hesitated.
'Has he said that he still feels the same for you?'

'Well, of course he does. We're best mates, always have
been.'

'Yes, but has he actually told you he loves you? Since
you've come home?'

Elaine's question hung in the air and cut to the quick,
mainly because it was something Abby had been tormenting
herself with since Thursday morning. She shook her head.
'No, not yet, but I'm sure it will come.'

'What makes you so sure? Didn't you tell him over and
over that he wasn't the one for you?'

'Please don't remind me of that,' Abby said.

'Look, I know we've talked about this already,' Elaine said, 'but I just wanted to clear something up in my head.'

'Hello? This is me and *Sam*, for God's sake. He makes me feel, just . . . how can I explain?' She tried to think of something that would satisfy Elaine without going into the deep, dark hollow of her heart. She tried to think of something that would satisfy herself and settle the confusion eating away at her and in the end she said, 'He makes me feel as though everything in my life is right again.'

'I'm sorry if things didn't turn out the way you expected, Abby,' Elaine said, closing the album.

'When did I say that?'

'You said Sam makes you feel that everything is all right again. What went wrong? Do you want to talk about it?'

Abby didn't reply at first, struggling for the right words. Why the hell was Elaine pouncing on every little nugget of anxiety that had started to find air time inside her jumbled-up brain? Her hands clenched around her mug as she said, 'If you must know, my life was somehow at a standstill. It was kind of meaningless. Then Sam came along. He's always been there for me.'

'Yes, I know, but as a best mate. I'm sorry if your life ground to a standstill, but why did you need Sam to pick up the pieces?'

In the tense silence that followed, Abby put some cheesecake into her mouth and tried to swallow it. She hated the way Elaine was talking, voicing her fears and plucking them out into the open, naked and defenceless. She hated the way she was regarding her with a steady, thoughtful gaze.

'Think about this for a minute,' Elaine persisted. 'Does Sam make you feel passionate? Wonderful and amazing?' Elaine pressed. 'He never made you feel like that before. That's how Colin makes me feel, and he'd need to, to help me put up with him at times,' Elaine gave a half smile. 'Look,

I'm trying to help. It seems to me there are a few crossed wires around here and I'm trying to save a few people from making some really flaky mistakes.'

Something crumpled inside Abby. 'Like what?'

'Like supposing Sam realised all those years ago that you were right to turn him down? And then, what if he met someone when he came home from Italy?' Elaine said gently.

As Elaine talked, Abby felt as though she was crying somewhere deep inside. But it was much too far away for her to reach.

Elaine was still talking. 'You know it would never work with you and Sam. It wouldn't have worked years ago and it's only fantasy to think it would work out now.' Her voice was soft and determined, which made it all the more credible. 'My sister and Sam are . . . involved. I didn't know anything about it until – well, we sat up all last night talking and Paula told me everything. He told her he was afraid to break the news to you because he didn't want to hurt you. Right now she's deeply unhappy, and Sam's angry on account of a misunderstanding. I want to help sort it out. Has he talked to you about any of this?'

'Yes, but it's ridiculous,' Abby blurted, unwilling to face this painful new reality even though it had been staring her in the face since Thursday morning and hating the feeling that she was clutching at straws in an attempt to avoid facing up to painful truths. 'Paula spent her life treating the three of us as though we were some form of killer disease!'

'You're exaggerating. Okay, she didn't have much time for us, but maybe we were at fault as well. I think Paula and Sam are perfect for each other, believe it or not. At the same time, you're my friend and I don't want to see you hurt.'

'Oh, really?' Abby's voice shook. 'Me and Sam go back forever. My life is nothing without him.' She heard the echo of her voice as though she was standing outside of her body and wondered why it sounded so odd.

'Nothing? Abby, your life doesn't revolve around him. It never did. You were always your own, free-spirited, independent person. And a brilliant friend to me. What's happened to you? What about all your dreams? Why do you need Sam to shore up your life? You seem to have lost yourself somewhere. Talk to me,' Elaine urged, reaching forward and squeezing her arm. 'Tell me what's going on. I'm saying all this because I care for you. Sam cares for you as well, but as a good mate. Do you understand?'

She couldn't answer Elaine any more than she could find a way through her muddled head. She made more coffee and tried to contain her bewilderment, some tiny instinct warning her against alienating Elaine completely. Then she changed the subject and asked about Ruth. Elaine was clearly relieved to talk about something safe and neutral.

'Just have a think about what I've said,' Elaine said as she prepared to leave. 'If you need to talk or a shoulder to cry on, I'm not that far away. I'm not sure what's going on with you, but I know you'll get over it. You're the most plucky, courageous person I know. Most of all, you deserve someone really special, not someone who just makes you feel right. You know deep down that that's not anywhere near enough.'

Abby felt stiff when Elaine tried to give her an awkward hug at the hall door.

'You'll be there next Saturday, won't you?' Elaine asked.

'Yeah, sure. Of course I'll be there,' Abby said.

'Colin and I will collect you on the way to Malahide if you like.'

'Good, ta.'

'Are you okay about . . . ?'

'Yes, I'll be fine.'

'I'll talk to you next week.'

*   *   *

The house felt different after Elaine left. Something had shifted. Abby walked around the quiet rooms, recalling the bubble of excitement she'd been swept up in as she'd packed for Australia. So impatient to get going and spread her wings that she'd never spared a thought for Sam.

She picked up her phone and dialled his number. He hadn't replied to the text she'd sent him on Thursday. Or Friday. At the very least, she could close her eyes and listen to his voicemail greeting. It might help to stem the peculiar feeling that everything was falling apart inside her. To her surprise, he answered immediately.

'Sam, hi, you're around.'

'Abby. I'm in my music room. What's up?'

Did there have to be anything up for her to phone him? What happened to all the times they had simply chatted and hung out together as friends and talked about nothing in particular? 'Did you get my texts? Saying thanks for the other night? It was good of you to come.'

'No prob. You're okay now, though? No more spooks?'

'No more spooks. I was having a bad moment and you happened to be around, so thanks for being there. Sorry if I gave you a fright.'

'You didn't give me a fright,' he said evenly.

'Anyway, I'm fine now,' she assured him.

'Good, I'm glad to hear that. See you next Saturday?'

'Yeah, sure.'

She didn't really deserve his kind patience, Abby agonised when she put down the phone. She'd told Sam that she loved him, but she couldn't ignore the stark fact that the words had sounded so odd on her lips. Neither could she ignore the fact that the safety and security of Sam's arms hadn't been anywhere near enough all those years ago and would never be enough.

Elaine had said she was plucky and courageous, but she

wasn't, not really, Abby thought sadly. Because deep down inside she was causing herself far more distress by denying the true love of her life and acting as if he'd never existed. And she'd blanked it out for far too long because she didn't have the guts to deal with the crushing pain, never mind face up to the part she'd played in his loss.

48

Lia was wrestling with the second draft of *Imperfect Murder* and half listening to the *plock plock* of tennis racquets that drifted up from the courts in the corner of Sadlier Square park.

It was a bright Sunday morning with a distinctly lazy feel to the day and Lia would have preferred to be going for a stroll around the square and getting some fresh air, but she was so far behind in her work that she'd sat herself down at her desk early that morning and any fresh air she was enjoying was courtesy of the opened sash window adjacent to her desk.

Abby's phone call was a welcome distraction.

She'd already talked to Abby twice that week and her daughter had sounded like her usual bright and breezy self. Lia told herself she'd obviously made the right decision after all in sending Abby back to Dublin and was relieved that there were no repercussions after her revelations of the previous weekend. She could just about cope with her own bitter memories, her long-buried sense of anger and outrage, once Abby was okay.

'Any word on Alejandro?' Abby asked.

'No, no more developments,' Lia said. 'I'm still trying to put the researchers off the scent.'

'Good for you. I didn't say anything to Sam or Elaine. They don't need to know. The reason I was phoning you, Mum . . .' Abby hesitated.

'So it wasn't just from daughterly concern,' Lia joked.

'I just thought I'd ask you again if you wanted to come over for the party? It's next Saturday. We'll all be there.'

'No, Abby.'

'I'd really love to have you over. We could go to the party together.'

'You know the party, reunion, whatever, is the last thing I want to go to. Wild horses couldn't drag me over. I thought I explained all that to you.'

'Yes, but I'm asking you to change your mind. Look on it as a favour for me.'

'Abby, that's impossible. Ask me anything, but not that.'

'Look, Mum, you're the one who told me that the past was the past, to move on and make the best of things. There's no point in letting something that happened years ago, a lifetime ago, stop you from going to a bloody party. And that's all it is. A party. Not an execution of sorts.'

Lia closed her eyes. This, now, coming on top of everything else that was going on in her life, was just too much. How come everything that she'd considered carefully locked away was gradually crawling out of safe and secret hiding places? Well, almost everything. She had one last secret that she was determined to protect for dear life. No way was that going to be revealed to all and sundry. She continued in a genial tone of voice, 'You've your friends to go with, Sam and Elaine, haven't you?'

'I'm not sure about that,' Abby said slowly.

'How do you mean?'

'Sam and I, well, we seem to be . . . I dunno, it's not working out quite as I expected.'

'I thought he was pleased to see you?' Lia's voice was sharp.

'Oh, he was. We're just not in a relationship, as such.'

'A relationship?' She obviously meant they hadn't slept together yet, Lia thought, deciding not to go there. 'You might just need some patience,' she went on. 'Maybe you're expecting too much too soon.'

'Yeah. Thing is, Mum, he's kinda friendly with Paula.'

Abby's voice sounded breathless, as though the words had rushed out, and Lia felt a stab of unease. Maybe her bombshell had upset Abby more than she realised. 'I wouldn't let that worry me too much if I were you.'

'Wouldn't you?'

'Sam could never take his eyes off you when you were growing up. And maybe you were too young to remember, but Mark and Paula had some kind of fling and, well, I just can't see Sam getting too involved there, especially when Mark lands home.'

'But Mum, that's the thing, you're mistaken.'

'What?' Lia was feeling irritated. She was tired from sleepless nights, anxious lest the whole Alejandro thing blow up in her face, fretful that the past was stretching out a mocking hand towards her and now Abby was trying every last ounce of her patience. All of a sudden, she found it difficult to maintain an even voice.

'Oh, never mind. Forget it,' Abby said 'I still wish you'd come home anyway.'

'Look, you'll all be better off without me there. Just put last weekend behind you and go out and enjoy yourself. What exactly are the arrangements?'

'The plan is to meet up in Sam's place in Malahide, then a meal and some clubbing in town, then back out to his place to stay over. There's a barbeque on Sunday afternoon.'

'Sam must have plenty of room.'

'Yeah, four big bedrooms all en suite, I believe, and there'll be six of us including Colin and Elaine as well as Paula.'

There was a silence.

'Abby? Are you there?' Lia asked.

'Yeah.' Her daughter's voice was faint.

'What's the matter?'

'Nothing, Mum. I better go. Talk to you soon.'

The connection was broken and Lia didn't know whether to be relieved or annoyed.

On Sunday afternoon, Paula stood on the pavement outside her apartment block and said goodbye to Elaine.

'Don't ever bottle stuff up again,' Elaine told her firmly. 'And if I ever get my hands around that scumbag Alan's neck, he'll be sorry he ever messed with my sister. I still don't understand why you couldn't tell me.'

'I just couldn't,' Paula sighed. She jingled her keys in her hand and felt the breeze lift her hair as she stood on the pavement. 'I felt so stupid about the whole thing, so used. So ashamed of myself for being led up the garden path.'

'And now?'

Paula shrugged. 'I don't feel anything at all for him. I could pass him by in the street and it wouldn't bother me. I wouldn't even waste my energy getting upset.'

'Good,' Elaine grinned. 'Anyway, it's all ancient history now. Sam is different. He's kind and intelligent. And gorgeous. I won't mention the obvious in case you think I have designs on him. I don't understand what fantasy land Abby is living in. She wouldn't confide in me. Maybe she'll talk to me in time. I just hope I've reassured you that there's nothing between them, so don't let her come between you and Sam.'

'It's not even about Abby any more. Sam just doesn't want to know me. He thinks I was only after his sperm. I really don't see how I can begin to put it right.' All of a sudden, her teeth were chattering, a reaction, she supposed, to the whole emotional see-saw of the last few days. Or else it was the recollection of his face as he'd marched out of her office.

'I'm sure when he's cooled down he'll be ready to listen to you.'

'Maybe I don't want to talk.'

'For heaven's sake, don't let your stupid pride stand in the way, Paula. Please. Life's far too short not to go after what you really want. Just sit him down and tell him exactly how you feel. What's wrong with being perfectly honest with him? You've nothing to lose, have you?'

'This is a funny place to be having this conversation,' Paula attempted a joke.

'Who cares? I'm just so thankful that we're having it.' Elaine fished her car keys out of her bag and gave her a hug. 'Whatever you do, don't stand by and do nothing. Go out there and fight for what you want. Supposing it was your business on the line, being threatened by a rival competitor?'

'Yes, but that's clear-cut business. I could devise a strategy for that. Emotions are far more complex.'

'That's only a cop-out. I thought you were supposed to be the clever one,' Elaine grinned as she climbed into her car.

Maybe it was a cop-out, Paula considered as she waved her sister off, but so what? At the very least, she would avoid having further damage inflicted on her heart, and what could be cleverer than that? She strolled back into her apartment block in the sunny afternoon, telling herself that she had her priorities sorted out now once and for all.

Afterwards she laughed at herself at that moment, and her supreme conviction that she had everything under control. For little did she realise how her whole perspective on life would change on account of a single, throwaway remark.

49

Paula was conscious of an overriding calm surrounding her as she sat behind her desk, even though Monday morning in Stevens was extra busy in Kate's absence. The calm after the storm, she thought wryly. Just before her coffee break, she summoned Maeve into her office.

'Am I fired?' Maeve asked, her defiant words at odds with her nervous body language.

'Relax, Maeve, I'm not going to fire you,' Paula smiled encouragingly at her junior consultant, realising that a few short weeks ago, she'd have had no compunction in terminating her contract.

Maeve bit her lip as though she wasn't entirely convinced. She gave Paula a look that said she didn't quite trust her smile and said, 'Did you have a problem with my leave last week?'

'The main problem I had was that you couldn't discuss it with me in the first instance,' Paula said.

'Yes, but I'd never have got the job here, would I?' Maeve pointed out with alacrity. 'And a wedding, of all things.'

'What do you mean, of all things?' Paula looked at her curiously.

'Well, you'd probably regard time off for a wedding as frivolous,' Maeve said, fidgeting with her biro. 'I mean, it's not as if I needed time off for college exams or something worthwhile like that.'

'I see. This might surprise you, Maeve, but I think weddings can be very worthwhile events. But let's leave the matter there, shall we? I'm not firing you, but in the future, I'd prefer if you could be a little more communicative with me. I called you in to discuss some additional administrative duties now that Kate's on leave. I think you should be able to handle them.'

'Sounds good.' In an instant, Maeve's face changed and grew more animated. Then, as if remembering where she was, she sobered up and adopted a suitably composed expression. Suitable in front of her boss, Paula considered a little uncomfortably.

'I'd be happy to take on more responsibility in Kate's absence. Just let me know whatever you want me to do.' With her biro poised over her notebook, Maeve was waiting to hear a list of instructions. 'You still like your coffee black, and at half past ten?'

Paula sat back, rather at a loss. Her coffee? Did Maeve think she was incapable of making her own? Just what did that say about her? She surprised herself by changing the subject and asking, 'Tell me, Maeve, are you happy here?'

'Of course! I love it here.'

'Why do you love it here?'

'It's the whole feeling of being part of an exclusive, premier recruitment firm, the dynamics of working with top-class institutions and enthusiastic job-seekers. Some days are very challenging, but I enjoy stepping up to the plate. I also like to think that my contribution to the team is important, especially when you find the right person for the right job. I know there are good advancement opportunities in the company . . .'

Paula smiled. Now that she had relaxed, Maeve's enthusiasm was catching. It was refreshing to talk to Maeve like this outside the structured confines of the interview or boardroom, and she threw out some ideas she had for staff incentive schemes, inviting Maeve's opinions. The younger woman was confident, poised and sharply savvy in a way that Paula knew would bring her places.

'So you're not fazed by the demands of the job or extra responsibility?' she asked. 'And I don't mean my coffee, thanks all the same. I think I can find my way to the staff canteen,' she smiled wryly, realising that she needed to be out there, mixing with her staff and not hidden behind her desk in her inviolate office.

'No, I'm not fazed.' Maeve's eyes were honest. 'On the contrary, I'm looking forward to it. I do have some faith in myself.' She smiled a little bashfully before she left the office.

Faith in herself.

Paula fidgeted with a yellow Post-it note before eventually screwing it into a ball. Then she had to hurriedly straighten it out again to read the message. She crossed to the window and opened it, gulping in the fresh air that swirled around her office. Maeve's throwaway remark had hit home, illuminating something in the deep recesses of her mind. For faith in herself was something that Paula was sadly lacking – unless it was a tangible thing that could be measured with a gold star or a framed scroll.

Instead of lunching alone at her desk, she went for a walk in the summery day and had coffee and a sandwich in a cheerful cafe, her thoughts crowding in. She might be on a stellar rise to the top in her field of business, but she had no faith in herself when it came to her feelings. No faith in her attractiveness, so she compared herself unfavourably with Abby; no faith in her desirability when Sam told her that there was something big happening between them and he wanted to give it a chance to grow; no faith in herself when he insisted that an old friendship shouldn't mess it up.

Back in her office, she called up spreadsheets and looked at figures, her mind elsewhere as she clearly saw for the first time that she was blaming Sam for her shortcomings. She was latching onto the fact that he was being friendly with Abby and using it against him to justify her own flaws and imperfections instead of being comfortable enough to accept their friendship as simply that – a relic of their childhood.

She drove home slowly that evening, realising that if she had more faith in herself, she might begin to believe him and trust what he said. Otherwise, she gulped, she'd never again turn around in bed and feel Sam's warm skin next to hers. She'd never meet his eyes as she shared a laugh and a joke with him. She'd never again fall over his feet as she struggled with dance footsteps only to be pulled, laughing, into his arms, or entwine her fingers with his across a table in their favourite Italian, or watch him sloping across the pub, drinks in hand and have the warm, comfortable, glowy feeling that he was with her, and that as soon as he sat down, his arm would curve around her. She slowed to a stop in the car park as she realised that even the fact that they'd already progressed to *having* a favourite Italian was a further cause of grief.

Yet how come it was the small things in life that ran through her mind, as though they'd be missed the most? The answer to that floated quite easily into her consciousness as she took the lift to her apartment, for the small things were only for starters. The big things, such as marriage and babies – Sam's babies – well, they didn't bear thinking about.

At first, Lia didn't recognise the feeling. It had hummed inside her since Abby's phone call on Sunday afternoon, much like an out of tune guitar string, making her feel vaguely uncomfortable. It interfered with her revision and caused her to be snippy with Gary when he phoned her on Wednesday morning, reporting that there was, in fact, nothing to report.

'Nothing whatsoever?' she'd asked.

'Nothing beyond the fact that the *Lunchtime with Rachel* researchers are meeting the Spanish contingent in Madrid later this week,' he'd said.

'And you call that *nothing*?' she said in a derisory tone of voice. 'Would it be too much to ask, when they're all gathered in the one place, that some kindly flying saucer might descend on top of them and suck them away into Neverland?'

'I think you're mixing up E.T. with Peter Pan,' Gary said in a deadpan voice.

Something painful flickered inside her. 'That's not the point,' she snapped before putting the phone down.

She got up from her desk several times and went into her kitchen to make coffee. Throughout the morning she decided that her cabinets urgently need to be cleared out, that her whole wardrobe needed to be examined and rearranged and even that her make-up brushes needed sterilising, but she somehow managed to resist these attempts to lure her away from her laptop. She found her eyes drawn more and more to the window outside and away from her screen, her thoughts focusing firmly on her daughter rather than her plotline.

It took her a while to realise that she felt definite stirrings of guilt because she'd refused Abby's request to return to Dublin for the party. Which was ridiculous. They were both adults, and her well-travelled daughter scarcely needed her mum around to hold her hand or prop her up. Besides, Abby would be among friends, whereas she, Lia, would most certainly not be. It would feel rather like – what had Abby said so blithely? An execution? Yes, that was it. To Lia, the party would feel like an execution of sorts.

She powered down her laptop at lunchtime, totally dissatisfied with her morning's work, then lifted the phone and called Abby. Some light-hearted chit-chat would soothe her guilty conscience. Of course, there was also the possibility that Abby may still be hurt and annoyed with her for refusing to return to Dublin, thus piling more guilt on Lia's head, but she had to take the chance.

However, there was no reply. The phone rang out in Mayberry Lane. Lia tried Abby's mobile, only to be directed to her voicemail. She sighed and stared into space and decided that Abby was deliberately ignoring her, much in the way she'd ignored her calls in the immediate aftermath of the Christmas row.

The post was late arriving on Wednesday in the Stevens offices. Paula had gone through the previous couple of days feeling as though she'd turned a familiar corner only to find the landscape startlingly different. It was so disconcerting that she was relieved to be busily absorbed in the normal office routine. She opened her post in her usual efficient manner, taking little notice of the private and strictly confidential instruction handwritten on the thick cream envelope. When she slid the sheet out, the words jumped up and down in front of her vision, for this was the kind of letter she'd heard about now and again but never personally experienced.

She wished her hand wasn't shaking so much as she held the letter and tried to absorb the content. Phrases leapt out at her: '*Accordingly, I would like to request a full account ... the decision-making processes ... disregard me as a suitable candidate ...*'

Madeline Jones. Obviously trying to find out if she had a case to take to the Equality Authority, probably with the assistance of her alpha male brother-in-law.

As she sat at her desk, Paula was conscious of two things. If Madeline took a case against her, it would certainly damage her business. Two or three months ago, this would have sent her into a tailspin, but any hysterics Paula might have indulged in were quickly squashed, for a little purposeful voice unlatched itself from the dark well of gloom that had occupied a corner of her mind in recent days and made itself heard.

It wasn't the end of the world. Not really. And there was, of course, one person who could help her. If she could run the risk asking him.

On Wednesday afternoon, Abby walked out of the terminal building at Naples airport into the broiling heat of an Italian afternoon and shaded her face from the sun.

She jumped into a cab, reverting to her fluent Italian with ease. The journey to Sorrento took an hour, and when the outskirts of Naples were left behind and the cab took the coastal route, she felt her heart quiver with a sense of recognition as flashes of the rippling bay, the picturesque coastline and the tumble of marmalade roofs appeared.

After the long, lonely nights and empty grey dawns in the echoing house in Mayberry Lane, her heart brimmed with a sense of homecoming. She hadn't told anyone of her plan to return to Sorrento. Acting on some impulse she couldn't quite define, she'd booked her flights and phoned ahead to a hotel. Besides, there was no one to tell, for thanks to her determination to lock the past far away and out of sight, there was no one who'd understand.

But she couldn't have spoken about it or explain why she needed Sam to shore up her life, for she didn't have the courage to open the door on it all, to struggle for the right words, feel the crushing pain in her heart and relive every horrible, guilty moment. Then, as if that weren't enough, she would be at the mercy of everyone's sympathetic glance.

She lifted her chin as the cab wound its way along the cliff road high above the town of Sorrento. Abby Lacey had never been at the mercy of anyone's pity or sympathetic glance. She'd desperately needed Sam and Elaine to see her and treat her as the bright, sparky Abby of years ago, and not a sad, sorry victim.

She stared through her sunglasses as the cab rattled through the narrow Sorrento streets and she recognised familiar landmarks. There was something else that was causing her a lot of anguish – how could she have insisted that she now had feelings for Sam when someone else had claimed her heart? Then there was the appalling prospect of coming under Paula's blue-eyed scrutiny, especially if they were directed at her across the breakfast table on a Sunday morning after she'd spent the night in Sam's bed. It was a realisation that had made her go hot and cold as she'd talked to her mother on Sunday afternoon about the party arrangements and the number of bedrooms in Malahide.

The cab swung to a halt in front of a pretty hotel with drowsy, sun-drenched gardens, and she hopped out and gave the driver a handsome tip. She'd asked for a room with a view of the hills and she stood on her balcony in the summery afternoon. As she lifted her face to the curving skyline and felt the heat of the sun on her limbs, suddenly the reality of Raffaele's loss swept over her in a wave of overwhelming grief.

She missed him so much. She needed to breathe him in and taste his nearness, but never again would they laugh together, love together. She felt the tears bubbling over and she sank down on a patio chair and cried her heart out.

50

When Maeve phoned through on Thursday just before lunch and announced that a Mr Ryan was outside in reception, Paula began to shake.

She'd gathered the strength from somewhere and left a message on his mobile the previous evening, and he hadn't just phoned her back, he'd arrived in person. She was full of gratitude as she told Maeve to bring Mr Ryan through, hold all calls and leave her undisturbed. Sam strolled into her office, his presence so close and so gorgeous that all her nerve endings danced and jangled and came together in a frenzy of longing.

'Paula. Hi. I got your message. You wanted to see me?' His voice was courteous but his face didn't give anything away.

'Thanks for coming so promptly, I appreciate it. Please sit down. I'm looking for some advice,' she began, cursing herself for her formality. 'In the area of legal expertise. I need to know where I stand on this.'

He sat down and at first he ignored the letter she passed across the table. 'So is this all you wanted me for? Some advice?' He shot her a disbelieving look.

'Yes, that's what I said,' she regarded him gravely, terrified, now that he was there, to reveal what was in her heart. This was far, far worse than any of her challenging business presentations.

'For a minute there . . .' He looked at her ruefully, shook his head and laughed dismissively. 'Never mind. Let me have a look.' He picked up the letter and read it once, twice, while she covertly studied his profile and thought how delicious it would be to look into his eyes and kiss his mouth. He slanted a glance at her and caught her staring and she furiously looked away.

'Has this Ms Jones any basis on which to believe she might have been discriminated against?' he asked.

'I suppose on the grounds of her pregnancy?'

'She doesn't actually mention that or refer to it in any way. Why do you think it might be an issue?'

'Because she was about five months pregnant when she applied for the position in question.'

'And you noticed this in the course of the interview?'

'Yes, of course I did. It was obvious.' She arched her eyebrows in true Ms Stevens fashion and inwardly wept that she couldn't shake her off. And why were they wasting time talking about this, Paula fretted. There were a million and one other things, far more important things, that they needed to discuss. It was crazy that she was allowing Madeline Jones and her bolshie letter to take centre stage.

'Hmm,' Sam frowned. 'But you scarcely let that influence your decision? I mean, a visionary woman such as yourself would no doubt be encouraging to your female staff?'

'Wouldn't that be positive discrimination?'

'Not necessarily. They might regard you as a role model and feel they could strive to have it all, the career and the baby.'

There was a hard edge to his voice and some of her fledgling hope evaporated. Sam would never forgive her. She'd been foolish to expect him to forget all about it. He must have noticed the downturn of her mouth, or something in her eyes communicated itself to him, for he went on, 'Don't tell me you did discriminate against her on account of her pregnancy?'

Paula remained silent. Sam watched her face for what seemed like forever. 'Paula? You didn't, did you? What on earth possessed you?'

'I don't know. I suppose I was jealous.'

'Jealous?' His eyebrows shot up.

'Yes, Sam, the green-eyed monster and all that,' she swallowed. 'I remember the day I interviewed her quite well. I felt she'd never attain the business heights that I'd reached but that she had something more precious, which was a baby of her own.'

'More precious? So you were jealous she was having a baby? We'll come back to the discrimination in a minute. Is that when you decided that it was your biological imperative to enlist my assistance and reel me in?'

'Now you're getting personal.'

'Of course I'm getting bloody personal.' His eyes glittered. 'We were very personal up to a week or so ago, remember? So tell me, was this around the time you decided to enlist me, albeit unwittingly, in your plans for motherhood?'

'Well, technically.'

'Technically? So you admit it?' He looked ready to explode and she was afraid to continue.

'Sam, I never denied it, but you didn't – you *wouldn't* – listen to the rest of my explanation. Or how things . . .' her voice was shaky but she had to say it, 'how it all changed for me. You were far too angry to listen to me.'

He sat back, arms folded across his chest. 'Can you blame me? After everything I thought we had between us . . .' Now he looked bleak and her heart clenched.

Paula took a deep breath, forced her shaking knees to stay still and took a huge leap of faith in herself. 'Then why are you here now?' she asked quietly.

'I came because I had to,' he said. 'Any excuse to see you again. Because the last week has been pure, unadulterated hell. I scarcely moved beyond my music room because everywhere I went I saw reminders of you, and it made me feel furious and bloody well hurt.'

There was a long silence.

'The last week has been hell for me too,' she said. 'I was glad of an excuse to see you again.'

What she saw in his eyes when he looked at her made her heart fizz with anticipation.

'Maybe I was a bit off the wall that day,' he went on, sounding subdued. 'Maybe I'm more prepared to listen to you now. So tell me, Paula. Enlighten me. What do you mean, things changed?'

Paula curled her hands tightly together under her desk and told herself to have a little more faith in herself as she went on to explain why she'd asked him out in the first place and how she'd planned to seduce him.

He sat still, poker faced, not betraying any of his thoughts.

'And then,' she went on, 'the night we walked out of the restaurant . . . remember? We got caught in the rain?'

He nodded, his eyes guarded.

'Well, that night, everything changed for me.' She looked away. Bit her lip. Forced herself to look back at him. 'You see, Sam, against all my intentions, all my best-laid plans, I started to fall in love with a great guy, a smashing guy, that night.'

She fell silent. She felt weak and defenceless, yet in that very vulnerability she felt stronger than ever before. Something flashed across his face, yet still he didn't reply.

Paula summoned enough faith in herself to continue, 'And from then on, the last thing I wanted to do was to use you. So although I once thought that it might be convenient to become pregnant with your baby—'

'Say that again,' he interrupted. 'The last bit.'

'Become pregnant with your baby?'

He closed his eyes and opened them again. This time, when he looked at Paula, his eyes were incredibly tender. 'That too,' he said softly. 'But I want to hear what you said just before that.'

Now her throat felt dry and her head was spinning. 'You mean what I said about starting to fall in love with you?'

'Would you mind repeating that?'

By the time she'd repeated the words, her voice was reduced to a whisper, for he'd come around to her side of the table, pulled her to her feet and wrapped her in his arms.

'Paula . . .' He snatched his mouth from hers momentarily.

'Yes?'

'I'm not starting to fall in love with you.'

She drew away and stared at him.

He laughed gently. 'I've loved you since the beginning. Since the first time I dropped in here and you showed off your qualifications, your scholarly achievements. Your big blue eyes looked kinda embarrassed behind all the haughtiness, and I got a feel for the real person camouflaged by that God-awful desk. And Paula, just to be clear about Abby—'

'Shh. It's okay. I trust you.'

She smiled at him. Breathed him in. He began to kiss her again. Her body was alive with need. Her jacket was off and his hands were swift on the buttons of her shirt, then sliding into the velvety softness of her cleavage.

She gasped.

He drew away. 'Sorry. Forgot I was in your office.'

'Don't stop,' she ordered, arching her back.

'Hey, watch it, if we go any further . . .' His voice was urgent. 'Hell – we're in your office.'

'So?' It was as if a giddy madness had taken hold of her, but if felt so right that it couldn't be denied. 'The phone's on hold. No one will dare disturb me.'

It was also terribly wild and wicked, but she so needed to be wild and wicked.

'That desk is very tempting, but I've a better idea,' he murmured. 'That plan you were talking about, the one to seduce me, just what exactly was in it?'

'All sorts of things. Let me see . . .' Already breathless, she could barely get the words out. She slid out of her killer heels, stood on her tippy toes and leaned into him so as not to break the connection.

'Sounds promising,' he said hoarsely. 'So why don't you bunk off? Right now? Look, Mark's flying in later this evening. I'm collecting him at the airport. I've to go back to Malahide to do a last-minute tidy-up and stuff; things got kinda neglected the last few days. Why don't we jump into your car and go out to Malahide together? Now?'

Paula wavered. She glanced at the files on her desk and saw her phone line flashing.

His hands cradled her head. 'I don't know about you, my love, but the last week has been bloody torture and I've missed you so much that I can't bear to say goodbye to you now, even for a few short hours.'

Neither could she bear to say goodbye to him. She needed to make love to him, to fix her sore heart with an intimacy that went above and beyond any words.

'I don't think there's any urgent stuff. And – God – I have to formulate a reply to Madeline Jones.'

He held her at arm's length and feigned surprise. 'So it's authentic? You mean you didn't just concoct that letter as an excuse to see me?'

She made a face.

'So you really were only looking for my expert opinion? Using me again, huh?'

He was teasing. She smiled. 'Well, of course.'

'I'll help you with your reply, not that you deserve any

help, but I can't stand idly by and have you carted off to jail. I do have a conscience, unlike some power-wielding women of my acquaintance.'

'Your *acquaintance*?'

'I'll show you exactly what I mean by that. Later.'

He pulled her close again and sifted his hands through her hair. She closed her eyes and wanted it to be later already. She eventually disentangled herself from his arms.

'And,' his voice was teasing, 'it might be our last chance to use the hot tub for a couple of weeks.'

'That's a major consideration.'

'So why don't you play truant for once?'

If the staff of Stevens noticed that their imperious boss was blushing like a schoolgirl as she summoned Emer and Maeve into her office, they wondered if it had anything to do with the sexy guy who was waiting impatiently in the reception area, the sexy guy who'd landed in without an appointment and had been seen straight away.

Although he was some kind of lawyer, wasn't he? And he'd called in before. So it probably was purely business.

They watched in silent admiration as she came out of her office and walked out to join him in the reception area. They asked the receptionist what had happened in the foyer between the bloke and their boss, but she merely reported that he'd taken her by the arm as he escorted her to the lift simply because her new Louboutins were causing her a bit of bother.

They asked Emer and Maeve what exactly had she said to explain her unusually short-noticed absence, but they merely reported that she'd told them she had urgent unfinished business to attend to.

Some of them idly bandied the words about as they gossiped over a prohibited afternoon tea break, and bearing in mind the cuteness of the bloke she'd gone off with, they couldn't help colouring her explanation with a sexual connotation and taking an entirely different meaning to the one Ms Stevens surely intended.

For that would never be Ms Stevens, they all agreed.

Not in a million years.

51

On Saturday afternoon, Sam stood in his kitchen and peeled back the foil from the top of the chilled bottle of Dom Pérignon. For the third time in his life, he was angry with Abby.

The first two occasions had been when she'd laughingly turned up her nose at his marriage proposals. Okay, so she'd been quite right as it happened, for his raw, youthful pride was the main thing that had been injured. But that didn't make it all right for her to mess up his carefully-arranged plans for Mark's party. Elaine and Colin had planned to collect her en route, but they'd arrived half an hour ago in Colin's silver BMW, minus Abby, and announced that she wasn't answering the door in Mayberry Lane.

'She's not answering her mobile either,' Elaine had said, looking crestfallen as she stepped into the hall with a bouquet of flowers and champagne. 'I haven't heard from her since I texted her on Monday. Although I had a few things to say to her last Saturday, so she could be avoiding me.'

'Don't worry about it. She seemed fine when I talked to her last weekend,' he said, swallowing his annoyance in front of Elaine, kissing her in greeting and shaking hands with her husband. 'Colin, hi, you're very welcome.'

He showed them to their room and brought them out to the patio in the landscaped back garden where Mark and Paula were chatting under the striped umbrella. He smiled at Paula as Elaine fell on Mark like a long-lost friend.

Then Paula rose to her feet to greet her sister, and he loved the way Elaine deliberately turned towards him to include him in her big, happy, meaningful grin.

'Champagne coming up,' he said, loping back inside to the kitchen.

Now he squashed the foil off the top of the champagne bottle into a ball between his fingers. He aimed it at the bin, missing it completely.

To hell with Abby. He wasn't going to let her mess this up.

Truth was, he'd been quite surprised when Mark had run with the idea of a reunion. He'd scarcely ventured home from the States in all the years he'd been there, and when Sam had talked about bumping into Abby, getting her home and organising everyone, he'd said he'd consider it. Sam had half expected that that would be the end of the matter until Mark had announced that he'd booked his flight. And until he'd actually come through arrivals in Dublin airport on Thursday evening, looking happy and relaxed and in holiday mode, Sam had harboured doubts that he'd actually appear.

So Abby or no Abby, they would party on regardless.

Sam stuck the bottle of champagne into a bucket of ice, opened a glass-fronted wall press and took out five crystal flutes.

'Sam?'

'Yes, love?'

Paula smiled at him as she came into the kitchen. 'Need any help? Here, I'll take out the glasses. You know,' she looked at him hesitantly, 'it might be an idea if you phoned Abby. She might answer you,' she suggested, and he loved her for her unselfishness as much as her trust.

'No, it's okay, leave it for now,' he said. 'She'll probably turn up at the Four Seasons tonight.' He followed Paula back out into the garden, grateful that the memory of that lost, empty week without her had faded so quickly. He was still getting used to having her in his life – to watching her sleep, waking beside her in the morning and taking hard-to-believe peeks at the wonderful prospect of sharing his life with her. Already, he couldn't imagine life without her.

Growing up, she'd always been slightly off-the-radar, distant. All that had changed the day he'd walked into Stevens and felt the undeniable spark when her blue eyes had fastened on him as she sat behind the shelter of that desk. Since then, she'd touched him and excited him in ways he'd never expected. Getting to know all about the real, grown-up Paula Stevens had been like discovering a wonderful gift.

He felt so protective of her that he hoped he'd never come in contact with that sad bastard who'd betrayed her, for if he did happen to run across him, he'd surely end up on the wrong side of the courtroom. Now, this weekend, and whatever about Mark, he was damned if he was going to let Abby upset Paula in any way with her deliberate absence. She'd already caused enough trouble between them. So tough shit if she was playing the drama queen.

Paula put the glasses down on the wooden patio table.

'Am I missing something here?' Mark asked. 'What's wrong with Abby?'

'Everything and nothing,' Sam said. He lifted the bottle out of the bucket and prepared to pop the cork. 'Everyone got a glass? Mark, I can't believe I finally managed to get you home from the States. That's worth a celebration in itself, never mind you going over the hill!'

And he popped the cork with a flourish.

Saturday night in the Four Seasons was a laugh, Paula looking particularly animated and smiling secretly at him when he squeezed her thigh under the table. He was glad in a way that Abby wasn't there, especially if she was in a sulk, because Abby Lacey in a thundercloud sulk was a sight quite difficult to ignore. Paula clung to him in the electric frenzy of the nightclub, and again he was slightly relieved that Abby wasn't there to observe them. Elaine said she'd forgotten what it was like to have a night off and she promptly announced that she was falling in love with her husband all over again. Mark, in an ice-white shirt and black jeans, could have had his pick of an endless stream of glamorous babes, yet he paid them little or no attention.

Sam couldn't figure what the hell he was waiting for.

'How come Mark's still unattached?' Paula asked him as she snuggled into him in bed that night, or rather the early hours of the morning. After the nightclub, they'd shared a people-carrier cab back to Malahide and he'd taken out his guitar and played music long into the night.

He lay with his arm curved around Paula, loving the scent of her and the feel of her soft, silky body pressed close to him. 'Why? Do you fancy changing his status?' he asked.

'No, thanks. One Ryan is about all I can handle,' she laughed, splaying her fingers across his chest. 'It's just he's so attractive and successful. And he could have had his pick of anyone tonight.'

'I dunno, honestly. He was always private about his girlfriends. Blokes don't really talk about that stuff the way girls do. Hey, we're wasting time. Let's talk about us.'

'Talk?' she murmured, reaching up to kiss the side of his face.

They were all up late the following morning and Sam commandeered the kitchen and organised a big fry-up for his guests. Elaine and Colin left for home as soon as brunch was over. 'It was a brilliant night, Sam, thanks for everything, but we have to get back to Ruth and release my mother-in-law,' she said. 'Enjoy the barbie, and Mark, we'll see you again before you head back.'

Mark rose from the table to hug her goodbye and shake hands with Colin. 'Sure we will.'

Sam strolled out to the driveway with his guests. It was a summery August morning and his heart felt full as he watched Paula hug Elaine goodbye. She looked gorgeous in white jeans and a pink top and her blonde hair shimmered in the sunlight.

'Let me know when you talk to her,' he heard her say.

'Are you still worried about Abby?' he asked as he stood with his arm slung around her while they watched Colin's BMW disappear through the gates, Elaine waggling her hand out the window.

Paula shrugged. 'I just want to make sure she's okay. Anyway,' she smiled up at him, 'I know what it's like to want Sam Ryan and to have to do without him.'

He squeezed her tightly. 'You haven't taken me away from Abby,' he pointed out. 'I was never really in *love* with her. I never saw her in my life the way I see you.'

He was pleased with the success of the barbeque that afternoon, the caterers pulling out all the stops. He was proud to show off Paula to extended family members and friends. In the early evening, he took out his mandolin and joined Dave and Rory and as the lively music drifted across the garden, he realised that he felt happier than he'd felt in years.

'Are you glad you came home?' he asked Mark, patting him on the back as he went through to the kitchen at one stage.

'Yeah, sure, it's been great so far. And you're a lucky bastard, because she's wonderful,' he nodded at Paula.

'I know,' Sam said soberly.

'It's great to see you two guys together. I never would have guessed you'd connect. I think she'll be good for you.'

'What about you, Mark?' he ventured. 'How come you managed to escape the altar rails all these years? I mean, take last night – you weren't short of admiring babes.'

Mark shrugged. 'There was someone, once,' he said, surprising Sam with his candidness. 'But it didn't work out, and after that,' he shrugged, 'well, it spoiled me for everyone else.'

Sam eyed him keenly. 'You must have fallen very hard. Or else it's all or nothing with you.'

'I guess you could say that.'

'Which was it? You fell hard or she was the "all"?'

'Both, actually.'

On Monday evening, Sam brought Mark over to Paula's apartment for dinner. She'd left the office earlier than usual to cook a good old-fashioned roast beef. Her face was slightly flushed when she opened the door to them and he felt a surge of tenderness as she looked particularly cute.

'Smells good,' he said, kissing her pink cheeks.

'I'm just proving my cooking credentials in front of Mark,' she laughed. 'Here,' she said, handing him a bottle of Châteauneuf-du-Pape, 'make yourself useful!'

'You don't need to prove anything to me, Paula,' Mark said. 'Not if that delicious aroma is anything to go by.'

After the meal, when they were relaxing with coffee on Paula's sofas, Elaine phoned. Mark took his coffee over to the windows to stare out at the Dublin city skyline while Paula chatted to her sister. When she put down her mobile and told him that Elaine still hadn't managed to contact Abby, something pinged in the corner of Sam's mind, like a bell striking a distant chord.

'It seems a bit odd,' he said. 'I thought she just wanted to avoid the party and the prospect of you and me together. I don't understand why she's still ignoring Elaine. And it's over a week since I've spoken to her.'

'Elaine hasn't talked to her since last Monday. You don't think there's anything wrong, do you?' Paula asked.

'I dunno – for all we know she's gone off kayaking or hang-gliding,' he said, secretly hoping that that was the case.

'Then why didn't she tell you? She was bound to be pissed off with me and you, but surely she'd talk to Elaine, or at least text her? I hope there's nothing wrong. I wonder if it's worthwhile contacting Lia?' Paula suggested.

'Lia? Jeez, we don't want to go off on a wild goose chase,' Sam said, trying to dismiss his flicker of uneasiness. 'I think we should check out Mayberry Lane first, make sure she's not just avoiding us.'

'And if she's not there, it might be an idea to contact Lia. If she knows where Abby is, fine,' Paula said.

'Yeah. Do you have a phone number for Lia?'

'I haven't talked to her in years. Doesn't she have a website like most celebrities? With contact details?'

'That's usually an email address,' Sam said. 'God knows how often she checks that.'

Mark turned from the window. 'There is another option,' he said. 'If Abby's not at home and you feel it's urgent, we could always contact Lia through her publishers.'

The next day, when there was still no answer at Mayberry Lane, Sam logged onto Google and looked up Gaynor-Munro.

52

'Are you sitting comfortably?' Clarissa asked.

'Yes,' Lia said, 'I'm at my laptop, hands poised. Relaxed and in the zone. Where else would I be on Tuesday morning?'

'Look, Lia,' Clarissa's voice changed. 'I don't want to worry you. It may be a false alarm.'

Alejandro. He'd been discovered. To hell with Gary for not warning her first. To hell with the private detective she'd quietly hired, promising to pay him double.

'It's Abby.'

'Abby?' Everything was swept away as Lia's heart fell soundlessly to her toes. 'What's wrong? Tell me quickly.'

'There may be nothing wrong. I've had a phone call from one of her friends who'd like to talk to you.'

'Sam? Elaine?'

'Sam. Apparently Abby hasn't been in touch with either him or Elaine in over a week and she doesn't appear to be at home. He thought you might know where she is. He contacted me in Gaynor-Munro and gave me his phone number.'

Lia felt the breath leave her body.

'No, I don't know where she is. She hasn't been answering my calls either. And this weekend was supposed to be party weekend, so I thought she was out enjoying herself. She asked me to go over for the party but I refused. What the hell have I done?'

'You've done nothing wrong that I know of,' Clarissa

remarked brightly. 'Talk to Sam. He sounded sensible enough.'

'Too sensible to be making wild goose chases,' Lia said. 'You'd better give me his number. I'll get back to you when I find out what's going on.'

For a long time after she spoke to Sam, she sat still as her thoughts flew around in her head. Wild horses couldn't drag her back to Dublin, she'd said, but a missing daughter did what nothing else could do. After a while, she logged on to the Internet and booked a one-way flight, then phoned Clarissa to update her.

She went into her bedroom and watched her hands mechanically open drawers and wardrobes and put clothes into a suitcase, feeling as though she was having an out-of-body experience. She wished that there was some kind of master switch she could throw on her feelings so that the pain in her heart would abate, even a little. She arrived at Heathrow in a kind of trance, barely avoiding mutinous, overloaded trolleys and wavering suitcases being dragged by bulldozing, over-enthusiastic holidaymakers. Right then, the prospect of heading off on a sunshine holiday was so removed from her own journey that it was laughable.

In her distraught state, she perversely felt like phoning Gary and telling him she was finally Dublin-bound, and then she was horror-stricken at the thoughts of being spotted by an eager fan. However, when she went into the ladies and saw her reflection in the mirror, she realised thankfully that no one would recognise her. Her face was pale apart from a smattering of freckles standing out against her pallid skin, and her hair was already mussed and frizzy around the ends. A far cry from the image of the glittering, glamorous novelist.

And that's all it was, she knew, staring at her amber eyes. An image, a façade, and all put together for the benefit of

. . . well, who exactly? And why? Lia swallowed, astounded to realise that it was far too difficult to answer those questions. All she knew was that this was her, now, the real thing, first and foremost a mother, Abby's mum, feeling heartsore and anxious, and all she wanted was to wrap her arms around her daughter and hold her close.

The evening flight to Dublin was full. It took ages to board and she tried to stem her rising irritation as she asked herself where the hell everyone was coming from or going to. Sam had said he'd be waiting for her in Dublin. She knew him immediately when she came through arrivals, even though he was far more in command of himself than she'd ever remembered. Tall, tanned and athletic-looking, never mind outrageously sexy, she could see straight away why Abby had had a major change of heart about him. He drove her straight to Mayberry Lane, where she produced the spare key she'd held onto. Then she let them into the house and held her breath.

There was no trace of Abby. And she hadn't just gone shopping or out for the day, for the house felt empty, the bathroom was clear of clutter and Abby's bedroom was silent and tidy, save for a small plastic figure of E.T. sitting on her dressing table. Then Lia dropped onto the bed and began to cry.

'Hey, Lia.' Sam was beside her in an instant. 'We'll find her, don't you worry. Abby's a born survivor. Hasn't she been all around the world and back again? She was a bit pissed off with me, so in a way I blame myself that she's gone off somewhere without telling any of us.'

'She was very cheesed off with me too, Sam,' Lia said through her tears. 'So if anyone's to blame, it's me. What am I going to do? I don't know how to begin or where to look for her. Oh, God, I've just realised that if she phones me in London I won't even be there.'

'What about your mobile?'

'I don't have one, believe it or not. I always thought it was an intrusion, and I hated the way people could get hold of you wherever you were, but maybe I should have, for times like this.'

'No worries, Lia. We'll find her. I can make a few calls, unofficial of course, and track her down. And there's no point in you being here all alone. Come over to my house and bring your case, I've plenty of room.'

'I think I'd rather stay here.'

'And what good would that do? Abby doesn't know you're here, so what difference will it make? Come over to Malahide and we'll sort everything out.'

She allowed herself to be led from Mayberry Lane, casting a final glance around just in case her daughter jumped out as though she was playing an elaborate game of hide and seek. She sat silently as Sam drove home, barely noticing the impressive gates and the imposing house that he halted in front of. He ushered her in through the door into a wide, tiled hall and directed her into a large maple-floored sitting room that ran the length of the house.

Paula jumped up from the leather sofa, a different Paula to the one she'd remembered growing up, a more sophisticated, glamorous, confident-looking Paula. She was surprised to see her there, until she remembered that as recently as her last phone call, Abby had talked about her in the same breath as Sam, and Lia had dismissed her daughter's conclusions. She wrapped her in a warm hug and Lia caught the waft of expensive perfume.

Something flickered at the back of her mind – the realisation that perhaps Abby had been doubly hurt on top of the bombshell she'd delivered. Surely that would have been too painful by far for anyone to cope with, wouldn't it?

Behind her, the sitting room door opened again and she

saw Paula's eyes look past her to the person who'd just come in.

Lia whirled around. Her heart crashed inside her and she felt a searing pain of recognition as she came face to face with the man with the seductive eyes.

'Hello, Lia,' Mark said.

53

Time stopped. Stood still. Reversed.

She is walking up Mayberry Lane in bright autumn sunlight, the trees already golden and russety, fallen leaves crispy underfoot. She is wearing a calf-length wraparound skirt and a long, multi-coloured scarf. She might be twenty-seven years of age, but when it comes to enticing drifts of autumn leaves, she's every bit a child as ten-year-old Abby, so she aims a kick and laughs at the slow motion whirl of russet and golden and burnt amber.

Laughter echoes behind her. She turns around and comes face to face with Mark.

'Good shot,' he says.

'How's college?' she asks, allowing him to draw near before she continues her stroll up the lane.

He makes a face. 'It's okay. I'd rather be playing music than studying it, but I guess I need to get the mechanics of it right.'

'Some day you'll be famous,' she says.

'Hey, that's not what I want. I just want to spend my time doing something I love. And be with someone I love.' He looks at her meaningfully.

They stop and stare at each other, immersed to their ankles in a drift of leaves.

'I wish you wouldn't say that,' she admonishes. 'You can't. You shouldn't.'

'Why not? It's true.' His eyes are holding hers, dark eyes,

dark and seductive and somehow intuitive. Eyes she has somehow grown to love and trust, despite the gulf – no, the yawning chasm – between them.

The lane is quiet and watchful, no passing traffic, just an occasional leaf falling in a dizzy drift from the line of sheltering oak trees. There is the scent of damp air, pungent with the onset of autumn, and the sun glinting through the silhouette of semi-naked branches. He shrugs off his satchel, bends down, picks up a curling leaf and holds it against her hair.

'The colour of the trees reminds me of you,' he says. 'All amber and russet, and glorious shades in between.'

He is standing too close, yet she is held transfixed by his gaze. She is painfully aware that his mouth is inches from hers. Then he chuckles softly, moves even closer, pushes back her hair in a slow, languorous gesture and kisses her.

Despite all her misgivings, she closes her eyes, leans into him and kisses him back.

'It's a while since you pair have seen each other,' Sam said.

In the sitting room in Malahide, with light flooding in from large picture windows, Lia blinked and stared at him for a long moment, not sure what he meant.

'You and Mark,' Sam went on. 'When was the last time you saw each other?'

'It was just before I went to the States,' Mark said. The quiet, measured voice was faintly accented with American tones. He threw her a glance that was half rueful, half challenging. She didn't make a move towards him, nor he towards her.

If Sam noticed the absence of any warm greeting, he ignored it. Instead he went on, 'Well, you'll have a lot of catching up to do, no doubt, two celebrities together. Funny how you're both from the one small lane yet you're famous and successful in such divergent arenas.' Lia sensed that his voice was deliberately cheerful, as though he subconsciously registered the slight charge in the atmosphere.

Lia realised that if she didn't sit down soon, she was likely to faint. In all her wild imaginings, she'd never pictured this moment. Everybody older, Sam finally grown into the attractive, personable man who'd been lost in Abby's shadow; the tense, inhibited Paula now beautiful and sophisticated, yet with a kindly warmth to her eyes and a soft radiance about her face; and Mark, the longish hair he'd sported in his student days now neat, yet still reserved and self-contained, the bloom of success resting easily on his shoulders, and to judge by his expression as he stared cross the room, when it came to Lia, he was distant now and proudly aloof.

But none of this mattered, for Abby was missing. Her daughter was hurting so much that she'd chosen to disappear without warning.

'Lia, would you like some coffee, or perhaps a drink?' Paula's concerned face swam in front of her.

She was sitting down without knowing how she's got there. Maybe she had simply collapsed into the chair.

'I think Lia needs a brandy,' she heard Sam say solicitously.

She was dimly aware that Paula went to fetch her drink, as though she knew her way around Sam's house. She finally let herself realise that that piece of knowledge had consequences far beyond the dent she imagined it must have made in Abby's heart.

The brandy brought some heat back into her chilled bones. She sat for several moments in the comfortable armchair, waiting for the dizzy feeling to pass, watching the interaction between Paula and Sam as they sat down together on the sofa, letting it filter into far corners of her mind. Mark flipped the lid on a can of beer and poured some into a glass. He too sat down, but thankfully at the opposite end of the room to Lia.

'Right, then, where will we start?' Sam said. 'Who was the last person to talk to Abby?'

'I talked to her last Sunday week,' Lia said. 'She wanted me to come home for the party, but I refused. I said she'd be with her friends, but she seemed to think . . .' Her voice trailed away. She saw Sam and Paula exchange glances and his hand close over hers, finally catching the full significance of their body language.

'Are you both . . . ?' she hesitated again.

'Yes. Paula and I are, well, an item, for want of a better word,' Sam said.

'Paula and you? But Paula, weren't . . . ? Surely you . . . ?' She couldn't help throwing a glance at the silent man in the corner and then back at Paula, lost now for words, unable to phrase it correctly.

Paula frowned. 'Did you also think that Mark and I were somehow involved way back on Mayberry Lane?'

'Weren't you?' Lia's breath was squeezing her chest. It felt like a physical pain. She was acutely aware of him sitting silently, watching, observing.

Paula laughed softly, a laugh that resounded in Lia's mind. 'No, never,' she said. 'Abby and Elaine had other ideas. They took it into their heads that we secretly fancied each other, and between hoax phone calls and fraudulent blind dates, made some rather brilliant, never mind not-so-brilliant, attempts at trying to get us together. I went along with a certain amount of it purely to save my adolescent dignity. So I can't blame you if you got the wrong end of the stick.'

Then Sam was talking. Lia struggled to listen to him.

'Abby was finding us hard to accept,' he said, going on to briefly explain what had happened. 'So you see, I feel responsible for this. She's annoyed with me big time.'

'I think it's my fault she's gone running,' Lia quietly admitted. 'I'm afraid I gave her some rather difficult news when she visited me recently in London.' She took a deep breath and raised her chin. 'You see, I told her the truth about her father.'

Sam said, 'But we all know the truth of that fantasy story.'

'Do you?' It was something she'd already feared, that her secrets had been divulged, and she couldn't help her eyes flicking to Mark. He stared back at her impassively. 'In any case,' she went on, 'it will probably be common knowledge before too long that Alejandro wasn't Abby's father.'

'Wasn't he?' Paula's gasp bore all the hallmarks of surprised shock.

Sam looked perplexed. 'What do you mean, he wasn't her father?'

Lia felt weak. She looked slowly from one to the other. 'I thought you said you knew,' her faint voice trailed away.

'All we know is that you were highly inventive about his fantastic travel exploits in the way you weaved mystical tales about him, but we'd no idea that Alejandro wasn't Abby's father,' Sam said.

She was grateful that in his total surprise, Sam was oblivious to the silent look she gave Mark, who met her contrite expression with polite guardedness. 'I'm not going to go into the details right now,' she said. 'I've no wish to discuss it, as some secrets are best left like that, but I can tell you that it was rather a shock to Abby.'

'Why did you feel the need to tell her now, after all this time?' Mark asked. It was the first time he had addressed her directly apart from his initial greeting.

'Because a certain tacky television programme has come up with the idea of finding Alejandro and reuniting me, Alejandro and Abby on live daytime TV.'

'Good God.' Sam shook his head. 'What are you going to do?'

'I'll deal with that another time. Right now I have to find Abby. She could be anywhere.' Lia bit down a sob.

'Have you any idea at all where we might start to look?' Sam asked. 'Where were her favourite places?'

'The whole world was her oyster. But lately she did seem to be very settled in Italy for some reason or other.'

'That's a starting point. With your permission, Lia, I'll make some phone calls and pull a few strings,' Sam said. He rose to his feet and patted her on the shoulder. 'I didn't want to do anything until I'd spoken to you and checked out the house, but if you agree, I'll get onto it straight away. I may not have any answers, though, for a while.'

'Thanks, Sam.'

He confirmed Abby's details, including her date of birth, then left the room with Mark. Lia tried to make small talk with Paula until the men returned.

'We'll have some information this evening,' Sam said, sitting back down beside Paula, 'so you'll just have to be patient for a little longer.'

'Thanks, Sam, I really appreciate it.'

'How about some food?' Paula suggested. 'Lia? Can I get you something to eat?'

'I'm not hungry. Although I haven't eaten since I spoke to Sam this morning,' Lia admitted.

'I'll get something light ready.'

'By the way, Sam, I've just realised – what made you think of phoning Clarissa?' Lia asked.

'Mark suggested it.' Sam nodded at his brother.

'I saw her name on the acknowledgement page of your latest novel,' Mark explained, looking discomfited. 'It seemed the quickest way to get to you.'

'Thank you. Good thinking,' Lia said, daring herself to meet his eyes.

*   *   *

A short while later, Paula called them into the kitchen. Sizeable and all as it was, with a long, refectory-type table and high-backed leather chairs, Lia knew that it brought her far too close for comfort to Mark. He sat down just a few feet away from her, the man who'd poured out his dreams to her, the man to whom she'd entrusted her secrets, yet now, as then, the divide between them was insurmountable. Contrary to her fears, it was clear that he'd kept her secrets. Contrary to her imaginings, neither had he been involved with Paula.

Paula chatted away as she arranged breads, a salad bowl, smoked salmon, cold meats and cheeses, obviously deciding that light-hearted conversation was the way to go. Sam followed her lead, the intimacy between them plain to see, the same intimacy that had no doubt upset Abby.

She let the conversation flow over her head, realising that if anyone noticed she was quiet, they would surely think she was anxious on account of her daughter. She tried to eat, the food tasteless on her lips. From time to time she stole furtive glances at Mark, that last final scene with him going around in her head, and she was incredibly touched by the fact that he'd not only bought her novel, but had read and remembered the acknowledgement, so much so that he'd known to phone through to Clarissa in order to reach her as quickly as possible. She absorbed the sound of his voice as he joined in the conversation, slightly different yet achingly familiar. She let it wash over her and seep like warm liquid into her parched and jangled senses. Now and again, she felt his eyes rest upon her, thoughtful and intent.

There was something bugging Mark.

Sam gulped the last of his coffee and threw him a glance, unable to figure it out. Behind his outward appearance, his brother was stiff with tension, as though he was on some kind of high alert. Could be he was overly concerned about

Abby. Whatever it was, he was a changed man to the Mark who'd laughed and joked as he circulated with his party guests on Sunday afternoon, or the Mark who'd relaxed in Paula's apartment only the previous night. As the day had unfolded, with the fruitless visit to Mayberry Lane and the subsequent phone call to Gaynor-Munro and Clarissa, Mark had become more and more subdued. But now he was radiating a nervous, charged energy. And he'd been like that, Sam swiftly cast his mind back, ever since Lia had arrived.

Ever since Lia . . . ?

Sam froze, then took a breath and looked curiously at Mark. Then hairs rose on the back of his neck as he intercepted a swift glance that his brother darted across the table towards the equally tense and pale-faced Lia, who was nervously pushing some food around on her plate.

Holy shit.

He'd no time to follow this train of thought, for just then, his mobile shrilled. He picked it up, excused himself and stepped out into the conservatory, Paula joining him as he listened to the voice at the other end. Several moments later, he returned to the kitchen, where Mark and Lia sat as if frozen in some kind of waxwork tableau.

'We've found Abby,' he said.

Lia's face crumpled. 'Where? Tell me.'

'You were right, she's in Italy. She flew into Naples airport last Wednesday—'

'Last *Wednesday*?'

'She's staying in a hotel in Sorrento. She seems to be fine.'

Lia's eyes filled with tears. 'Sorrento. I should have known she'd be there. Why didn't I cop on before now?'

'Lia, don't blame yourself.'

'You don't understand. When I saw Abby at Christmas, she was upset about something and I handled it all so stupidly. Something had gone wrong in her life, but before she had a chance to confide in me, I stomped all over her feelings. We ended up having a row and she flew straight back to Italy and to whatever was keeping her there.'

'Abby might not have confided in you anyway,' Sam said. 'I've asked her several times if anything was wrong because she seemed kind of needy,' he paused, anxious not to upset Lia further, 'but she kept insisting she was fine.'

Paula went around the table and gave Lia a hug. 'Please don't be hard on yourself. At least we know where she is.'

'I'm going to Italy,' Lia stood up, looking, defenceless and very much alone. 'I need to talk to her, to see her for myself. How soon can you get me on a flight, Sam?'

Sam glanced at Mark and tried to marshal his thoughts. 'Probably tomorrow, if that's okay. But Lia, I really hate the thought of you heading off on your own like this,' he stalled. 'I can see you're anxious and upset. And I don't think—'

He felt an excitement surge through him when Mark spoke from the other side of the table, his voice deliberately neutral. 'If you like, I'll come with you, Lia.'

54

Abby was glad that it was quiet at this time of the evening, with the coach parties and tourists returned to their hotels. She was able to admire the panorama for herself and feel as though its spectacular beauty was flaunting itself for her and her alone.

The light had changed and the sun had slipped behind the western mountains so that half of the village of Positano was a fudgy sugar-cubed whiteness, basking in late evening sunshine, the other half cloaked by the shadow of the mountain, the tumble of buildings thrown into three-dimensional relief in the shade.

She'd forgotten how definitive the shade of blue across the swell of the Golfo di Salerno was, how calm the vast expanse seemed from this vantage point, how perfectly the colour complemented the paler sky. She looked to where the scatter of sailboats crawled imperceptibly across the smooth lapis lazuli surface, much in the manner of scraps of white confetti sprinkled haphazardly upon the deep. She stared down into the serene, secretive depths, tasted the warm scented breeze and felt it riffling her hair, and everything that had happened since she left Italy drifted through her mind.

Then she realised that although everything looked the same as it had a few short weeks ago, the scene had somehow altered, changed, reshaped itself irrevocably in an indefinable way. Maybe the few weeks in Dublin had distanced everything so that it wasn't quite the same, for the intensity of feeling had already softened.

Yet it was still her favourite place in the world.

'Your favourite place?'

She heard his voice as though he was standing there beside her.

'Yeah. I thought it was yours too.'

'It was, once, but the world is so big and fascinating that it's hard to have just one favourite place.'

'Well, I've been around the world, and this is mine.'

She tried to ignore his voice as she turned back and looked down at the steep plunge from the edge of the precipice, measuring its fall. For a second it had seemed to be the answer to everything – by the time the sun would have set behind the mountains, it would all be over.

'You'd never survive that,' he said.

'I'm a very good swimmer,' she automatically boasted. 'I've swum with the dolphins in Akaroa.'

'So you've told me. But I doubt if you'd even make it to the water. Not with those jagged rocks.'

'Maybe it's what I deserve. What happened to you was all my fault.'

'Abby! *Cara mia,* don't blame yourself. I don't blame you.'

'Anyway, I couldn't do it.'

'Good. You've far too much going for you to want to do something rash.'

'What makes you think that?'

'I see it in your face, a curiosity, a light, a spiritedness. It's what I loved about you from the beginning.'

'I don't feel so bright at the moment.'

'Maybe you don't, not right now, but who knows what's around the next corner? You know what they say about the darkest hour.'

'Yes, I know.' She was impatient. 'But that doesn't make it any easier.'

The sun had shifted westwards, throwing more of the

village into the shade, and the breeze had risen. Although she was alone on a viewing ledge above the boundless sea, she didn't feel the least bit nervous or afraid. It was suddenly easy to talk, to voice her fears, to listen to the whispers in the wind and summon up his voice.

'Alejandro wasn't my father,' she said.

'I see.'

'Is that all you have to say?'

'Who was your father, then?'

'I can't tell you that.'

'Are you going to start searching all over again for him?'

'No. As far as Mum is concerned, Alejandro should have been my dad, so therefore he was my dad.'

'Then it seems quite simple to me.'

She lifted her face to the last of the evening light. 'How so?'

'If your mother felt that Alejandro was your father, and you're not going to look for your real dad, then it seems to me your mother is right in her thinking.'

'Yeah, that's what I'm trying to tell myself. That's one of the reasons why I came here, to sort it out in my head. I've rather a lot of stuff to sort out,' she admitted.

'What else is troubling you?'

'I met an old boyfriend from Ireland and I followed him home because he made me feel safe again and reminded me of a time when life was full of promise. I thought he'd mend my heart, but it was all a bit confusing.'

'In what way?'

'I thought I'd find myself in his arms again, but all I found was an echo of our childhood friendship, a safety net, the comfort of his hug, which has nothing to do with real passion.'

'And you'd know about passion?' his voice teased.

'Yes, thanks to you I know how it tastes, how it feels, how it inflames all the senses.'

'You're lucky. Not everybody manages to have that experience. You said you wanted to feel safe,' he went on. 'Is that important to you? More important than passion?'

'I thought it was, but no, it isn't. I think that after a while, I'd get bored with feeling safe.'

'I think you would too.'

'I miss you so much. I knew you'd understand.'

'I've always understood you, and will always love you. *Ti amo, bella Abby, sempre.* But you must look forward and not back. You must pick up your dreams again, for life is out there, waiting for you.'

She fell silent for a while and let the resonance of his voice echo in her head.

When Abby looked out across the blue expanse again, she realised why it appeared to be different. Now, for the first time, she saw, out beyond, the call of the horizon.

55

Sitting in the window seat, struggling with the buckle of her seat belt, Lia felt stricken with shyness.

It had been okay in Sam's lovely home, both the previous night and that morning, where he and Paula had smoothed the awkward pauses between them with plenty of light conversation. Then, in the busy airport, check-in procedures had kept them occupied and given them some neutral talking points. Once through security, Lia had taken refuge in the duty-free, pretending she needed to stock up on Clinique, then disappearing into Hughes & Hughes, pretending to browse the shelves. If Mark noted that she returned to the boarding area just as their flight was being called minus any purchases, he kept his silence. Courteous and respectful, he fell into step beside her as they walked down the carpeted tunnel to the airplane. She was grateful for his presence. The journey was fraught enough without having to undergo it alone.

But now that she was buckling her seat belt, the full realisation that Mark would be sitting in close proximity to her for the duration of the journey was sweeping painfully over her and rendering her tongue-tied.

Added to that was the knowledge that they had to take two flights, much as Abby had done, travelling out to Naples via Gatwick, and that thought troubled her. Abby had touched down in London almost a week ago, and she hadn't even known about it.

'Okay?' Mark asked her, smiling a little diffidently as the plane taxied out to the runway.

'Fine,' she replied. Her mouth felt woolly and she racked her brains for suitable conversation.

'Tell me about Abby. How did she sound the last time you talked to her?' he asked.

She was grateful for the question. She cast her mind back to the previous Christmas, and even further to her daughter's emails of the previous autumn, and she told Mark everything that had happened, feeling that although she was ostensibly talking about her daughter, she was communicating with him all the time on some deeper level. Their eyes met and held, their hands brushed as he passed her airline coffee. She was acutely aware of his shoulder next to hers in the confined space, his elbow touching hers on the narrow seat rest between them.

And above all that, she was acutely aware that she desired him still, had never, in fact, stopped wanting him.

As she spoke and he listened, interjecting now and again with a question or a comment, she was highly conscious that they were slowly but surely absorbing each other all over again, much in the way they had all those years ago when they began to get to know each other on Mayberry Lane.

It had all started the night she brought Abby to see *E.T.*

Perhaps if she hadn't brought Abby to the movies that particular night, Lia thought afterwards, or maybe if she hadn't been caught with gushy tears in her eyes, their paths in life might have run in altogether different directions.

She'd never paid much attention to him before that. She'd known that a family with two sons were living in the bungalow up at the end of the lane and that Abby had become friendly with Sam, the younger lad, and had asked him to her birthday tea, along with Elaine, a little blonde girl who lived next door.

Lia's life was busy between her job in Value Centre and looking after Abby when she got home from work. She rarely socialised, so she enjoyed bringing Abby to *E.T.*, as it was a night out at the movies for her too. She hadn't expected the compelling story and evocative music to grab at her heartstrings and send her into meltdown. After all, she was twenty-four and all grown up. When they exited the cinema and bumped into Mark Ryan in the foyer, Lia was embarrassed at being caught with a puffy face and red eyes by the pimply adolescent from the end of the lane. He was alone and had obviously watched the screening by himself, and Lia thought briefly that his girlfriend must have let him down. Although he was barely old enough to have a girlfriend, she considered, glancing at his immature, sensitive-looking face and solemn dark eyes, eyes that regarded her a little shyly. Seven-year-old Abby was excited and giddy and Lia was grateful that her excitable daughter chattered nineteen to the dozen as they strolled to the bus stop together.

Abby climbed to the upper deck of the bus and commandeered the front seat, ordering Mark to sit beside her. Feeling rather helpless, Lia sat immediately behind them. Abby began to make faces out the window and Mark turned around to Lia. His face wasn't all that pimply, she noticed, just a couple of spots on his chin that were more endearing than off-putting.

'What did you like best about the movie?' he asked her.

'I wouldn't even know how to start answering that question,' she laughed. 'What about you?'

'For me, it was the music,' he said. 'That's why I went to watch it. Could you imagine a movie without music? Go on, think about it for a minute. Think *Jaws* without that introductory music sequence.' He smiled at her, and she thought it was an extraordinarily beautiful and knowledgeable smile for a teenager.

She considered what he'd said and then smiled back at

him. 'Gosh, no, you're right. A movie without music – how dull and dry.'

'Mummy, can I get an E.T. bike?' Abby got fed up making faces and squirmed around in her seat.

'What's that, darling?' Lia asked.

'A bike with E.T. sitting in front,' Abby said hopefully.

'You mean a bike with a basket on the front?' Mark asked.

'Yes, that's what I said, an E.T. bike.'

'Maybe for Christmas,' Lia said.

'How long it is 'til Christmas? What are you getting?' Abby's chirpy voice was directed at Mark as the bus pulled away from the terminus and she barely stopped talking as they journeyed out to Mayberry Lane.

A couple of days later, Mark appeared at the door with a miniature E.T. He'd bought it for her, but full of embarrassment, she'd given it to Abby. After that, he stopped to chat when he bumped into her occasionally. And a couple of years later, when he was seventeen and had suddenly, overnight, shot up to almost six feet tall and filled out a little, Mark Ryan started working part-time in the same branch of Value Centre.

'It's just a few hours a week, mostly in stores, evenings and weekends,' he told her when she bumped into him in the canteen and almost dropped her tray in surprise. 'I'm hoping to go to college to study music next year,' he went on. 'I'd like to have some dosh of my own. Can't be begging off the parents all the time.'

It was the most natural thing in the world to suggest they travel home together when their finish times coincided. Buses to the north Dublin village nearest Mayberry Lane were few and far between and meant a long walk from the nearest stop. Months later, when Lia learned to drive and bought a second-hand Fiat, she gave him a lift whenever they were clocking off around the same time.

He spoke to her of his love for music, and she talked of her writing dreams. Music was his passion, he told her. He wanted to spend his life making music. Writing was her passion, she said. Now that Abby was a little older, she was trying to find time to write in the evenings.

And then, as they travelled home together on occasions, Lia found herself sneaking glances at him, noticing his loping stride as he came towards her in the car park, his sensitive eyes full of enthusiasm as he sat close in the car telling her about his hopes, the way his mouth curved in a smile and the way he used his lean fingers to shove his dark hair away from his face.

She felt as though she was being caught up in a dangerous whirlwind. She was twenty-seven now. She had a daughter of ten. Alejandro was part of the dim and distant past. Abby's father, likewise. This music lover from down the lane, who was handsome in a broody way, was doing mad things to her blood supply and her breathing. Problem was, he was nine years younger than her – an insurmountable chasm at their stages in life.

No one on the lane thought anything beyond the fact that she was merely giving a neighbour an occasional lift home from work.

Lia told herself she was imagining the attraction growing between them, the electrical current that was a living thing. In any case, she was playing with fire, for Mark would soon have lots of girlfriends. She waited to see if he would start to get involved with some of the younger assistants in Value Centre, or the prim and studious Paula next door, whom she'd seen throwing glances in his direction.

Then one night when she was leaving him home, instead of getting out of the car, he leaned over and kissed her. Just the briefest of touches, a feathery kiss, yet it scorched her mouth.

'Mark! You shouldn't. You mustn't.'

Even in the shadowy darkness of the November evening, she could see the hurt on his face. 'Why not? You must know I fancy you, Lia.'

'Get away, Mark Ryan!' She attempted to make a joke of it. 'Pick on someone your own age!'

He continued as though she hadn't spoken. 'Ever since the time I saw you coming out of *E.T.* and I saw your face, I fancied you. I think – oh, Lia,' he hesitated, then it came out in a nervous rush, 'I think I love you.'

She was shaking and her face was hot. 'You can't say things like that. You daren't. And you can't talk of love, you're far too young. You don't know what you're saying.'

'I'm not too young. I know how I feel about you and me and that's the most important thing. Don't treat me like a stupid teenager.'

'You're far too young. There is no you and me.' She switched on the ignition with trembling fingers.

She tried to avoid him in work, but it was impossible, just as it was impossible to avoid bumping into him on Mayberry Lane from time to time. Impossible not to kiss him back when he put his mouth to hers, or to feel shivery when he put his arms around her. She was amazed that no one suspected, no one took heed of her flushed cheeks or heard her thumping heart. When Mark started college, he held onto his part-time job in Value Centre, and she was amazed that no one in work suspected either. All they saw was the quiet, private, single mother with the carroty hair giving her neighbour a lift.

She brought Abby to Scotland to talk to her about Alejandro, but also because she needed a break away from the lane and hoped to sort out her head. She talked to Abby all right, but she didn't – couldn't – sort out her head.

Then kissing and hugging wasn't enough.

'I want us to make love, Lia,' Mark said. It was the end of November, and a year since he'd first kissed her. They'd been working late on Christmas orders. By the time they were driving home, it was after ten o'clock. At Mark's insistence, Lia had pulled in to the kerb before they reached the lane. They needed to talk, he urged. It was better, she thought, to pull into an anonymous, poorly lit side road rather than risk being seen parked on the lane with him for any length of time. She switched off the engine.

'Did you hear me?' he asked into the thick silence.

'No.' She wanted it too, though, something she'd never thought she'd desire – intimacy with a man. Intimacy with Mark.

'Yes.' He pushed her hair away from her face in a gentle gesture. 'I need to make love to you. Properly.'

She started to shake. 'I can't.'

In answer, he caught her lips with his and kissed her deeply, and she was shaking even more by the time he lifted his head.

'I want you, Lia, do you hear me? You're driving me mad, crazy.'

'It's just your testosterone talking,' she said lightly, her heart hammering. 'You're infatuated, that's all.'

He drew back and in the shadowy confines of the car she sensed his hurt, palpable and raw.

'Please don't treat me like a child. I'm not a pimply kid any more, I'm twenty, almost twenty-one, a man who wants a beautiful woman.'

'Me, beautiful?' Lia laughed. 'You need to be with girls your own age, not the likes of me. I'll soon be thirty years old!'

'Girls my own age don't interest me.' He spoke with the earnestness of youth. 'They only giggle and talk about pop stars and clothes and want a good time. I can talk to you about my dreams and my feelings. *Our* dreams. You're the one person I've always been able to talk to. I feel we understand each other. I think you're beautiful, Lia. I want us to be really close, to be together. I want to show you how much I love you.'

Without warning, Lia burst into tears.

Mark was immediately contrite. 'What's the matter? Have I upset you? God, I'm sorry.'

'You don't know me,' she sobbed. 'You don't know the real me. If you did, you'd never say I was beautiful. I'm ugly inside, warped and ugly.'

'Why are you so upset? Surely you know how lovely you are.' He kissed her gently on the forehead. He was full of tender awkwardness as he put his arm around her and stroked her hair.

'You don't know what really happened. No one does.' Lia struggled for breath. 'Or why I can't make love to you. Ever.'

'Why not? What's wrong?'

'I can't tell you,' she groaned. 'It's far too horrible.' She cried again, sobbing into his shoulder, hearing the muffled sound of her cries in the car. He held her close for a long time, waiting patiently for her to finish and to draw a normal breath.

'What's so horrible? Did someone hurt you, Lia?' he asked eventually, his voice tender.

'Yes,' she whispered, hanging her head.

He reached across and lifted her chin. He touched his mouth to her tears and kissed the corners of her mouth. 'Who? When?'

'After Alejandro.'

'Abby's father?'

'He's not, he was never, Abby's father.' Lia's voice was a whispery echo. 'It was just a brief holiday romance that went nowhere, we never even slept together. He was going back to Madrid, to college. On the way home on the boat I got upset and had too much to drink . . .' Lia shivered. 'Oh God, I can't go on.'

Very gently, Mark's hand caressed her hot face, wiping away tears, pushing back her hair, smoothing it as you would a frightened child. 'It's okay. You don't have to go on.'

'I think I'll go mad if I don't speak of it now.'

'Then tell me. Tell me what's making you cry.' He was holding her as though she was infinitely precious to him, and in that moment, she trusted him enough to share her deepest, darkest secret.

56

Even then, she blessedly couldn't recall the finer details of what exactly had happened on that fateful night-time voyage across the Irish Sea, having blotted out so much of it in her attempt to cope.

She'd been unable to sleep and, already missing Alejandro, had slipped out of her bunk, headed to the bar and ordered a Bacardi and Coke. She'd seen it advertised and thought it sounded exotic, but she hadn't a clue how strong it was, or how easily it could make everything so distant and unreal.

The alcohol had rushed to her stomach and equally fast to her head, taking the edge off everything and turning the pain of her sore heart into a bearable, indistinct fuzz. She remembered feeling amazed at its ability to help her forget all her troubles so that she could laugh and joke with the young man who'd perched on the stool beside her and told her she had gorgeous hair.

She couldn't even remember his name.

She thought afterwards that that small, bald detail had been the worst thing to get her head around. And it hadn't exactly been rape, she'd told herself in the immediate aftermath. Especially when she'd allowed him to bring her down to his cabin, far too drunk and incapable of making a proper decision for herself, to stop him when he'd . . .

She'd never spoken of the pain and terror of those moments, never told anyone what had happened, especially not her bereaved mother. When she discovered, two months later, that she was pregnant, it was far easier to pretend that Alejandro was the father. And when Anne Lacey suggested that at the very least he needed to know, she told her mother quite fiercely that apart from the fact that she hadn't got his address, she never wanted to lay eyes on him again.

Now, wrapped in Mark's arms and sitting in her little Fiat parked in a quiet, shadowy side road near Mayberry Lane, she haltingly told him the truth.

'I met someone at the bar. I went back to his cabin . . . Oh, God.' Lia broke into a further torrent of weeping. 'Please don't ever tell anyone, not Abby, not my mother,' she said in a harsh, ragged voice. 'Please, Mark.'

'Of course I won't. But Lia, what happened? Were you attacked?'

'No. Yes.'

'This man, did he . . . ? Back in his cabin?'

'Yes, but it was my fault for getting drunk, so I was just as guilty.'

'What? *Guilty?* Lia, darling.' He gathered her even closer. 'You aren't guilty. He was way out of line, the bastard.' He rocked her back and forth. 'You are a special person, the loveliest, most beautiful person I know. What happened to you . . . Jesus, it was terrible, but no way are you to blame. He took advantage of you, can't you see that?'

She sobbed into his shoulder as he murmured the same reassuring words over and over. After a while, her tears stopped and she felt a curious calm. She moved slightly out of his arms and tried to mop her face. His profile was partly visible in the light slanting in from a nearby streetlamp. He was barely twenty-one and she'd told him something shocking, yet he was still looking at her with such an expression of love and tenderness that her heart leapt into her throat.

'I want to make it up to you, Lia. I want to make love to you and show you how special it can be with us.'

'You deserve better than me, Mark. I'm damaged goods.'

'How can you speak about yourself like that? What about Abby?'

'What about her?'

'Isn't she the most gorgeous, bright and bubbly daughter?'

'Yes, but—'

'You'd never say there was anything wrong with her, would you?'

'No, of course not.'

'Well then. She's a reflection of you, something wonderful that resulted from that night. That's all you need to hang on to. He was the guilty one, not you. But you have Abby as a result, and she's all you, brilliant and amazing.'

'I've always thought of her as being Alejandro's daughter. It was the only way I could live with it.'

'There's nothing wrong with that.'

'It was a way of saving Abby from knowing the awful truth as well. Unless, God forbid, she ever wants to trace him.'

'Did you ever, well, think of going for counselling? Or talking to someone?'

'No way. I never even wanted to put it into words until now. And I don't want to put it into words again. I want to forget all about it,' she said, wiping her eyes, some of her spirit returning. 'I want you to forget all about it. As far as I'm concerned, it never happened.'

'Surely it's better to talk it through with someone, someone professional, rather than let it cloud the rest of your life? Or even talk to your mother?'

'I can't turn around now and tell my mother, no way, and it won't cloud the rest of my life. I've shared it with you. As far as everyone is concerned, it never happened. Okay? Please, Mark.'

'Okay. If that's what you want, it never happened,' he repeated. Then he kissed her so softly on the lips that she started to cry again.

A few weeks later, against her better judgement but finding it impossible to ignore the yearning in her heart, Lia went to bed with Mark.

He was full of youthful tenderness and passion. He was painstakingly slow as he kissed every inch of her trembling pale flesh, then he teased her freckles, soothing and caressing and calming her skin as though she was treasured beyond price, and he dispelled each and every memory of that shocking and revolting night, renewing her soul and replacing terror with trust and pain with passion, as well as giving her the kind of pleasure she'd never expected to feel.

They went to bed together a few times, always in Mark's bungalow at the end of the lane when Lia could slip away and the coast was clear. Lia was torn between this new and wondrous dimension in her life and the cold hard fact that Mark was nine years younger than her.

Nine years!

Then Paula Stevens brought everything crashing down upon her.

One April evening, when the evening sky was bright with the onset of spring, Lia arrived home from work and got out of the car to find her younger neighbour watching and waiting in her adjacent front garden.

'You haven't seen Mark, have you?'

Lia's heart squeezed. Did she know? Did anyone suspect?

'You obviously didn't give him a lift home,' Paula went on in that clipped voice of hers. 'Was he by any chance in work today?'

'Actually, no.' Lia forced her heartbeat to return to normal. 'He wasn't in work, or if he was, I didn't run into him.'

Paula gave her an abstract smile. 'No worries.'

'Were you supposed to be seeing him?' Lia ventured. Paula shrugged as though it was no concern of Lia's.

Suddenly she was raging with jealousy and all the insecurities that went with it. It hit her with the force of a sledgehammer. Paula, much younger and with that fresh, dewy bloom of youth that she didn't even know she possessed, was surely far better girlfriend material for Mark than Lia, nearly thirty and burdened with a whole heap of baggage.

Then the following weekend, she heard Mark being called to the phone over the public address system.

'Is everything all right at home?' she asked as they drove home that evening.

'Yeah, why?'

'I heard you being called to the phone.'

'Oh. That was just Paula.'

Paula. How come he was mentioning her name? Was he trying to remind Lia of her existence? Drawing her gradually into conversations, the easier to explain that he had feelings for her? The easier to let Lia down gently?

'What did she want?'

'I dunno. She seemed to think I was looking for her.'

'And were you?' She felt like his mother, questioning him like this.

Mark frowned. He looked incredibly young and vulnerable. 'No, of course not.'

Naturally, he'd deny it, Lia thought. He was scarcely going to come straight out and admit that he fancied her. Now that he'd gone to bed with Lia and slaked his desire, he fancied a slim, blonde, intelligent girl who was going places, as opposed to a practically middle-aged mum who'd been through the wars.

Then Mark gave up his job in Value Centre.

'I'm coming up to my finals,' he explained as they drove

home on a bright sunny evening. 'I can't afford to have any distractions. Of the work kind, I mean.' He threw her a smile. 'I have to get stuck into the books.'

'I can understand that,' she smiled a little sadly.

'I knew you would. I'll miss our journeys home, talking to you, but it's only for a little while. After my exams, we'll have to have a serious talk about where we're going, okay?'

'Okay.'

He was slowly starting to move away from her, she felt. It was gradual, but he was putting a distance between them all the same. She missed him, missed the chats she would have had with him on the car journeys home from work, missed being in his arms, as he didn't have any spare time what with all the cramming he had to do. And in the bright summery evenings it wasn't so easy for her to wander innocently up the lane to his bungalow.

Then she heard Abby chatting to Elaine about Paula and Mark in the same sentence, in the same breath, as though they were an item. The first couple of times she ignored it, but on the third occasion, she couldn't help but ask Abby, 'What's that you were saying to Elaine? About Paula and Mark?' She felt incredibly foolish and silly but needed to know.

'Oh,' Abby was offhand. 'We were just talking about their romance. Do you think they make a nice couple, Mum?'

'How would I know?'

'Elaine and I really think they're suited.'

Lia felt as though a knife was twisting in her heart. She'd asked for this. She'd known all along that she'd only end up getting hurt. She'd been stark raving mad to listen to Mark Ryan, to think she could trust him. He was a man, after all. She might have known he couldn't be trusted.

Then came the evening she pulled into the driveway, a college evening for Mark, one of his last before his exams, and Paula was heading down her driveway all done up, looking anxious and nervous.

'Are you off somewhere special?' Lia asked, dreading the answer.

'Just off to the movies. With Mark.'

'Oh?' Her face pained. 'Where is he, then?' she went on, feeling foolish.

'I'm meeting him outside the cinema in O'Connell Street. He's going there directly from college. I think he needs a break before his exams.'

She'd watched at her bedroom window for hours and her heart stopped when she saw them coming up the lane together. She didn't wait to see if he gave Paula a goodnight kiss. She wondered if he'd told Paula about her, the carroty-haired mother with the guilty secret.

She heard Abby say to Elaine that she was delighted they'd finally seen sense and got together at last.

'I think it's best if we finish,' Lia said, stony faced. 'I'm setting you free, Mark.'

Abby and Elaine had gone into the city centre for a meal with Sam and his parents to celebrate his birthday. Mark wasn't going, Abby had announced, as he was too busy cramming for exams. It was the only opportunity, Lia decided, to get him alone and talk to him.

Mark looked bewildered in the face of her determination. He ushered her into the kitchen, where his music theory books were spread across the table. 'What? What's going on?'

'Don't pretend. You know we've come to the end of the road.'

'Sorry, Lia, I don't get you. What's up?'

'I know you've been seeing Paula.'

'Seeing Paula? No way.'

'Oh, come on, Mark, I'm making it easy for you, believe it or not. I know you went to the movies and there's something going on between you two.'

'I was set up. By Abby and Elaine. We both were. Anyway, one visit to the movies doesn't make me and Paula an item. I don't know who was more embarrassed, her or me. Look, Lia, I'm nearly finished with the exams. I thought you'd understand why I can't see you all that much.' He looked ill at ease. Was he annoyed he'd been caught out?

'I do understand,' she said, feeling tired and dispirited and every day of her thirty years. 'But there's far too big a gap between us. I can't blame you for wanting someone younger, more attractive.'

'Lia, please,' he urged, 'you're the only one I want. You're wonderful and amazing and there's something special about you, something that goes beyond your age.'

'Yes, my age,' she stormed. 'Thanks for the reminder that I'm thirty and you're only twenty-one. It's crazy to think we have any kind of a future. Because we sure as hell haven't.'

'Lia, I love you.'

'That's only the sharp pull of your testosterone talking. You can't possibly love me, Mark. It's ridiculous. And you need someone your own age. Like Paula. I've seen you with her, and you look right together.'

They argued until Lia's throat was closing over.

He said he wanted to bring her to America, her and Abby, so that they could start a new life together. That's where he saw their future.

'That's out of the question,' she said, stony-faced. She felt he was taking the easy way out, using America as a convenient lever. Surely he realised she'd never leave her mum or take Abby away from the only security she'd ever known? She stormed out of the house, fighting back tears, and it took a long time for her to forget the sight of his shocked, pale face.

In the long reaches of the night, after Abby told her that things must have gone pear-shaped with Mark and Paula because he'd upped and left for the States almost overnight, she told herself that he'd been too young and immature, too young to know what he was saying or what he really wanted in life. But it didn't assuage the pain in her chest or prevent her from feeling he'd somehow been disloyal after she'd given him her heart and her soul, and when she unavoidably bumped into Paula from time to time, until Paula herself moved away from Mayberry Lane, she barely spoke to her.

57

'Ladies and gentlemen, we will shortly be starting our descent into Naples airport. May I remind you that seat belts . . .'

The disembodied voice brought Lia back to the air-conditioned aircraft, the flurry of activity as flight attendants passed down the cabin checking last-minute preparations for landing and the quiet, self-contained man by her side.

In spite of the passage of years and the painful gulf between them, there was a gut-wrenching familiarity about him in the way her hand scorched where his long fingers happened to touch it, in the lift of his eyebrow and in the same silent leap in her soul whenever his compelling eyes met hers. At forty, Mark Ryan was in his prime. The enthusiastic, passionate young man had been tempered by life and buffed with success. He was gracious and respectful as he escorted her off the plane, through the melee of Naples airport and out into blazing Italian sunshine, summoning a cab immediately.

He must have sensed, she thought gratefully, that her legs were buckling beneath her, now that she was getting closer to Abby.

At first they sat silently, Lia oblivious to the passing scenery. It was only when they reached the coast road and she saw the vista in front of them that she instinctively craned forward and felt some of her anxiety slipping away.

'Beautiful, isn't it?' she whispered.

'Yes, indeed,' he said.

She was glad he was beside her as they swept along the cliff-hugging coast road alongside the glinting sea, and that he was sharing it with her. Although that was silly and foolish, she chided herself. He had a full, successful life of his own in San Francisco. She'd seen him surrounded by a bevy of glamorous women when she'd watched her DVD recording of his BAFTA award ceremony and had occasionally seen his name linked to beautiful A-list celebrities in glossy magazines. Accompanying her to Italy had merely been a generous gesture from one old friend to another one in trouble. The Mark Ryan of today was light years away from the boyish student who'd spoken of his dreams and who'd made love to her with youthful passion. If there was any kind of subtext between them, she was surely imagining it.

The garden fronting the hotel was a riot of colour, lush with carefully-tended lawns, flower arrangements and lemon trees. Wooden benches and occasional tables were sparsely occupied. To one side, partly secluded by a line of palm trees, Lia caught sight of a swimming pool from where she could hear the splashes of children and the echoing laughter of voices. Inside, the hotel was cool and dim and marble tiled, and the last of a straggling line of holidaymakers had just finished checking in as they reached the desk. Sam had already phoned ahead and booked two adjoining rooms. It was the same hotel that Abby was staying in and Lia was thrown into a sudden panic.

What if Abby resented this intrusion? What if she had gone off to find some peace and space of her own? Supposing she strolled into the lobby right now and was angry at their appearance? She felt frozen to the spot as Mark completed checking in and passed their baggage over to the attendant. Mark had a few words with the concierge and established that a Signorina Lacey was indeed staying at the hotel but that she was out at present. A message could be left for her in the pigeon hole, which would certainly be handed to her along with her key on her return, but Lia declined.

'I'm afraid it might send her running off again and I'd really like to see her,' she explained to Mark.

He saw her to her room and opened the door for her. She felt the brush of his fingers as he passed her the key.

'I'm just next door,' he said. 'Lia?' he hesitated.

'Yes?'

'I don't want to intrude. Now that I've got you this far, you might not want me around when you manage to contact Abby.'

He clearly wanted to go home now that she was safe in Italy. 'Whatever you want, Mark. Thanks for bringing me this far.' It was awkward and she felt suddenly stilted until he smiled. Courteous, polite, but still a smile.

'No problem. I suppose I might as well hang around until you're safely reunited. Sam would kick my ass all the way back to the States if I didn't see you two together. What would you like to do now?'

So he was here because he was doing Sam a favour. Sam, in asking Mark to wait until Lia caught up with Abby, was somehow purging his guilt for the part he'd played in sending Abby running.

'Give me half an hour to freshen up and I'll meet you in reception. Then we'll go looking for Abby.'

Lia sat in the Piazza Tasso with Mark and picked at a dish of fettucine.

'I don't know what I was thinking,' she said. 'We'll never find her in these busy streets. I guess we'll have to wait around the hotel until Abby comes back.'

'That's always an option,' Mark said.

She fell silent, observing the traffic, hearing the roar of

the scooters, watching the milling throngs of tourists, some hurrying, others strolling idly by in warm sunshine. This was where Abby had lived for over six months. She'd walked these busy streets, strolled down the alleyways, had probably sat drinking cappuccinos in this very square, had shopped perhaps in the Standa supermarket they'd passed. Something, someone, had held her captive here, so much so that she'd come back for more.

'Abby was working here as a wedding planner,' she said to Mark, quite forgetting that she'd filled him in on all this on the journey over, just needing to talk about Abby and to fill the silence between them. She felt suddenly alarmed and self-conscious at the situation she found herself in. Mark Ryan, who she hadn't seen for half a lifetime, was sitting opposite her sipping coffee as though he was oblivious to the passion that had once swirled between them. He also looked as though he hadn't had much sleep the night before. He was probably still adapting to his jet lag, she told herself. And he was only here, apparently, on the orders of his brother, who was concerned about his childhood friend.

All of a sudden, her breath was trapped in her throat. She felt the prickle of sweat on her face and even though she was sitting down, the edges of the Piazzo Tasso began to blur. She gripped the table and tried to relax by taking slow, measured breaths.

'Are you all right?' Mark had noticed.

'Fine,' she smiled. 'I'm just not used to the heat.'

'Would you like a cold drink? Some water?'

'No, thanks,' she said as she pushed her plate away. She felt incredibly tired as she rose to her feet and smoothed down her skirt. 'I think it's best to wait for Abby at the hotel.'

'*Grazie,*' Abby said as the waiter removed her empty coffee cup.

'*Prego.*'

'So you don't want to come back?' Rosita asked.

'No, thanks, Rosita, I think my wedding planner days are over.' She adjusted her sunglasses and stared across to the gardens of the monastery, the same gardens where all those months ago she'd come face to face with Sam. She remembered Sam's shocked face that fateful afternoon, and her stubborn defence of her job.

'And you're happy you went home to Dublin?'

'I'm glad I went home,' she said. Even though it had been for all the wrong reasons. She'd been crazy to think that time could somehow be turned back so that she and Sam could resume just where they'd left off, and it was crazy to have expected him to mend her broken heart. She'd also spent far too long in frozen denial of the tragedy that had befallen her love.

'But you had to come back to us for a visit.'

'I suppose you could say that, yes.'

They chatted for a while and then Rosita checked her watch, gave a little cry and leapt to her feet. '*Scusa*, Abby, I must go, I'm late.'

'I'm going too.' Abby rose to her feet and hugged her friend.

'Don't forget,' Rosita said, 'we always have work for calm, patient Abby.'

Calm, patient Abby?

She didn't feel eerily calm any more, Abby realised as she headed back to the hotel. She felt as though she was simmering with anger – anger that she hadn't taken note of the weather warnings that fateful afternoon, anger that she'd left her mobile phone behind on a hotel dressing table. Guilt that she'd dragged him across to Scotland in the first place, to the lure of the purple-shaded mountains. Anger that on account of her stupidity he was gone, so suddenly out of her life, almost as suddenly as he'd come into it.

However, whether she liked it or not, it was finally time to face reality. She had phone calls to make. First her mother, then Elaine and Sam, because although she was dreading it, sympathy or no sympathy, it was about time she told them where she was and what had happened.

Abby Lacey could do lots of things, she mused, but turning back the clock was well and truly beyond the scope of her capabilities. And she didn't really want to go back to her childhood on Mayberry Lane. Growing up, Sam had always been her safety net, but never her passion. In her distress, naturally enough, she'd instinctively run to him seeking solace. But solace, she'd soon realised after she'd cried into his chest that night in Mayberry Lane, was a million miles away from the intensity of joy that great passion brought.

There was no rationalising what had happened to her and Raffaele, any more than she could comprehend what had happened to her mother one night on board a ferry boat, she told herself as she walked along the warm, sun-drenched Sorrento streets. There were times when life was incomprehensible. She just had to live it, to put one foot in front of the other, much as her mother had done, and accept the fact that some things in life would never make sense, no matter what way you looked at them.

She turned in at the entrance of the hotel and saw her mother and Mark Ryan sitting together on a bench under the shelter of lemon trees in the hotel garden, and in spite of all the chaos in her head, when she registered the look on their faces just before they spotted her, something came together and made the greatest sense of all.

She swiftly put that aside for now, for her mother saw her, sprang to her feet, and Abby began to shake.

58

Lia felt Mark patting her on the shoulder before he melted away. Then Abby stood in front of her, silent and shaking.

'Abby? What's wrong? Please tell me.'

At first Abby was incoherent and Lia's heart contracted, for the images sketched out by Abby's jerky words were quite unbearable, never mind incredulous. Lia closed her eyes for a moment. 'Abby, take it easy. Start again from the beginning.'

'I can't.' Abby's lips trembled.

'Yes, you can.' Lia reined in her whirling thoughts, summoned every ounce of self-control and tried to anchor Abby in a steadfast gaze as though she could silently communicate some of her inner strength to her daughter.

'Talk about it. Please. Tell me what happened to you.'

'That's the thing, Mum,' Abby said in a thin, distressed voice. 'I don't feel as though it happened to me. I feel removed from it all, as though it happened to someone else. That it wasn't really me in that cold, dark place.'

Lia smiled sadly. 'Believe me, I understand that Abby, more, perhaps, than anybody else would.'

'It seems unreal and kind of weird. And it's a load of crap as well.'

'I know. If it makes it easier, why don't you tell me as though you're telling me a story about somebody else? Like the way I spoke to you of Alejandro when you were small? Tell me about that cold, dark place. Describe it to me. Speak to me about it.'

'You mean, as in once upon a time?'

'Yes, if you want.'

Lia was relieved to see that Abby had calmed down a little and that some of the colour was returning to her white pallor. So far, Lia hadn't touched her, nervous of invading her space, for the space around her was crackling with tension. Now she tentatively reached out and caressed Abby's arm in a soothing gesture.

Then Abby sat down and began to talk, and Lia still found it difficult to comprehend the terrible, awful scenes she was conjuring up.

From what Abby was telling her, she'd fallen in love with a gorgeous Italian guy she'd met on the safari in Africa the previous October. In their whirlwind romance, they'd even got as far as talking about marriage. Then something had gone horribly wrong. She'd brought him to Loch Lomond and there had been a dreadful accident. He'd slipped off the mountains in the mist and fallen to his death.

Lia's heart somersaulted. It was tragic beyond belief. Yet what had Abby been doing there? And why hadn't she told her mother before now? Why had she bottled it all up? Lia ignored her own questions as she tried to follow the sequence of how Abby's trip to Africa had led to a tragedy in Loch Lomond and then in turn to Italy. Abby's face was angled with pain as she sketched out the details.

'When did the accident happen?'

'Last November. You were away in Australia at the time, or maybe New Zealand.'

'I can't believe you didn't try to contact me somehow. I would have dropped everything and come home to you in an instant.'

'Mum, I was in shock. I didn't know what I was doing. I didn't even know what part of the Antipodes you were in and I'd no phone number for you. As well as that, I was swept along in some kind of frozen hysteria and I wasn't thinking straight. It all happened so fast, a few short weeks from the time I first met him until it was all over. It was like a crazy dream, a nightmare. And afterwards ... well, it wasn't exactly something you could explain in an email. Besides, I blocked it all out because it was the only way I could cope and then I felt as though it had never really happened to me or had nothing to do with my normal life,' Abby halted.

'That time, at Christmas, when you came to London, were you going to tell me then?'

Abby shifted on the seat. 'I might have. But it was as though I was still in major denial. I didn't know if I'd be that way forever. That's why I was asking about you and my— Alejandro. But then you were . . .'

'I was so disparaging about love and so totally unsympathetic. I jumped to the conclusion that someone had let you down badly and I didn't want to see my daughter wallowing in lost loves or self-pity. So I tried to jerk you out of it, the totally wrong thing to do.'

'I was angry with you for being so cynical and dismissive.'

'Of course you were. Come here.' Lia held her daughter close. 'I don't know what to say, Abby, I'm still in shock myself. Tell me, what was his name?'

'Raffaele. His name was Raffaele.'

At the mention of his name, Abby's composure fractured. Tears ran down her face and Lia silently handed her a tissue.

After a while, when Abby had recovered a little, Lia said, 'Didn't you mention him in a couple of emails from Africa?'

'I did, just casually. It was so special that I was keeping it to myself for a while.'

'Did you, well, obviously you loved him to bits?' Lia asked after Abby had recovered herself a little. It was imperative to keep her talking, she sensed, that Abby get it all out into the open so that she could start to heal and not have it festering in her heart forever more.

'Yeah, it was instant attraction,' Abby smiled through her rivers of tears, 'from the time I saw him in Heathrow airport where the group were getting ready to board the flight for Joburg. We sat together on that long-haul flight, the two of us. We started to talk. It was his first time doing any serious travel. He was amazed I'd seen so much of the world. Then when I told him all the places I had seen, he asked me something nobody else ever has.'

'What, love?'

Abby's breath heaved. 'He asked me what I was searching for. I felt we were on the same wavelength, that he touched something deep inside of me. And do you know what I told him, Mum?'

Now Abby had a faraway look in her eyes and Lia knew she was back on the night-time flight in the skies above Africa, where the cabin lights were dimmed and secrets and intimacies were easily shared. 'I told him all about Alejandro, and I said that in a sense I was searching for him, had always been searching for him. All these years, I had half hoped that maybe he'd followed his dream after all and that maybe I'd bump into him, or someone would see me and think I resembled the exotic Spanish traveller who'd recently passed through.'

Lia was stricken with confusion. 'God, Abby, why didn't you tell me?'

'I didn't want to upset you, or make you feel guilty that I didn't have a father in my life, or that you and Gran weren't enough for me. And maybe it was just as well I stayed quiet, the way things turned out.'

'I don't know what to say.'

'And that's why I brought Raffaele to Loch Lomond, as soon as our African trip was over. It was to be my last adventure, my way of saying goodbye to the search for my father, in the place where it all began. Where I thought *I* had all begun . . . After that, I was going to come to London as soon as you were back, to tell you everything. But then when it – the accident . . .' Abby closed her eyes. Lia gripped her hand tightly and willed her daughter to articulate it, to talk about it.

'When Raffaele fell . . .' She struggled to take a breath and went on in a high, thready voice that clutched at Lia's heart, 'I heard him cry out, that was all. Then there was a horrible silence.' She shivered violently and Lia held her closer. 'I stayed in the same spot for ages, but all I felt was the cold, nothing else. I couldn't feel anything in my heart. Then a search party found me. The alarm had been sounded when the mist came down and we didn't get back to the hotel. I had to phone his parents. They flew in immediately and took charge of everything because I was completely out of it.'

'Abby! How terrible!'

'Yes, it was. I came straight back to Italy with them for the funeral, and . . . oh, God, he's buried up the hillside in Positano, in a spot that looks right out over the sea.' Abby's voice was reduced to a whisper. 'He was from there originally, although his parents now live in Naples. The day he was buried, I still couldn't feel anything in my heart. I just remember the breeze on my face and the scent of lemons, and the sound of his mother crying out his name.'

'I can't believe you went through this alone. Why didn't his parents try to contact me, seeing as you were in shock?'

'They didn't want to know about me. They were also distraught and grief-stricken and they blamed me, you see. Even *I* blamed me, and so I was guilty on top of everything else.'

'*Guilty?* No, Abby,' Lia protested.

'Well only for me, he wouldn't have been gallivanting around Scottish mountaintops. I was the one who dragged him over there.'

'It was an accident,' Lia said in her most implacable tone.

'Even if I'd listened properly to the weather warning. I should have been clued-up enough to do that. Or maybe if I'd had my mobile with me to summon help immediately, it might have made a difference.'

'It was an accident,' Lia repeated, injecting her voice with as much stern command as possible.

'Afterwards I got a job as a wedding planner and stayed on here because I just couldn't bring myself to leave. It was as though I was numb, frozen in time. At the same time, it made me feel close to him and our dreams,' Abby went on. 'He talked of his lovely country, you see, and spoke of us getting married in the Cloisters, so although I'd never be married there, I took on the job to help other brides have the wedding they'd always wanted as though it could absolve my guilt a little. Then Sam came along and, well, I realised I was living a fantasy in a way. Then I foolishly thought I could turn back the clock and go back to the way we were on Mayberry Lane as if nothing awful had happened, and that was why I went home.'

'Tell me about Raffaele. What was he like?' Lia asked softly.

Abby alternately talked and cried as she poured out her heart and spoke of the young man she'd loved for just a very short time. Finally she managed to smile, hold out her wrist encircled with a turquoise bracelet and say, 'This is all I have left of him.'

'Darling, you have your good memories. And you'll always carry his love. He must have been very special. And you've been very brave and courageous,' Lia said, reaching out to her. 'You'll survive this, I know you will. One day, life will be good again, I promise.'

Holidaymakers strolling past were probably intrigued as to why two grown women with red eyes were clutching each other and weeping as they sat on a bench in a quiet part of the garden under the lemon trees. The Italians, used to displays of emotion in public, merely smiled.

'There's just something I don't understand,' Lia asked. 'How come I didn't get to hear of the accident? Surely it was in the newspapers or something? Or even when I was there in Loch Lomond recently? Your name is not all that common, surely people made the connection?'

It was early that evening and they were sitting in the hotel bar sharing a bottle of Chianti, having come in from the garden and showered and changed, trying to get back to some semblance of normality. There was no sign of Mark.

'But everyone assumed I was Italian,' Abby explained. 'We spoke Italian together and they took it for granted that we were an Italian couple. Even in the hotel they just asked for one passport, for Raffaele's. I went along with it because even before the accident I didn't want anyone to make the connection until you knew about us. Afterwards, I was too shocked to correct any wrong impressions. Then when his father arrived he took over and didn't waste any time bringing Raffaele back home. He gave the family address in Naples.' Her face darkened. 'He has my mobile number but has never contacted me since the funeral. I know there'll be an inquest later this year, so he'll probably contact me then, as I'll have to go back to Scotland for that.'

'Well at least you won't be facing that on your own. You'll have me by your side. For now, though, have you any plans, or are you going to stay on here?'

'No, I just want to hang out for a couple of days and say goodbye to it all before I move on with my life, wherever that will take me. That's all I came back for. Then I want to go home to Dublin to talk to Sam and Elaine. They need to know what happened and deserve some sort of explanation for my weirdo behaviour. God, when I think of it. And they were so nice to me. Also, I have some photographs of Africa and Raffaele that I want to download. I haven't even looked at them yet. Maybe we could look at them together.'

'I'd like that, Abby. I'd love to see your photos. I also . . .' Lia hesitated.

'What, Mum?'

'I'd like you to think about counselling.'

'Why?'

'Just to give you the best possible chance of moving on properly. And to understand that you shouldn't feel the least bit guilty. Abby, don't let this unfortunate accident cloud the rest of your life. Believe it or not, I'm thinking of talking to someone as well.'

'You, Mum? On account of . . . ?'

Lia smiled. 'Yes, darling. Even though it was years ago, some parts of it still linger and I don't want it to colour the rest of my life. You see, I've realised that I was wrong to act as if it hadn't happened and wrong to tell you that I'd put it behind me. We do have a duty to make the best of things, but we also have a duty to acknowledge the bad things for what they are, to take them out and speak of them and give voice to our deepest outrage instead of letting them fester.'

Abby was silent. Then she said, 'You should have told Gran what happened to you.'

'I know that now,' Lia acknowledged. 'I thought I was saving her from more worry and upset, but in reality I was short-changing her. The human spirit is far stronger than we realise. She was great, but I should have given her the opportunity to support me even further at the worst time in my life and be there in the way I really needed her. Anyway, Abby, never forget that the upside is that I had you, and you brought us both great joy.'

'Thanks for coming after me, by the way,' Abby said.

'I was afraid you had run back here on account of me and my bombshell. It was wrong of me to send you back to Dublin so quickly. I should have followed my gut instinct at Heathrow airport. But that was me, trying to put a good face on things.'

'Don't beat yourself up, Mum. Something else you said is that you're still you and I'm still me. That's important to remember.'

'And afterwards, when all this is sorted and when you feel up to it, if you'd like to take a break from your travels and try something different, I think you should seriously look at all the emails you've sent me over the last few years. They're fantastic, Abby, and so full of colour and life. Maybe you could think of putting together a proper kind of journal or travel diary?'

'Hmm. Maybe.'

'Then we have to put together a plan to get one step ahead of the *Lunchtime with Rachel* campaign.'

'What's happening with that?'

'Sam told me last night that he'll be able to pull some strings and find Alejandro for me quicker than any private investigator.'

'Jeez, I really owe Sam and Paula an apology for my behaviour.'

'They've already forgiven you. They seem . . .' Lia hesitated. 'They seem very happy together. Is that okay with you? Sam was afraid you'd run off because you were upset on account of him and Paula.' She watched her daughter's face carefully, but Abby seemed to be okay.

'I'm fine with it, Mum, honestly. Sam's a good friend, nothing more. I was just temporarily unhinged when I threw myself at him. He was very kind about it all and so was Elaine, and that did help me in a way to face up to reality. But what about you? What will you do if and when he finds Alejandro?'

'Hopefully he's alive and well. I'll talk to him, see if he even remembers me and is prepared to listen to my side of the story.'

'Maybe he'd like his moment of glory on daytime television.'

'Too bad. Although he could be married with children and his wife might take a very dim view of everything. No, I was thinking of mounting a counterattack,' Lia smiled. 'Once I'm satisfied that Alejandro knows what to expect and is okay with it, I'm hoping to appear on *Oprah* and spill the beans. Gary will love me altogether.'

'Mum!'

'Not the real beans, Abby. I'm keeping some of my secrets. No, I was planning to make a sort of confession and stick to the truth as closely as possible. Tell the world at large that I embellished the story of Alejandro and used him as a scapegoat, because I was really involved in a torrid, illicit liaison with a very prominent man and I was sworn to absolute secrecy.'

'Mum!'

'You don't mind?'

Abby grinned. 'It's all the same to me, so long as the very prominent man is not supposed to be a cabinet minister. How about hinting that he was a famous rock star? Or a celebrity billionaire? That'd give me some classy prestige. Let me think about it a little more. Anyway, whatever happens, I don't think you'll be facing this one on your own.'

She had a funny glint in her eyes, Lia thought. A kind of benevolent, encouraging look. She had the sense that her daughter had come through the wars and was already emerging as a stronger, wiser woman.

'And I don't mean me,' Abby said, very firmly indeed.

Lia was immediately discomfited. 'Why, who else?'

Abby smiled. 'I saw the way you and Mark were sitting together in the garden. What gives?'

'As if. You've an even better imagination than I have,' Lia scoffed, secretly wondering what exactly Abby had seen, but equally terrified to ask her.

Abby remained silent, merely smiling hopefully at her for a long, knowing moment before Lia's face broke into a smile too.

Then Lia said, 'I was wrong about something else too, Abby, when we talked at Christmas. I take back what I said about romance just being for losers.'

Mark sat on a bench overlooking the Bay of Naples and asked himself if the woman he'd loved all his life was going to reject him again. The woman whose expressive eyes he'd carried everywhere in his heart and whose beauty and passion had inspired him to the heights of success with his evocative music.

Yet all the success in the world didn't make up for the fact that she wasn't there by his side, sharing his life, or sharing her life with him.

He'd often wondered what might have happened had he remained on Mayberry Lane and bided his time. Many a long, lonely night he'd bitterly regretted his impetuous flight to the States and the stubborn pride that had prevented him from contacting her again. Other nights he'd found comfort in an anonymous pair of arms, but it was a bleak and empty comfort that failed to quench the deep longing inside him. Now, just looking at her was enough to recapture the youthful passion of the twenty-one-year-old who'd taken her to bed and felt as though he'd found the reference point for his life.

He'd followed her career with interest and if anyone

happened to mention that her novels were littered with chilling moments of terror and populated with the underbelly of humanity, well, he knew exactly where that came from. It was one way, he suspected, of working through her angst and exorcising the pain. He waited for the day when she would produce something different, something reaffirming about the soul of humankind, but so far that hadn't happened.

He asked himself if he was being foolish to take it as a sign that there was still an empty unhappiness at the heart of her life.

In London earlier this year, he'd been acutely aware that she was living somewhere in the busy, cosmopolitan city and he'd almost tried to contact her, chickening out and regretting his dismal failure on the long flight back to the States. So when Sam had invited him home for a reunion, he'd leapt at the idea. She might just conceivably be there, especially if Abby was coming. If not, well, London was only a short flight away . . .

Now, this evening, as he watched the slow swell of the tide across the bay and felt the warm breeze on his face, he tried to work out if he was simply having a mid-life crisis and would be better off returning to Dublin to get on with the remainder of his holiday, or if he should be bold, take a chance and risk being rebuffed all over again.

'Here he is now, Mum,' Abby said.

Lia's heart jumped. They were still sitting in the hotel lounge. She saw Mark come through the entrance foyer and hesitate for the briefest moment when he spotted them. Then he waved hello, but rather than coming over to join them, he continued across the tiled foyer out of her line of sight.

'He's gone across to the elevators,' Abby said, her eyes following his progress.

Lia willed herself not to turn around.

'Now he's pressing the button for the lift,' Abby went on.

'Abby, that's enough. What am I supposed to do?'

'He's waiting for the lift. Hmm. He looks good in those jeans. Kinda sexy. You have my full approval. Go for it! Follow him, Mum.'

'What do I want to follow him for?' Lia asked.

'I'm not stupid,' Abby said. 'The minute I saw you two together, it was obvious. I don't know how on earth I missed it beforehand, but for God's sake don't waste any more time.'

'Yes, but I'm heading towards fifty and he's—'

'Mum!' Abby's voice was so loud that people nearby turned to look. 'Age has nothing to do with it,' she insisted. 'Raffaele was just twenty-five. It's the feeling inside that counts.'

'What did you say?'

'It's all about how you feel. Now if you don't follow him, I'm going to—'

'You're going to what?' Lia asked, her flat voice belying the turmoil in her heart.

'Actually, I don't have to do anything.' Abby had straightened up and was smiling impishly as she looked across the foyer. Her voice carried a sudden excitement. 'He didn't get into the lift. He changed his mind. He turned around and he's walking back across the foyer; wow, looks like he's coming straight over to you . . .'

Once again, the holidaymakers relaxing in the gardens of the hotel in Sorrento were treated to the sight of the flame-haired lady in the long green skirt sobbing her heart out in the quiet, partly secluded corner. But this time it was different. This time she was wrapped in the arms of the good-looking guy and they were tears of happiness.

They knew they were tears of happiness because they'd spent some time engrossed in deep conversation before embracing in a long, passionate kiss. And now he was holding her as though he'd never let her go.

EPILOGUE

She looks at dazzling sunshine slanting across the open-air Cloisters of San Francesco and blazing whitely along the colonnade of pillars. She stands quietly at the back of the courtyard as the bride and groom exchange wedding rings and promises. She hears the ripple of Italian music drip melodies across the Cloisters.

Then the all-encompassing feeling of his presence wraps around her much as his love once did.

She has come to say goodbye.

She doesn't want to move or even look away, for she knows it will break the connection. She wants to hold onto this moment, right now, because she knows in her heart of hearts that this time, when she lets go and says goodbye, it will be forever.

Then the little flower girl, bored with the pomp and ceremony, wriggles out of her seat and fidgets restlessly. She finds the waiting basket of rose petals. She gives a childish giggle as she leans right in and burrows her arms deep into the soft, scented pile. With a sudden flourish, she raises her arms and sends a shower of petals whirling up into warm afternoon air.

And Abby looks away, her attention caught and held by the swirling petals as they spin and drift and freely swirl up, up, up into beckoning blue sky.